PRAISE FOR MARY BURTON

THE SHARK
"This romantic thriller is tense, sexy, and pleasingly complex."
—*Publishers Weekly*

"Precise storytelling complete with strong conflict and heightened tension are the highlights of Burton's latest. With a tough, vulnerable heroine in Riley at the story's center, Burton's novel is a well-crafted, suspenseful mystery with a ruthless villain who would put any reader on edge. A thrilling read."
—*RT Book Reviews*, four stars

BEFORE SHE DIES
"Will keep readers sleeping with the lights on."
—*Publishers Weekly* starred review

MERCILESS
"Burton keeps getting better!"
—*RT Book Reviews*

YOU'RE NOT SAFE
"Burton once again demonstrates her romantic suspense chops with this taut novel. Burton plays cat and mouse with the reader through a tight plot, credible suspects, and romantic spice keeping it real."
—*Publishers Weekly*

BE AFRAID
"Mary Burton [is] the modern-day Queen of Romantic Suspense."
—Bookreporter.com

THE HANG MAN

ALSO BY MARY BURTON

The Forgotten Files

The Shark
The Dollmaker

Morgans of Nashville

Cover Your Eyes
Be Afraid
I'll Never Let You Go
Vulnerable

Texas Rangers

The Seventh Victim
No Escape
You're Not Safe

Alexandria Series

Senseless
Merciless
Before She Dies

Richmond Series

I'm Watching You
Dead Ringer
Dying Scream

MARY BURTON

THE HANG MAN

Montlake
Romance

Published by Montlake Romance, Seattle

www.apub.com

Amazon, the Amazon logo, and Montlake Romance are trademarks of Amazon.com, Inc., or its affiliates.

ISBN-13: 9781503943698
ISBN-10: 1503943690

Cover design by Mecob Design Ltd

Printed in the United States of America

THE
HANG
MAN

PROLOGUE

Tuesday, August 15, 1992, 1:00 a.m.
Richmond, VA

"I should have been a Boy Scout," he said as he secured the cord into a square knot between the woman's small breasts. Standing back, he admired the slender red ropes wrapped in a figure-eight pattern around her torso.

As she watched him with nervous anticipation, he reached for the noose dangling above her, slipped it around her neck, and secured it tight until she coughed and gasped for air. He lifted his gaze to the woman's sharp blue eyes. There was panic now. Still a faint desire to please. Confusion. Fear.

Good.

"This is pretend, right?" she rasped.

"I'm not playing, Rene," he said. He softly caressed the underside of her chin.

"You said it would be fun." Rene had been too proud to ask questions up until this point. She was streetwise, savvy; she didn't want to show weakness. But now, her fears had gotten the better of her.

"You aren't having fun?" he teased.

She closed her eyes and shook her head slowly as she tried to move her arms, now twisted and bound behind her back. "No."

He traced his index finger around her erect nipples. "No? Do you want to stop?"

"Yes."

He kissed her on the lips. "I don't want to stop."

Her eyes widened, curious and worried. "You paid for an hour. You said you wouldn't hurt me."

He shrugged as he stepped back. "I lied. You're going to be here much longer. And it's going to hurt."

Alarm magnified uncertainty in her eyes. "Tell me you don't mean it. Tell me this is part of the game." When he didn't do either, she said, "Stop. I don't want to do this anymore. You said you'd stop if I asked."

"You said you wanted a walk on the wild side," he said. "And we're just getting started."

"I changed my mind."

"Sorry, darling. No stopping now," he said, his face inches from hers. "We have to play this game to the end. You see, this isn't about your suffering or my fun. It's about sending a message."

Her nostrils flared as she pulled in a breath. "Message? What message?"

"You're going to teach everyone about loyalty."

"No one cares what I have to say."

"You won't be speaking in words. Your body will be talking. And the right people will understand the significance."

"What people? The people I know don't matter."

"That's not true. What about the people you shared all your secrets with?" he prompted.

"What secrets?"

"You've seen things you knew you shouldn't have discussed. And yet you did."

Her eyes watered as understanding bloomed. "I didn't talk to anyone."

He brushed a lock of brown hair from her eyes. "A little late for lying now, don't you think?"

She closed her eyes. "I didn't tell."

"You told enough." He reached for a rag.

Terror glinting in her eyes, she opened her mouth to scream, but he was ready with the balled rag as well as a strip of duct tape. She gagged as she glanced toward the shadows by the warehouse door where the red light of a video camera glowed.

"No one's coming," he said. "No one is going to help you."

He pressed the tape over her mouth and sealed her lips closed. Soft whimpers rose in her throat as Rene violently shook her head and strained against her bindings. He watched her struggle for a minute until she slumped forward, winded and light-headed from the bindings and gag that restricted her breathing.

"The more you fight, the tighter the ropes get." He moved behind the woman, drawing a fingertip along her bare shoulder. She flinched. Her breathing grew faster.

A sob rumbled deep in her throat. She shook her head, and the ropes tightened around her neck, forcing her to relax into a slump.

When she slowly and carefully raised her head again, his face was inches away. "I'm your whole world. I control everything. Should I end it now? Or prolong it?"

Her brows rose, but she'd already learned not to move or the ropes would punish.

"How much pain should I dole out? It's all mine to decide." He sucked in a breath; his power over her vitalized him. "This is such an exciting, heady rush in a world that can make a man feel powerless and unworthy."

Tears glistened in her eyes.

He tugged on the rope above her head, testing the steadfastness of the beam above. "We don't want the beam breaking under your weight. The whole point is to suspend you. It's supposed to take time."

She strained against her bindings as a scream caught in her throat.

He wound his fingers through her thick hair and tugged her head back so that they both could see the rafter above. "It took me time to find this place. I needed space and privacy. The beams look strong, but it never hurts to be careful."

He released her head and moved to the rope lashed to a structural support pillar. He unknotted it and yanked once. Immediately she rose up on toes with nails painted a bright crimson. She was small-boned and petite. Lifting her was easier than he expected. She struggled to replant her weight back on the ground. Another tug on the rope and those pretty toes would flitter free.

A deep moan rumbled in her chest as she increased her struggles. The rope tightened. She gagged.

Groaning, she shook her head. A renewed bid for freedom tightened the noose around her neck and cut off most of her air. Shock and desperation widened her eyes. Her nostrils flared and her breasts heaved as she pulled in precious little oxygen.

Grinning, he yanked until she was suspended two feet off the ground. He wound the rope around the bracket screwed into the pillar. "Be a good girl, and you might live a little longer. It's up to you."

Tears dropped from her eyes as she mewed like a dying animal caught in a snare.

"I knew this was going to be interesting, but I had no idea I'd feel so euphoric." His skin tingled, and his erection was rock hard.

Her kicks slowed. Breath gurgled in her chest.

"You're as light as a feather," he said. "Might take the bindings a little longer to do their job, but I'm in no rush. I've all night."

As he stood back, he had to admire his work. He'd studied the knots carefully for months, practicing first on himself and then on women willing to surrender control.

Her eyes closed, and her body twitched. He counted to three, then lowered the rope until her feet touched the ground. She slumped forward and gasped. She hadn't suffered enough yet.

But she would.

Her betrayal had earned her a slow death.

He moved to his duffel bag, fished out a sandwich, and took a seat on an old bench across from her. Carefully he peeled back the wax wrap, excited at the prospect of eating his meal.

He studied the thinly sliced pieces of roast beef and white American cheese with mustard pressed between two slices of homemade bread. "I could tell you the secret to making a great sandwich, but this is a lesson about keeping secrets, isn't it?"

Rene struggled to turn her neck to loosen the tension and allow more air down her windpipe, but the ropes held her head in place. Panicked, she looked up at him.

He finished off the first half of his sandwich and wiped the crumbs from his fingers with a paper napkin. Carefully he bit into the second half. By the time he ate the last morsel and balled up the wax paper, Rene had regained some of her senses.

He shoved his trash back in his duffel. He stood and walked up to her, stopping inches short of touching her. "You know why I'm doing this, don't you? You do understand that you deserve this, right?"

She shook her head as tears filled her eyes. Her nostrils flared, starving for morsels of air.

"Nobody likes a snitch," he said.

"Nobody," a voice whispered in the shadows.

Rene tried to shake her head no.

"Say what you want," he said. "But you know I'm right. You were given trust, and you squandered it."

He pulled on the end of the rope again. Her feet rose above the cement floor, and this time, when he tied off the rope, she was suspended three feet above the ground. She struggled, kicking her feet as the rope cut off the air to her lungs. Soon her eyes rolled back in her head.

He waited, then again lowered her to the ground, giving her a bit more time to recover. He repeated this a half-dozen more times before he tied the rope off for good. Her rising chest and twitching limbs stilled. He left her hanging.

He checked his watch. After fifteen minutes, he said, "I think a bit more time. Better safe than sorry, right?"

"Yes," whispered the voice.

"Yes, what?"

"Sir. Yes, sir."

"You got all this on tape?"

"Yes, sir."

"Good."

The shadow in the corner shifted, and he knew today's lesson in loyalty had been heeded.

Five minutes later, he moved behind Rene and pressed his fingertips to her wrist. No pulse. Her feet were turning dark purple, a sign her heart no longer functioned and blood was settling in the lowest parts of her body.

"You can shut off the video camera now. This should be enough proof."

CHAPTER ONE

Sunday, October 29, present day, 11:01 p.m.
Richmond, VA

Flashing lights from the patrol cars and fire engine made it easy for City of Richmond detective Tobias Novak to find the Church Hill murder scene. He parallel parked at the end of the block, climbed out of his SUV into the bitter cold, and burrowed deeper into his overcoat as he made his way up the brick sidewalk past century-old row houses, some looking every bit their age.

It was his evening off, and he was not happy about leaving behind a warm bed and the woman in it. Blame it on the lunar cycle or Halloween week, but the dispatcher had every on-duty detective already committed. He was needed.

A uniformed officer stood by the strip of yellow crime-scene tape tied to a wrought-iron fence encircling the small front yard. A "Rice Renovation" sign was planted in a bed of overgrown weeds. He'd seen the company's signs around the old Church Hill and Fan District neighborhoods and knew similar companies were buying and remodeling these vacant old homes for empty nesters hungry to move back into the city.

The uniformed officer was lean, muscular, and in his early twenties. "Detective Novak," the officer said as he raised the tape.

"What do we have?" Novak asked.

The officer shifted his feet and rubbed his hands together to chase away the night chill. "Neighbor across the street spotted a fire on the first floor and called it in. Crews put it out in fifteen minutes. It appears electrical, but they're calling in the arson investigator. The house's new owner was alerted. You received the call when they found the body in the basement."

Novak blew warm air on his cold fingers. "Is the death related to the fire?"

"Doesn't look like it."

"How can you tell?"

"You'll have to see it for yourself, sir."

Novak stared up at the peeling gray-white paint of the early twentieth-century row house. The wide front porch had rotted in several places, a section of the portico roof had collapsed, and two of the four floor-to-ceiling windows were broken. Six faded "No Trespassing" signs were nailed across the front of the house.

"Who's inside now?" Novak asked.

"Another uniformed officer, and the forensic technician has been on scene for nearly an hour."

Across the street, a couple of dog walkers huddled close as they stared at the scene. At least there were no television news crews, so he might have more time before this went public.

Novak climbed the front steps, crossed the rotted porch, and entered the foyer. He'd been in countless city houses like this before. Called shotgun houses, the homes were built with a staircase on the left, a long hallway leading to the back, and two rooms on the right.

The front room was dark, filled with trash and several stained pieces of upholstered furniture. The pungent scent of smoke grew stronger as he moved closer to the adjoining room, which was blackened from smoke and flames. Jagged burn marks originated at an outlet and crawled up the wall. Water dripped from already-peeling wallpaper.

Under the scent of charred wood lurked hints of mildew, dust, and urine, but no signs of human decay. The cold snap would have slowed decomposition, but there was still generally some smell of death.

Temporary lighting set up in the kitchen illuminated the hallway, which was filled with more rubbish and fallen ceiling plaster. In the kitchen, a set of dark cabinets dating back a half century hung over a filthy porcelain sink filled with trash. The black-and-white linoleum on the floor peeled and buckled in several spots.

Noise echoed up from the basement and pulled him toward the open door that led to a wooden set of rickety stairs. He climbed down into the basement.

The ceiling and ductwork were low and only inches higher than his six-foot-three frame. In the far right corner, he found the uniformed officer and a forensic technician who was aiming her camera into a small room.

Novak moved toward the tech. In her midtwenties, Natasha Warner was short and slender with dark hair pulled into a ponytail. He'd worked scenes with her before and knew she was sharp and ambitious and cut no corners. Novak fished latex gloves from his pocket and worked his large hands inside them.

"Officer Warner," Novak said.

Natasha turned and lowered her camera from her angular face. "Detective Novak."

Novak nodded before stepping past her into the small room. The air was dry, but there was no scent of rotting flesh. "Natasha, what do you have?"

Her gaze sparked with keen curiosity. "A woman who was locked in this room, which was probably a root cellar at one time. By the looks of her clothes, I'd say she's been here around twenty-five years."

"Twenty-five years?" Novak pulled dark-rimmed glasses from his pocket and slid them on as he accepted a flashlight from Natasha. "Were you born twenty-five years ago?"

Natasha glanced in her viewfinder. "Barely. You?"

"Very funny," he said. The forensic technician looked like a kid. Natasha Warner couldn't have been much older than his daughter. Frequent workouts kept Novak's body trim, but the glasses and the flecks of gray at his temples gave away his approaching forty-second birthday.

Lying on the floor were skeletal remains of a body appearing to be lying on its back, arm and leg bones outstretched. The mandible, or lower jaw, was slightly agape. The clothing was intact and amounted to what remained of a faded pair of jeans with yellow and white flowers embroidered on the pockets and a pale-blue blouse with a wide collar and cuffs. What had been the victim's long red hair remained partially intact and still knotted into a braid that draped over her shoulder.

"You said female," he said.

"Clothing is one clue, but the deciding factor is her brow ridge. It's thin, indicating female."

"She's only bones."

"In Virginia's hot and humid climate, this kind of decomposition is expected. And she's intact because she was in a sealed room. Animals would have scattered her bones if she had been outside."

Novak studied the position of the arms and legs. "She looks posed."

"Or she did it herself," Natasha said. "I worked a suicide once that was like this. The woman took a couple handfuls of pills and then laid herself out on her bed."

"Presenting herself to the Almighty?" Novak asked.

Natasha shrugged. "Her husband said they'd argued that morning and she'd promised to 'show him.' He said the suicide was an *f-you* message to him."

The summary struck a sharp nerve. His late wife had killed herself. But she'd not chosen pills. That was too passive for Stephanie. No, she'd driven her car into a lake. The kicker had been that she'd strapped Bella, their one-year-old, into her car seat. Fortunately, someone had seen Stephanie's car plunge into the water. Bella had been pulled out as Stephanie screamed and fought to be left alone. The lake had quickly sucked under the car, and by the time Stephanie had been pulled from the water, she was dead.

Two days later, a letter from Stephanie posted the day she died had arrived at their home. In it, she blamed him for her dark moods and miserable life. At the time, he'd been too damn angry to care about *why*. She'd tried to kill Bella, and that was unforgivable.

His father had moved in with them, helping with child care while Novak worked. From then on, his priorities had been simple. Raise Bella and catch bad guys. She'd been an easy kid. Smart. Funny. Strong. His father had passed two years ago, and when Bella had left for the University of Virginia last year, he'd thought he'd finally get a chance to enjoy a bachelor's life. Instead, the house remained too empty. Too quiet. Until a few weeks ago, he'd pacified the restless silence with extra work.

Novak thought again about the woman he'd left in her warm bed. For the first time in a long while, he resented the job. "Any sign of a weapon or pills?"

"None." Natasha nodded toward the far corner behind Novak. "I did find a purse in the corner, but I haven't opened it yet."

"How about a suicide letter?"

"None that I've seen."

Novak studied the skull still attached to the neck vertebrae. A small heart-shaped gold pendant winked at the base of what had been her throat. He crouched by the remains and inspected the skull closely. "What's this on the underside of her skull?"

Natasha came around to the other side and turned the skull gently until a one-inch round fracture became visible. "I take back what I said about suicide."

"Looks like the size of a hammer's head," he said.

"I'll leave the cause of death to the medical examiner."

"Is the medical examiner's office sending someone?" The medical examiner had jurisdiction over any crime-scene body. Sometimes they sent a technician, and sometimes they allowed the local jurisdiction to transport the remains to their morgue.

"Dr. Tessa McGowan is on call. I spoke to her and told her what we have. She'll be here in about a half hour."

Dr. McGowan was new. He'd crossed paths with her once and had been impressed. "You check the dead woman's pockets?"

"All empty."

"Mind if I have a look at the purse?"

"No, go ahead. Let me photograph you as you go."

His long legs crossed the confined space in a couple of strides. He squatted in front of a small black purse trimmed with fringe. As Natasha photographed, he slowly opened the purse.

Inside was a smooth leather wallet. The folds creaked and protested as he opened it. Natasha took more pictures. There were fifteen one-dollar bills in the side pouch, and in the change pocket were a few nickels, a dime, and a penny. The coins dated back to the sixties and seventies. One penny was minted in 1991. He shifted to a small compartment, which contained a Virginia driver's license for a Rita Marie Gallagher born in 1969. Her address was a suburban Far West End apartment complex located near the hospital. He snapped pictures of the license with his phone.

Rita Gallagher's identification picture featured a smiling young woman with long bright-red hair and a round face. She was wearing the same gold necklace as the corpse. The license stated her height at five foot three inches. "The body matches the description on the license.

Unless the medical examiner finds evidence to suggest otherwise, I'd say this is Rita Gallagher," he said.

In the wallet were a handful of receipts. One from a fast-food chain that was so faded he couldn't read the date. Another was from a clothing store. It was handwritten in blue ballpoint pen and detailed the purchase of a new pair of jeans and blouse on November 1, 1992, at a Regency Square Mall. The description on the clothing receipt matched what she was wearing. "The receipt places her at the mall over twenty years ago." Rita Gallagher would have been twenty-three in 1992 when she had purchased the last outfit she'd ever wear.

In the wallet's back compartment was a photograph of a dark-haired man in his thirties with a young girl who appeared to be about six or seven. The man's smile looked weary. The girl had a round face, braids, and a bright smile. The child's olive-toned coloring told Novak she couldn't have been Rita in her younger days. However, he recognized the location. It had been taken at a popular soccer complex. Bella had played soccer, and he'd spent many an afternoon there on the sidelines with his dad.

Oddly, the man looked vaguely familiar, but he couldn't place the face. His body was lean and fit, and his bearing suggested former military or cop.

"Could you hold that up for me?" Natasha asked.

He held up the wallet with the picture.

Natasha snapped a dozen images. "The picture looks like it was taken at least twenty years ago. The dude looks a little retro."

"When did the early nineties become retro?" he asked.

"If you have to ask . . ."

Novak let the comment pass. "Can I pull the picture from the wallet?"

"Hold it by the edges and move slowly. If it sticks at all, stop," Natasha said.

Novak pinched the edge and pulled gently. The plastic casing cracked and bent enough to allow the picture to pull clear.

He studied the man in the picture closer. A name danced out of reach.

He turned the image over and found writing on the back.

Jim and Julia Vargas. Soccer practice, September 1992.

"Jim Vargas," he said, more to himself. *Damn.* The man's daughter, Julia Vargas, was a cop. "He was honored at the Chamber of Commerce's award ceremony a few weeks ago."

"Yep. He was a homicide detective in Richmond."

Novak had been at the event, and he'd read Jim Vargas's bio in the program. The man had been a legend in the narcotics and homicide departments. This guy's world-weary features barely resembled the police academy picture used in the program.

"There was controversy at my banquet table over his receiving an award twenty-five years after he died," Natasha said. "Some weren't happy about listing him."

When Jim Vargas's name had been called out, Julia, a tall, slim woman from the table beside his, had risen, walked to the podium, and accepted the award. She said thank you and promptly left the banquet hall.

"Vargas investigated the Hangman cases," Natasha said. "He shot himself. There was no note, but some thought he'd known more about the Hangman case than he'd let on."

"Strung up his victims by their necks. They all asphyxiated."

Novak studied the face of the smiling young girl standing so proudly by her father. She barely resembled the lean woman who'd carefully guarded her emotions. Julia.

"The daughter, Julia, became a cop," Natasha said. "She works for the Virginia State Police. She was in the news with her partner about a month ago."

Novak knew the case. He had first heard of Julia Vargas when Bella showed him the article about a killer dubbed the Dollmaker. Bella wanted to be a cop and had homed in on the female agent's success. He'd been smart enough not to comment, still betting college would change her course toward medicine or business. Shit, he'd even settle for basket weaving, just as long as it didn't involve guns and dark alleys.

Two days after the article had come out, he'd collected his citation at the banquet and quietly slipped out. He'd found Julia in the stairwell leaning against a cement wall, fingering an unopened packet of cigarettes and clutching her old man's award in her hand. Slim pants accentuated her long limbs, and a white silk blouse and black blazer drew his attention to her full breasts. When his gaze lifted to her thick ebony hair, deep-set brown eyes, and high cheekbones, he was hooked.

They'd stumbled through small talk. He'd suggested a drink. She'd agreed. And they'd been in a hotel bed two hours later. The sex had been hot, but she'd been cool and distant when she dressed in the morning. He'd thought that was that. But forgetting her had been impossible. He lasted only two days before he called to ask to see her again. Since then, they'd been in bed a half-dozen times in the last three weeks, but he knew little else about her beyond the headlines. It was her bed he'd left an hour ago.

He pulled off his glasses. Julia was tense by nature, and she never talked about her childhood or her father. The couple of times he'd tried to turn a conversation toward her past, she found a way to make him so horny he couldn't think.

He took a picture of the father-daughter image and carefully put it back in the wallet.

He rose, left the purse with Natasha, and moved back toward the uniformed officer. "Where's the new homeowner?"

"His name is Mike Rice, owner of Rice Renovation. He's out front in a squad car. He closed on the property last week and was supposed to begin demo in a month. If not for the fire, we'd have found her soon enough."

"He never did a walk-through before he bought the place?"

"Bought it sight unseen."

Novak looked at the door leading to the room. He saw a freshly cut padlock dangling from a hinge. "Who cut the lock?" he asked Natasha.

"When the fire crew inspected the basement, they saw the lock and used bolt cutters. As soon as they shone a light in here, they saw the victim."

"Good. Thanks, Natasha. Is there anything else I need to see?"

"No, but check with me tomorrow. I may have more."

"Thanks."

Novak searched the corners of the basement. The space was filled with old chairs, a broken stove, a claw-foot bathtub, and a marble mantel.

"Are you going to call Julia Vargas about the picture?" Natasha asked.

Novak wanted Julia to hear it from him. "Yes."

He climbed the stairs and moved outside. He found the home-owner now leaning against a squad car, a cup of hot coffee cradled in his hand. One booted foot tapped impatiently.

Novak introduced himself. "And you are?"

"Mike Rice. They said a detective was coming and I had to wait until I talked to you before I could leave."

Novak dug a notebook and small pen from his breast pocket. He flipped the notebook open. "Thank you for sticking around."

"That's all right." He shoved out a breath.

"Have any idea how the fire started?"

"The captain asked me that several times. I have no idea. It could be anything with a run-down old house like this."

"This has to be a first for you," Novak said.

A calloused finger scraped at the side of the coffee cup. "The first walk-through on places like this always has a surprise or two. Usually it's mold, rotting wood, or vagrants. This is my first dead body."

"What do you mean by *places like this?*"

"The property has been vacant at least ten years, maybe more. Lots of damage happens to a house when it's abandoned."

Novak clicked the top of his pen a couple of times. "Whom did you buy the house from?"

"From the city. They took it over about two years ago when back taxes weren't paid. I can't tell you who they seized the property from, but the title search turned up clean."

"I'm going to send a cadaver dog through the house. Just in case."

Rice glanced toward the house, his frown deepening. "Holy shit, you think there are more?"

"Let's hope not, but I'd like to check."

"Sure. I'll be ripping out walls as soon as you let me back inside. Be nice to know there are no more unwelcome surprises."

"Right."

"How soon can I get into the house?"

"It will be at least a week. But right now, until we complete a full search of the property, I can't make any promises."

The guy ran thick fingers through thinning hair. "That's not so bad."

"That's assuming we don't find other bodies or evidence."

The man pinched the bridge of his nose. "Damn it."

"Right."

Novak gave him his card, then reached for his cell. He dialed Julia's number, knowing he was waking her up with unwelcome news. As he stared at the houses lining the street, he also knew tomorrow would have him knocking on each door. Someone always sees something.

CHAPTER TWO

Sunday, October 29, 11:30 p.m.

The dream always begins with bloodred apples.

A collection of six bright Red Delicious arranged in a white bowl centered on her mother's kitchen table. Ripe. Delicious. Ready to burst. Julia runs into the kitchen to greet her father but the ground under her feet turns slick, and the beige tiles melt into crimson puddles. She skids. Slips. Her gaze settles onto her father's body slumped over the kitchen table. One of his hands stretches toward the apples, and the other dangles toward the floor where his service weapon rests in a puddle of blood. His glassy eyes are wide open, mirroring joyless surprise, and his slack jaw presses into the table. Her mouth opens to scream, but it's her mother's anguished cry she hears behind her.

The shrill of a phone pulled Agent Julia Vargas toward consciousness. Heart racing, she sat up. She groped the nightstand beside her, fingers skimming over an opened pack of cigarettes before she found her phone.

Making no effort to clear the sleep from her voice, she glanced at the clock's red digital numbers. It was well after eleven. "Yeah."

"Julia?"

She blinked and cleared her throat. "Yes, who's this?"

"Tobias." His rough, gravelly tone chased away the fog of sleep.

"Novak?" Phone pressed to her ear, she looked toward the pillow to her right. A faint impression still remained, evidence he'd been there. "I didn't hear you leave."

"You were sleeping soundly. I didn't want to wake you."

She had been sleeping unusually well until the dream. "Where are you?"

"I'm at a homicide in Church Hill. You'll want to come and see it."

She pressed the bridge of her nose. "Novak, if this is your idea of pillow talk, it's not working for me."

"Julia." Warning hummed under the word.

"Can you give me more details at least?"

"I'll text you the address."

She cleared her throat again and swung her legs over the side of the bed. Earlier today, she'd worked a homicide with Agent Dakota Sharp. After nineteen hours nonstop, they'd traced the killer via a series of violent texts made to the victim, his ex-girlfriend. The accused was in cuffs by 7:00 p.m., and by 9:00 p.m. she was in bed, swearing she'd not move before dawn. But she'd been too wired to sleep. So she'd texted Novak.

"Why me?" she asked. "I'm technically off duty. And I'm surprised you'd be reaching out to Virginia State Police." Though she worked for Division One, which covered the Richmond metro area, the city had sufficient resources and usually didn't call in the state police.

"Trust me on this one."

She picked up the pack of cigarettes and tapped it against her thigh. Novak was no nonsense. No drama. A call from him meant the case could be big. "You're going to have to do better than that, Detective."

"Victim is female. Young. Blunt force trauma to the back of her skull."

Rising, she paced, hoping to clear her head. "Seriously, why me?"

"It appears the victim knew you."

She flipped back a lock of dark hair. "Stop dropping bread crumbs for me to follow, Novak. I've crossed paths with a lot of people."

"Look," he said, lowering his voice. "This is a topic I'd rather not get into with you on the phone. But I strongly suggest you look at the crime scene."

She looked back at her still-warm bed. "You can't give me a clue?"

"No."

When he didn't offer anything else, she checked the clock on her nightstand. It read 11:40 p.m. *Damn it.* She had court at ten and a meeting near Quantico in the early afternoon.

Resigned, she crossed to the long window and peeked through the blinds. The streets were quiet. She lived in Richmond near the Shockoe Bottom district in an apartment over a bar called Billy's. The bar was outside the financial district, but not quite in the historic section. A not-so-charming no-man's-land.

If it all went perfectly, she could dress quickly, check out Novak's scene, and be home to catch at least another few hours of sleep. *Perfect.* She'd yet to have a murder scene unfold neatly in front of her.

"Okay. I can be there in thirty minutes."

"I'll be here."

She ended the call and willed away fatigue. The edges of her faded police academy T-shirt brushed her thighs as she surveyed the room.

"Shit," she muttered as she ran fingers through a tangle of dark hair.

Automatically she removed her second to last cigarette from the pack, but then caught herself. Last night, she'd taken the capture of the killer as a sign to ditch the dirty habit. With a twinge of regret, she threw the pack on the rumpled sheets. "Damn it."

Across from her bed was a large gilded mirror; its streaked and faded silver backing hinted at its decades in an old hotel lobby. Below it, her secondhand dresser, painted a bright indigo, was covered with perfume bottles, makeup, and earrings. A rocking chair in the corner was draped with yesterday's jeans and a white T-shirt. Beside it were ankle boots kicked off midstep in her rush to get into a hot shower and wash away today's homicide scene.

Controlled chaos. Just as she'd left it when she went to bed.

Julia hustled to her closet and yanked on slim dark pants and a black T-shirt. She threaded a worn leather belt through the loops. The belt buckle had been her father's and doubled as a knife. Fastening it, she shrugged on a jacket.

Her black hair curled around her face as she tugged it up into a ponytail. High-heel boots and a collection of beaded bracelets around her wrists made her look more like a rocker than a cop. She secured her service weapon, badge, and handcuffs to her belt. She tucked the cigarette pack in her pocket for good measure.

Julia had been with the Virginia State Police for eight years. As all agents did, she'd started as a trooper and worked the highways for six years before she landed an uncover gig in Virginia Beach. Turned out she had a knack for slipping into pretend lives and found working back alleys and smoky bars preferable to a cruiser. Six months ago, her arrest record had landed her a promotion to the criminal investigations team in Richmond.

Her single-cup coffee machine spat out a strong blend, and with travel mug in hand, she made her way down a back staircase leading to the alley where she'd parked her unmarked car. She drove east on Cary Street and then up to Church Hill. She turned north toward Broad and spotted the blue lights flashing atop three city cruisers. She parked in front of the smoldering old town house. Rolling her head from side to side, she drained the last of her coffee. She stepped into the cold night air. Cursed.

Julia spotted Novak's tall, broad-shouldered frame. He stood by his unmarked vehicle, feet braced and a cell phone pressed to his ear. He was one hell of a cop. One of the good guys. One day he'd figure out she hauled too much emotional baggage around and leave, and their late-night encounters would end. *Too bad.* Because if she could have liked a guy, it might have been him.

She stepped into his peripheral vision, and he turned, holding up a finger. She shifted from foot to foot, folding her arms over her chest, telling herself she wasn't really that tired or cold. He quickly finished his call.

"Julia." His tone wrapped an unwanted familiarity around her name.

"Novak, this better be good."

He tucked his phone into his breast pocket. "Nothing excites me more than meeting you at a crime scene in the middle of the night."

The dry humor tempered some of her irritation. "So seduce me with sweet talk. Make me glad I'm not at home asleep in a warm bed."

"Asleep?"

"Or whatever."

Lights from a squad car highlighted the small smile that didn't soften a carved jawline shadowed with the hint of stubble. "The house caught fire, and crews found a nasty surprise in the basement. Hence the call to you."

"You said a young female."

"Correct."

"How long do you think she's been dead?"

"That's the odd part. Better to let you see than me tell."

"The plot thickens." She waited for the grin that had literally charmed her pants off a couple of weeks ago to flicker at the edge of his lips. When it didn't come, she slid long fingers in her coat pocket and retrieved a pair of latex gloves. "How long have your people been on scene?"

"I've been here close to an hour."

"Scene's been processed?"

"The forensic technician has done a preliminary sweep, and the medical examiner's rep should be here in a matter of minutes."

"Lead the way."

His booted feet crunched the cold earth as they moved into the glare of spotlights illuminating the house with a wide front porch. "The generator is running what lights we have. No electricity to the house, but if there were, it wouldn't matter. The light fixtures were stripped a long time ago."

Floor-to-ceiling windows flanked the front door. In the foyer, the floor was coated in decades of dirt, though there were a couple of spots cleaned as if pickers had salvaged some of the flooring. The heavy scent of fire lingered in the long hallway.

She studied the wall with black scorch marks. "Place was torched."

"Maybe. Or it was electrical." He led her into a kitchen that was a throwback to the sixties.

"I bet torched."

Novak motioned toward a doorway leading to a basement staircase. "Let me go first. Stairs are shaky."

"Of course. Bet there are also spiders, too." The hang-up began when she was a kid. And in the last year, the annoyance had bloomed into real anxiety.

"You're afraid of spiders?"

"I am not. But I hate tight spaces."

"Didn't know that."

There was a lot he didn't know about her. That's why it worked for them.

He descended wooden stairs that tunneled toward the bright forensic lights that cut through most of the soggy darkness. A small creature scurried in the corner where the light didn't reach. It was always the shit you couldn't see that bit you in the ass.

Novak's towering frame skimmed under the low ceiling, and in a couple of spots he ducked under a low-hanging duct. The air was cold and stale.

"How old is this place?" she asked.

"Built around 1920."

The basement was L-shaped, and around the bend the lights of a camera flashed. She tugged at the edges of her gloves and braced herself as she rounded the corner.

A forensic technician snapped pictures. It could be years before some cases went to trial. The technician's notes and images would help put the images in proper context while she was testifying in court.

At the center of the activity was the door leading to a root cellar or furnace room. "No smell of decomposition," Julia said.

"Wait," Novak said.

Julia braced herself again. She'd seen some horrific sights during her years and had learned emotional distance was the best way to cope.

What she saw in the room was a first. She didn't speak as she studied the woman's skeletal expression. Her mouth appeared open, and her eyes were empty sockets. Death had frozen her as she'd dragged in her last breath. Bony fingers lay palms up, and her legs were spread, feet turned out.

The low dark ceiling made the room oppressive. *Jesus.* What a place to die. Julia imagined the woman's final terrified seconds. The panic. Fear. As an undercover agent, she'd learned to bury her true feelings and discovered the talent translated well in moments like this.

Stoic, she moved toward the body. The victim was dressed in faded, distressed jeans and a pale-blue top. A collection of metal bracelets banded a wrist, and a burgundy ring encircled her left ring finger. Her hair was red, and pierced earring hoops lay on the floor.

"Do you have any identification?" she asked.

"We found a small purse in the corner. Inside was a wallet. ID says she's Rita Gallagher." He nodded to the tech. "Natasha, can you show her the purse?"

"Will do." Natasha handed her a clear evidence bag containing a black purse. "We've inventoried it, but be careful. Touch as little as possible. I want to do a work-up in the lab."

"Sure. Thanks, Natasha." Julia held up the bagged purse as she faced Novak. "What am I looking for, Detective?"

Novak shifted his weight. "You tell me."

"So this is a game?"

"I want you to have fresh eyes when you look at it."

She arched a brow, in no mood for a game that she knew she had to play. She carefully removed the purse from the evidence bag. Squatting, she flattened the bag on the ground and laid the purse on it. She poked around in the faded cloth interior. Lipstick. Small knife. White pills in a small brown glass vial. She saw nothing out of the ordinary. She opened the wallet and read the name on the ID card. Rita Gallagher. The picture matched the remains lying just a few feet from her.

Julia squinted to read the girl's stats. "She was born in 1969, and judging by her clothes, she was in her early twenties when she died. That puts time of death almost twenty-five years ago."

"That's what we're thinking. Assuming the medical examiner confirms the theory."

Julia looked up at Novak's stone features. "She had a shitty ending to a short life, but it doesn't necessarily warrant a call to me."

"There's a small pocket in the wallet." He clicked on a flashlight.

A sigh leaked from her lips as she accepted the light and shone it into the pocket. Carefully she worked a gloved index finger between the fabric folds and grabbed the tip of the picture with her fingers.

Julia held up the picture of a man and a child. Her first assumption came quickly, but she immediately dismissed it as too out of the box. She blinked and refocused. "Is this some kind of sick joke?"

Cops played pranks on each other, and after the remarks she'd heard at the awards banquet about her father, she wouldn't be surprised. Still, this was in poor taste, and though she could fit all she knew about Novak on an index card, she didn't peg him as the type to pull a stunt like this.

He searched her face, clearly trying to dig below the layers as he often did. "I don't play jokes like this, Julia."

Her gaze returned to the picture, studying the man's grinning face and the young girl. The man's thick dark hair brushed off chiseled features that had earned him the nickname Devil.

He draped one relaxed arm over Julia's shoulder. She was wearing a white soccer uniform that was covered in mud. Her knees were muddied and her braids plastered against her face with sweat. The sky was clear, and there were green soccer fields in the background. She remembered the game. It had been one of her best, and she'd defended against three goals.

The little girl leaned easily into her father, savoring a rare father-daughter moment. He'd not been around most of her life until those last few years when he'd left narcotics and joined homicide. She was still getting to know him, to trust that he wouldn't take off again.

"You recognize it?" Novak asked.

She cleared unwanted emotion from her voice. "It's the last picture taken of my dad and me."

CHAPTER THREE

Monday, October 30, 12:30 a.m.

Julia stared at her father's smile. Of all the pictures she'd seen of him, he'd never looked happy except for this one. It was their one perfect moment, and now a goddamned crime scene had tainted it.

"How—" She cleared the emotion from her voice again, aware that Novak and the forensic tech were watching her. "How did this picture end up here?"

"That's my question. Do you know this woman?" Novak asked.

"No. Or if I did, I don't remember." How had this woman gotten this picture? "She's been here over two decades?"

"The receipt in her pocket dates back to November of 1992."

"About eight weeks after this picture was taken."

"I recognize the setting. My daughter played soccer."

Novak had a kid. She should have known, but neither had talked about themselves beyond establishing that they were both single. The new information surprised and intrigued her. She reminded herself the less she knew, the easier it would be when it ended between them.

"I'm hoping the medical examiner will be able to give us a better date. I'm running the woman's name through the police database to see if she had any record."

Julia studied the woman's driver's license picture. Pretty. Round face. Red hair. She was smiling. Back in the day, DMV took color pictures and allowed a smile.

"No idea why she might have this picture?" Novak asked.

"No clue. I was seven when my dad died, and though she clearly knew me, I don't remember her at all. My mom died three years after Dad, but I can ask my aunt and see if she knows her." She snapped a pictured of the ID.

Novak shoved his hands in his trousers and rattled loose change. "When exactly did your father die?"

"November 1, 1992. Shot himself."

"The anniversary's in a couple of days."

"So it is." Anyone who worked homicide had heard about Jim Vargas. Cop communities were like small towns. Secrets got around. "How long have you worked homicide? Six, seven years?"

"Yes."

"Then you've heard the stories."

"Sure. I heard."

To Novak's credit, he'd not asked her about her father. She put the purse back in the evidence bag and handed it to Novak. "My aunt has a good memory for faces. If anyone remembers this woman, it will be her."

"She's local?"

"She owns the bar below my apartment." He was very familiar with the back staircase that led to her place. Thankfully, he had enough tact to not comment in front of the technician.

"Your aunt owns the restaurant?" he asked.

"And the building for about forty years."

"I've eaten at that restaurant. Great burgers."

"I'll pass compliments on to the chef." She pulled the picture up on her phone. "My aunt's name is Cindy Stafford. She's my mother's sister, so not everyone makes the connection to the Vargas name."

"Have you seen another picture like this one?"

"In a box. After my mom died, I went on a mission to find all the pictures I had of my parents. My aunt handed me a small box that contained a paltry collection of Vargas family memories. Dad was gone a lot when I was a kid, working undercover operations."

"You still have the other family pictures?"

"I'm sure they're around somewhere." She shook her head. "This is a bit ironic."

"How so?"

"I had some time on my hands earlier this year and was cleaning out my aunt's attic. I found several videotapes that got me to thinking about the Hangman's case."

"What kind of tapes?"

"Tapes Jim made while he was investigating the case. They made me want to have a look into the case again. That's why I'm taking some time off this week. I'm going to do some digging."

"You call your father Jim?"

"I have since he committed suicide."

"Why?"

"Easier to distance myself from a Jim than from a Dad."

Novak studied her a beat, and she knew he was trying to get a read on her. But she was too good to give him any clues.

"The cases happened in Richmond. I can help," he said.

"Thanks, Novak. But I have this."

His jaw tightened, released, but he didn't comment.

She drew in a breath. "What else do you have?"

"An abandoned house in a run-down section of the city is a great place to hide a body. I talked to a couple of curious dog walkers while

I was waiting for you. This building has become the place for kids to drink and for vagrants to sleep. They were glad to have new ownership."

Julia studied the victim's hollowed face. *Who are you? And how do you know my father and me?*

The forensic technician's phone buzzed, and she answered it. "The medical examiner is here," Natasha said. "Twenty-five years entombed in a basement qualifies as unusual enough to warrant a medical examiner's visit."

Julia felt Novak's gaze on her as she shifted her attention back to him. "Thanks for the call, Detective. I'll ask my aunt if she recognizes the picture taken of me or the victim."

"Keep me posted."

"Of course."

She extended her hand, and he wrapped strong fingers around hers and studied her closely. "I'll be in touch."

She moved out of the confined basement space up the stairs to the front door and out to the porch. The sky was starlit and the moon full. Five hours until dawn was a lot of time to think. She drew in a breath.

Her father's life had been shrouded in secrets. Her mother had always said it was a holdover from his undercover work. The strain of those secrets coupled with long absences and rumored affairs had finally been too much for her mother. Shortly before Julia turned seven, Amy Vargas moved out with her daughter. Just as her parents were considering reconciliation, Jim killed himself.

She looked back at the old house as Novak stepped onto the porch. The look in his eyes was unsettling. He wasn't looking at her like she was a cop, colleague, or lover. Instead, his gaze was guarded. He knew she didn't like to talk about herself. Now, he had to be wondering what she was hiding. She was a part of his investigation.

The medical examiner's gurney rattled, and she looked up to see Dr. Tessa McGowan. Julia raised her hand. "We have to stop meeting like this."

Tessa smiled. "Agreed. Next time a cozy tapas bar."

Julia held up a thumb. "Done."

She checked her watch, sensed Novak's gaze, and looked back at him. "I'm in court later this morning, but I'll get back to you."

"You know how to find me, Julia."

***

Novak followed Dr. McGowan and an assistant to the basement. He stood outside the small room so the two had time to adjust to the scene. She issued firm commands as her assistant unzipped the body bag and opened the sides to make way for the bones. The two laid the bones in the bag while Natasha Warner worked the scene.

"Any thoughts on cause of death, Doc?" Novak asked.

She examined the face and reached around to the back of the head. "The base of her skull feels damaged. My guess is that the blow would have been enough to knock her out, and maybe kill her," Dr. McGowan said. "Without flesh, there's no way to determine if there were ligature marks on the neck." She pushed up the brittle shirt. "Tox screens won't be possible."

"Let me know when you do the autopsy. I'd like to be there."

"We'll get her scheduled in the next day or two."

"Thanks."

Dr. McGowan zipped up the body bag and, with the help of her assistant, lifted it to the gurney before securing it.

The concrete floor where the body had lain was stained with the victim's outline, but there were no large dark stains suggesting old pools of blood. If she'd been struck hard, it hadn't been here. Where the body had been was a strip of rope about two feet long with the ends cut clean.

Novak watched as Natasha photographed and bagged the rope. "Dr. McGowan, be on the lookout for any marks on the bone that might suggest blunt force trauma or a knife wound."

"Will do."

He followed the pair to the stairs, and when Dr. McGowan moved to heft her end of the stretcher, he nudged her aside and took the weight. It was unwieldy more than heavy and slow going up the stairs. It took maneuvering to get the stretcher around the tight kitchen door corner. When they cleared it, he and the assistant carried the gurney out to the sidewalk.

"Thanks," Dr. McGowan said. "I'll never say no to a bit of brawn."

"How well do you know Agent Vargas?"

Since Novak and Julia had started sleeping together, he had resisted the idea of learning more about Julia Vargas. He respected her privacy and halfheartedly believed she would eventually open up to him about herself. Now, asking about her didn't feel as intrusive. She was part of his case, so it was business. And when it came to a case, all bets were off.

"She's worked with my husband, Agent Sharp, on a couple of cases. She's new to the criminal investigations unit. She's dedicated. Did a couple of years' worth of undercover work near Virginia Beach. We've been out for drinks once, so I can't say I know her well."

"Does she ever say much about herself?"

Dr. McGowan cocked her head. "If you want to ask her out, then do it."

"It's not like that. We found evidence connecting her to this body."

"This body? She would have been a kid when the woman died."

"I know."

"What did you find?"

"A picture of her with her father in the victim's wallet."

Dr. McGowan brushed a strand of hair from her eyes. "Did you ask her?"

"I did. She didn't recognize the woman's name or face." And if she had, he wasn't sure she'd have told him. She guarded her thoughts closely. "I thought you might know about her family."

"Like I said, we went out the one time, but she never mentioned her family."

"What's she like in general?"

"When it comes to a case, Julia's a straight shooter. She'll tell you what she thinks. If she says she didn't know the victim's name, she didn't know."

"I'm not questioning her integrity. Have you heard about her father?"

"She doesn't talk about family, but I know he was a cop. I was at the awards dinner when she went to pick up his award."

"I was there as well. She didn't stay long."

"Can't be easy. Not everyone was happy that Jim Vargas received recognition."

When Novak had been in Julia's apartment, he'd glanced around for the award, but there'd been no sign of it.

Wouldn't hurt to have a look at the Hangman's files—and poke around in Jim Vargas's life.

CHAPTER FOUR

Monday, October 30, 7:00 a.m.

When Novak pulled into his driveway, he was dead tired and could have used an hour or two of sleep. But the dark-blue four-door sedan parked in the driveway told him his daughter, Bella, was home. He reached for his phone and checked the texts. Nothing. She was supposed to let him know when she was on the road.

He ignored the fatigue and pushed through the front door. "Bella? Everything all right?"

"Came home last night to do laundry and study in a quiet place. Where were you?"

He loosened his tie and shrugged off his jacket. He moved to the small cabinet in the entryway, unclipped his gun, and locked it in one of the drawers as he'd done since she was a baby. "Crime scene. Why didn't you text me and let me know you were coming?"

He found her sitting at the counter, a cup of coffee cradled in her hand. She'd pulled up her hair in a sloppy ponytail, and her eyes were still puffy with sleep. "I don't know. Guess I wanted to surprise you."

"I would have told you to stay at school."

"Is it a crime to visit my father?"

"No."

She grinned, sensing she'd already won this round. "So, how did it go last night? What's the case?"

Novak opened the refrigerator and pulled out the carton of eggs. This was her second year away at school, but he still bought groceries in case she showed. He rolled up his sleeves and washed his hands. "A woman. Looks like she's been dead about twenty-five years."

"How do you know she's been dead that long?"

"Right now it's based on receipts in her purse and the state of her body." These moments with Bella were now few and far between, and he knew, as she got older, he'd see less of her. He was sorry he'd not been here last night when she'd arrived, but he wasn't sorry he'd been with Julia.

Bella had never shied away from case details. "How'd the victim die?"

He fished a bowl from the cabinet and cracked a few eggs while the pan heated. He whipped them up and poured them into the pan. "I'll soon have a date with the medical examiner to find out."

She sipped her coffee. "I wish I could come. Maybe I could drive back after classes on Friday and discuss the case like you did with Grandpa?"

He was proud of his girl. But he didn't want this life for her. "Stay at school. Enjoy the weekend. Besides, I'm not crazy about you driving back and forth on the busy roads." He pushed the eggs around until they were cooked, then served up most on a plate for her.

Bella accepted a fork and jabbed it into the eggs. "Who cares about weekend parties when there's such an interesting case?"

He poured himself a cup of coffee. He liked it when they could have breakfast. "Be a kid while you can."

She rolled her eyes. "Because by twenty-three you and Mom were married and I was on the way."

"Exactly." He wouldn't have traded Bella for the parties or freedom, but parenthood was hard. It sure had been on his wife. He'd never figured out why his wife had snapped.

"I don't need a college degree to be a uniformed officer."

"You need a college degree. End of discussion." His phone buzzed with a text. It was from Julia.

Let me know when Gallagher autopsy is scheduled. I'd like to attend.

A half smile tugged the edge of his lips as he typed back.

Will do.

"Is that a hot date?" she asked, watching him closely.

He shoved the phone in his back pocket. "It's work."

She pointed the end of her fork at him. "Your face looked like it could be a date."

"It's a date with an agent at the medical examiner's office."

"But she's pretty, right?"

The kid was too sharp. "She is."

Bella grinned. "Maybe you should ask her on a date. Have some fun. I'm out of the house. No more excuses."

He ate the eggs on his plate. "How about we agree that you shouldn't date until you're thirty?"

"Right."

When they were finished, he cleaned the dishes while she grabbed the laundry she'd done last night. When her car was loaded, he shoved fifty bucks into her hand, kissed her on the cheek, and reminded her to stay under fifty-five miles per hour.

"I'm not a baby, Dad."

"You'll never convince me of that."

After Bella drove off, Novak's thoughts turned immediately to the Gallagher case. He showered, changed, and drove to the office.

Novak exited the elevators and made his way to his desk, located in the center of a busy room with phones ringing and people talking. He shrugged off his coat and settled it on his chair. He kept his desk organized, files stacked and pencils sharpened. The lone personal item was a picture of Bella, taken when she was two.

His desk butted against his partner's. Detective Samuel Riggs had muscled shoulders and a broad chest that hinted at his years playing football for Virginia Tech. Riggs dressed well, and his quick smile always caught the ladies' attention. He was one of the sharpest minds in the department. At forty-one, he and Novak were the same age, but Riggs had no wife or kids. Wasn't ready to retire from the field, as he liked to say.

Novak sat, checking messages. The arson investigator on the case would be on-site this morning at nine. The cadaver dog handler could also walk the property. He checked his watch. He called the handler and arranged for a nine fifteen meeting.

Riggs rounded the corner, approaching his desk with a fresh cup of coffee from the café across the street. A pressed blue shirt and red tie set off mocha skin. He smelled of expensive aftershave. "I heard about the bones."

"Too bad you missed it."

"Dealing with a shooting. Lucky me." He set his cup on his desk and tugged at starched cuffs secured with gold links before sitting. "Is it true about you hooking up with Jim Vargas's daughter?"

Novak had told no one about Julia, but that didn't mean word hadn't leaked out. He slowly looked up from a stack of messages. "*Hooking up* isn't the right phrase for it."

"You called her to the scene, right?"

"Yes."

"I've seen her picture in the paper." He whistled. "She's smokin'."

Very true. "And prickly when called to a homicide scene in the middle of the night."

He chuckled. "Wouldn't you be?"

"Maybe." He unfastened his cuffs and rolled up his sleeves.

"Is it true about the picture in the victim's wallet?" Riggs asked.

Word traveled fast. "Yep."

"What're the chances? How'd Vargas take it?"

"Difficult to get a read on her."

"Had to be a kick in the balls. Did she know the victim?"

"She says no. But she was seven at the time of the victim's death. You said you saw her picture in the paper. What do you know about her?"

"A buddy of mine told me she worked undercover in Virginia Beach. He said she had a solid record. Some have said she's a natural like her old man."

"Why did she leave?"

"I'm not sure if it was her choice. The last bust captured a shit-ton of drugs, but it went sideways, and she nearly died."

"What happened?"

"One of the guys she was shadowing during the operation made her as a cop. Started beating her. There was some confusion about whether she was in trouble, and when the backup team finally busted the door, she was in bad shape. Had to take six weeks of paid leave to recover."

He thought about her smooth pale skin. How sometimes she flinched a little when he touched her face. A rush of anger and outrage made it hard to keep his voice steady. "Bad shape, how?"

"Beaten up and then some. The paramedics wanted to order a rape kit, but she refused. Said it wasn't necessary. They didn't press, but my buddy said the cops had their doubts."

"About a rape?"

"Yeah. But she denies it happened."

Shit. He leaned back in his chair trying not to imagine Julia Vargas beaten and bloodied. Raped. She wore her pride like a mantle, and to think some animal had tried to strip that away. "Did she ever see a counselor?"

"How am I supposed to know that?"

"You know it all, my friend. If anyone knows what's going on in any department in Virginia, you're the man to ask."

Riggs grinned. "I make an effort to keep up. You don't."

"What about Vargas seeing a shrink?"

"That, I'm not privy to." Riggs held up a large index finger.

Novak thought about the first time he'd touched her. He'd sensed tension. Nerves. He'd figured it had been a while and she was edgy. "Keep your ears open."

"Always."

"You get my text last night?"

"Yes, and I've requested all the files on the Hangman's case. Records promised them this morning. And by the way, they told me your pal, Julia Vargas, put in a similar request while she was on leave. She made copies of all the files."

"Last night she told me she was reopening the case."

"She decided to put to rest the rumors about her old man?"

"Maybe."

"There are a few who think the past should stay in the past."

"I suspect when she sets her mind, there's no changing it."

"What do you think of her?" Riggs asked.

"She's tough. Has a temper." Her old man had killed himself, and an assault could leave deep scars. Both were red flags.

"Hotter looking in person?" Riggs teased.

"Yeah." He reached for his telephone.

The reality of a detective's job was hours of tedious phone calls, knocking on doors, record searches, and walking crime scenes. And yet, in a second, violence out of nowhere could shatter the tedium.

"Who's your contact in Virginia Beach?" Novak asked. "I want to ask him a few questions about Vargas."

Riggs scrolled through his phone and sent the contact information to him. "Why?"

Novak couldn't articulate why he should care. Instead, he said, "You know her old man killed himself."

"And you think the apple doesn't fall far from the tree?"

"I don't know. I do know suicide makes a hell of an impression on a kid."

"Bella's doing fine."

"Yes, she is."

Shaking his head, Riggs turned back to his computer. "If you think Julia's hot, ask her out."

He tried to look like he didn't care one way or the other. "Now you're a matchmaker?"

Riggs grinned as he sipped his coffee. "You don't make a move, I might."

Novak met his partner's gaze and before he thought, said, "Don't."

Riggs raised a brow. "Well, all right. Looks like the old man might be back in the game."

"I don't know what I am."

"But she's off-limits?" Riggs said, laughing.

"Yes." He dialed the number of Riggs's contact at the beach and found himself in voice mail. He left his name and number and asked for a callback.

Irritated, he refocused on the case. The first order of business was to determine the history of the homeowners where Rita Gallagher had been found. He made calls to the city records offices and was given the name of William Delany, who had owned the property until his death early in 1992. Delany's son, Marcus, inherited the property but had failed to pay the taxes in the last couple of years before the city had taken it over. Marcus Delany was in his early fifties and living south of the city in Chesterfield County.

Next, he pulled up the arrest record for Rita Gallagher. He learned that by her twentieth year, she was convicted three times for prostitution and once for possession. At the time of her last prostitution conviction, she was looking at several years in jail, but a day before trial, charges were dropped. No reason was given.

Her next of kin was her brother, Brad Gallagher. He helped her make bail the first time. The contact information listed was twenty-five years old.

He rose, pulling his jacket off the back of the chair. Riggs was on a phone call as Novak headed out to his car. His first stop was the crime scene so he could meet with the arson investigator, and then he'd knock on a few doors.

It was almost nine when he parked in front of the old Church Hill home behind the fire vehicle. Out of the car, he ducked under the crime-scene tape and made his way into the building.

He found a burly man with a thick mustache, wearing a city fireman's uniform, inspecting the socket in the room where the fire had done the most damage.

"Captain Fletcher, I'm Detective Novak. What do you think?" he asked, nodding to the socket.

The man rose and shook Novak's hand. "The socket was rigged. Someone shoved a wire inside, which short-circuited the outlet and caused the fire." He pointed to black burn patterns on the wall. "Area is also testing positive for accelerant. My guess is gasoline. When the socket short-circuited, fire sparked and caught the area on fire. Gasoline fires burn hotter and leave a residue."

"I didn't think the house had electricity to it?"

"When Rice Renovation took it over, they had it turned back on. All someone would have to do is screw in a fuse."

"Any prints on the fuse?"

"No." Fletcher studied the scorched wall as if reading words on a page.

"Was it enough to destroy the building?"

"Never can say with fire. In this case, the flames stayed contained in this room."

"You see a lot of arson in this area recently?"

"No more than the usual. And from what digging I could do this morning, Rice Renovation is a solid company."

"Right."

"Any more information on the woman in the basement?"

"Still working on that one." The burn patterns in the wall were black and dark all around the outlet, but as they climbed the wall they diminished. "I'm going to have a look upstairs."

"Sure."

Novak heard a dog bark and looked toward the front entrance, where a young woman stood with a hound dog. She had blond hair pulled into a thick ponytail, which emphasized her brown eyes and full lips. He moved toward her and introduced himself.

"Officer Sara Young," she said. "This is Charlie. You want us to search for cadavers?"

"Crews have been through the house, but I don't want to overlook anything."

"Where do you want us to start?"

"How about upstairs."

"Will do." She left Novak, and she and her dog climbed stairs that creaked and groaned with each step. He followed.

The second floor was dark, and if not for the sunlight streaming in the windows, it would have been hard to navigate. He pulled a flashlight from his pocket and clicked it on as Charlie moved into the first room, sniffing as Officer Young spoke softly to him.

There were three bedrooms and one bathroom upstairs. A string dangled from an attic pull. The canine checked the first bedroom. It was small, and a soiled twin mattress lay on the floor. The second bedroom wasn't much different, though this one had a window that overlooked the brick wall of the town house next door.

He moved toward the front room and found a series of yellow numbered tents that he guessed Natasha had left behind when she'd moved her investigation upstairs. He knelt in front of the tents, which were placed on dark spots that stained the room.

Charlie moved to the brown spot and sniffed. He wagged his tail and barked.

"He's alerting me that he's found something. Likely blood."

"Looks like the forensic tech spotted it."

Charlie barked again as Officer Young rewarded him with a treat. "We'll move downstairs and to the basement."

Fishing his phone from his pocket, Novak texted his number to Young and, after the pair left the room, called Natasha.

Her voice was heavy with sleep when she answered. "Natasha Warner."

"It's Novak. Did I wake you?"

"Taking a short break. Just in from the Church Hill home an hour ago."

"Why the yellow tents on the upstairs bedroom floor?"

"Field test showed the presence of human blood."

"Okay."

"I'll have a better idea when I run more tests, but someone bled out in that room. However, I don't know when."

"DNA can match it to the victim."

"It might. That's assuming we can pull some kind of DNA from her teeth or bones. Still too early to tell given the house was ground zero for countless homeless people."

"You find anything else while you were upstairs?"

"Place is full of trash. I'll be back later and sift through what's there. Again, will let you know."

"Right."

"I'll be in touch soon."

"Thanks."

He stood and stared at the brown stain. If she'd been killed up here, it would explain the lack of blood in the basement. Twenty-three years old. She was young, but he'd seen younger kids die.

Novak checked in with Officer Young one last time and drove to Marcus Delany's house, located in a community twenty-five minutes south of the city. He wound his way down the center drive to a two-story brick colonial with a wide front porch furnished with a handful of white rockers.

Novak parked at the top of a circular drive and climbed the front steps. He rang the bell. Within seconds, the door opened to an older African American woman, who peered at him over half-glasses. "Can I help you?"

He held up his badge. "I'm looking for Marcus Delany. And you are?"

"Susan. I work here. What's this about?"

"Questions about one of his properties."

"He's in the sunroom reading. Let me tell him you're here. Wait here." She closed the door, leaving him to stand on the porch. He waited a good five minutes before she returned. "He'll see you."

"Thank you."

She pointed down the hallway. "Follow me. Second door on the left."

Novak followed, taking in the expensive modern art on the walls and the vaulted ceiling.

"Mr. Delany," Susan said. "You have the police here to ask you questions about some property."

Novak found a lean man sitting in a chair by a large window as he read from a laptop. "Mr. Delany, Detective Novak."

Delany looked up from his screen and rose. "What can I do for you, Detective?"

Novak moved toward him and showed him his badge. "I've questions about a property you inherited from your father."

"Pops left me several properties. Which one?" Delany sat and motioned for Novak to do the same.

He pulled up a straight-back chair and sat. "This is a 1920s row house a block off Broad Street in Church Hill."

"I turned that over to the city a couple of years ago. I'm in the land development business, and my fortunes rise and fall. A few years ago they were low, so I stopped paying the taxes on that place. Does the city want to give it back to me?"

"No. Nothing like that."

"Hell of a location to own property. Has a lot of potential if you can wait for the real estate market to turn. It still hasn't really taken off in that particular section, which I suppose explains why I couldn't sell it when I needed to unload it. In the end, I had to walk away. Maybe the current owner will have better luck."

"The newest owner has a troubling problem. The body of a woman was found in the basement."

"What does that have to do with me? I've not had access to that property in years."

"We think the victim has been in the basement twenty-five years. You had possession of the property at the time of her death."

"I did inherit it from my father while I was trying to launch my land development project in the Far West End. Another great location, but I lost my shirt in the early nineties. I was getting back on my feet by the end of the decade."

"Looks like you've done well for yourself."

"Like I said, the fortunes rise and fall."

"Was the Church Hill property vacant in the early nineties?"

"It was not. There was a guy whom I allowed to live there. He needed a roof, and I didn't care as long as he paid the utilities."

"What was his name?" Novak pulled out his notebook and flipped to a fresh page.

Delany raised a thin hand to his chin and scratched as he dug for the name. "Scott Turner."

"When is the last time you saw Mr. Turner?"

Delany shook his head. "He packed up his stuff without warning and moved out of the house right about the time you're asking about. He gave no word to me that he was leaving. And he stuck me with one hell of a heating bill. I haven't seen him since."

He scribbled the man's name on a clean sheet. "What did Mr. Turner do?"

"He bartended in the Slip and worked odd jobs. I met him at one of my construction sites. Likable guy."

"Did Turner ever mention a woman named Rita Gallagher?"

"Hell if I know. Like I said, I was letting him squat in the place." He sat back, uncrossed and recrossed his legs again. "I can tell you the guy was good-looking, a real ladies' man. If half the tales he told on the construction site were true, there were a lot of ladies in and out of his bed." He shifted in his chair. "Is this Rita Gallagher your victim?"

"Yes."

"Do you think Turner killed her?"

"I don't know. I'm trying to piece together what happened in and around the house at the time. And you've had no contact with Scott Turner at all since?"

"You know, I think he moved to California. Heard one of the boys on the job talking about him. Turner owed him money."

"Turner have any friends in the area?"

"I was his boss, not his friend. I didn't keep up with him."

"Did anyone else live in the house?"

"After Turner bolted, I couldn't get anyone to live there for free, let alone for money. The area was rough, but I had hopes the real estate market would improve around there. I locked the front door and waited for property values to come around. And as you know now, they didn't move fast enough and the city took the place."

"Did you have anyone check on the property over the years?"

"I didn't invest a dime in the place. My properties in the West End took all my energy. And when they paid off, I set my sights even farther west. I'm always looking for the next big real estate score."

Novak handed the man one of his cards. "If you think of anything else about the house, let me know."

"Yeah sure. So who was this woman?"

Novak rose, not willing to discuss details. "I don't know much at this stage. Like I said, I'm still pulling the pieces together."

Delany stood. "And she's been in the house for twenty-five years?"

"Looks like it."

He shook his head. "Damn. I'm glad I didn't know. She can't be much more than bones."

Novak didn't comment on the state of the body. "Thank you for your time."

"Sure. Call me anytime."

In his car, he drove toward the Far West End to the last address listed on Rita Gallagher's driver's license. The Maple Tree Apartments were next to the area hospital and in the early nineties had been new. The development had been updated with a fresh coat of gray paint, but the design and building materials hearkened back to that decade. The landscaping was neat and crisp and the lawns mowed.

He parked in front of a rental office and, once inside, found a petite strawberry-blond woman with large glasses sitting at the reception desk. "I'm Detective Tobias Novak with the City of Richmond Police."

"I'm Wanda Richardson, the manager."

"I'm hoping you can help me with a former tenant. The name is Rita Gallagher, and she listed her last address as 702 unit D."

"Sure. Let me see what I can find." Smiling, Wanda turned to her computer and typed. "You're lucky. We digitized our records several years ago. When was she here?"

"Around 1992."

"Why're you digging into twenty-five-year-old records?"

"We found Rita Gallagher's body last night. I'm trying to trace her last steps."

Wanda adjusted her glasses as she looked up. "You just found her?"

"Yes, ma'am."

"I didn't see any mention on the news."

"We've not released any information yet, but I imagine it will make the evening news."

"Did you find her in a grave?"

"I can't say."

"Right. Sorry. Not the kind of question I should be asking." She nodded and turned her attention to the computer. "We've been through a couple of management changes since 1992."

"How long have you been here?"

"Since '96. Sorry."

She keyed in the name and leaned in to read the screen. "She lived here with a roommate, Charlotte Gibson. They were in the apartment for a year. According to a note from the property manager, Rita Gallagher moved out and defaulted on her share of the rent. Ms. Gibson was able to finish paying the last two months, but was late both times. Ms. Gibson moved out at the end of 1992."

"Do you have any forwarding information for her?" He pulled out his notebook and flipped to a clean page.

"I have an address where we sent the remainder of her security deposit." She rattled it off. "But it's twenty-five years old. Not sure if it will help."

"It's a start." He looked up. "Was there employment information on file for Rita Gallagher?"

"She listed her place of employment as a bar called Billy's, located on Main Street in the city."

Julia lived above Billy's now. He didn't like all the leads trailing back to her. He scribbled the information. "Thanks."

Wanda frowned as she read the computer screen. "Charlotte and Rita lost most of their security deposit. The carpet in the back bedroom was destroyed. I have a note here that Charlotte came in and complained about us keeping her deposit. She blamed the stain on Rita. She received ten dollars and two cents back from her deposit."

"Does it say how the carpet was damaged?"

She read the files, scanning lines of neatly written notes. "Nope. Says it was a rust stain. Floorboards also had to be replaced. When the floorboards have to be redone, that's usually pet damage. At that time we had a no-pet policy, but people break the rules all the time."

"That color usually associated with pets?"

"Depends. There's mention of a rust smell, which we usually don't find with pet damage."

"Can you print out what you have on file for me?"

"Sure." She turned to a printer and collected the pages. "Just because they weren't supposed to have a pet doesn't mean they didn't. If this job has taught me any lesson, it's that people lie. Some more than others."

"Right."

Rita had been killed by blunt force trauma to the back of her head. There'd been no blood at the basement crime scene, but blood upstairs. She could have been struck in her apartment and brought to the Church Hill house to die. Or neither stain could be of relevance. At this point, he suspected he was dealing with multiple crime scenes.

CHAPTER FIVE

Monday, October 30, 10:00 a.m.

As Julia slipped into the courtroom, the commonwealth's attorney and the defense attorney were huddled in front of Judge Robert Bischoff, an athletic man in his late sixties. The judge did not suffer fools gladly and had a reputation for imposing the maximum prison terms allowed by law.

Bischoff scowled as he stared over half-glasses at the sleek, tall female defense attorney dressed in designer black and then at the thirtysomething male prosecutor in an ill-fitting suit. Today was sentencing day for drug trafficker Benny Santiago.

Julia looked toward the defendant's seat and noted the wide shoulders of the man in the conservative dark-blue suit. Benny Santiago had cut his long dark hair into a sensible style that now highlighted flecks of gray he normally dyed. There was no sign of the bird tattoo on the right side of his neck, and she guessed the attorney had used stage makeup to cover it up. Benny Santiago was presenting himself as Respectable Man in a play called *A Judicial Travesty*.

She didn't need to see Benny's face to know that the sleeker hairstyle enhanced his angled olive-toned features. He was as beautiful to look at as he was vicious.

When he lifted his arm slightly to adjust a cuff, she noted the tattooed snake on the back of his wrist. She knew from experience the tattoo wound up his arm and coiled around a muscled bicep. Beneath the bland cotton shirt and traditional suit beat the heart of one of the cruelest drug dealers in the mid-Atlantic. And he was here today to learn how much time he'd serve in prison.

For seventy-one days, Julia had worked undercover as a dealer and bartender in El Lobo, a bar ninety miles east of Richmond in Virginia Beach. As she slung drinks, the wire embedded in a necklace had video recorded Benny and his crew as they made deal after deal. She'd blended well into the rough culture, easily losing herself in the role of Jules Glover. She'd been so close to finding out who supplied Santiago with his drugs.

And then, the last night of the operation, someone had told Benny a police takedown was in the works. Benny had gone wild with rage and turned his anger toward a familiar target, his young girlfriend, Lana Ortega, a full-figured blonde with dark-brown eyes. He'd pinned Lana up against the wall and, always careful not to harm her face, drove his fist into her belly. He'd cocked his fist and hit her again as he demanded to know who had betrayed him. She'd crumpled and whimpered, begged him to stop as a bar full of Benny's boys watched. He'd pulled her up by her hair and raised a gun to her temple.

Julia hurried around the bar. "Shit, Benny. Leave her. If what they're saying is true, you need to get out of here now."

"Who the fuck are you to talk to me?"

"The only one here who has the guts to give you good advice."

Benny turned on her in a blind rage, grabbed her wrist, and twisted. The pain made her drop to her knees. "I've seen you talking to Lana."

Before she could speak, he hit her with a bone-rattling punch to the jaw. She landed hard on the floor. He grabbed the necklace and ripped it off. "What the hell were you two bitches talking about?"

He rolled her on her back as a crowd gathered. He drove a fist into her ribs. The pain overwhelmed her, and she struggled to reach the small service weapon strapped to her ankle.

Lana stumbled to her feet, her hand pressed to her gut, and watched as Benny reached for the snap on Julia's pants. "Benny, she wears a gun in her boot."

Benny's fingernails scraped along her leg and pulled the gun from its strap.

"Nobody gets in my business, bitch," Lana spat.

The judge's gavel brought Julia back to the present. The attorneys returned to their seats as the courtroom doors opened.

As Julia tried to relax against the hard bench, a plump blonde wearing a tight red skirt and a form-fitting white sweater made her way to the front of the courtroom. A thick trail of perfume followed her.

Lana took a seat behind Benny. "Hey, baby."

As Benny turned to smile at Lana, his gaze swept the room and, for an instant, hitched onto Julia. A small smile tipped the edge of his full lips. Without a word spoken, she understood he considered her unfinished business.

Julia didn't budge or allow her line of sight to waver.

Lana's gaze trailed her boyfriend's, and when it settled on Julia, her lips rose into a snarl. She wore her hatred as plainly as the fresh heart tattoo above her right ankle.

Julia remained as still as stone. She could hide her thoughts and feelings better than Benny. He was an amateur.

Judge Bischoff's gavel drew Lana's attention to the front of the court. Benny winked at Julia before he slowly turned to face the front of the courtroom.

The female attorney, Elizabeth Monroe, was on retainer for many of the drug dealers in the area, and Julia knew exactly how Benny had been able to hire her. Monroe beckoned Benny to stand. The commonwealth's attorney and his assistant also stood and faced the judge.

"The defense has petitioned the court for a one-month delay in sentencing," the judge said. "It states Mr. Santiago is still recovering from wounds sustained in an attack against him in the city jail."

Julia had heard about Benny's beating, which had taken place in the common area near the phones. Benny knew the gangs on the floor ran the phones and that he needed their permission to make a call. He'd not asked for approval as he reached for the receiver. Three men had beaten the hell out of him. She'd bet money he'd orchestrated it all as a way to delay sentencing.

"However," the judge continued, "I don't concur. Mr. Santiago, you have been tried and convicted." The judge listed each of the charges, pausing before he slowly cited Julia's assault. "Therefore, I sentence you to the maximum prison term of twenty years. Your sentence begins immediately."

Julia tipped her head back until it touched the wall. She waited for a sense of relief to wash over her, but none came. There was only emptiness.

As Lana groaned over the loss, Julia rose, slipping her purse on her shoulder. She didn't bother to glance back toward Benny or his girl, refusing to give either one the idea she cared. That was the trick to undercover work. Dump the true emotions in a bottomless hole.

She automatically fished in her purse for a cigarette. Her fingers brushed the pack, and she pulled it out, but she couldn't locate her lighter. She'd been serious about quitting yesterday but now could think of nothing else.

Out of the courtroom, she moved toward the stairs, her head bowed. She wanted fresh air. Needed to decompress before any reporter—or worse, attorney—approached her.

"Running for your life, Vargas?" The deep, gravelly voice of her sometime partner and favorite smoker had her turning to face Agent Dakota Sharp.

"Sharp."

"I thought you kicked the habit again."

A sly smile tipped the edge of her lips as she kept walking toward the stairs. "Nobody likes quitters. Now tell me you have a light."

He held up empty hands, his head slowly shaking. "Three weeks since I've had a smoke."

"Damn it. If there was anyone I thought I could count on, it was you, Sharp."

"Blame it on Tessa. She's not a fan of the smokes."

"Since when did Agent Sharp let anyone tell him what to do?"

He laughed. "Happy wife, happy life—isn't that right?"

She rolled her head from side to side. "Maybe you're smarter than you look."

As they paused at the stairs, he nodded toward the open courtroom doors as people filed out. "How did the Santiago case go?"

A shrug. "Sentenced to twenty years."

"So Benny's not too injured to be sentenced."

"Apparently not."

"That must feel good."

"Almost as good as the cigarette I'm not having right now."

Sharp looked as if he'd say more when his gaze settled on a point behind her shoulder. "There's a woman headed toward you."

She didn't turn around. "Don't tell me. Big blond hair, tight skirt, and an attitude?"

"Yep."

"That would be Lana Ortega. Benny's girlfriend."

Sharp's fingers slid subtly to his waist, inches from his weapon.

Julia turned to face the approaching woman. She didn't speak as the woman's four-inch heels clip-clopped on the tile floor.

With the thick scent of perfume circling her, Lana walked up to Julia, stopping short of entering her personal space. "You think you're so smart. But my Benny is smarter than any cop. He's going to appeal this bullshit conviction."

"That so?"

"He's a good man," she said. "He's innocent. You entrapped him with your lies."

"Did you think he was such a good guy when he was using you as a punching bag? How many stitches did it take to close the cut in your skull?"

Heavily lined eyes narrowed as she absently fingered the diamond bracelet that probably had been part of his apology tour. "You made him lose his temper. If you hadn't come into our world, he never would have gotten so angry."

"If he does by some miracle beat this on appeal, do you think he'll be sorry when he finally loses it and beats you to death? You and I both know that's a matter of time."

Lana tipped her chin up. "You don't know my Benny. He loves me."

Julia wouldn't waste her breath arguing with the girl. The case was out of her hands now and the responsibility of the attorneys. "Whatever you say."

"You know, you're a real bitch," Lana said.

"Am I? Good. Better a bitch than a victim."

Lana leaned in, her eyes now feral. "Cunt. Whore. The way you turned on us when we treated you like family."

Elizabeth Monroe came up and placed a manicured hand on her shoulder. "Time to go, Lana."

Lana shrugged off Monroe's hand. "I have more to say to this bitch cop."

"No, you don't," Monroe said. Sleek fingers banded around Lana's wrist. "We leave now."

Lana jerked free of Monroe's grasp and moved to within inches of Julia. "Watch your back, bitch."

As Sharp reached for Lana, Monroe jerked her away with such force that Lana stumbled to keep her balance in her platform shoes.

"Excuse us, Officers," Monroe said.

Julia stood, silently watching the anger flash and burn across the young woman's face. As tempting as it was to spar, she didn't move. She wasn't going to let a police harassment charge derail this case.

"This is not over," Lana said.

"It is for now," Monroe said.

After Monroe and Lana left, Julia rushed down the stairs and out the front door. She paused to breathe in fresh air.

Sharp stayed on her heels. "Isn't it time you headed north? You have an appointment, correct?"

She checked her watch. Sharp's work with Shield Security on a cold case had prompted her to ask him about the Quantico, Virginia, security firm's new mission to help law enforcement officers dig into cold cases. He'd been one of the few she'd told about her meeting. "I have time."

"Who are you meeting with?"

A sigh shuddered through her as she dumped the cigarette pack in her purse. "Garrett Andrews. He works for your buddy, Clay Bowman, at Shield Security. Andrews has agreed to help me with data searches."

"I didn't realize you'd reached out to them."

She shrugged. "You know me. Never afraid to ask. I've been reading my father's old files on the Hangman case. I want to take a crack at it."

"Why?"

"It was a big case in its day. No one ever caught the killer, and I'd like to remedy that. And so that you hear it from me, my old man shot and killed himself during the investigation. Some think he was involved with the killings. Whatever the outcome, I want solid answers."

"Tall order."

Yes, it was, and she hoped she could back up her claims. "If there's no challenge, what's the fun?"

"Right."

Julia smiled. "I heard Bowman respects you."

"He's a solid guy."

"Any words of wisdom?"

"You're a good cop. You know your case. Be yourself."

She laughed. "Ah, so you mean overly direct and irritating?"

He smiled. "You said it."

As she dug keys from her purse, she asked, "What if they don't take the case? What if twenty-five years is too long a stretch for them? What if they buy into the rumors about my father and believe the case is closed?"

"They wouldn't allocate their time today if they didn't think new evidence could be found. It's their job to find answers, whether you like what they find or not."

"I don't—*can't*—believe my father did it."

"Then you've nothing to fear."

"Right. I'll keep that in mind."

"I know, easier said than done."

"I've gone through all the files as well as my father's case notes. But I'm concerned the Hangman did too good a job covering his tracks and whatever mistakes he did make are now lost in time."

"What about your father's police partner?"

"Ken Thompson? I've talked to him twice, but there's a wrinkle there. He has Alzheimer's. He still appears okay to most folks, but I can see he's missed a step or two."

"I'm sorry to hear that."

"Yeah. He's a good man. Hell of a way to end. He's also my last tangible link to the Hangman case." She patted her coat pockets for cigarettes, half hoping she'd find one, when she caught herself. Jesus, why was it so hard to stop? "Not that many people know what's going on with Ken, so keep it under your hat."

"Sure."

"Ken kept in touch after Jim died. He never missed a birthday or Christmas. Mom wasn't ever thrilled to see him, but he kept coming. Always had a gift for me. And when she died, he was a rock. I think he blames himself for Jim's suicide."

"Cops are good at second-guessing. It's what enables us to do the job. The problem is those questions are hard to turn off."

She understood self-blame, second-guessing, and replaying an event over and over. It didn't take a shrink to link what had happened in Virginia Beach with the dreams of her father's suicide that had been plaguing her for the last eight months.

The ripple effect of her father's death had changed life for Julia and her mother. When Jim shot himself, Amy Vargas embodied every nightmare of a cop's wife. The cops didn't distance themselves from Amy and Julia intentionally, but they did it nonetheless. She'd learned at a young age that victims were ultimately rejected because no one wanted a living reminder of how bad it could get.

Catching the Hangman would win her a couple of get-out-of-victim-jail cards. Her father would be vindicated and maybe what Benny did to her, forgotten.

"You're tough," Sharp said.

That's what everyone said about Jim Vargas. Ballbuster. Pit bull. Hell of a man. And he'd cracked under the pressure of the Hangman case. "Yeah, I'm tough."

Sharp was silent for a moment before saying, "You're right to pull in Shield." He clicked his key fob, and the lights of a dark SUV flashed. "And if they refuse the case, talk to me. I might be able to lend a hand."

The rush of gratitude was quick and sharp, sending her scrambling toward sarcasm. "That's pretty damn touching, Sharp."

He smiled. "What can I say? I'm one hell of a guy."

Grinning, she slid behind the wheel of her SUV as Sharp got in his vehicle and drove off. She sat in the car, letting the heat from the sun warm the chill in her bones. Finally, she pulled on her sunglasses.

As she checked her phone for messages, she spotted a flash of red silk in her peripheral vision. Her fingers slid to her weapon as she set the phone down. She turned to find Lana, sans her watchdog, closing in on her vehicle.

"Give me patience," she mumbled. Tightening her hand on the grip of her weapon, she wrestled with going toe-to-toe with the woman. Not long ago, she'd have thrown open the door and not thought twice about consequences. But working undercover had leashed that impulsive streak.

Lana knocked on her window and motioned for Julia to roll it down. "It's only you and me now, bitch."

Julia counted to ten and started her car as she muttered to herself, "You've bigger fish to fry, Vargas."

Lana knocked on the window again, her long bony fingers clutched into a tight fist. Rap. Rap. Rap. "Open this fucking window, bitch. Don't pussy out on me."

Julia drummed short nails against the door handle as common sense told her to remain calm. A confrontation wouldn't accomplish anything. Refusing to be baited, she clicked on her seat belt.

"I'd love to chat, Lana, but not today."

"Chickenshit! Coward." Lana slammed both palms against the driver's side window so hard one of her red gel-tip fingernails snapped.

Julia put the car in reverse, backing out as the girl continued to follow and beat fists on her window. Julia moved carefully, inch by inch. By the book.

"How do you sleep at night, you fucking whore? You betrayed Benny and me." Tears glistened in the woman's eyes. "We treated you like family!"

When Julia had been undercover, she'd made a point to befriend Lana. It didn't take long for the woman, starved for attention, to bond with Julia. She'd played on Lana's insecurities and weaknesses to learn all she could about Benny's operation. The more she'd learned about Lana's wretched past, the more she'd come to pity the insecure girl who saw Benny Santiago as a step up from the shit hole where she'd been raised.

The night it all went wrong, when Benny had shifted his anger away from Lana to her, she had made eye contact with Lana as the girl swiped blood from her split lip. Julia had seen the hurt and then anger flash in Lana's gaze as the girl realized the person she'd trusted, confided in, shared her dreams along with Benny's secrets with, had betrayed her.

Outside, Lana beat on the trunk of Julia's car.

Julia's heart raced as she pulled away, watching in the rearview mirror as Lana threw a high-heeled shoe at the car. It hit the trunk and bounced off.

A flash of light caught Julia's attention, and she spotted a man recording the entire scene.

CHAPTER SIX

Monday, October 30, noon

Julia drove across town, willing her shoulders to release their tension. She used the time to crank a rock tune and let her body absorb the beat that always elevated her mood. Wrapped in the rhythm of the bass, there were no doubts of her upcoming presentation or worries over what she'd do if Shield refused her.

When she parked in the gravel driveway of a suburban brick rancher, she paused as the song wound down. Drawing in a breath, she was out of the car, ready to face what came next.

The front garden beds were filled with neatly trimmed hedges, and the grass was freshly cut and raked. A tall oak in the yard had begun to shed its autumn leaves, and the long crooked branches stretched up to the blue sky like fingers. Ken was a yard guy, and since his retirement last year, he was making the most of his passion for landscaping.

She noted a standard cop four-door parked in front of the house. Ken's cronies didn't visit often anymore, but when they did, they rarely stayed long. She was sorry she'd have to break up whatever visit was happening because she knew he enjoyed them. But they had to get to

Shield. Initially she'd wanted to go alone, but he'd insisted on coming, assuring her there was still enough of him left to help. Pride and fear had coated his words, and she'd reluctantly agreed.

She walked to the front door and rang the bell. Seconds later, the clip of determined footsteps approached the door before it snapped open to Wendy Thompson, a trim woman in her early fifties. She and Ken had been married for twenty-five years. Ken had intended to work a few more years, but then his memory began to slip. Small things at first. Keys. Reading glasses. A cup of coffee. All small enough to chalk up to senior moments. But then the lapses grew. Keys became a lost car parked in a lot. Reading glasses became the checkbook.

Eighteen months ago, Wendy took Ken to the doctor when he'd started having trouble remembering. After a series of tests over the course of last year, the doctor diagnosed Alzheimer's. Ken retired, and Wendy left the city's forensic department.

"Julia, you're right on time," Wendy said.

"I see Ken has a visitor," Julia said.

"Yes. It's a nice surprise."

Julia checked her watch. "I hate to be a killjoy, but we're going to have to get on the road soon. Is Ken ready to go?"

Wendy motioned her inside. "I'll get him going."

Male laughter rumbled along the hallway. "Who came by to visit?" asked Julia.

The house smelled of pine cleaner. "Detective Novak from Richmond homicide."

"Novak?" Tension banded around the base of her skull. "What does he want?"

"Said he wanted to catch up when he called an hour ago. I thought it would be nice. Ken misses the job."

"Really?"

Wendy arched a brow. "What's that mean?"

"Nothing."

"I've known you too long, Julia."

"Novak called me into a homicide last night. Body's been entombed for twenty-five years. Found a picture of my dad and me in the victim's purse."

"Who?"

"Rita Gallagher. I don't have any idea who she is." It bothered her she didn't know anything about a woman who appeared to have been close to her and her father.

Wendy stared at Julia. "And her body was just found?"

She ignored her unease. "Yes."

More male laughter drifted down the hallway from the sunporch.

Julia checked her watch again. She didn't have time to visit even if she hustled when she drove up I-95 to Quantico. "We're going to have to leave in the next few minutes."

"Right. I'll get Ken's coat."

Julia moved to the bright sunporch and saw Ken sitting in his chair, laughing like she hadn't seen him do in years. Novak had his back to her. However, as soon as her foot touched the threshold, he rose and turned.

"Julia," Ken said, looking up. "You know Tobias Novak?"

"I do," she said. "We met at a crime scene last night." She didn't expect her thing with Novak to last, so she saw no point in mentioning when they really met.

At sixty-two, Ken remained lean and fit. He had a thick shock of white hair that he brushed off from a round face. He looked healthy. The model of perfection, which perversely made it all the more sad. "That's what he was telling me. He said he found a picture of you and Jim in a victim's pocket."

Made sense the call was business. Ken was an obvious choice to question about Jim Vargas. "That's right."

"Good to see you again, Julia," Novak said.

No one on the force other than Ken used her first name. She was Vargas to everyone, except for Novak, who'd always called her Julia. The familiarity was unsettling.

She slid her hands in her pockets. "You, too, Novak."

"What was the woman's name, Novak?" Ken asked.

"Rita Gallagher." Novak's gaze didn't shift away from her.

"I don't remember Jim mentioning her," Ken said. "But I have lots of old notes from my cases. I told Novak I can read through them."

She'd seen his office, a study in mile-high stacks of paper and chaos. A search for Rita Gallagher constituted a needle in a haystack. "Great idea."

"I found out she worked at Billy's," Novak said.

"Billy's," Julia repeated. "My aunt's bar?"

Novak nodded. "Interesting, don't you think?"

She frowned, not liking the newest connection. "Small world."

Novak studied her a beat before saying, "I asked Ken what he remembered about the fall of 1992 when he and your father worked the Hangman case."

"Okay." Novak was a good cop and didn't ask random questions.

Ken looked at Novak. "Julia wants to see if she can crack it."

"Why now?" Novak asked.

"Time is running out, I suppose," she said. "Witnesses are getting older. Evidence is degrading. If not now, then most likely never."

"And it's no secret that my memory is also fading. I told Julia several times not solving that case always bothered me," Ken said. "Catching the Hangman is top on my bucket list."

Julia had promised Ken she'd never patronize him. "Ken's right. It's now or never. Speaking of which, if we're still going to Quantico, we'll need to get going."

Novak studied her. "Quantico?"

"We're working with Shield Security over there. They'll be helping us with data searches and DNA retesting," Julia said.

"Odd Rita Gallagher was found as you're reopening the case," Novak said.

She'd wondered about the odd coincidence as well. Clearly, he didn't believe in divine timing either.

"Gallagher died within weeks of the last Hangman victim. She lived and worked in the same area as the victims. Maybe Shield can figure out if she's connected to the Hangman."

"You'll keep me posted." Novak hadn't tacked a question mark on the end of the sentence.

"Sure. I didn't think you cared about cold cases," Julia said.

"The killings happened in my jurisdiction. And there's no statute of limitations on murder."

"Sure. I'll keep you in the loop," Julia said.

Novak shook Ken's hand. "I might come back and pick your brain some more."

"You're welcome anytime," Ken said. "Wendy, we're leaving."

Wendy showed up with his coat in hand. "I heard you." She handed him his coat.

Novak walked them to her car, watching as Ken settled in the front seat beside her. Until now their relationship had centered on physical pleasure. He'd asked questions about her, but she'd been able to deflect them easily enough. Now, she sensed the next time they were alone, she wouldn't be able to easily dismiss his questions.

"I'll never get used to not driving," Ken said, clicking his seat belt. "I always drove when your dad and I were partners."

She started the car. "We'll make better time with me behind the wheel."

"Still, it sucks."

She glanced in her rearview mirror. Novak was still watching them. "What did Novak have to say?"

"Like he said, wanted to know about Rita Gallagher."

"And you don't remember her?" She focused on the road and shoved Novak to the back of her mind.

"No. But your dad didn't tell me everything. He guarded his secrets."

"You haven't talked much about the days you and Jim worked together." She knew basic facts. They'd been partners for three years, working dozens of homicide cases in the city. The Hangman case had been their last.

"Your dad was a tenacious son of a bitch. You remind me a lot of him."

"I heard that from my mom and aunt once or twice."

"Jim could never let a case go. He worked it until it cracked or the brass pulled him off."

After several conversations with him in the last couple of weeks, she knew it was best to let him talk. If she pushed for details, he could get confused or sidetracked. So she kept her gaze on the road and waited for precious details about her father's career.

"You know he came from vice," Ken said. "He worked undercover. Had a hell of a knack for slipping into the skin of anyone."

The last undercover assignment had come when she was three or four, and she had vague memories of seeing Jim with long hair and a beard. Jim Vargas had been gone a year before he'd made his case. He'd dismantled a large heroin ring and received a promotion, but the work came with a personal price. A lesson she now understood all too well.

"The narcotics department made a dozen arrests based on the evidence he gathered from that last undercover operation. And not low-level street punks. He snagged some big damn fish. Made a lot of enemies, but he didn't care. Homicide must have been tame after that kind of work."

"Did he say that?"

"He was always restless. He tried to settle into the new life, but it was never easy."

"It takes time adjusting to your real life again," she said. "Hard to shut off the adrenaline."

"Is it that way for you, Julia?"

She heard the concern behind the words. "No. I'm fine." She tossed in a grin to sell it. "Really, don't worry about me."

"You always say you're fine."

"Because I am. Please don't worry."

"How can I not?"

She didn't speak as she searched for words—or maybe it was courage—to ask what she'd been unable to ask until now. "Why do you think Jim killed himself?"

Ken frowned. "I've spent countless sleepless nights replaying our last conversations. I never remembered one hint of trouble. I figured your dad would go on forever. He was indestructible. I never saw it coming. I still haven't gotten over it."

"He never said he was upset?"

"Not a word. I know it was rough for him after your mother moved out with you. He wanted the marriage to work, but he always wanted to close cases. It's impossible to do both. Your mom was tired of the job always coming first."

"She loved him. She said it enough times before she died."

That's why they'd been at the house that day. Her mother was moving back and willing to give their marriage another try. *It's going to be good this time, Julia.* She met her mother's watery gaze in the rearview mirror. *We're going to be a real family this time. No more pretend.*

And then she and her mother had discovered the blood and destruction waiting for them at the house.

The medical examiner had put Jim Vargas's death at about five in the evening. Later, when Julia became a cop, she'd accessed the police reports from that day. According to what her mother told the police, they'd arrived home shortly after five. They'd pushed through the front door of their house minutes after her father had shot himself.

So close to seeing him alive. Maybe stopping him. Close, but no cigar.

"Did you and Jim ever feel like you were close to catching the Hangman? You listed suspects in the files, and I read the interviews. Was there anyone who stuck with you more than any other?"

"I didn't like Gene Tanner. He was the husband of the first victim. We leaned on him hard. When the press got wind of it, they chased Tanner and dug into his personal life. But then the second body showed and he had a solid alibi, so we backed off."

"Did anyone know all three victims?"

He didn't answer immediately, as his gaze drifted to the strip malls giving way to woodlands as they drove north on I-95. "We spent countless hours going through the interviews. The evidence. But there was never one guy that stuck out to us." He shook his head, plucking a thread from his pant leg. "And after Jim died, well, I lost a good bit of the fire in my belly to solve the case. I had wanted this killer caught so badly. And then the killings stopped, and I wondered if maybe the rumors about Jim were true. And if you tell anyone I said that, I'll deny it."

She shifted in her seat. He'd never told her any of this before. "You thought he might have been the Hangman?"

"Working undercover can change a person, especially if they're under for a long time. Jim and I went to the academy together. The job took its toll on us both, but especially him."

She was silent.

"Jim could be short-tempered, and he wasn't afraid to bend the law to catch a suspect. In the darkest parts of the night, I thought maybe he was the Hangman. That the job had transformed him."

Julia sat still, barely breathing.

"It was a year after his death before I could get really motivated about much. Like I said, there were no more deaths, and the case was shoved to the back burner. Until you. And now Novak." He stared out the window. "By the way, Novak asked about you today."

"Me?" Her fingers tightened on the steering wheel. "What about me?"

"General stuff. Mainly why you care about the case."

"And what did you tell him?"

"The party line. The last case your old man worked deserved to be solved."

"It's not a party line. It's the truth."

His gaze narrowed, like he smelled something was off. "Don't bullshit me, Julia. You think solving that case will somehow explain Jim's suicide, and maybe send a message to the friends who distanced themselves from you and your mother after his death."

"We did fine."

"It's okay to say you're suffering."

"But I'm not."

"Novak thinks you are."

"Really?"

His gaze cut toward her. "What's going on between you two?"

She adjusted her sunglasses. "We had a case last night."

He shook his head. "I'm not so far gone that I don't see the way he looks at you. What's the deal with you two?"

"Nothing."

He chuckled. "Maybe nothing for you, kiddo, but I don't think Novak received the memo."

CHAPTER SEVEN

Monday, October 30, 1:45 p.m.

Julia took the Quantico exit and let the GPS guide her along side streets to the security station where a guard stood. Ken, who had been silent most of the trip, sat straighter.

"Agent Julia Vargas," she said to the guard, showing her badge. "And this is retired detective Ken Thompson. We're meeting with Garrett Andrews."

The guard studied her identification before handing it back. "I need to see his identification."

Julia smiled. "Ken, where's your driver's license?"

The hint of uncertainty in her voice clearly irritated him. Frowning, Ken reached in his breast pocket and produced his ID. He handed it to the guard.

"You're on the list," the guard said. "Follow the road to the back."

"Got it," Julia said.

She followed the road and parked in a visitor spot by the front door. Out of the car, they made their way to the sleek five-story office building. The smoked-glass front was opaque, but she sensed every move they made was monitored by someone on the inside.

"Ready to wow the committee?" she asked Ken.

He tugged at the edges of his sports jacket as he stared at the building. "You're doing most of the talking, right?"

"That's the plan, but they may ask you questions. Is that okay?"

He jutted out his chin. "Of course it's okay. I miss details from time to time, Julia, but I'm not an invalid."

"I'm sorry. I'm really worried that they'll turn us down."

The lines around his eyes softened. "No one says no to you."

"Sure they do."

A smile crunched the edge of his lips. "And the poor bastard lived to regret it, didn't he?"

"Maybe a little." She straightened his tie.

When they stepped into the lobby, a formidable man stood by the security desk. In his late thirties, he wore a well-tailored suit that hugged a trim waist. The shoes were polished. The red tie was straight, and the thick blond hair was cropped close. Scars on the back of his left hand suggested he'd been badly burned.

"Agent Vargas," the man said. The voice was deep with hints of rust on the edges.

"Yes, sir. I'm Julia Vargas." She moved toward him, her hand outstretched.

He wrapped long fingers around her hand and squeezed. "I'm Garrett Andrews."

Matching his grip, she met his gaze. She'd read up on the company and its principal partners. Andrews was the firm's computer expert, though some considered him a genius. He'd served with Special Forces in Iraq until an IED explosion had blown up his vehicle. He was the only survivor of the explosion. "Good to meet you, Mr. Andrews. This is Ken Thompson, my father's former partner."

Andrews extended his hand to Ken. "Pleasure to meet you. I've read the case files. You did some impressive work on the case, Detective Thompson."

Ken accepted his hand, no hint of worry in his lined face. "But I didn't solve it. The killer is still free."

"You're here to fix that."

"Damn right," Ken said.

She'd briefed Andrews on Ken's medical condition and had worried he would patronize Ken. But Andrews's demeanor didn't suggest even a whiff of pity.

"Excellent," Andrews said.

Ken nodded toward her. "Julia is the driving force behind this case now. I'll help wherever I can."

"I bet you still have some moves," Andrews said.

Ken gave a slight nod.

"Let me show you both to the conference room." He crossed to the elevator with long confident strides and pressed the button. The door opened, and when they stepped inside, he swiped a key card and pressed "5" before the doors closed.

The elevator doors opened to a reception area, and a pretty redhead sitting behind a polished desk smiled.

"We'll be in the conference room, Naomi," Andrews said.

"I've notified the rest of the committee," Naomi said. "They're on their way."

"Thank you." He extended his hand toward the long hallway. "It's right this way."

As Julia and Ken followed Andrews, her mind ticked through the key points she wanted to make to the committee.

The west wall of the conference room consisted of a bank of windows offering a clear view of the woods and a lake. A dozen office chairs surrounded a long polished conference table. Under a flat-screen television, a matching credenza was filled with drinks, fruits, and doughnuts. Doughnuts. Cops and their doughnuts.

"Can I offer you a drink or snack?" Andrews asked.

"A coffee would be great," Ken said. "Black, one sugar."

Andrews poured a cup and handed it to Ken. "Julia, what about you?"

"I'm fine, thank you." She all but lived on caffeine, but right now she was too hyped to risk another cup. "Where would you like us to sit?" She heard the clip in her voice and tried to soften it with a smile.

"At this end of the table," Andrews said.

She slid her purse from her shoulder and into the chair to the left of the head spot, which she'd give to Ken.

"Sure I can't get you a beverage?" he asked.

A pack of cigarettes. A shot of tequila. Maybe bourbon. "Thanks, but I'm fine."

Two men entered the room. Her homework had also told her the striking man with short black hair was Clay Bowman, the company's new CEO. Bowman was dating a Virginia State Police trooper and had worked with Agent Sharp on a cold case last month. To his left was a fit man in his midsixties. That would be Joshua Shield, founder of the company.

Andrews made introductions. Hands were shaken.

"Dakota Sharp speaks highly of you," Bowman said.

Julia held his direct gaze. "He's one hell of a cop."

"Agreed."

Bowman and Shield sat opposite Julia and Ken.

"Agent Vargas kindly sent me her presentation, and it's now uploaded into our system," Andrews said.

"We're ready whenever you are, Agent Vargas," Bowman said.

Andrews handed Julia the remote. The lights in the room dimmed, and the first image, a warehouse located in Richmond's Shockoe Bottom, came up. "This area of Richmond is the old tobacco warehouse district of the city. Today, it's been revitalized and is home to many young professionals." She clicked through more images of the area. "In the midseventies and eighties the area was in decline, but by 1992 was beginning to see a significant uptick in traffic. The promise of the city's new flood wall encouraged more businesses to relocate to the area. However, drugs and prostitution weren't uncommon, and there were many old tobacco warehouses yet to be renovated."

Unable to sit, Julia rose when the slide changed to the twenty-five-year-old image of the now-defunct Shockoe Bottom bar Stella's, owned by the first victim. "The Hangman was a serial killer who stalked Shockoe Bottom in the fall of 1992. As I said in my application, my father, Detective Jim Vargas, worked with Detective Ken Thompson to solve the murder of three women. All three victims were found within a three-block radius of Stella's, located on the eastern fringe of Shockoe Bottom."

Julia stole a glance toward her audience and found them all paying close attention.

A click and the screen image changed to the mug shot of a young woman with long brown hair and blue eyes. Mascara smudged under defiant eyes that stared at the camera. "This is the first victim. Her name was Rene Tanner. She worked at and co-owned Stella's with her husband, Gene Tanner. According to her husband, she took the evening off to go out with friends. She never came home. Her body was found hanging in a nearby warehouse six days later. The investigators focused on Gene Tanner, who until the death of the second victim was their primary suspect. Tanner didn't report his wife missing for three days, and when asked about the delay said his wife often took off."

"He was a hostile witness from the start," Ken said. "He was irritated and angry each time Jim and I interviewed him. He was uncooperative and considered unstable."

Julia clicked to a crime-scene photo displaying a naked body hanging in a bleak warehouse. "Note the bindings securing the victim's hands and feet. The knot work wasn't elaborate and was associated with some bondage fetish cultures."

"Do you think she was a willing participant?" Bowman asked.

"I think she knew her killer. She was arrested for prostitution and drug distribution several times. The medical examiner tested her blood and found high levels of cocaine."

"There were no signs of bruising on her body, suggesting she might have known her killer," Ken said. "Another reason we focused on Gene Tanner."

The next slide featured a young African American woman. "This is the second victim, Tamara Brown, who was age twenty-one at the time of her death. Tamara also had an arrest record for prostitution and drugs. She was found in an abandoned warehouse two blocks from Stella's." The next image featured Tamara Brown's lifeless body suspended from a beam.

"She's displayed differently," Shield noted.

Julia nodded. "Yes. The knots were more complex, and her arms were extended as if she were a puppet. The medical examiner believed she asphyxiated over several hours."

"That's slower than Tanner. He was prolonging the kill," Bowman said.

"That was the theory." Julia clicked to a series of forensic slides. "Hair and semen samples were found on her body and tested for DNA, but there were no hits. I'm hoping subsequent technology might discover what wasn't available to the lab in 1992."

"The clothes were found near their bodies in all three cases," Andrews said. "Was DNA pulled from their clothing?"

"Yes," Ken said. "The lab results were inconclusive."

Andrews raised a brow. "From all three cases?"

"Yes," Ken said.

Andrews stared at the screen. "Continue, Agent Vargas."

"Brown had been dead approximately four days when discovered," Julia said. "During that time, Gene Tanner was in Atlantic City with dozens of witnesses corroborating an alibi. Security cameras also had him on video."

"There were no large blocks of time during his trip that he was unaccounted for?" Bowman asked.

"There was a five-hour stretch at four a.m. when he left the casino and went to his room," Ken said. "There was no record of Tanner flying back to Virginia. And he'd have to have averaged one hundred and eleven miles per hour to make the round-trip during the gap. And that leaves no time to commit the murder."

"Private plane?" Shield asked.

"No flight plans were filed at any of the small airports within one hundred miles of Richmond during this period," Ken said.

"So Tanner was out as a suspect," Andrews said.

"Correct." She pressed the remote. The second victim appeared. "Because the temperature was unseasonably cold, Tamara Brown's body was intact. This time, the victim had bruising on her cheek that suggested a struggle," Julia said.

"Jim and I spent hours at the scene searching for evidence. We found nothing. Whoever this killer was, he was meticulous."

"The detectives' notes suggest they thought the murders were sexual in nature. As I said, the bindings are similar to bondage and discipline, sadism and masochism, known as BDSM," Julia said.

"Jim and I interviewed dozens of people in and around the club where Brown worked. Only a handful made the short list, but we couldn't prove anything."

Julia clicked to the next slide. "Ten days later, victim number three, Vicky Wayne, an exotic dancer, was discovered in a warehouse a block from the first. Her body was suspended from the second-story support beams, and it likely took her hours to die." The next slide featured the DMV photos of Rene, Tamara, and Vicky. "The primary connection to all three was that they worked within several blocks of Stella's."

"What about the original witnesses?" Andrews asked. "How many are still available for interviews?"

"I made a list of the ten primary suspects and witnesses. The only suspect I can't locate is Stuart Lambert, who worked in a video porn shop located on Cary Street."

Andrews made a note on a small pad. "Have you made contact with any of the witnesses?"

"Not yet."

"What do you want from Shield Security?" Shield asked. "The state lab could retest the DNA."

"There's a long waiting list of active cases. Our cold case has twenty-five-year-old DNA and has the lowest priority. This could drag out for years without your assistance."

"Are there any similar cases like this one anywhere else in the country?" Bowman asked.

"I did an extensive data search and found no other killings that had any similar hallmarks," Andrews said. "The killer either went dark after the third murder or died."

"One theory was that Jim Vargas was the killer," Shield offered.

Ken's gaze rose. "Hey, now. That bullshit theory was never proven. Came down to a bunch of reporters angling for headlines and bylines."

Shield drew in a slow breath. "You have DNA collected from the clothing of three victims. All samples tested inconclusive. That seems statistically unrealistic."

Ken might have had his doubts about Jim, but he wouldn't allow speculations outside his inner circle. Julia sensed this and laid a hand on his shoulder. "There were multiple problems with the lab that fall. The Hangman wasn't the only case that had trouble."

"So if we retest and find Jim Vargas's DNA on the clothing of the victims, then what?"

Julia nodded. "Mr. Shield, we follow up on any and all leads regardless of where they take us. If you find evidence proving my father was the killer, I'll accept it."

"Are you sure about that?" Bowman's demeanor had sharpened.

"I'm sure, Mr. Bowman," Julia said. "I want it solved."

"Jim Vargas didn't leave a suicide note, is that correct?" Shield asked.

"He did not," Ken said.

"This isn't some attempt to clear his name, is it, Agent Vargas?" Shield challenged.

Shield was playing devil's advocate, but he no doubt echoed the thoughts everyone on the committee harbored. She admired their candor.

"Nothing changes the fact that three women were slowly suffocated until dead and displayed for everyone to see," Julia said. "These women deserve closure. With or without your help, I'll work this case. However, I would rather work with Shield Security. You have tremendous resources."

"Do you really believe you can work with us?" Andrews asked. "The risks you took as an undercover agent nearly got you killed."

"I do take calculated risks, Mr. Andrews. It's part of being a cop. Yes, I paid a price for it during my last undercover job, but a large-scale drug dealer is now on his way to prison and facing twenty years."

"It was my understanding that the operation was aiming higher than Santiago," Shield pressed. "And the investigation was compromised. Whatever leads you had to the very top evaporated."

"Undercover operations like that are fluid," she said. "Everyone can plan all they want, but things can go sideways in a heartbeat."

"So you're saying you'd take a risk if the situation called for it in this investigation?" Shield asked.

"Absolutely, I sure as hell would. I don't see how—" Hearing her temper bubbling around the words, she paused. "I'm a professional. My objective is to solve this case."

Shield's expression was impossible to read as he studied her.

Bowman tapped his finger on the table. "Agent Vargas, I think we've heard all we need to. We'll contact you by close of business today with our decision."

The abruptness of his dismissal caught her a little short. She'd expected more questions. This likely didn't bode well. She'd shown her temper and now sensed a *hell no* by close of business. Not the best first impression when trying to woo an ally. *Shit.*

"Thank you for having us." She reached for her purse. "Ken?"

Ken rose, frowning at the group. "She's one hell of a cop. You'd be a fool not to work with her."

Color burned her cheeks. She didn't need anyone defending her. If she'd fumbled this interview, so be it. She wasn't going to apologize.

Shield rose and came around the table, extending his hand first to Ken. "Thank you for coming." Cool, steely eyes shifted to her. "It's good to have passion, Agent Vargas."

Bowman came around the table and shook Ken's hand and then hers. Again, another unreadable expression. "Thank you for coming."

This was the politest brush-off she'd ever received. "Thank you all for hearing the presentation."

"Mr. Andrews will escort you out," Bowman said.

A fitting end. "Great."

She and Ken moved toward the elevator, but she didn't bother to glance back at Bowman and Shield. She pressed the button to head down.

The doors opened. Ken and Andrews stepped in after her. She pushed the first-floor button. A dull headache throbbed, and she set her sights on a cigarette and a shot of tequila.

Andrews escorted them to the front door and thanked them again, and they left the building and crossed to her car.

Inside the SUV, Ken clicked his seat belt as she slid behind the wheel. "That didn't go well, did it?"

"Not as well as I'd hoped." *Stay positive. Stay positive.* "They were trying to amp us up to see if we really cared about the case."

He shook his head. "I shouldn't have defended you. Made you look weak."

"You had my back. Thank you."

He twisted one of the buttons on his jacket cuff. "I wish I could have done more."

"You were great. I dug my own grave, Ken. I'm too much of a cowboy."

"Like your old man."

"Yeah."

"Hey, they didn't say no."

"They will by close of business." She slowly backed out of the spot, hoping it wouldn't be her last time at Shield Security.

CHAPTER EIGHT

Monday, October 30, 4:45 p.m.

Julia's phone dinged with a text as she arrived at Billy's. Her aunt had owned the bar on Main Street for forty years. It had belonged to Julia's grandfather, who'd left it to her aunt and her mother. After Julia's father died, she and her mother had moved to the upstairs apartment, and her mother returned to tending bar, as she had been doing when she first met Jim Vargas.

She parked and checked her phone, expecting a message from Shield. It was from Novak.

Rita Gallagher's autopsy is scheduled for 8:30 tomorrow morning.

She texted back: I'll be there.

Inside, she went upstairs and changed into jeans and a Billy's T-shirt. Since the academy, she'd worked here on her days off, enjoying the camaraderie of the regular customers and knowing all she had to do was mix drinks and listen.

Down the back staircase, she moved behind the bar and reached for an apron. Her training here had allowed her to effortlessly slip behind Benny's bar. Though this place attracted the young professionals and Benny's lured bikers and drug dealers, she found after a drink or two everyone wanted to talk to the bartender. She'd heard a lifetime's worth of dreams and sad stories.

"Julia." The greeting came from Cindy Stafford, her mother's older sister.

Julia smiled. "Aunt Cindy."

"Good, you remembered to cover my shift tonight."

"I wouldn't forget your rare night off."

Julia hadn't told her aunt about digging into the Hangman case. Anything associated with Jim Vargas had always been a sore subject with Cindy. Seeing as Rita was now connected to Jim, she opted to hold off asking about their connection until she heard from Shield. She didn't need to be knee-deep in an argument when they called.

She pulled her phone from her back pocket and checked to make sure the volume was turned up. Close of business for Shield Security was exactly fifteen minutes from now. "I don't suppose I can bum a smoke off you?"

"I thought you quit."

"I did."

"But . . ."

"I'm a work in progress."

Cindy laughed. "In the back office. You know where I hide my purse."

"Thanks."

Julia ducked under the bar and moved toward the back to the office. A simple desk butted against a wall under a bulletin board covered with invoices, to-do lists, and pictures of the staff. Front and center was a picture of thirteen-year-old Julia standing with her aunt and mother.

She found Cindy's purse and fished out a pack of cigarettes and matches. She glanced at the clock. Ten minutes to five.

Curling her fingers around the cigarette, she moved to the back alley. Outside, a cool wind teased the edges of her ponytail. She leaned against the brick wall while staring toward the orange sun as it dipped into the horizon.

She rolled the cigarette between her fingers. Waited until five o'clock. When her phone didn't ring at five, she cursed.

Propped against the building, she was already dissecting how she'd tackle the Hangman case by herself. She'd read the case files several times and figured if she pulled some strings, tossed in lots of doughnuts sprinkled with *pretty please*s, she'd get her DNA samples bumped up a few places in the line.

The back door opened, and Cindy popped her head out. "There's someone up front for you."

"Who?"

"Didn't say. A suit."

A cop? Or someone who worked with Benny? Suits hid a multitude of sins.

"Be right there."

"He's cute."

Cute didn't mean squat. Some of Benny's associates were attractive, and they'd cut her throat if ordered to do so. "You didn't get a name?"

"Honey, I'm trying to get out of here so I can get home to my bookkeeping. Come up front."

Her phone now read 5:02 p.m. No call. "Right, I'm coming."

Julia knelt and removed the off-duty service weapon from her ankle holster. Knowing she could need her gun fast, she pulled the bar rag tucked in her apron and wrapped it around the weapon. She headed inside, the chatter of the night's first customers doing little to calm her nerves.

Tonight's waitress, Tammy, was seating the first to arrive. Julia's gaze roamed the place, searching for any man who might, well, look out of place, like he'd been sent to shoot her.

Everyone fit. No strange man. And then Tobias Novak turned from a group of men who looked like detectives. Not a trained assassin, but still trouble.

He caught her gaze and moved away from the others, tracking her as she moved behind the bar.

As he sat on one of the stools, she knelt and tucked the gun back in its holster.

"Expecting trouble?" he asked.

She tossed a bar towel over her shoulder. "Just careful."

He nodded, keeping whatever questions he had about the gun to himself. "Shield going to help?"

"They said close of business. And we're past that. So not looking good."

"Do you need them?"

"It would have been nice. They're a huge asset."

He scooped up a handful of peanuts from a bowl on the bar. "I'll lend a hand."

"Don't you have a full caseload?"

"I need community-service credits for my merit badge."

It was a touching gesture. "There are more entertaining hobbies."

"Agreed, but this one will include you."

That startled a half laugh out of her. "Right."

He shifted topics. "This is a nice place. It's been a while since I came in through the front door, though."

He'd been to her apartment several times, but they'd always used the back staircase leading off the alley.

When she didn't respond, he asked, "You moonlight?"

"Helping my aunt out for an evening. She's got to do bookkeeping and payroll tonight."

"You ask her about Rita Gallagher?"

"No." She leaned forward. "Cindy won't be happy about me reopening the Hangman case. Anything or anyone linked to my father puts her in a foul mood. But I need to ask now. She's changing. She'll be down soon."

"Great. I'll wait."

Of course he would. And now was as good a time as any to tell her about the Hangman case. "Drink?"

"Sure. A draft beer."

Grabbing a mug, she expertly filled it with just the right amount of head and set it on a napkin in front of him. "Any leads on Rita Gallagher?"

He sipped. "Some. Spoke to the former owner of the house where her body was found. He had a renter who went missing in 1992. Scott Turner. Working on tracking him now. So far, nothing. Also spoke to Rita's former landlord."

"You've been busy."

"Rita and her roommate lost a security deposit because there was a large rust-colored stain in Rita's bedroom."

"Blood?"

"No way of knowing."

"She have an arrest record?"

"She did. Files should be on my desk tomorrow."

Cindy appeared wearing her purse on her shoulder and a fresh coat of red lipstick. "I'm off."

"Cindy, before you go, I want you to meet Detective Novak. He's working a homicide and has a question for you."

Cindy grinned, sticking out her hand. "Detective Novak."

Novak rose and accepted it. "Ma'am, nice to meet you."

"What can I do for you?" Cindy asked.

Novak pulled his cell from his clip. "We found a woman's body. Driver's license says she was Rita Gallagher. I pulled her employment records from a rental application made in 1992, and she listed Billy's as her place of work." He showed her the driver's license picture on his phone.

"Rita Gallagher?" Cindy asked. "Yeah, yeah, I remember Rita. It's been ages since I've seen her."

"You remember much about her?" Julia asked.

"Rita was hard to forget," Cindy said. "Are you saying she's dead?"

"Her body was found last night," Novak said. "She's been dead at least twenty-five years."

"That's about the time she took off. She worked here about six months and then, without a word to anyone, didn't show again. Where did you find her?" Cindy asked.

"I can't really discuss it. What do you remember about Rita? You said she was hard to forget."

Cindy studied Rita's face. "Same smile. And the red hair caught a lot of attention." She handed the phone back. "Friendly with the customers but terrible with numbers. Always screwing up the cash register. Couldn't count to save her life. But she could make people laugh, and she could sell drinks. I used to say she could peddle a truckload of ice to an Eskimo in winter."

"She ever say what she did on her off-hours?" Novak asked.

"I don't remember that, but I do recall she left unexpectedly right around the time Julia's father died. The family was in turmoil. Amy was a wreck. There was also a big convention in town, and Rita's disappearing act left me in one hell of a bind. I worked nonstop for a week until I could hire someone else."

"They found a picture of Jim and me in her purse," Julia said as she pulled up the image on her phone. "It was taken on my team's soccer field before he died."

Cindy's frown deepened with confusion. "Why would she have a picture of you and your father?"

"That's the mystery," Julia said.

"The fact that Rita worked here fills in several pieces," Novak said. "I'm assuming she had access to the bar's office."

"Yeah. And upstairs. She seemed like a good kid." Cindy studied the picture of Julia and Jim. "I do remember the day this picture was taken. Julia was seven." She smiled up at her niece. "You were so excited about playing in the game. You were champing at the bit to get to the field that day."

"Mom came along that day, right?"

"She did. I held down the fort at the bar so Amy and Jim could enjoy the day with you. She was so excited to have your dad back in your lives again." Her smile faded a fraction. "He'd been gone so often. The loneliness was hard on your mom. She kept saying it was for a good cause. Never complained once. But it bothered her when he wouldn't call her."

"Cindy, Mom and Jim were separated when Jim died in November. Why'd they separate?" Julia asked.

"Amy never said what it was, but she was upset."

Julia had resented her father. He'd left them again and again, and in the end, used a bullet to take himself away for good. "Do you have any guesses as to who took the picture?"

"I suppose your mother took it, but couldn't say for sure." She handed Novak back the phone.

"Could Rita have stolen the picture from upstairs?" Julia asked.

"Sure, it's possible."

"When I cleaned out the attic in the spring, I didn't see any pictures of Mom and Jim."

"There are a few more closets to clean out back at my house," Cindy said. "I'll look."

"Anything else you remember about Rita?" Novak asked.

"She dated a guy named Jack," Cindy said. "I gather from what she said about him, he was a solid fellow and was nice to her. She worked hard. Took off a little too much sometimes. She liked to party. I always thought she had another guy on the side besides Jack."

"Why do you say that?" Novak asked.

"I'd catch her talking on the phone. When she saw me, she'd hang up. Not my place to judge as long as she did the work."

"And she vanished?" Julia asked.

Cindy shrugged. "One day here, happy and laughing. And the next she was gone."

"What about Jack?" Novak asked. "Did he ask about her?"

Cindy frowned. "I'm pretty sure I never saw him again."

"You remember his last name?"

"Afraid not. How did she die?" Cindy asked.

"I don't know for certain yet," Novak said. "The medical examiner's office has her remains now, and they'll be doing an autopsy in the morning."

Cindy shook her head. "Damn shame."

"If you think of anything else, will you let me know?" Novak handed her one of his cards.

"Yeah, sure." Cindy glanced at the clock. "Listen, if I don't get going now, I'll never get my work finished."

Novak smiled. "I know where to find you."

Cindy kissed Julia on the cheek. "Thanks again, doll."

"Sure."

After Cindy had left, Novak asked, "When are you going to tell her about the Hangman case?"

"Soon."

"You hold a lot inside, Julia."

"Hazard of the business." Julia's phone rang. It was Garrett Andrews. "Excuse me a second. It's Shield Security."

"Sure." He appeared in no rush to leave.

She turned and faced the line of liquor bottles. "Julia Vargas."

"My apologies, Agent Vargas," Andrews said. "I couldn't break away to call you by five."

Julia held her breath. "No worries."

"Shield Security has agreed to work with you on the Hangman case."

Relief washed away the tension gripping her gut. "I'm very glad to hear it."

"We'll provide all the lab testing and computer analysis. To start, I'll do a data search on the key parties involved in the case. Current address, police records, et cetera. I'll have a list of current addresses by tomorrow. Get me the DNA samples from the lab and I'll have them retested."

"That's great. Thank you."

"I'll be in touch." Andrews hung up.

She stared at the phone, allowing a grin over this victory.

"Looks like good news," Novak said.

"Yeah. It might be."

"Shield is taking the case."

"They are. Their help will save legwork."

He tapped his fingers on the bar. "The Hangman was high profile. Ken and your father would have been working nonstop."

"It was an election year, and when the media learned of the story, the powers that be put big pressure on the cops. Ken said the entire department was involved." Novak studied her, listening, watching. She liked the kind of distraction he offered. "I'm hoping fresh eyes will do the trick."

"You have nothing to prove."

His words hinted at unspoken emotions that had her ducking her head toward a lime in need of slicing. "I owe it to Mom, more than anyone. That last day we were driving home to see Jim, she was happy. Excited. Said a couple of times how much she loved him. And then, he was dead. The rumors about him being the Hangman always bothered her."

Even now, if she closed her eyes, she could picture her mom's smile while the wind blew her dark hair as they drove across town. "You Give Love a Bad Name" by Bon Jovi had been playing on the radio, and her mother had been singing along.

Seeing her father's blood had tainted that memory along with so many others.

Novak frowned. "You okay?"

Julia shook her head. "Don't worry about me; I always land on my feet. I know what I'm doing."

Novak's gaze didn't waver. "The case took a toll on your father, according to Ken. And from what he said, you're like him."

She tipped her chin up. "I'm not going to crack, Novak. I'm not going anywhere. What I'm going to do is catch this killer."

Again, he was quiet. Peeling off layers as fast as she piled them on. "I'll see you tomorrow at the medical examiner's office."

"I'll be there." She watched as he walked out of the bar. Broad shoulders. A subtle swagger she'd noticed the first night he'd found her in the stairwell avoiding the loud crowds.

She'd broken her number-one rule when she'd slept with him: don't date cops. Though *dating* wasn't the right word. At least they'd not worked together. But now that they had a professional relationship, the sex would have to end. Her focus had to be on this case. Maybe that was for the best. She'd sensed that the last time they'd slept together, he wanted to get closer, get to know her better. Maybe if she was a different kind of person, a better person, she might let him. But she wasn't.

***

It was past eight when Andrews entered Bowman's office. He should have called it a night, but the Hangman case had already gotten under his skin. He hated the idea of a killer escaping justice.

A need to right the world's wrongs had prompted him to join the army after he graduated college. His physical and mental quickness had caught the attention of his superiors. He'd moved up through the enlisted ranks and, within four years, was enrolled at OCS in Fort Benning, Georgia. He served for fifteen years on active duty until an IED explosion in Iraq ended his military career.

He couldn't change what happened in Iraq, but he could help Vargas catch the Hangman.

"I delivered the news," Andrews said. "Julia Vargas is ready to get started."

Bowman sat back in his chair. "What have you found out about Jim Vargas?"

"He's a hard one to pin down," Andrews said. "Lives weren't posted online twenty-five years ago as they are now, so no cells to trace or online profiles to build."

"I know you. You've found something."

"He had ten thousand dollars in credit card debt. Most of the card transactions were cash advances, so I have no way of knowing what he spent the money on. He also took out a second mortgage on his house. His death was ruled a suicide, so there was no life-insurance payout. His widow lost the house and moved into the apartment above her sister's bar with Julia."

Every man reacted differently to death. He'd seen the meekest push through the worst and the strongest break like glass. Jim Vargas broke.

"And there wasn't a note?" Bowman asked.

"The wife said no. The first cop she called was his partner, Ken Thompson, and he was first on scene. He backed up her story about the note."

"Partners look out for partners."

"Possible."

"Signs of foul play?" Bowman asked.

"None was detected. But his death rattled a lot in his ranks. The department opted not to give him a formal funeral."

"Do you think he was the Hangman?" Bowman asked.

"Hard to say. A few cops talked anonymously to the media about it." He had nothing but contempt for anonymous sources. They reminded him of the politically obsessed who'd distanced themselves from him after the explosion. "But there was never any solid proof."

"You think Julia Vargas really wants to get to the bottom of the case?"

"Not my concern," Andrews said. "I follow the facts. And if she doesn't get to the bottom of it, I will."

***

It was minutes after 1:00 a.m. when Lana stood outside of Billy's watching as Julia locked the front door and flipped the "Open" sign to "Closed."

"Bitch," she muttered.

She staggered back into the shadows, cursing the extra shots of tequila that made her head spin. Benny always said she got sloppy when she was drunk. He'd be pissed if he saw her now.

But Benny wasn't here. He was locked up. Awaiting a transport to prison that could eat up the rest of his life thanks to the dirt that bitch cop had dug up. His attorney still might get an appeal, but it was a long shot.

It wasn't fair. Benny had taken Julia Vargas into his life and given her his trust. Treated her like family.

If she'd let Lana take her beating, then Benny would have gotten over his anger. He always did. He might have escaped the raid. And they'd still be together.

"I should torch this bar with you inside," she muttered.

Smiling, she staggered as she turned to find herself standing face-to-face with a man. His face was hooded, his hands gloved. Immediately, she tensed. Tried to step around him.

He blocked her path.

"I don't want any trouble, man," she said.

"Neither do I."

His voice had a very familiar ring, and she dug for a smile. "Do you work for Benny?"

"Let's say I'm doing him a favor."

The snap of a stun gun came seconds before voltage cut through her body. Her knees buckled, and he caught her, pulling her close against his side.

"Breathe," he said. "And keep walking unless you want more of that."

"I didn't talk to no one," she whispered. "Tell Benny I'm doing what he said to do."

"You're looking to make trouble for that cop, aren't you?"

He'd been watching her. *Shit.* This was bad. "Look, maybe we can go somewhere and have some fun."

"That's what I was thinking."

The dark glint in his eyes sent a jolt of fear through her. Instinctively Lana balled trembling fingers into a fist and reared back to hit him. As she raised her arm, he zapped her again.

Her entire body constricted, and she nearly vomited. He dragged her down the concrete sidewalk to a van. The side door slid open, and he dumped her inside and climbed in beside her.

"Benny," she rasped. "Did he want me killed?"

He quickly bound her hands and feet. "Benny knows you talk when you drink too much."

She tripped and struggled to right herself. Her head was spinning. "I didn't talk to anyone."

White teeth flashed. "You talked to that cop last year. He knows you were the one who betrayed him to the cops." He shoved a rag in her mouth.

She shook her head as a scream rumbled in her throat. She didn't know that bitch had been a cop until it was too late. If she'd known, she'd never have talked.

She shook her head no.

"You shouldn't have talked." He stunned her again, and she crumpled. "Time to play, Lana."

CHAPTER NINE

Tuesday, October 31, 8:00 a.m.

Julia arrived early outside the medical examiner's office. She'd closed up the bar after midnight and then spent a couple of hours reading the Hangman case file. And when she had closed her eyes and nodded off to sleep, she'd dreamed again of apples and blood. She'd awoken twice last night, her nerves rattled and her hands trembling. Now, her eyes were burning and the countless cups of coffee weren't putting a dent in her fatigue.

In the lobby she showed her ID and took the stairs to the basement. After one final swig of java, she dumped her cup in the trash. She pushed through the doors to the autopsy suite.

Dr. Addison Kincaid, one of the top medical examiners in the country, was tugging on latex gloves when she looked toward Julia. The doctor had pinned her hair in a neat bun and wore a face shield that accentuated bright-green eyes full of curiosity. The medical examiner's technician wheeled in the sheet-clad remains and positioned the gurney under the overhead light. Behind the gurney was a long stainless-steel sink equipped with bottles filled with solutions, extra supplies, and instruments.

"Agent, which autopsy are you here for?" Dr. Kincaid asked.

"I understand you're autopsying Rita Gallagher's remains now."

"That's correct. Is this your case now?"

"No. She belongs to Detective Novak. I've an interest in the case, and he's letting me tag along."

"Ah." Questions lingered behind the statement, but Dr. Kincaid rarely bothered with the jurisdictional questions of an investigation. She already had enough to worry about.

Julia shrugged off her jacket. "Is Novak here yet?"

"He called to say he was hung up at the forensic lab. He should be here any minute. Generally, you can set your clock by him."

Julia pulled a hair band from her wrist and coiled her hair on top of her head. Then she suited up.

The technician pulled back the sheet, revealing the yellowed bones of Rita Gallagher. The clothes were gone, and the bones had been laid out in anatomical order. The mandible gaped as empty eye sockets stared sightlessly toward the ceiling.

"Where are her clothes?" Julia asked.

"They've been sent to the state lab for processing," Dr. Kincaid replied.

That explained Novak's visit to the lab. Honestly, she was glad to be here first. Gave her a moment to get her bearings and shore up her barriers. Novak was very perceptive, and if anyone picked up on her fatigue, it would be him. She straightened her shoulders, determined it would not happen.

The doors opened to Detective Novak. He wore a dark suit, crisp blue shirt, and a red tie. Shoes polished. Always so pulled together.

"Agent Vargas and Dr. Kincaid," he said. "Sorry I'm late. I was at the forensic lab."

A glance at the clock nailed him as one minute late. "No problem," Dr. Kincaid said.

"Just started," Julia said. "You checking on the victim's clothing?"

"Spoke to Natasha about them. She'll have something for us in a few days."

"Great."

Novak slid off his jacket and carefully laid it over a chair before donning a gown and pulling on gloves and eye protection. Julia stood across from Dr. Kincaid, while Novak slid into the spot beside her. His aftershave was barely noticeable, just like an expensive aftershave would be.

"Any theories on when she died?" Julia asked.

"There was a clothing receipt in her pocket that Natasha was able to enhance," Novak said. "It dates to November 1, 1992. Because the line items match the clothing she wore when her body was discovered, we believe it confirms Ms. Gallagher was still alive until that day. Your aunt said Gallagher went missing after your father died. She also didn't make her rent in November. My guess is she died around the first of November."

"Any family?" Julia asked.

"A brother. Still trying to track him down."

Julia shifted her attention back to the bones. "Twenty-five years alone and forgotten in that room."

"Let's see if we can find out how she died," Dr. Kincaid said.

Dr. Kincaid moved up to the exam table and positioned the overhead microphone closer to her mouth. She leaned in and asked her assistant for tweezers. She spoke her name, the date, and the names of the persons in attendance. "We took X-rays of Rita Gallagher's skull and body. As was noted at the crime scene, she suffered a blunt force trauma to the back of her skull. A closer look reveals she wasn't hit once, but twice in the same spot. The blows would have been enough to knock her out and likely cause severe cranial hemorrhaging." She turned to the X-ray pinned to the lit monitor. She pointed to the fractures, which were the size of quarters and slightly overlapped. "Note there are two sets of edges, indicating two strikes. One would have knocked her to the ground, and the second was so violent it caused this small fracture that radiated up to the center of her skull."

"Did the second blow immediately kill her?" Novak asked.

"If it didn't, I think she would have died of her injuries within hours. I doubt a team of surgeons could have saved her."

"So she might have been alive when she was left in the root cellar room," Julia said.

"It's possible," said Dr. Kincaid.

"The killer would have taken a big risk walking Gallagher into the house, surrounded by close neighbors, down into the basement and then bludgeoning her in such a small, cramped dark room," Novak replied.

"Other injuries?" Julia asked.

"Her hyoid bone is intact, which suggests she wasn't strangled." The delicate horseshoe-shaped bone centered in the throat was often snapped under extreme pressure.

The doctor closely examined the victim's arm bones. "If you look closely, her right humerus and scapula are slightly larger than the left. That suggests she was right-handed. The muscles decompose, but their influence on the bone doesn't vanish."

The doctor tipped back the victim's skull, revealing yellowed teeth. "She was a tooth grinder as evidenced by the wear patterns on her molars, and she had several cavities." She gently plucked a red strand from a back tooth. "A fragment of cloth."

"In her mouth?" Novak asked.

"It was shoved in her mouth," Julia said.

"Why do you say that?" Novak asked.

"I don't know. Maybe I've read too many files about the Hangman, but I can't help but note Rita died about the same time and within a half mile of the other victims. And the killer stuffed the mouths of his victims before he hung them."

"Like Rita."

"Yes." Julia swallowed, remembering how Benny had shoved a dirty cloth in her mouth to silence her screams. She'd coughed, gagged, and struggled to breathe. The memory made her heart pound against her chest like a jackhammer.

Breathe. Her therapist had said memories would come back when she least expected it and time would soften their power. Eventually they'd feel more like a dull ache than a sharp pain. Julia had hoped that day would have come by now; she was losing patience.

She pressed her thumbnail into her palm, letting the discomfort override the fear. She glanced up to find Novak studying her.

Julia cocked her head, held his gaze. He didn't look away, forcing her to break eye contact. Fuck him for sensing anything. "Could she have suffocated?" she asked.

"Possibly. But if she'd already been struck, a gag in her mouth would have made her labored breathing nearly impossible. Either way, she'd have died soon from the head trauma." Dr. Kincaid paused, apparently struck with a thought. "Or she could already have been dead when the rag was put in her mouth."

Julia resisted the urge to raise her hand to her throat. "Why shove the rag farther into her throat after she was dead?"

"Doesn't seem logical," Novak said, shifting attention to Dr. Kincaid. "But many killers aren't logical. I no longer bother to guess why people do the things they do."

"Rita bought nice clothes on November 1," Julia said. "She'd been hopeful and excited about something."

The doctor moved along the body. "There were no bullet or stab markers on the bones. We've extracted some marrow and will send it off for testing along with strands of her hair. We might find hints of drug use, but no telling after all these years."

Dr. Kincaid inspected the carpal bones. "Looks like her right thumb was broken." The doctor continued to study the remains, then moved to a small side table and pushed it toward the necropsy table. She uncovered it and revealed a small collection of bones. "This was found in her abdominal region under what remained of her pants. She was at least twenty weeks pregnant."

Julia didn't respond. Didn't even blink.

Novak's expression didn't change, but the fingers of his right hand curled into a fist. "Can you run DNA tests on the fetal bones to determine who the father was?"

"I'll see what I can get," Dr. Kincaid said. "But don't hold out hope."

Dr. Kincaid continued her analysis of the body. The bones in Rita Gallagher's sacrum had not fused, which, the doctor explained, occurred around the age of twenty-three. The young woman had also suffered some malnutrition. A healed spiral fracture on her right wrist suggested possible abuse. In the end, the bones had painted a picture of a troubled young woman.

"Thank you," Novak said. "Can you keep me posted on the results of the tox screen?"

"Will do, Detective."

"Thanks," Julia softly said, turning from the bones as Dr. Kincaid pulled the sheet back over the remains. She stripped off her gown and tossed it in the trash. Slinging her purse over her shoulder, she quickly moved into the hallway, up the staircase, and out to the sidewalk. The sky was ripe with thick gray clouds, and the air held the hint of colder weather coming soon.

"What's chasing you?" Novak asked.

Julia started at the sound of his voice. She didn't face him. "Never comfortable in that place. I guess it's the smell."

He stood beside her. "I'm used to it. Not sure what that says about me."

"You can't be in this job without it changing you."

"That's what I keep telling my daughter."

"How old is she?"

"Nineteen. She's a sophomore at the University of Virginia."

"Must be a smart kid."

"Beautiful, too."

No missing the pride in his voice. She wondered if her father's tone of voice had changed when he'd spoken about her. "You and her mom must be proud."

"My wife died when Bella was a baby."

"I'm sorry."

He grimaced. "Bella wants to be a cop."

"I already had my sights set on the police academy at her age. I wasn't a fan of college, but my aunt insisted. I signed up for the academy the day before college graduation."

"That's what I'm afraid of."

She fished in her purse for her keys. "She might grow out of it."

"Maybe." A frown knotted his brow. "What happened back there?"

"What do you mean?"

"I saw the way you paled when we discussed the gag."

"I've a weak stomach."

He shook his head. "You're a bad liar."

"I'm a great liar with a weak stomach."

"You can talk to me, if you need to. It wouldn't go any further."

She saw the steadiness in his gaze. She believed him. He was one of the good guys. But everyone wanted to help the victim. At first. Then when they really knew the terrible truth and were confronted by its emotional aftermath, they flaked. "There's nothing to tell, Novak."

"I don't buy that."

"That's your issue, not mine."

***

In her car, Julia pulled the list of the businesses in the Shockoe Bottom district that had been around during the time of the Hangman killings. Three were still there. She'd talked to one restaurant manager, but he was barely old enough to remember the early nineties. The same was true for the bookshop owner. However, Angie's Pizza, located a block from Stella's bar and two blocks from one of the murder scenes, was still owned and operated by the same man. Mark Dutton had opened the place in 1990 and remained the sole proprietor.

His pizza had been voted Richmond's best several years in a row, and in the last couple of years it was catching a new buzz with a migration of thirtysomethings moving into expensive condos that had been carved out of the old warehouses.

She parked on the cobblestone streets and walked quickly to the pizza shop. She pushed through the front door, savoring the fresh scents of oregano, tomato, and basil. A portly man standing behind the counter wore a white T-shirt, jeans, and an apron. Thinning white hair was brushed off his round face. He pressed a sticking key on an old brass register.

"Be right with you," he said, frowning at the key.

"No rush," Julia said.

The shop was long and narrow, and the brick walls were covered with several dozen photographs taken in the shop over the years. One of the first pictures featured a thin and wiry Dutton in front of his pizzeria. His hair then was thick and dark, and his eyes bright and full of excitement as he grinned broadly. Beside him was a woman wearing a ruffled shirt, jeans, and permed hair. Written in the corner was "1990." The pictures progressed through the years, Dutton's hair becoming thinner and whiter as his waistline thickened. A lifetime captured on the walls. As she scanned back toward 1992, she spotted a picture of Ken and her father standing with Dutton. All three were grinning.

She stared at her father's smiling face. The particular day wasn't recorded, but she'd guess early fall because the three still had their summer tans, but a patron behind them was wearing a sweater.

He didn't look like the kind of guy who'd kill himself by the end of the year. He looked comfortable, in his element. He'd never been like that at home. She understood smiles could mask all kinds of sadness. And she knew everyone had a breaking point. She'd been near that edge, but she'd never been tempted to jump over it.

"What can I do for you?" His accent quietly gave away his Brooklyn roots.

She turned toward the man, recognizing him as Dutton, as she reached for the badge clipped to her waistband. "I'm Julia Vargas with the Virginia State Police. I have a couple of questions; it'll only take a moment."

"I got a few minutes. Expecting a delivery truck, so I might have to multitask."

"I'm looking into the Hangman case."

He shook his head, resting thick fists on his hips. "I hoped I could live the rest of my life without hearing that god-awful name again. The son of a bitch nearly killed my business."

"What do you remember about it?"

"I'd opened the shop a year or two before. I was getting traction. All the drunks coming out of the bars with huge appetites, and they kept me in business."

"Why did you choose this area?"

"Rent was cheap. I always thought I'd make enough to springboard to a better location."

"But you stayed?"

He shrugged as he reached for a rag and began to wipe the counter. "After my wife, Gina, died, I didn't see the point. She was the one with the big dreams and the one who wanted the chain of stores. When she was gone, this place was enough."

"When did she pass?"

"Ten years now. She had cancer. Hell of a woman. I stay here to be close to her."

"Did she worry about the Hangman?"

"Sure. But she was never alone in the restaurant after dark. I saw to it. And we both figured this killer went after a certain type of woman."

"What type?"

"Hookers. The working girls back then were real scared. They didn't go out alone during that time but stayed in pairs after the second body was found. They'd stand near this store because they knew I was open until one a.m., and I kept my .45 behind the counter. I was more worried about a robbery, but if I'd come across that son of a bitch, I'd have gladly shot him, too."

"Did you know the victims?"

"I remembered Rene. She was nice. And Tamara. She hung out on the street corner by the shop sometimes."

"The johns would pick her up out there?"

"Yeah. Like I said, it got a little rougher around here after midnight. Hell, we still get some of that crap happening here today. And frankly, they aren't any subtler than they used to be."

"Any of Tamara's johns stand out?"

"No. I made a point to keep my nose in my own business."

"Did the cops ever speak to you?"

"Sure. I spoke to them a bunch of times. First the uniforms and then the detectives. Mutt and Jeff I called them."

"Mutt and Jeff?"

"Don't get me wrong, they were sharp and tough guys. But they stuck together like glue. They could finish each other's sentences. I gave them slices of pie, and they made a point to stop by to check in while they were working the case. Got to know them pretty well. Solid guys. Sorry to hear the one died."

She pointed to her father's picture on the wall. "That's him, isn't it?"

Mark came around the counter. "Yeah, that's him. Jim and Ken. Mutt and Jeff."

"Jim also worked the area as an undercover officer."

"I remember him saying that. He said once he came into the shop undercover for a slice. I told him later I didn't recognize him, and he laughed. He said *good*. His job was to slip into another identity as easily as a suit. I asked him if he had trouble keeping it all straight."

"Did he?"

"Never quite gave me a clear answer. The guy had a million-dollar smile, but he also had an edge."

"What do you mean by *edge*?"

"Short fuse. He never lost his temper around me, but he didn't appreciate it when someone got in his face."

"Who got in his face?"

"That guy, Tanner, whose wife was murdered. He was in here buying a pizza when Mutt and Jeff came into the pizzeria. Tanner accused them of harassing him. Said to do their job and find the real killer. Mutt didn't like that."

"Mutt being Jim."

"Right."

"What about his partner, Ken? How was he?"

"Smooth, jovial. I always figured he was the good cop, the one that softened you up for the bad cop. Ken came by regularly until about a year ago. Where's he?"

"Retired. You ever suspect anyone who might have killed those women?"

"A lot of crazy people come in here, and I keep my .45 close. Everyone talked about the crime, but no one had the faintest clue who it was. No one was holding back."

"I read their reports of their interview with you and your wife. They noted how much they liked the pizza."

"Really?" Dutton beamed.

"Yeah. One report had a tomato sauce stain on it."

He glanced up at the picture on the wall. "Your name's Vargas?"

"Yeah."

"Father?"

"Yeah."

"You look like him."

"I get that a lot," she said.

"I wish I could help you."

She pulled a card from her jacket pocket and put on her best smile. "If you think of anything, give me a call. Just sleep on it."

He flicked the edge of the card with his index finger. "Sure. And if you see Ken again, tell him Mark has got a complimentary pie waiting for him."

"Will do."

"Sorry about your dad. I sincerely liked him."

"Thanks."

She spent the next hour walking up and down the brick sidewalks trying to imagine herself back in 1992. What was it about the victims that had drawn the Hangman? Was it because they were easy prey, or was there more?

She found herself standing in front of the first murder scene. The tobacco warehouse had long been converted to condos, and what had looked rough and run-down in crime-scene photos now looked trendy and chic. Time had marched on and had forgotten those women.

"I haven't forgotten," she whispered.

***

Andrews found Bowman in his office. On the credenza behind his desk was a picture of Bowman and his girlfriend, Riley Tatum. A part of Andrews envied Bowman's happiness, but a bigger part of him feared it. With gain there was the potential for loss, and he'd lost enough. "Have you seen the website called the Hangman?"

Bowman arched a brow. "I don't prowl the Net often."

"The site appeared about a month ago," Andrews said. "It profiles the original Hangman victims as well as the detectives working the case."

Bowman sat back in his chair, folding his arms over his chest as he waited for Andrews to continue.

"Judging by the level of detail, the creator did his homework."

"Who put the site up?"

"A man by the name of Vic Carson," he said. "He was in town during the 1992 killings and, by his own admission, became obsessed with the killings. He only just got around to putting up the website. Guess he figured he'd cash in on the anniversary. He's already making decent money with his advertising sales."

"Where's he now?"

"According to his digital trail, he's in California at a conference."

"Let Vargas know. She'll want to put him on her list of people to interview."

"I've added him to the witness-suspect list I sent her."

"How many of the original witnesses and suspects did you find?"

Andrews arched a brow. "All of them."

"I shouldn't have expected less."

"No, you shouldn't." He was one of the best trackers alive, and in the two years he'd been with Shield he'd proved his skills over and over. He could find anyone who left a digital footprint.

"What's their status?"

"Of the fifteen names she gave me, several of the witnesses are in prison for nonviolent infractions, and the remaining nine are living and working in the area."

"I know you did a background check on all of them. Anything they've done in the last twenty-five years that catches your eye?"

"No. The Hangman fell off the face of the earth. When he killed his last victim, he either stopped or died."

"Which adds to the argument that the killer might have been Jim Vargas."

"McLean delivered the DNA samples, and testing has begun. I'll test them all, but Jim Vargas is still topping my suspect list."

***

Rita Gallagher's arrest file hit Novak's desk that afternoon. He opened the yellowed file, and immediately his gaze dropped to the mug shot of the young woman who stared wide-eyed at the camera. Her head was slightly tilted and holding the placard with her arrest date and booking number. Red hair was teased high, and her tube top barely covered her ample breasts. The gold heart necklace that had been found with her hung innocently around her neck.

According to one interview, Rita had moved to Richmond when she was seventeen and gone to work on the streets for a pimp. Rita had bounced around the city for a couple of years, managing to get noticed and sometimes arrested by just about every cop in the district. Her last job before landing at Billy's had been at a Northside bar called Ollie's. The bar had been a known hangout for the newly arriving Russian immigrants. She'd been a cocktail waitress. After one of her arrests, the officer had taken her to the emergency room because she'd been beaten pretty badly. One of her injuries included a broken thumb.

Rita's last arrest had been for cocaine possession. She'd been holding enough to be charged with intent to distribute, but the commonwealth attorney had dropped the charge. The attorney who'd been representing her had been Jack Holcombe.

"Jack," Novak said to himself. "You the boyfriend?"

He turned to his computer and did a quick Internet search. Jack Holcombe had practiced law in Richmond for a firm called Ricker, Davis & Michaels between 1980 and 1996. He'd died at the age of forty-five of a drug overdose. "Another dead end."

CHAPTER TEN

Tuesday, October 31, 11:00 p.m.

Halloween night, and the streets and bars of Shockoe Bottom were packed with partygoers dressed in every kind of costume imaginable. He appreciated each reveler's ability to slip on a creative mask and become someone else.

However, several blocks south, where it was quiet and dark, he was doing his own form of creation.

He wasn't fond of the name the press had given his alter ego. The Hangman. Not inspiring or original. The name implied a lack of finesse and beauty. He wasn't sure who in the media had come up with it, but it sucked. Still, it was easy for the common folk to recall, and he did want to be remembered. Over the years, he'd thought twice about reviving the Hangman persona but knew he had to wait for the right time. Timing was everything.

He hefted the blonde's unconscious body out of the back of the van and, bracing booted feet, hoisted the limp weight onto his shoulder.

Lana was small, likely not more than 120 pounds, but he struggled to steady their combined weight. This was a young man's sport.

Through the ink black of the moonless night he negotiated the uneven pavement that he'd walked a thousand times before. He knew every rut, every crack, and basically every inch of this area.

He pushed open the back entrance of the warehouse, knowing he'd unlocked it hours ago in preparation for this moment. He was meticulous and always prepared. Call it paranoia, but he never killed unless he had calculated all the possible ways a gig could go sideways.

He obsessed over all the details, including the cops' schedules, security cameras, the precise location of where death would occur, area traffic patterns, electrical hookups, and which homeless individuals frequented the area. He did not want his work discovered unfinished. His subjects deserved the very best from him.

Soon he'd post keywords on social media to bring his fans to his gallery, but for now he needed silence and time to create.

He stepped inside the warehouse, noting the dank, dusty air and maybe hints of tobacco that had once filled this riverfront location. All the old places along the river in the district had been reclaimed to create apartments, restaurants, and trendy shops. He supposed it was good for the city, but it left him feeling a bit like a lion losing his hunting ground.

The woman slung over his shoulder moaned. The rope of her bound hands moved against his back as she began to waken. *Good.* He liked it when they were awake. He liked it when they watched as he killed them, inch by inch, with his rope. He wanted them to know that their life was slowly being squeezed out of them and that there was absolutely nothing that they could do to prevent his art from freeing their souls.

He laid Lana on a tarp. Her wrists and ankles were bound with rope so she couldn't run. Soon he'd unwind the crude knots he'd tied to subdue her and would bind her in the creative web of knots that had been the hallmark of the Hangman.

He'd killed for many reasons: passion, pleasure, and money. But regardless of the motive, no one who had seen his work was ever quick to forget.

Clicking on a small light, he moved to a large duffel bag he'd left here earlier. It was filled with rope, enough to suspend her from the hooks he'd secured to the beams over two weeks ago. He pointed his light up toward the heavy oak beam and caught the glint of the metal hooks dangling like drops of silver.

The woman moaned through her gag and rolled on her back. She blinked, her gaze reflecting panic as she searched the dim light for context.

He shone his light onto her face. "Trying to figure out what's going on, Lana?"

She whimpered and tugged hard at the ropes binding her hands. She struggled, and when she couldn't break free, her fear fueled rage. This one had a temper. She was a fighter.

He'd watched the way she'd gone toe-to-toe with Julia at the courthouse yesterday. There was a lot of the street in this one. So full of righteous anger when she stood in defense of her thug boyfriend who, if given the chance, would gladly be beating her within days of his release from jail.

"You can struggle all you want, but I've been practicing my knots for years, and they're good. They may not look like much at first, but I can promise you that you'll be impressed once you give them a chance. The city will never forget Lana Ortega, and you have me to thank for that," he said softly.

Lana drew back as if she'd been struck. Her history suggested she came from a world of anger and raw violence, but not gentleness.

Women like this one were so accustomed to brutality that the tiniest bit of kindness overwhelmed and scared them. Kindness offered a false hope that was worse than the beatings.

If he had the time or the inclination, he could teach her how to crave compassion like a drug. Soon she'd do whatever he asked just to see the approval shine in his eyes.

But he didn't have the time or the inclination. He had a job to do.

He squatted beside Lana and rubbed his gloved hand over her blond hair. She was a beauty, and though she was only twenty-one, he could already see that by thirty-five she would be a distant memory to Benny.

"In the big picture, I'm doing you a favor. The next decade is going to be cruel. And when the world has stolen all it can from you, you'll die alone. Now at least you have your beauty, and you have me. I'll remain with you to the end."

She shook her head and began to pull hard at the bindings at her wrists.

He caressed her gently along her thigh, then turned to his duffel. He unzipped it and removed a coil of rope and slowly began to unwind it. She continued to struggle. That was expected, of course. They always struggled in the beginning. But as the ropes grew tighter, they calmed as the inevitable overtook them.

He stared at the taut line of her legs outlined by the black leggings. He always started with the legs. Thinking ahead, he knew if the legs were bound, no matter what happened, escape would be difficult if not impossible.

He grabbed the bindings around her ankles and wrists, carried her to the center of the room, and set her down under the harness dangling above. "I've put extra thought into your exhibit. I was a little worried I wouldn't get it right, but then I watched my videos from the first three scenes. I also read the notes the cops made, and I have to hand it to Jim Vargas. He preserved every detail he could on these cases. In fact, you might be the Hangman's best creation yet."

Screams caught deep in her throat as she flailed her head from side to side. Soon, Lana's struggle would succumb to acceptance.

He slowly ran a hand up her leg and over her flat belly. He squeezed her breast. She tried to scream louder. He pinched her nipple. She tried to raise her legs to kick, but he pressed a knee to her thighs, trapping her.

"A little pain never hurt anyone," he said as he twisted harder. "It's actually liberating."

Clear, bright, angry eyes stared up at him as she shook her head. No tears for this one. *Good*. He'd never been a fan of the tears.

"I bet you like pain. It's an old friend, isn't it?" he asked.

She watched.

"You must like pain or you wouldn't have stayed with Benny or defended him so passionately at the courthouse." He smiled. "Maybe all that anger at the courthouse didn't have to do with defending Benny, but hurting Julia. She tried to save you, but you turned on her. Did she get under your skin? Did she make you hope? Her betrayal must have stung terribly."

He smiled. Another pinch and twist. "I know all about Benny."

She shook her head.

"No need to be in denial. There're many who like pain and degradation as much as tenderness and love."

A scream, muffled by the gag, reverberated from her chest. He took no notice of it.

"Lucky for you, I'm now here to fill your need for abuse and attention. When you're dead, I'm going to create such a spectacle with your body that the cops, and especially Julia Vargas, will not forget you for a long time."

She closed her eyes and shook her head.

"If you think Julia's going to rescue you this time, you're wrong. She won't. Before this is all over, she won't even be able to save herself."

He drew back and unfurled his rope. Grabbing two sections, he pulled hard and savored the snap of the taut line. Gently he dragged the rope over her face and belly.

He reached in his pocket and pulled out a switchblade. With the press of a button, a shiny, sharp blade flicked into place.

Lana stared at him as he took the tip and ran it down her leg. This time she didn't flinch. She braced. "So I'm right. The pain doesn't scare you, but tenderness does. Interesting."

He slid the tip of the knife under the rope between her ankles and began to slowly saw the nylon. "You do understand that if you fight me, I'll catch you and I'll cut you. Not enough to kill, but enough. The slash of a tendon in your leg would work."

Tears filled her eyes, and several slipped down the side of her face.

He cut the remainder of the rope around her ankles, and immediately she began to kick as he suspected she would. She was a spitfire, this one.

He watched as she rolled on her belly and tried to scramble to her feet. Defeat was always more bitter after the taste of freedom. He knew in these seconds as Lana looked toward the door that she thought she could escape.

He let her clamber to her feet, but when she took her first full step, he lunged forward and shoved her hard. She fell, and the ground leveled a hard blow.

She reached out with her hand, clawing at the floor. She'd kill anyone to survive.

And so would he.

With the swift flick of the knife, he sliced into tendon. Pain washed over her, stealing her breath and her fight.

Blood pooled under her legs, and he found himself mesmerized by the warm crimson puddle. He dipped his fingertips into the blood and rubbed it between his fingers.

He rarely resorted to bloodshed, finding it made too much of a mess. Too many chances to carry away DNA that could be traced back to him. But now, as he raised his fingertips to his nose and inhaled the coppery scent, he discovered he liked the smell. The feel, and yes, the taste. Later, he would have to burn his clothes and destroy everything he'd touched, but for now he reveled in the moment.

He began to tie his first knot.

CHAPTER ELEVEN

Wednesday, November 1, 7:00 a.m.

As Julia crossed the alley behind Billy's to the green dumpster, she hated the stiffness in her body. Another bad night of restless sleep had left her irritable. She heaved the trash bag from her apartment with practiced precision, and as she turned to head toward her car, a flicker of movement caught her peripheral vision. Her hand moved to her gun as a matter of reflex; her heart beat faster with adrenaline as she looked at a noose dangling from a lamppost.

Pulling her weapon from its holster, she glanced from side to side and behind the dumpster, expecting to see someone lying in wait. When she'd worked undercover, she never came home directly from the field for this reason. She would drive in the opposite direction of her apartment and then circle around the block at least four times, knowing that carelessness could get her killed.

"Shit."

The message swayed gently in the morning breeze. Holstering her weapon, she reached for latex gloves tucked in her back pocket and tugged them on. There was no note. No threat. Nothing verbal. Anyone else would have dismissed the rope as a kid's prank. She didn't.

She touched the red nylon looped cord. Anger replaced worry.

Benny was in jail, but Lana hadn't been shy about showing her anger. One word from Benny, and Lana would gladly have done her lover's bidding. Or the Hangman might have gotten wind of her interest in his case and was making a statement.

Either way, the rope's message was clear: *Today's the anniversary of your father's death, and I know where you live.*

"You're going to have to do better than that," she whispered. She pulled a plastic evidence bag from her purse and lifted the noose free from the lamppost. She fought the urge to stomp on it, and instead, gently inserted the rope into the evidence bag.

The back door to the bar opened, and Cindy emerged with a sack of trash in her hand. Julia tucked the bag in her jacket.

"You're leaving? I didn't hear you get up," Cindy said as she flipped open the dumpster lid and let the sack loose.

"Yep."

"Where you headed?"

Julia's lips tipped into a wary grin, knowing she'd avoided this discussion with Cindy long enough. "I'm searching out the old Hangman suspects. Andrews at Shield forwarded me a list of current addresses last night, and now it's time to knock on doors."

Cindy frowned. "You're doing what?"

"I'm reopening the Hangman case."

Cindy cursed. "I thought you were taking time off or at least going at a slower pace!"

"I am."

"*Off* means not working and *a slower pace* means sleeping in, Julia." Her voice rose.

"I'm not *working* working. Exactly. Going to swing by the forensic department and ask a couple of questions, then chat with a few people."

Cindy flexed her fingers. "That case poisoned what was left of your parents' marriage. It's the reason Jim shot himself."

"That's why I'm reopening it," she said softly. "I have to finish what Jim started."

Cindy was silent as she shook her head before she said more slowly, "What does Rita have to do with this?"

"Novak and I think she might have been a victim of the Hangman."

Cindy stared at Julia and then sighed. "When are you ever going to sit and just be?"

"Once I see this case through, I'll kick back."

"You know what today is?"

"I do. And I'm okay."

"You sure?" Tears glistened in Cindy's eyes.

"Yes." Julia kissed her aunt on the cheek and hurried up the back staircase to her room. There she pulled the rope from her pocket and stared at the noose. She'd been threatened before but never at her own home. She thought about asking Andrews to have a look at it, but this was outside of the original case parameters for the Hangman. And Andrews had enough on his plate. She was still in control.

She put the rope in her backpack and hustled down the stairs. A buddy at the state lab might be able to help.

"You're off in a big rush." The deep timbre of Novak's voice stopped her midstep on her way to the SUV. She turned to find him leaning against a parked car.

"What are you doing here?" she asked.

"Thought I'd stop by." He looked toward the sky like he was taking in the morning sun. "Where are you headed?"

"Running an errand. And yeah, I'm kinda in a rush."

He slowly glanced around, making sure they were alone. "Does your urgency have anything to do with the noose you found in the alley?"

"How do you know about that?"

"I arrived about two minutes before you came downstairs."

"I didn't see you."

"I know." He rose to his full six-foot-plus height. "Were you going to tell me about it?"

She was tall for a woman, but he was a good four inches taller than her and was pressing on the edge of her personal space. "Not sure there's anything to tell."

"Really? You don't see the significance?"

Her fingers tightened around the shoulder strap of the backpack. "Look, I can take care of myself. And again, what are you doing here?"

"I came to see Cindy. She said she'd get those other pictures of you and your father."

"She didn't mention you were coming."

"Seems communication is not a strong suit in your family."

"Appears not."

Cindy arrived with an old box. "Detective Novak, I found the pictures."

"Where were they?" Julia was a little annoyed her aunt had not mentioned Novak's visit while they'd been in the alley.

"Attic of my house. Back corner. Really tucked away." She set the dusty box on the hood of the SUV. "These are all the pictures taken while your dad was still alive. When he passed, your mom didn't want them around, so I boxed them up and put them away. I wasn't a fan of Jimmy Vargas, but he was your father and I thought that one day you'd want these."

Julia let her backpack slide to the pavement and opened the box. "I've never seen these." She'd learned at an early age that mentioning her father to her mother or aunt triggered the same response. Time hadn't changed much.

The first set of pictures was of her as an infant. She was about three months old, and her dad had long hair and a beard.

"He was working undercover then," Cindy said. "He came home every few weeks to see you two. But he was also gone a lot."

Feeling a rush of unwelcome emotion, she set the picture aside and dug for the stack that would have been taken at the park. Midway through the pile, she spotted the park location. She handed them off to Novak, not wanting to do the digging. "Here are your pictures."

He took them. "I'll get them back to you."

"Keep 'em."

"No. I'll get them back to you." He slowly folded back the yellowed envelope flap of the drugstore photo developer and pulled out about ten pictures. He laid the first on the hood like a playing card. The picture looked identical to the one found on the body. The next two were the same. However, the fourth was of Julia and Rita.

Rita was wearing a bright-yellow dress, and her red hair flowed in soft curls around her shoulders. Julia was standing close, grinning.

Julia cleared her throat. "She was at the soccer field that day. Where was Mom?"

Cindy frowned. "I thought she was at the game as well."

"In 1992 your league hosted a tournament on September 15," Novak said.

"You looked up my team?" Julia asked.

"I needed the timeline," he said.

"Cindy, why did Jim take me to the game?"

"He was trying to be a father. I didn't think it would last, but you were so glad to see him, I hoped he'd stick around this time."

"Why was Rita there?"

"I don't know," Cindy said.

Novak laid out the remaining three pictures. Two more were of Rita and Julia, and the last was of the three of them grinning.

"I don't remember her at all. You'd think I'd remember," Julia said.

"Your father's death really rattled you. There's a lot from that time and the year after that you didn't recall," Cindy said.

"Like what?"

"Nothing too dramatic, just details. You were in a fog for a good year."

Novak carefully stacked the photos and placed them back in the envelope. "We are working the same case, Julia."

We. He spoke about them as if they were a team. The last time she'd been a part of a team, she'd nearly gotten killed. "Thanks, but I have Shield helping me."

"Computer work doesn't take the place of legwork," he said.

"What about your caseload?" she challenged.

"I've doubled up before." A wry grin tugged at his lips. "We make a good team."

"I'm not a team player, if you haven't noticed."

"I think it's a good idea," Cindy said. "Julia, you're too close to the Hangman case. He will see the facts with an uncolored view."

Both were right. But Novak saw too much.

"Worried I'll steal your thunder?" Novak challenged.

Julia's practiced smile brightened. "You're welcome to all the credit for all I care. I want answers."

"We want the same thing."

He brought objectivity to the case. And she had only five more days before her vacation was up and she would be back to working her regular cases. "Sure. Let's do it. Makes good sense."

"That makes me feel a lot better," Cindy said to Novak. "She goes it alone too much."

"I've noticed that," he said.

"I'm standing right here," Julia said.

Novak slowly closed the flap on the photo envelope. "Cindy, any fresh coffee in the bar?"

"You bet."

When Cindy was out of earshot, Novak said, "Now, tell me who you think left the rope."

"I have this under control."

He grabbed her arm. "Whoever did this also knows Cindy works here. Your stubbornness could get her hurt."

She cared about Cindy's safety more than her own.

He tucked the pictures in his breast pocket. "Talk to me, Julia."

If not for Cindy, she'd have blown him off. "I think it was someone associated with Benny Santiago."

"Tell me about his case."

The nudge of the painful memories scratched inside her.

"Long story short, I hurt Benny's operation worse than he hurt me."

He was silent for a second. "Why hasn't Benny sent one of his people after you?"

"I'm sure it's on his to-do list. Right now his goal is to compel his very expensive attorney to file an appeal. Benny may have a hair-trigger temper, but he'll get his revenge when it suits him best. I'll be watching my back for a long time with this guy."

"You don't look too concerned."

"Believe me, I'm concerned." She shook her head. "More and more, I understand why my father stayed away from us. He was trying to keep Mom and me safe."

"So you tried to save the girlfriend, and she turned on you?"

"I ruined a good gig for her, sans the beatings, when Benny was arrested. I guess she thought that like before, she could take the beating, he'd cool off, and life would go back to normal for a while longer."

"And if it's not Lana?"

"Benny has lots of people who work for him. Lana might have voiced her frustrations loud and clear with me at the courthouse yesterday, but she's only posturing. I'd wager his crew is acting on Benny's behalf. Hurting me could leverage anyone up Benny's food chain."

"Let's drop it off at the lab. Then we can walk the old crime scenes."

"Sure, we can do that."

He looked around the alley. "You don't think it's odd that you grew up and still live near the site of the murders?"

"My mom needed a place to live after Jim died. Cindy's bar was here, and the rent was free. None of this area had much significance to me until I read up on the case. And I don't plan to stay here forever. But Cindy's getting a little older, and she likes having someone on the property after she goes home at night."

"Good place to be until this case is solved. You never forget about it."

"Doesn't matter where I live. I never forget about it." The intensity of Novak's stare had her shifting her stance, eager to get going. "You don't have to come with me to the lab."

"We're a team."

"Maybe we should get jerseys and a mascot."

"Smart-ass."

She muzzled a grin. He was right. The lone-wolf act had not cracked the case so far. And yes, Shield was helping, but no guarantees there. Still, this case was a deeper quagmire than a guy like Novak deserved, especially with her on the team. "Be patient with me. I'm not the easiest person to work with."

A dark brow rose. "You're funny." He pulled keys from his pocket. "I'll drive."

"We're standing by my ride."

Cindy emerged, carrying two to-go cups of coffee. "Julia takes her coffee black. How about you, Novak?"

"That's perfect." He accepted the cup.

"Take care of her," Cindy said.

Julia sipped coffee. "I'm still here."

"I will," he said to Cindy, and then to Julia, "I'll drive."

"I can drive."

Behind the smile lurked steel. "Not today."

"I like this guy," Cindy said.

For her aunt's sake, she accepted this small concession. "Have at it."

As they headed toward his SUV parked on the street, she asked, "What're you going to do with the pictures?"

"Go through them."

"Why?"

"They relate to my case."

She was getting edgy for no rational reason and had to rein in her need to control. "Makes sense."

Novak chuckled. "See, that wasn't so hard, was it?"

He clicked his key fob, and the lights of a black Suburban winked. She climbed into the passenger seat, flexing her fingers, already itching to be behind the wheel of her own car.

"Play nice," she whispered to herself. "He's a means to an end."

Novak put the photos in the backseat, then slid behind the wheel of the car.

"The easiest way to get there—" Julia started to say.

"Thanks, I got this," Novak interrupted as he put on sunglasses.

She clicked her seat belt. "Sure."

"What was your cover when you worked in Benny's bar?" he asked.

She tensed, knowing where a question like that led. "Doubleheader. Bartender and a drug dealer." It was a little more involved than that, but the less said the better. "I'm a natural seeing as I grew up slinging drinks."

"I've pulled Benny Santiago's arrest record. Heavy into drugs and prostitution."

"You've really been busy."

Novak didn't take the bait. He moved easily in and out of the Main Street traffic. "You were saying about the undercover work?"

She'd feed him tidbits like she did everyone else. "I played up the fact that I was in the drug world. I created fake track marks on my arm and was quite the tease. I had a good feel for it most of the time. Soon Lana was my best buddy. And talking."

"How badly did Benny beat you?"

Cut to the chase. Novak looked like the all-American guy next door, but she sensed a ruthlessness matched by the likes of Benny. "Don't you know?"

"No one is saying much about that."

"Good. I'm not interested in a pity party."

He slid into a parking space across from the lab. "How bad, Julia?"

"Bad enough." She looked out the window, staring at the city's tall gray buildings.

He put the car in park and shut off the engine, but didn't move. He just kept looking ahead.

"It's water under the bridge," she said.

Novak pulled off his sunglasses and looked at her. She sensed the patience of Job.

"When I kissed you the first time, you tensed," he said.

She gritted her teeth. "Things heated up pretty quickly between us. And I don't remember any complaints."

"No complaints whatsoever. But I wondered why you tensed."

"I'm high-strung by nature. And it had been a while since I'd been out with a guy," she said. "Like I said, what happened at the beach is water under the bridge."

Out of the car before he could ask another question, she pushed through the front door of the state forensic lab and showed her ID to the receptionist as Novak came up behind her. "I'm Agent Julia Vargas. This is Detective Tobias Novak. I'm here to drop off an item for testing."

The receptionist buzzed them in, and they made their way to the elevators. As the doors opened, he stepped in close to her. When they closed, she pulled in a deep breath. The ride was only a couple of floors. The confined space was manageable.

When the elevator stopped, Novak held the door and allowed her to go first. She made her way down the long hallway past a series of glass windows that offered a view into the lab. At the end, she found the office and knocked.

Inside, a woman with graying hair and wearing a white lab coat and glasses looked up at her. "Can I help you?"

Julia pulled out her badge and introduced herself again. "Is Lucy Franklin here today?"

"She's not in today. What can I do for you?"

"I have a section of rope I need tested," Julia said.

The woman rose and reached for an evidence label. "The rope is in regard to what case?"

Julia pulled off her backpack and removed the bagged rope. "I'm not sure. It was left outside where I live." She dangled the bag with the noose. "If it was meant to be funny, it failed."

The woman nodded. "You want latent fingerprints and DNA?"

"If you can get them. Maybe you can lift them where the knot forms. Any touch DNA would be great. I'll take what I can get." She hoped whoever was sending her this message had also touched the rope with bare hands and left behind skin cells.

Frowning, the woman peered over her glasses. "Did you report the incident?"

"It's a fluid situation," Novak said. "Right now, your lab is our best shot."

"Do you have any suspects in mind?" the woman asked.

"I think it might have been left by a woman by the name of Lana Ortega," Julia said. "She's not a fan, and this would be her way of trying to intimidate me. Be nice to know who left this little memento."

The woman accepted the bag and attached a label. "Okay. I'll call you as soon as we have any details."

Julia left her card, and minutes later they were outside.

Novak fished his keys out of his pocket, jangled them in his hand. "You're pretty calm about this."

She didn't dare permit fear as they got into the car. If she allowed it, others would sense blood in the water. Game over if that happened. "I focus on what I can control. And right now, I've done all I can do. I'll worry later when I have more facts. Ready to view a crime scene?"

He started the car. "Sure."

"The warehouse crime scene where the first victim, Rene Tanner, was found has been converted into a restaurant on the bottom floor and upscale condos on the top levels."

As she paused, he said, "The second Hangman murder site is now an apartment building." He drove down Cary Street, which cut through the heart of Shockoe Bottom.

"I bet your mom had the bumper sticker 'My Kid's an Honor Roll Student,'" Julia said. "And that you also sat in the front of the class and asked lots of questions."

Novak slid into a parallel parking spot. "I know this area well, and I spent a good portion of last night getting up to speed on the Hangman case basics, like that the site of the third murder has remained relatively unchanged."

They walked the brick sidewalk under the bridge toward the long dark building that hugged the James River. Ten years ago, this entire area was submerged in water after a freak storm. So if by some fluke evidence did survive, it would likely have been destroyed.

"I'm mostly interested in what the space looks like. Why choose warehouses? What was it about this building that attracted the killer?" Julia asked.

He reached for the warehouse door posted with a "No Trespassing" sign, ratting the lock. Then he pulled a small case from his breast pocket and opened it, working with two small picks. The lock yielded in seconds.

"I'd be impressed if I actually saw that."

They stepped inside the dark structure, where Novak found a light switch and turned it on. Large fluorescents buzzed overhead and gave off a faint glow. Even in the dim light, the stain left on the walls from the flood was visible. A dank, musty smell clung to the air.

From her backpack, Julia removed a crime-scene photo tucked in her case folder. She angled the image until she had the exact space in her sights. "Our luck is turning," she said, grinning.

A chill passed through her as she thought about her father standing in this exact spot, staring up at the body of the third victim, Vicky Wayne. Like her, her father had studied the same beams, smelled the same moist, dense air, and walked the wood floor.

Novak stepped back; his gaze methodically swept over the open warehouse space. "What do you remember about your father?"

"He wasn't around much, and when he was, he was bone-tired and on edge. He was also a good guy, and he loved us." A distant memory coaxed a small smile. "He always grilled hamburgers on my birthday."

"What did your mother say about him when he wasn't around?"

"Always positive, but as I grew older she said less and less. Said he was one hell of a cop. Aunt Cindy tries not to complain about him, but she never liked him. She always thought he took the easy way out."

"At least your father didn't try to take anyone with him when he killed himself."

She hesitated, waiting for him to expand on the comment. When he didn't, she handed him several photographs. The light above them had brightened, chasing away the shadows and revealing the old brick walls of the large barren room. He held up the crime scene captured in the photograph.

In the picture, the woman's suspended figure was front and center in the shot. Her body was wrapped in a series of knots that began with coils around her ankles. The ropes twisted around and up her legs until they banded around her waist. From there the rope snaked across her breasts and then around her neck. Her hands were bound behind her back.

"I also have video," she said. She dug a tablet from her backpack and selected a computer file created from the original VCR tape. She hit "Play" and handed it to Novak.

"We're at the third murder scene."

She recognized the deep baritone voice of her father. She wished she could say she had better memories of him reading bedtime stories, but she didn't.

"She looks like she was strangled to death similar to the other two," the voice continued.

A much younger and more muscular Ken Thompson stepped into the frame. While her father was forever frozen in time as a young man in the prime of his life, Ken had since become old. Seeing Ken's broad shoulders, thick dark hair, and trimmed mustache caught her off guard. She'd forgotten how handsome he had been.

Ken opened a small spiral notebook. *"I spoke to a dozen people in the area, and no hits."*

"No one who's around here is going to call it in even if they did see something. Only trouble comes here."

In the background, several officers grabbed the rope holding the woman, and while one cut, another held the body, digging his feet in so it wouldn't drop to the floor.

Slowly the woman's body came to the floor, the stiff legs and torso coming to an awkward rest. Her feet were discolored a dark blue.

"She's rigid, which means rigor mortis has set in. She's been dead, what, about twenty-four hours?" Ken asked.

"Give or take," Jim said as he moved forward, squatting beside the body. He rolled the woman on her back and studied her with a keen intensity. He brushed the hair from her face as he shook his head.

Novak hit the "Pause" button. "He looks at the victim as if he knows her."

She studied the frame, searching for what Novak saw. "He may have crossed paths with her on the streets. He worked the city for years."

"It's more than that."

"What's that mean?"

"It means his expression reads shock as well as sadness. He knew her well enough to be saddened by her death."

She challenged Novak as any good cop would. "How can you say that?"

"Come on, you worked undercover," Novak said. "I bet you read body language better than most."

Julia leaned into the picture, looking at her father, knowing he was a man of so many secrets. She hit "Play" and watched as he rubbed his temple and slowly blinked. "Maybe he knew her from one of his undercover jobs. Maybe a confidential informant."

"If I had to guess, I'd say it was more than a professional relationship," Novak said. "Look at his expression. The way he brushes the hair from her face."

"CIs are people, Novak. They have hopes and dreams. Cops working with CIs can see the good in them at times."

"That ever happened to you?"

"Sure."

But Novak was right. Julia had seen it, too. Jim's stoic expression didn't hide the grief the cop had for the victim.

CHAPTER TWELVE

Wednesday, November 1, noon

Novak and Julia found Gene Tanner, the husband of the first victim, in the back office of his sports bar, Touchdown. He was frowning at a wide-screen computer that displayed multiple columns of numbers, mostly red. With glasses perched on his nose, he glared at the numbers.

Julia moved to knock, but when she met Novak's gaze, she put him to work. "Batter up."

Nodding, Novak rapped on the door and waited for the man to look up. "Mr. Tanner."

The man's face scrunched with annoyance. "You're cops. What do you want?" He pulled off his glasses and tossed them on his desk. "You all look alike to me. It's like you go to a school to be trained to stick out."

Novak had carefully studied Tanner's profile in the Hangman files. He'd been one of the initial suspects in his wife's death. The detectives had leaned on him hard until the second victim's body had been found suspended in a nearby warehouse.

Novak pulled out his badge as Julia held up hers. "We're here to talk to you about the Hangman case."

Tanner's chair squeaked as he leaned back. "Hangman? I haven't heard that name in years. Why do you guys care about him?"

"We're reviewing the case," Julia said. "There's no statute of limitations on murder."

Tanner rose and ran his hand through his hair. "So what do you want from me? I was cleared of all charges in my wife's death when that psycho killer murdered those other women."

"Bear with us," Julia said. The strain in her voice suggested making nice wasn't her talent. "We're interviewing all those involved in the three 1992 cases."

"Those involved? Sounds nice the way you put it. You mean suspects, right?" Tanner asked.

Julia didn't rise to the bait. "Do you remember the last time you saw your wife?"

Tanner eyed her and didn't respond right away. Realizing the cops weren't leaving without answers, he sighed his resignation. "Yeah, sure, I remember. She was working at the bar. She was supposed to get off early that night so she could go out with a friend. It was a Tuesday. One of our slowest nights, so I told her to go and enjoy herself. She worked long hours to make the bar a success . . ." The man's voice trailed off.

"Where were Rene and this friend meeting that night?" Julia asked.

"I didn't know. Rene was a free spirit, and she didn't like it when I asked too many questions." He shifted, straightened his shoulders. "I told all this to the cops a million different times. They were so sure I had done it that they kept asking me the same question over and over again. But the answer was the answer. I didn't know where she went."

"You and your wife had a volatile marriage, Mr. Tanner," Julia said. "The cops responded to a couple of domestic disturbance calls."

"We had our ups and downs." He pointed to a scar on his forehead. "She could give as good as she got," Tanner said.

"Who was the friend she went out with?" Novak asked.

"That I do remember. Rita. I never got Rita's last name. She worked at another bar up the street."

"Rita?" Novak asked. A connection between the two women underscored his belief that the Hangman had killed Rita. "You sure about that name?"

"Yeah, I'm sure. Rita was coming around. She and Rene hit it off. It was hard to forget Rita. The woman had tits that could make a man sit up and beg for more."

"What can you tell us about Rita?" Julia asked.

"Is she the newest suspect?" Tanner challenged.

"She's a part of the picture," Julia said. "She might have been the last person to see Rene."

"Why aren't you talking to her, then?" Tanner asked.

Novak ignored the question. "What do you remember about Rita?"

"Other than the tits? Reddish hair. Big laugh. Easy on the eyes. Always good for business to have a hot working girl hanging around. She wasn't always so smart. Probably why she was arrested so much that summer."

"I don't remember you mentioning Rita's name in the initial interview," Novak said.

"I told 'em," he said. "I can't help it if they didn't write her name in the files. They wrote everything else down that I said."

Novak kept his expression blank. "The distance between Stella's and Billy's is eight blocks?" Novak asked.

"Stella's. I haven't heard that name in a long time. I sold the place a year after Rene died. Too many memories. But yeah, eight blocks is right. The area was different then. Rough. But the rent was cheap and it was a chance for Rene and me to get a start."

"You were partners with Rene in the bar, right?" Novak asked.

"Yeah. Half and half. And yes, I did inherit her half when she died. It was the motive the cops focused on over and over. And for the record, I sold the bar at a loss."

"Did anyone see her and Rita walking in the area that night?" Julia challenged.

"I asked around, but no one really noticed. Read the old case files. Those two detectives talked to everyone on the street. Acted like it was their personal vendetta to catch the killer."

"Isn't that what cops are supposed to do?" Novak asked.

"That's what happens in the nice neighborhoods, but it didn't happen around here much. Everybody knew this area was the Wild West back in the day when I first came here. Park a car too far down the hill and expect to lose hubcaps or tires. Walk alone at night, odds were you'd get mugged."

"So Rene leaves here about when?"

"Eight o'clock on a Tuesday night," Tanner said.

"And she doesn't make it home. What happened next?" Julia asked.

"When I woke up, I didn't notice she wasn't there right away."

"Why? She was your wife," Julia said.

"We weren't sleeping in the same room at the time. I've never slept well. Getting up and lying down all the time was driving her crazy. She moved into the guest room in our loft. It was supposed to be for a night or two, but by the time she died, it had been months. Honestly, I think she liked it that way. Rene wanted her privacy."

"So you wake up, get your coffee, and go on about your day?" Novak asked.

"Yeah. I almost looked in on her, but I had to get to the bar. We were expecting a delivery. The workday started, and I lost track of time. It wasn't until she didn't show up for her shift that I got worried."

"What did you do?" Julia asked.

"Called the apartment. The answering machine kept picking up. By the time I left the third message, I was pissed."

"You made nasty threats on that tape," Julia said. "I remember, *I'm going to mess you up if you don't haul your ass over here.*"

"How do you remember shit like that?" Tanner asked.

"I read the transcripts in the files a few times," she said.

Tanner shrugged. "I could talk rough to Rene when I was mad, but she could be the same way with me. Like I said, she gave as good as she got. Maybe it wasn't the healthiest way, but it's all we knew."

"So she wasn't answering the phone," Novak prompted.

"Yeah. So I went by our apartment, and she wasn't there. I thought she was sleeping one off. I called Rita at her work."

"Billy's?" Julia prompted.

"Yeah. Rita said she hadn't seen Rene since about midnight. They shared drinks and laughs, and then Rita met up with her boyfriend. Again, I thought it was a Girls Gone Wild kind of scenario. But when Rene didn't show after a few days, I called the police. They sent a beat cop to take my missing persons report. The cop didn't look too worried. He figured my wife would probably show up when she was good and ready."

"She ever take off for a couple of days?" Novak asked.

"Sure. Sometimes. But she always came back."

"They found Rene four days later in a warehouse three blocks from your bar," Julia said.

"Yeah. That's when the two detectives took over the case. They were so damn sure I was the one who killed her. But when they told me she was strung up by her neck and bound in ropes . . . shit. That was pure evil."

"Whatever happened to Rita? Did you tell the cops about her?"

Tanner shook his head. "Yeah, I told the detectives. At first, one of 'em thought I was making up the Rita story. They wouldn't quit. Kept asking me what I really did with my wife. But I kept telling them to ask Rita."

"And did they?" Novak asked.

"They said they did. They told me Rita lost track of Rene after that night."

There was no mention of any interview with a Rita or similar person in the notes. Ken didn't remember Rita, but that didn't mean he'd not known her.

"I never hated cops until then," Tanner said.

Novak ran his hand along his tie. "They established fairly quickly that you had an alibi when the second victim was found."

"Yeah. They told me I shouldn't leave town, but that was bullshit. I took off with a couple of buddies, and we went to Atlantic City to blow off steam for the weekend. That's when the second woman vanished and was found. I was off the hook." Tanner's eyes narrowed. "I saw your badges, but I didn't catch your names."

"Detective Tobias Novak, Richmond City Police."

"Julia Vargas. Virginia State Police."

Tanner cocked his head. "Vargas. Shit. I thought you looked familiar. There can't be too many of you running around. How did you know the detective?"

"He was my father."

Tanner shook his head. "Well, if you want me to make nice about the guy, I won't. He was a real son of a bitch. I didn't like him during the murder investigation or before."

"Before?" Novak asked.

"He worked in narcotics as an undercover in this area. I didn't recognize him at first when he and his sidekick interviewed me about Rene. He was all clean-shaven and wearing a suit. But when he spoke, I recognized the voice. Sounded like gravel." He cocked his head as he studied Julia with newfound interest. "You have his eyes. How old were you when he offed himself?"

"Young."

Novak heard the sharp tension in her response and sensed she needed a second to process. "So Jim Vargas was around the bar a lot before Rene died?" Novak asked.

"Yeah. I mentioned I'd seen him before, but he and his partner shrugged it off. Your old man was too wrapped up in the investigation. He pressed me hard to confess, and was relentless. It was like he was looking for a way to deflect the attention from himself."

"What did he do when he came by Stella's before Rene died?" Julia asked.

"Sat at one of the corner tables and drank. Guy could pound the booze. People would come by and meet with him. They'd talk in low voices so no one would hear. I knew he was up to some shit, but he didn't bother my customers, so I let it go. Not my business."

"Did Jim Vargas know Rene?"

"Sure. She served him drinks. And a couple of times I saw him chatting her up. He could make her laugh, which was a rare sight."

"You ever think something was going on between them?" Novak asked. Tension rolled off Julia, but she understood no question was off the table.

"I never had proof," Tanner said. "But Rene could keep her secrets."

"What kind?"

"If I knew that, then they wouldn't be secret." He shook his head. "Look, I don't want to speak against her. She's been gone twenty-five years, and she was my wife. I still did love her." He looked at Julia. "And sorry for what I said about your old man. I thought all those old emotions were dead and buried, but I guess they're still there. You were a kid. None of it was your fault."

Julia's smile held little warmth. "Convenient for you to be in Atlantic City when Tamara Brown was murdered."

"What's that mean?" Tanner asked.

"What's it, a five-hour drive?" Julia asked.

"Sure, without traffic, which is never," Tanner said.

"A small plane could do the trick," Julia said.

"That's enough," Tanner said.

"Tamara Brown's bindings were not as intricate as Rene's," she added. "Cops assumed the killer was in a rush."

Tanner jabbed a fat finger at her. "I'm trying to be nice, but I've had enough. I'm not doing this again."

"What?" she asked.

"Being strung up for a crime I didn't do."

"Did I hit a nerve?" Julia asked.

"I'm calling my attorney."

"Bad idea," she said. "No statute of limitations on murder even with the best lawyer."

Tanner cursed. "You need to leave now."

Novak didn't move. He sensed Julia wanted a pound of flesh. She wanted to find the Hangman so badly; he bet she could almost taste it. He'd had cases that had done the same to him. But at this stage it was better they both back off and regroup. "If we have more questions, we'll be back, Mr. Tanner."

Julia turned to leave, and he followed her along the hallway and through the empty bar. Outside, she stopped and stood staring at the bright sky. He sensed her irritation.

"What do you think?" he asked.

She shoved out a breath. "Other than the bombshell that Rene knew Rita? Hell if I know. His story checked out twenty-five years ago."

"That comment you made about Tamara Brown. That wasn't true. Her bindings were more intricate than Rene's."

"I know." A smile tugged at the edge of her lips. "But I was betting Tanner didn't have the full case details. Thought I'd throw a line in the water."

Novak grinned. "Interesting Rita was the last person Rene was seen with. Do you believe Tanner told Jim and Ken about her?"

"I didn't see Rita mentioned once in the files. And I made a careful list of witness names for Shield. No Rita on the list. What would the motive be for Tanner to now introduce Rita?"

"Maybe he told Jim and Ken about her during the initial investigation. Maybe Jim kept her out of the files intentionally. If she'd been a CI, he might have wanted her involvement and connection to him kept quiet."

"Sure, it's possible." She looked up at him. "Rita died within weeks of the other Hangman victims. We know she knew at least one of them. The Hangman could have been very aware of Rita, who fit his victim profile. Maybe he saw her with Rene that last night."

"Why hit Rita over the head? Why hide her body and not display it like the others?" he asked.

"Maybe she knew who he was. If he saw her with Rene, she might have also seen him. Maybe her relationship with Jim was also known. She could have been a loose end."

"All good theories now."

Her phone buzzed, and she glanced at the display before holding the phone to her ear. "Say again," she said into it after listening a moment.

After she hung up, he said, "What's going on?"

"Benny Santiago's transport has been delayed an additional month. He's complaining of chest pains," she said.

"What do you think his angle is?"

"He's buying time. Scheming."

"You think it has to do with you?"

"Yep," Julia said. "I cracked open Pandora's box, and there'll be hell to pay if he wins on appeal. The good news is he won't win on appeal, and if he does kill me, he'll do it himself. I betrayed him, so my death is personal to him. So I'm on layaway for two decades." Julia checked her watch. "We have time to speak with Tamara Brown's sister."

His gaze lingered on her.

"According to Andrews, Jocelyn Brown Smith works as a receptionist for a security office in the Far West End," she said. "She'll be getting off work soon. Care to join me?"

"Wouldn't miss it."

Julia didn't speak while he drove, but he sensed she was chewing on what she'd learned about Benny Santiago. He only hoped she was right and Benny would insist on killing her himself.

Novak couldn't stop thinking about her last night of undercover and the beating she'd taken. What Benny had done to her did not affect his case or his agenda, but still, because Julia was in the mix, he wasn't afraid to stick his nose in where it might not belong.

Ken had said the apple didn't fall far from the tree. Riggs had hinted that Benny had sexually assaulted her. If she was this good at hiding that secret, what kind of secrets had her old man been able to keep?

***

It was after two when they arrived at the security office as Mrs. Smith was leaving through the front door. She was dressed in her blue-and-white uniform and carried a small lunch box. Dark hair was twisted into a tight bun, and heavy-rimmed glasses sat atop her head.

"Let me talk to her first," Julia said. "Psychologically, a woman alone crossing a parking lot night or day responds better to another female."

"Agreed."

As they approached, Julia pulled her badge, holding it high. "Mrs. Smith."

The woman turned her head and halted, gripping her purse. "Yes?"

"I'm Agent Julia Vargas with the Virginia State Police."

The introduction did little to ease the woman's trepidation. "What do you want with me?"

"I'd like to talk to you about Tamara's death."

"Tamara?" she stammered. "She's been dead twenty-five years. Why would you want to know about her?"

Novak approached and introduced himself. "We're reopening the Hangman case."

A car pulled out of the crowded parking lot, and another quickly took its place. "Is there somewhere we can talk and maybe grab a cup of coffee?" Julia asked.

"It's been a long ten hours, and I have to be back here by six tonight for another shift," Mrs. Smith said.

"We won't take much of your time." Julia forced a slight smile. "I'll treat."

The woman sighed. "There's a diner right on the other side of the gas station. We can walk there. The lunch crowd has left by now."

"Good," Julia said.

The woman studied Julia. "What did you say your name was?"

"Julia Vargas."

Dark eyes narrowed. "Jim Vargas's kin?"

"He was my father."

"Why would you want to open that case up?" she asked.

"I want to know who killed Tamara and the two other women."

"You sure you want to dig into this?"

"Yes. Why wouldn't I?"

The woman shook her head. "Let's get that coffee."

Within ten minutes the trio was settled in a booth with their coffees.

"When was the last time you saw your sister?" Julia asked.

"Lord, I don't know. Even twenty-five years ago when the cops talked to me, I never could recall the exact date for them. Tamara was a troubled soul. She moved out of our parents' house when she was sixteen and took to the streets. We did what we could to get her to see reason, but she said she could take care of herself."

"You learned about her death from the police?" Novak asked.

"I did. It wasn't Vargas but his partner who paid me a visit. His name was Thompson, I think." She stirred her coffee absently. "Funny after all these years that I'd remember his name. But he was nice. Respectful. And I appreciated it."

"Was there anyone in her life who you knew might have been a threat to her?" Novak asked.

"I would say everyone. She ran with a rough crowd. She was hell-bent for trouble."

"She had several arrests," Julia said.

"She did. Drugs. Prostitution. I don't know what got into her. I tried to save her, but she thought I was jealous of her."

"What do you remember about Detective Vargas?" Novak asked.

"He wasn't as easy to deal with as his partner. And I knew him from before, of course."

"Before?" Julia asked.

"I saw him with Tamara at one of those bars a couple of years before she died. They were sitting in a booth talking to each other real close and quiet. His hair was longer, and he looked rougher, but I knew it was the same guy." She set her cup down as if the weight of the memory overwhelmed her.

"Are you sure it was the same officer?" Julia asked.

"I am. I made a huge scene. I was so sure I could save Tamara from herself. I went charging into the bar full of fire and brimstone. I marched right up to her table and told her it was time she came home with me."

Mrs. Smith paused, her expression pained, and Julia asked, "What did your sister say?"

Mrs. Smith choked up. "She said I was dead to her. She looked at that Jim fellow and acted like she was embarrassed to be seen with me. He told me to leave in that deep gruff voice that I'll remember longer than his face. He said he had it all under control. He scared me, but I stood my ground."

Julia had seen pictures of her father during his narcotic task force days. He'd grown his hair long and had a thick mustache. He looked like he belonged on the streets.

"I told him to mind his own business. I told him she was my sister. And then he was up out of that booth and grabbed me by the arm. He told me to stay away. Tamara would be fine with him." She shook her head. "I looked up into his eyes, and there was something I couldn't put my finger on. I was so tired of chasing after Tamara. I was so tired of waiting up for her. I looked back at her and asked her one last time to leave with me. She said no, and I left."

The woman picked up her coffee and stared into it. Her brow knotted as she shook her head.

"The last time was at the morgue when Ken Thompson called me to identify her."

"My father was working undercover when you saw him in that bar." Julia didn't question the need to defend her father. "I believe Tamara was working with him as a confidential informant."

"That's what he told me later. I suppose it was meant to make me feel better, but it didn't. I always wondered how different life would be if I'd dragged her out of that bar that day."

"Do you know what case she was working on with Vargas?" Novak asked.

"I asked her. She was too afraid to tell me. Said it was the kind of information that could get her killed."

The three spent the next half hour discussing Tamara. Mrs. Smith wanted to talk about the girl she'd been before she left home. She wanted to share the hopes and dreams their parents had had for them both.

When the check came, Novak intercepted it before Julia could and paid the tab.

Julia cleared her throat. "Tamara's autopsy report said she had a baby about eight months before she died."

A ghost of a smile warmed Mrs. Smith's round face. "Alicia. She's twenty-six. The county called and told me she had been born, and I went straight to the hospital. The baby was there, but Tamara was gone.

So I wrapped her up and took her home. Raised her as my own. She's getting her master's in nursing at VCU. Smart girl."

"So you know who the baby's father was?"

"Tamara never told. I figured she didn't know."

Julia thanked Mrs. Smith, and they walked her back to her car. Novak waited until she drove off before he started his car.

"Your father knew Tamara, Rene, Rita, and maybe Vicky. He and Ken did a good job of hiding that in the homicide files."

She rubbed the back of her neck, fearing what else she might find out about her father if she kept digging. "That wasn't lost on me."

As they hit Broad Street, his phone rang. "Novak." While he was listening, the lines in his face deepened.

When he hung up, his gaze took on an untamed edge that surprised her. The call wasn't good.

"What's happened?"

Novak jammed the phone in his breast pocket as he hit the lights, which flashed through the car's grill. He punched the accelerator, raced toward the intersection, and did a sharp U-turn. "The body of a young woman was found in the Manchester district."

She'd heard rumblings that Novak could be a hard-ass. The night they'd met, he'd received some kind of award at the dinner. The people at her table talked about the case Novak had broken that no one else could. But she'd been so wrapped up in her own issues, she couldn't remember what it was for. "If you can't drop me off anywhere, I'll grab a cab."

Novak shook his head. "The victim was bound multiple times and strung up from the beams of an old warehouse."

His steady, deep voice triggered an eerie stillness. She conjured a horrific image of the victim. "Oh Christ, he's back."

"Or a copycat." He glanced at her, his expression grim. "Either way, it's bad for everyone."

CHAPTER THIRTEEN

Wednesday, November 1, 4:00 p.m.

A ring of flashing cop cars greeted them when they arrived at the warehouse just across the James River from Shockoe Bottom. The sun hung low on the horizon and spattered the sky with bright oranges and reds.

Julia pulled back her hair and secured it into a tight ponytail before she and Novak approached the uniformed officer with their badges.

"Detective Novak. I'm with Richmond homicide." He nodded his head toward Julia. "Agent Vargas, Virginia State Police."

The uniformed officer nodded and raised the yellow tape for them both. They ducked under and moved across the rutted parking lot until they reached the entrance to the warehouse, now being prepped with floodlights and a generator that would be needed shortly.

Inside, lights illuminated the body of a woman whose face was hooded. She hung from ropes hooked to beams. Her arms were each tied with a rope, and her ankles fastened by two more bindings. A final rope wound tight around her neck.

Julia's chest constricted as she struggled to keep her reaction in check. Absently she reached in her pocket for gloves, but found she didn't have a set.

Without missing a beat, Novak handed her a pair as he worked his large hands into his own.

"Thanks," she said.

"No problem," he said.

She appreciated the gesture. "Who found her?" she asked a uniformed cop.

The cop was older, with gray hair and a sturdy build, but seeing Novak, he stood straighter. "A few college kids. They were looking to rent the space for a party. As soon as they opened the front door, they spotted the spectacle and obviously the odor."

A sigh shuddered through Novak. "Where are the kids?"

"A squad car took them back to the station. Detective Latimer is talking to them. They're pretty shaken up."

"Who's working the forensic end of this?" Novak asked.

"Natasha Warner."

"Good." Novak's jaw tensed as he looked past the officer to the suspended body.

"The brass wants you to take point, Detective Novak," the officer said. "This is going to be a media shitstorm."

"Yes, it is," Novak said.

Julia stared up at the woman, her hooded face tilted to the side, her limbs dangling from ropes like a marionette's. A surge of fury rushed through her body, stinging her nerve endings as she imagined the woman's last panicked moments of life. The blink of a camera's flash drew her attention to Natasha Warner, who was snapping pictures. "How long do you think she's been there?"

"No more than twenty-four to thirty-six hours," Natasha said.

Julia moved away from Novak and Natasha, her full attention on the victim. The thick scent of death infiltrated stagnant, dusty air and filled all her senses. Experience reminded her the human nose would soon block out the odorous scents if she didn't fight. Her stomach tumbled. A cold settled deep in her marrow. Easier said than done.

Jesus.

"Why's her face covered?" Novak asked more to himself, his deep voice calm and controlled.

She'd not heard him approach and couldn't stop herself from flinching. She cleared her throat. "That's a change from before."

He stood behind her, so close she imagined the heat of his body warming her chilled bones. "Copycat or original?"

"Did my investigation trigger this?" Julia folded her arms over her chest, fearful that Novak would confirm her worries. "Is she dead because of me?"

For several beats, he was silent. When he spoke, his voice was barely audible. "No, you didn't make this sick bastard do anything."

"I kicked a hornet's nest."

"The hornets were always there, and if you hadn't gotten his attention, someone else would have. Killers like this don't need an excuse."

She stared at the victim's hands and feet, darkened by the blood that had settled after her heart stopped beating.

With her gaze locked on the body, Julia took solace knowing Novak didn't bend to bravado. No drama. And she needed that right now as she shouldered the weight of this woman's death.

Natasha approached the two officers. "I've photographed the scene, sketched it, and had the uniforms search the area. Next step will be to cut her down." The tech studied Julia's badge. "Is the state taking over jurisdiction?"

"No," Novak said. "Agent Vargas is consulting. Take the body down now."

"Right," Natasha said.

They watched as Natasha and a couple of uniforms moved under the form. The two officers held the rope and braced for the weight when it released.

As Natasha recorded with a video camera, another officer used a pocketknife to saw through the rope that stretched over the large rafter in the ceiling. As soon as the final strands gave way, the body was slowly lowered to the floor.

Rigor mortis had stiffened the victim's limbs. Natasha shot more pictures over the course of the next fifteen minutes before an officer rolled the body on its back. The woman wasn't naked like the original victims. Her feet and the undersides of her arms were blue. She wore a thin white T-shirt and jeans that tightly skimmed her body. No shoes, but her toenails and fingernails were painted a dark purple.

Her shirt rode up on her right side, revealing two red prong marks that left no doubt about the use of a stun gun. That's how he had controlled her. Without that, it would have been hard to bind her limbs and hoist her up.

Novak moved to the edge of the tarp, knelt to get a better look at the body. He was a man of few words, which suited her fine. She hadn't been looking for conversation when they first hooked up, and even now, she wasn't warming up to it. His quiet strength communicated more than most people did with excessive words.

As he studied the victim, his frown deepened. Julia knew the feeling all too well. Any cop wanting to survive the job had to cope with the darkness. Otherwise, the work became too personal and the demons consumed you whole. Those damn demons had been circling close the night Novak had walked up to her at the awards banquet. She'd been drawn to his calm, his steadiness, and his indifference to the ceremony. When she'd seen the desire spark across his gaze, she'd found a way to push back her fears. What she'd not expected was to crave the same release with him again and again.

Natasha took more pictures of the body, close-ups of the woman's hands, feet, and neck. When the body had been completely documented, the technician inspected the coil of rope around the neck. "My bet is she died of asphyxiation."

"Like the original cases," Julia said. "The victims strangled to death under their own weight."

Natasha stepped back. "I'll leave the cause of death to the medical examiner. I'm also going to leave the ropes in place and let the medical examiner's representative inspect them. I don't want to lose one bit of evidence."

"Did you find anything else that belonged to the victim or that was out of place?" Novak asked.

"I found a crumpled white napkin over there beside a stack of boxes. In here, it wouldn't take long for anything white to get dirty. But it was sitting there, wrinkled and fairly clean, with what looks like a mustard smudge on it."

"So our killer had a snack?" Julia asked.

"Brazen enough to believe he had time for a sandwich," Novak said.

"If there's DNA on it, we'll find it," Natasha said.

The image of the dead woman still in her mind, Julia understood her father's fixation and drive to solve the case.

Activity at the warehouse front door had her turning to see the medical examiner's team. Julia recognized Dr. Tessa McGowan.

The doctor, a petite woman with short dark hair, crossed the room as another tech raised the expandable gurney and pushed it up to the yellow tape. She and an assistant unfolded a large black body bag and unzipped it.

Tessa crouched next to the body, laying a gloved hand on the victim's arm. Julia had seen the doctor do this before. She thought it odd that Tessa was giving comfort.

"I'd like to remove the hood from her face," Tessa said.

"We were waiting for you," Novak said.

Nodding, Tessa pulled the thick black hood away.

Julia simply stared at the too-familiar blond hair, full lips, and high sweep of cheekbones. She drew in a sharp breath and took a small step back.

"What's wrong?" Novak was so close now she could feel the heat radiating from him.

"I know her."

"Who is she?"

She steadied her voice. "Lana Ortega."

"Benny Santiago's girlfriend?"

"Yes."

Novak nudged her shoulder. "Outside. Now."

Without a word, she left the scene behind, needing to breathe in fresh air. Outside, she stripped off her gloves and tossed them in a waste bin. Her hands trembled slightly.

Novak appeared at the door. He jerked off his gloves, tossing them in the same bin, and came up beside her. He didn't speak for a few moments.

"Are you sure that's Lana Ortega?" he asked.

"Yes, I'm sure."

"Who did you tell about reopening this case?"

"The Shield people. Sharp. You. I also requested the files from the records department. Ken. His wife, Wendy. And stop looking at me like I'm a goddamned suspect."

"You're not a suspect, but you're in the center of this, Julia. What would you have me do?"

She searched his dark eyes, seeing the steady directness she'd come to expect from him. She shook off her frustration. "Exactly what you're doing."

He looked from side to side before softening his tone. "You told enough people for the story to get out. You know as well as I do that secrets get around fast in police departments."

"I thought I was careful."

"How reliable is Ken?"

"There was a time I'd have said rock solid, but now I'm not so sure. He wouldn't talk about the case intentionally, but he easily gets confused."

"And Wendy?"

"Wendy is former Richmond police. She and Ken met on the job right about the time the Hangman case broke. She's steadier, discreet."

"When did you request the files?"

"Eight months ago. I had them for a couple of weeks. Made copies and returned all the originals. I was careful with the files. Kept them in a locked closet at my place when I wasn't reading them."

"You are positive."

"Very."

A muscle twitched in his jaw. "Who saw Lana threaten you at the courthouse?" he asked.

"Dozens of people could have seen her in action. She didn't care. Elizabeth Monroe, Santiago's attorney, dragged her away." She shook her head. "Could this Hangman be watching me?"

"It all traces back to you. Someone knows what you're doing. Someone is watching you."

The idea sent a cold chill trickling down her spine. But it wasn't fear that made her nerve endings snap. It was anger. "I'm not a victim."

Concern softened his gaze. "I didn't say you were."

"No one ever says it out loud. But they think it."

"If I'd had any thoughts or opinions about you, you would have been the first to know."

"You have been direct."

"Because I care about you, Julia."

She raised a finger. "Well, knock it off. I'm not the kind of person you should care about."

He cocked his head, curious. "Why not?"

She slid her fingers into the front pockets of her jeans. "What we did was fun. Real fun. But don't confuse that with caring."

"Did." He leaned closer to her. "Past tense?"

She arched a brow. "We can't anymore."

"Why not?"

"We're working this case, for one."

"We wouldn't be the first couple who met on the job."

"We're now a couple? No. Not a couple. You're nice and normal; I'm crazy with issues. Not gonna happen."

A smile tugged at the edges of his lips. "You're not crazy."

"Trust me. I'm nuts. You don't want me long term."

"You aren't nuts. But maybe crazy in a good way."

The tightness always coiling her gut eased. "Fine line between the two."

"Miles apart."

"I should get you to put that in writing."

"Okay." He nodded toward his car. "There's not much we can do here now. Let's drive back to the station and talk to the kids who found the body."

A half hour later they were walking a plain gray hallway toward a muscular African American man with a detective's shield clipped to his belt.

"Novak," the detective said. "I was about to call you."

"This is Agent Julia Vargas," Novak said. "Julia, this is Detective Samuel Riggs."

Riggs extended a hand. "Hear you're working a similar case to the one we just grabbed."

She made sure her grip was firm, her gaze steady. "Unfortunately, yes."

"And as it turns out, Julia knew the victim found in the warehouse," Novak said.

Riggs's face lost all its jovial qualities as Novak filled him in on the case details as well as Julia's connection to the victim. "That's not by accident."

"No," she said.

"Can we talk to the kids that found the body?" Novak asked.

Riggs ran his hand along his silk tie. "I don't think they'll give you much. Dumb kids looking for a place to party. But have at it."

"Thanks," Novak said.

They walked into the interview room where two young women and a man sat at a table. Each was cradling a cup of coffee, and all of them looked shell-shocked.

Novak introduced himself and Julia. The tallest woman, a redhead, introduced herself as Emma. Her friends were Matthew and Sara.

Novak pulled out a metal chair for Julia and one for himself. His face had lost most of the cold hardness she'd seen at the crime scene, and when he smiled, he could have been any dad talking to his kid's friends at a soccer game or school function.

"Hey, guys," Novak said. "We won't keep you much longer. I know it's not been an easy night."

Novak's presence relaxed the kids. One stopped gripping her cup so tight, and the other two leaned back in their chairs a little.

"No one's in trouble here. We're trying to figure out what happened. Tell me why you chose this place," Novak said. "It's vacant and uninhabited."

"We got a message," Emma said. "Said if you wanted a cheap place to hold a party, then look at this warehouse."

"Can I see it?" Novak asked.

"It's already gone. It's only up for an hour before it automatically deletes itself."

"Who sent it?" Julia asked.

"I don't know. The handle was *Hangman*," Emma said.

Julia shook her head, enraged by the killer's arrogance. She had the sense he was taunting her.

"Anyone heard from the Hangman before?" Novak asked.

"I never have," Emma said as the other kids shook their heads no. She opened her phone and showed Julia the invitation.

It would have been a matter of time before someone stumbled onto the body, but for some reason the killer had wanted it found sooner than later.

"What kind of party was it?" Novak asked.

"We have regular parties on random days," Sara said. "Offbeat places. We provide the music, and it's BYOB. It's never gotten out of hand. Just a way for the seniors to blow off steam."

"You all in college?" Novak's smile was self-deprecating. "I must be getting old. Everyone looks like high school to me."

Emma frowned. "What was that hanging from the ceiling? Was it really a woman?"

"It was," Julia said.

"Shit," she whispered. "I've never seen anything like it."

Novak absently tapped his fingers on the table. "You see anything unusual when you showed up at the warehouse? Anything out of place that caught your attention?"

"The place felt off," Emma said.

"What do you mean?" Novak asked.

"We've partied in some odd places, but I've never been scared. This time I was scared. From the moment we got out of our car, I thought we were being watched."

"And then a dog started barking," Sara said. "That spooked me."

"You see the dog?" Novak asked.

"No," Sara said.

"Nothing real or solid," Emma said. "Just weird feelings."

"Okay," Novak said. "Detective Riggs has your contact information, correct?"

They all nodded.

"Then there's no reason to keep you any longer," Novak said, rising. He walked to the door and opened it. "If we have any more questions, I'll call."

Julia rose. "Thanks, guys."

As Novak escorted the students out of the building, Julia reached for her phone and called Andrews. He answered on the second ring. She briefed him on the new murder.

"So the Hangman uses social media that vanishes in an hour," Andrews said.

"Looks like it."

"You'll want to talk to Vic Carson," he said. "He runs a website called the Hangman. Big fan site."

"You're kidding. There's a fan site? Why didn't you tell me?"

"It popped up about a month ago, and I am telling you now."

"What do you know about him?"

"He was living in Richmond in 1992 and has always had a fascination with serial killers. He has a moderate following."

"I won't insult you and ask if he has a record," she said.

"He does. Small petty crimes in the eighties, but since then, no arrests. He's clean."

"Or careful."

"Agreed. He's still in California at a conference, but as soon as he returns to Richmond, I'll contact you. Sending his image now."

Her phone dinged with a text, and she studied the picture. "I've not seen him, but I'll keep an eye out for him."

"Considering the Hangman might be active again, this case is now a top priority. I'll expand my search and report to Mr. Shield and Mr. Bowman."

"To include what?"

"A much deeper look into the lives of the past victims and now current victim. Your father. People you've crossed paths with over the last few years. Think of it as casting a net. I'll let you know if I find anything."

"Novak is working the case of a Rita Gallagher. Her body was found three days ago, but she died around the time of the Hangman's victims." She recapped all that she knew about Rita and her connections to the Hangman's victims.

"I'll add her into the search."

"Keep me posted."

"Understood."

When she hung up, Novak reappeared and she filled him in on her conversation with Andrews.

All traces of the amiable, steady man who'd been talking to the teenagers vanished. "Going forward, you and Andrews will both keep me in the loop. If Shield Security gives you new data on the Hangman or Rita Gallagher, call me. You meet with Shield Security, I'm along for the ride."

The order stoked her temper before she reminded herself she was working in his jurisdiction now. "Sure. What I know, you'll know." She slid her phone in her back pocket.

"Dr. McGowan said they've scheduled the autopsy for the day after tomorrow."

"I want to attend," Julia said.

Novak shook his head, the corners of his eyes creasing. "We'll finish this together."

"Famous last words."

"We need to talk to Ken."

"He's likely asleep by now. Besides, evenings aren't good for him."

"Early in the morning. I'll pick you up."

Novak was a part of her case, and that she didn't mind. But he was now weaving into her life. She was depending on him. Looking forward to seeing him. None of that was good, because when it ended, she knew it would hurt like hell. "I'll be ready."

CHAPTER FOURTEEN

Thursday, November 2, 8:00 a.m.

When Novak and Julia arrived at the Thompson house, the sun had burned off the last of the morning fog. The air was crisp, and most of the trees had peaked with fall colors.

Julia got out of the car. Her heeled boots clicked on the sidewalk. Unhurried, Novak easily caught up to her.

He knocked on the door, and Wendy greeted them moments later with a smile.

"Come on inside," she said. "Ken is doing well this morning. I think working again has raised his spirits."

Julia moved through the house and found Ken in the sunporch. The room was lit with morning oranges and yellows. He sat at a desk, leaning over a computer that looked to be at least a decade old. Any kind of change had never been easy for Ken, but now it was impossible.

"Ken," Julia said. "Look who I have with me. It's Detective Novak." Ken remembered long-term facts well, but new acquaintances were harder for him to retain. She and Ken could still pretend that he remembered, but the encouragement might spark a recollection.

Ken looked up from the computer and pulled off his glasses. He smiled, but his eyes searched for a connection. "Novak, how are you? It's been a while."

Novak didn't point out that they'd seen each other three days ago. "Doing well. You look good."

Ken patted his fat belly. "Wendy is feeding me too much. I'm getting fat."

"Sounds like she's taking good care of you," he said.

"She's great." He pointed toward the floral couch flanked by a couple of matching chairs. "Have a seat."

Ken got up and took the chair on the right as he always did. Julia chose to sit close to him on the edge of the couch, and Novak took the opposite chair.

Ken sat back. "So, what can I do for you two?"

Julia smiled. "We want to ask you a few more questions about the Hangman case."

"Right, sure," Ken said. "Of course. What do you want to know?"

Novak leaned forward. "We've been talking to some of the former witnesses and family members of the victims."

"Good start," Ken said.

"According to Rene's husband, Gene, Jim hung out in Stella's bar when he used to work undercover."

"Makes sense," Ken said. "He was all over the area during those years."

"Gene believed that Rene knew Jim," Julia said.

"He might have," Ken said. "He knew everyone who worked in Shockoe Bottom."

"Rene was last seen with a woman by the name of Rita, but there's no mention in your notes about Rita," Julia said.

"There isn't?" Ken frowned.

"You said before you don't remember Rita. Are you sure about that?"

157

Ken shook his head. "I said that?"

"Yes."

"That's not right. Jim knew Rita, and he told me he'd trail her. When I asked him about her days later, he said Rita was a dead end."

"And you believed him?" Julia asked.

"Sure, why not."

"Maybe you saw her," Novak pushed. He opened his phone and produced the image from her driver's license. "Early twenties with red hair. Pretty. Attractive build, according to witnesses."

"A lot of 'em were pretty," Ken said. He studied the picture, his frown lines creasing.

"I know Jim wasn't a Boy Scout," Julia said. "I heard Mom and Cindy talk when I was growing up." Cindy had been furious with her mother for grieving for Jim, a man who'd loved his wife but couldn't be faithful. How many times had Cindy said that love wasn't enough? "So if you remember Rita, tell us."

Ken shoved out a breath and sat back. He looked at Julia a long moment. "Yeah, I remember the redhead," he said. "He met her at Billy's. Jim called her Red Hot Rita. She was sexy and had a crush on Jim. He was working homicide by then, but I could tell he was restless. Missed the excitement and adrenaline of working narcotics undercover. It bugged the hell out of him that the past wouldn't let him go."

"Did they sleep together?" Julia asked.

Ken nodded. "Yes, they slept together several times that fall. I think she's the reason Amy left him. When your mother left with you, Jim finally snapped out of whatever funk he'd been in and realized he needed to dump Rita. And he told me he did. He wanted to make it work with your mother. I know he loved Amy and he wanted his family back. After Jim died, Rita vanished. I never saw her again. What happened to her?"

"She was killed right around the time Jim died," Novak said. "We found her body a few days ago."

"She's dead?" Ken asked. "How?"

"Blunt force trauma," Novak said. "And it looks like she might have been pregnant."

Ken rose, running his hand through his thick white hair. "A baby?"

"About twenty weeks along," Julia said. She'd been an only child and more than once dreamed of having a brother or sister. To think, she almost might have had one.

"Was the baby Jim's?" Novak asked.

Ken tensed, glanced between Julia and Novak. "He never mentioned a baby to me."

"A pregnancy would explain why Mom left," Julia said. It must have shattered her mother to discover her husband had gotten another woman pregnant.

"But who killed her? Do you think she's connected to the Hangman?" Ken asked.

"She's a new piece to the puzzle," Novak said.

"Makes sense," Ken said, more to himself.

Novak leaned in toward Ken. "Sometimes cops have theories that they don't put into the paperwork. Maybe it's a gut feeling, or perhaps someone has a lot of political juice, but either way the details don't make the report."

Ken shook his head. "I was never one to leave information out. I put every detail in my notes. Jim was different. He was a little more selective."

"Why was that?" Julia asked.

"Had to do with his undercover work. He was never a fan of the paper trail. He worried a careless administrator could get him killed."

"Did he mention that Tamara Brown was one of his confidential informants?" Julia asked.

"No. He never said a word," Ken said. "But he didn't talk about his undercover work. I sensed it was a part of his life he wanted to leave behind, so I never pressed. Can you two pull those old files from the narcotics investigations?"

"Jim's undercover files are still sealed, and it's going to take someone with a higher pay grade to gain access," Novak said.

Ken rubbed the top of his head. "I knew the murders really troubled him, and he took them harder than I did. It never occurred to me Jim had a personal connection to the victims."

"Do you think Jim killed those women?" Novak asked.

Julia held her breath, afraid to move until he answered. Time slowed. When Ken glanced in her direction, his face tensed and she nodded. "Be honest, please."

Ken threaded his hands together, and she had the sense he was about to speak when Wendy entered the room with a tray of coffee cups. She said, "Jim didn't kill anyone. He was a good cop and not a serial killer."

Ken straightened as she set the tray down. Whatever thoughts he'd been ready to share had filtered away.

Frustration jabbed at Julia. "Ken, what do you think? Did Jim kill those women?"

Ken glanced at Wendy, who laid a gentle hand on his shoulder, and then back to Julia. "Jim *was* a great cop, kiddo. He believed in justice."

"You should talk to Neil Rogers," Wendy said. "He was the forensic technician on all three murders. I worked with him on several cases, and if anyone knew the details as well as or better than Ken and Jim, it was Neil."

Novak scribbled the name. "I read some of his reports. Solid work. We'll find him." He accepted a mug of coffee from Wendy.

Ken frowned, and his hand began to shake. He slid it into his pants pocket.

"Look," Wendy said. "I think it's time we take a break. Ken and I'll talk about it later, and I'll dig through the attic and see what I can find in his file boxes. But for now, he needs his rest."

Novak released a breath. "Sure. We can talk later."

Julia was frustrated. A critical piece of the puzzle had just danced inches from their reach. "You were a big help, Ken. Thanks. We'll come back another time."

"I must have some notes on her in my files," Ken said, clenching his fists. "I know the answers are there."

Julia patted him on the shoulder. "And we'll get at them. Just not today. Not now."

She and Novak showed themselves out. The sun was higher in the cloudless sky, but a wind added to the chill as it cut through her light jacket.

"He became agitated," Julia said.

"Yes, he did."

"Like he thought Jim might have been involved in Rita's death?" Julia pulled up her collar to guard against the wind.

"Next time, I'll talk to him alone without you or Wendy." No hint of hesitation. He was telling her what was going to happen.

"What happened to *team*?"

"If I were cutting you out, I wouldn't be telling you what I was going to do."

"Ken is family."

"I understand that. But I still need to talk to him. He'll be more candid with me and less embarrassed if we're alone. I'm a fellow cop. He thinks of you like a daughter and doesn't want to hurt you."

She understood the logic and what needed to be done. But she didn't like it. She checked her watch. "I'm calling Neil Rogers."

"We'll talk to the guy together." He adjusted his cuffs. "Foolish to double up efforts."

She could have used distance from Novak right now, but he was right. Territorial cops weren't as effective. "You're annoyingly logical."

The edges of his lips lifted as he fished keys from his pocket. "See, that wasn't so hard."

She slid into the front seat of Novak's car. He had a relaxed confidence that she admired. Sure, she was confident, but not calm or tranquil. He wasn't rattled easily, and she was a little jealous of that.

Novak called Neil Rogers and explained the situation. "Great. We'll be by in a half hour. Thanks."

When he hung up, she settled back into her seat.

Novak's phone rang. "Hey, kiddo," he said. His face and demeanor softened when he spoke.

Julia guessed it was his daughter. Feeling awkward, as if she were now intruding on a family conversation, she looked out her passenger-side window.

"You made it back without any issues?" he asked.

Julia didn't want to be curious, but she was.

"All right," he said. "Do you ever get instant messages for parties?" He frowned. "Do me a favor and watch out for any from the Hangman. He's very bad news. Yeah, I know I've said it before. Just be careful. Okay. Have a good time this weekend. And remember . . ."

She could hear Bella groan like she imagined a teenager would when talking to a protective father.

"But I enjoy hearing you run through the safety rules all the time. Run 'em again," he said. And then, "Love you."

He hung up and clipped his phone back in its holster. "My kid," he said. He scowled as he drove. "Why did you become a cop?"

No challenge, but genuine curiosity was enough to make her answer. "My mother always said I was like my father. She said some people are wired for this kind of work. Like me, you, and maybe Bella." When he frowned, she said, "Cheer up. Bella might not be suited for police work. One thing to say you want the job, but it's another to do it."

"She's a lot like me."

"Tell you what. If she still has an interest, she can shadow me for a few days over the holiday break. I'll take her to an overnight stakeout on the coldest night. I fill her up with sludgy coffee and stale candy bars."

He shook his head. "I don't think so."

"What, you don't trust me with your kid?"

"I don't know you that well, Julia."

It was a fair statement. "You mean, am I too much like my old man?"

"You hold a lot of feelings in tightly. Sounds like he did the same, and it cost him in the end."

"It's never crossed my mind to do what he did."

He shot her a glare as if she'd hit a nerve.

"I'm not Jim. Not your late wife."

"You could open up more."

"Look, part of the reason I can do what I do is because I can keep my feelings in check. You're the same. You'd have to be to do the job."

He stared ahead, silent.

"If Bella wants to see what being a cop is like, I'm a great resource. And I would never put her in danger."

"No offense intended, but you take chances."

"And you don't?"

"Calculated risks."

"They're the same in my book."

"No, not really."

Ah, they'd come full circle back to what happened in Virginia Beach. "You don't want me around your kid because you think I'll encourage her to be reckless, and one day a drug dealer will treat your kid like a punching bag, is that it?"

His fingers tightened on the steering wheel.

"Look, I appreciate that you're protective of your daughter. It's really damn charming. But let's face it, she's one example of the many reasons we could not go the distance." She took his silence as acceptance, and though it bothered her more than it should that they weren't couple material, she couldn't blame the guy. "I don't fault you for caring about Bella. In fact, I used to dream that if Jim hadn't shot himself, he would have settled down and been a great father to me. You know, the kind that cheers on the sidelines at soccer practices and threatens your prom date if he doesn't bring you home by midnight."

"Have you ever gotten pushback for your father's suicide?"

"Not outright, no. But some instructors at the academy recognized the name. And my captain at the beach brought it up in a debrief."

"Why?"

She shrugged. Her captain had meant well. He'd wanted her in counseling, and when he found out she only attended two of the four scheduled sessions, he pressed buttons. She finally agreed to complete the counseling sessions. "He was afraid I'd go off the rails like Jim did. He wouldn't be the first to wonder if I'd go a little nuts."

"I know you were pretty battered." His brow knotted. "Is the other part true?"

Her heart stilled, and her breathing slowed. She didn't answer.

"Did Benny rape you?" Each syllable sounded gnawed on and spit out.

For a long moment she didn't respond. "Who's saying that?"

"Riggs said you refused the rape kit."

"Maybe I needed to be left alone. Maybe the X-rays and the twenty-five stitches the nurse put in my arm were enough of an intrusion for one day. Maybe the noise of the emergency room was too much."

"You're deflecting."

No one other than her captain had had the balls to voice the question directly to her face, let alone push for an answer. "It's going to have to do. Like you said, you don't know me, Novak, and I sure don't know you."

"That's why I'm asking. I want to know."

She stared out the window, thinking. It would be so easy to open up and talk to Novak. And she nearly did before reason stopped her. She sidestepped back to Bella. "I remember how my aunt tried to talk me out of the academy. She hated the idea. At the time, I didn't understand her fear. I understand it now. I can talk to Bella about the job and what it's like for a woman. I can warn her and share war stories, but none of us really knows until we put on the uniform. But at nineteen, we all think we're bulletproof."

He accepted the conversation shift, not pressing about Benny's attack. "The goal is to get her to twenty-five, and then she can make any kind of decision she likes."

Laughter rumbled in her chest. "Have you picked out the convent she'll live in until then?"

"Not funny."

"Do you see me laughing?"

He sighed. "Bella's a good kid. Her mother wasn't easygoing, but she is."

"Lucky for you. I was a terror."

That tweaked a smile. "I can't imagine you being difficult."

"Let Bella figure her own life out, Novak. If her head is screwed on straight, she'll make good decisions."

He didn't speak for a couple of miles.

"You see the world as black-and-white," she said. "I see lots of grays."

Shaking his head, he said, "I don't know what the hell that means."

"Not surprising."

He was at ease behind the wheel, and she sensed that, like her, he was at his best when he was chasing a case. Nothing warmed the blood better than hunting bad guys and watching them go down. She and Novak had more in common than she originally thought.

***

Novak parked in front of the simple brick rancher located on a tree-lined street. The neighborhood dated back to the fifties, but the presence of children's toys in many of the yards proved the area was enjoying a renewal.

Julia walked up to the door and Novak followed, allowing her to ring the bell. Novak liked Julia. Liked her tenacity. Been hooked on her since the first night he'd seen her standing in the back of the ballroom. Also suspected she'd bolt if he told her so.

Inside the house, a steady beat of footsteps approached. Those steps then hesitated on the other side of the front door as Novak assumed Rogers was checking them out through the peephole.

A chain rattled, and the door opened to a slim man with a thinning stock of gray hair. Deep wrinkles lined his face, but his eyes were a brilliant blue. "Novak," he said.

"Good to see you again, Neil." Rogers had been on the way out when Novak had made detective, but they'd caught a few cases together. "This is Agent Julia Vargas with the Virginia State Police."

Julia extended her hand. "Thank you for seeing us."

"Anything for Novak. And Jim's kid. Come on inside." Rogers stepped aside, allowing them into a well-lit hallway that led into a living room and a kitchen beyond. Though the smell of burgers still lingered in the air, Novak could see the kitchen was clean, counters wiped, and dishes stacked in the drying rack by the sink.

The living room was also tidy. The television was off, but a steaming cup of coffee next to the television remote suggested he'd been watching the news.

"Can I get either of you a cup of coffee? Just put a fresh pot on."

"I'll take a cup," Novak said.

"Sounds great," Julia said.

Rogers moved into the kitchen and grabbed two white mugs from the cabinet. He filled each carefully, then reached for a bowl filled with sugar and creamer packets. "No fresh milk. I drank the powdered kind on the job so long I never could get used to real milk after I retired."

"Most of my meals come out of vending machines or fast-food joints," Julia said. "Hate to think what I'd do if I came toe-to-toe with a fresh vegetable."

Rogers held up a cup. "Novak?"

"Black works," he said.

The three sat in the living room, Rogers in a well-worn recliner and Novak and Julia on the couch that faced a large picture window.

Rogers swiveled his chair from the television toward the couch as he sipped his coffee. "You surprised me when you called. I haven't heard the names Vargas and the Hangman in ages."

Julia cradled her cup in long fingers that looked oddly graceful even with plain, shorn nails. "I'd thought about opening the case, but until this year didn't act on it. In my spare time I've been going through the files and reading my father's notes. Now I have a private security firm that's willing to retest some of the samples. I'm hoping something might pop."

"Since you phoned, I've been trying to recall the case. I made it up to the attic and pulled the notes I kept." He reached for a pad and pencil resting on another small table by his chair. "The forensic guys are light-years ahead of what we could do twenty-five years ago. DNA was only just being accepted by most juries."

"I've read your notes," Julia said. "Well written."

Rogers raised his cup to her. "Thank you."

"Did your notes jog your memory?" Novak asked.

"They did. I remembered that I found hair fibers on all the bodies. I sent them off for testing. Not uncommon for it to take months, even a year to get DNA tests back. After Jim Vargas died and the killer went dark, the case landed on the back burner and the results must have been lost in the shuffle."

"According to what I read, DNA couldn't be mapped," Julia said.

"When some suggested that Jim had been the killer, I wanted to cross-check the DNA scene samples with his. I called the lab and found out the samples had been compromised. They had been improperly stored in plastic. Mold and heat had destroyed them," Rogers said.

"All three were destroyed?" Novak asked.

"Afraid so."

"Who was in charge of the samples?" Julia asked.

"Everyone and no one. Procedures have improved considerably since then," Rogers said.

She and Novak exchanged glances. Who'd had access to the samples? The forensic team. Technicians. Cops. It could have boiled down to incompetence, but didn't seem likely with three separate sets. If Jim hadn't improperly stored the evidence, someone who knew him might have.

"We have another homicide case," Novak said. "Her body was found four days ago, but the woman was murdered within days of Jim's death." He recapped the details.

Rogers nodded. "Be interesting to see what forensic samples they can pull from her clothing."

"Agreed," Julia said. "We also have a recent murder." She told him what they'd found, keeping her voice steady and clear. "I knew the victim from my undercover days."

"Funny that you knew the victim. A couple of the Hangman victims knew your father."

"Jim told you that?" Julia asked.

"I don't think he told me. He could be pretty tight-lipped when it came to the undercover days. But his partner, Ken, mentioned it to me after Jim died. Ken had been drinking heavily, and his wife asked a couple of us to track him down. We found him in a bar and asked him what was wrong. That's when he started talking."

"We were just with Ken," Novak said. "He said he didn't know about Jim's CIs."

"He might not have known all of them, but he knew some." Rogers shook his head. "Jim confided in Ken. They were close. Went to the academy together. If Jim Vargas had any secrets and was inclined to tell them, then Ken Thompson would have been the one he confided in."

Was Ken lying? Or did he not remember? She'd had the sense that both Ken and Wendy were hiding something.

Rogers sat back in his chair, carefully setting his cup on a side table. "I was sorry to hear about your father, Julia. He was the last guy I would ever expect to commit suicide."

"Thanks. I appreciate it." She leaned forward, cradling her cup in her hands. "What was he like to work with?"

"He was a stud," Rogers said. "I don't think anything scared the guy. The risks he took while undercover made the toughest cops shudder. If not for him, Popov would never have been brought down."

"The Popov case made Jim's career," she said to Novak.

"Alexi Popov was a drug dealer and a nasty son of a bitch," Rogers said. "Left a trail of mutilated bodies along the East Coast. No one could get close to him, but your father did. It was a huge bust. Saw to it that the murderer died in prison."

"Neil, if you can give some more thought on the Hangman, it would be a help," Novak said. "Any detail would be appreciated. And I'm especially interested in those lost samples."

"Believe me, all I've thought about is the case since you called. I'll go through my notes again."

"Thanks for your help," Julia said.

"Keep me posted," Rogers said.

They rose and Novak took Julia's untouched coffee with him back into the kitchen. He drained both cups in the sink and returned to the living room.

Julia was at the front door. "Thanks again, Neil."

"You come by anytime. Jim's kid is always welcome here."

Outside, Novak dialed Riggs's number and landed in his voice mail. "I need you to look up the case files of an Alexi Popov. He would have done time for drug trafficking in the late eighties. Arresting officer was Jim Vargas."

He pocketed his phone and met Julia at his car. As she sat in the passenger seat, he slid behind the wheel. She was quiet as she stared at the house.

"You okay?"

"Why wouldn't I be? I've heard people talk about my father before."

"It doesn't bother you?"

"Does it look like it does?"

He studied her closely. "You can be hard to read."

"Good." A smile hitched the edge of her lip. "Keeps everyone guessing."

He shook his head. "I'm not a fan of puzzles."

"Another reason why we're excellent in the short term."

As he pulled onto the street, his phone buzzed. He glanced at the text. "Dr. Kincaid will be conducting the Lana Ortega autopsy tomorrow morning at nine thirty."

"She's efficient."

Her phone buzzed with a call from Andrews. She glanced toward Novak. "Andrews, I'm going to put you on speakerphone. I'm with Detective Novak now. He'd liked to be looped into your work."

"Understood," Andrews said.

She pressed the proper button. "Go ahead."

"A video has been uploaded on the Hangman site. The footage looks like it was taken by the killer."

She looked toward Novak, who frowned as he absently rubbed the worn section of his steering wheel with his thumb.

"It's the murder of Tamara Brown," Andrews said. "The coverage is about twenty-five seconds long and was taken with a VHS camcorder."

"Can you send the link to me?" she asked.

"On its way now," Andrews said.

She clicked open the attachment and tilted the phone screen toward Novak. The image was grainy and the lighting poor, but she could see the swaying, elevated body of the victim. The woman was struggling, her feet twitching as she clearly fought to get her last few breaths. The killer circled her body slowly, moving behind her and then back in front, catching every last gruesome spasm of her body as she strangled to death.

"Jesus," Julia muttered.

"You said the video was uploaded to the Hangman site? That's administered by Vic Carson, correct?" Novak asked.

"It is, but bear in mind that site is fairly easy to hack. I did it easily when I removed this video."

"So the footage is down now?" Novak asked.

"Yes," Andrews said. "Whoever uploaded the footage was careful not to leave a trail. It'll take me some time, but I'll find them. I've been able to find the address of Stuart Lambert," he said.

"He worked in the porn shop located on Cary Street," Julia said, confirming what she knew.

"Correct. He was seen with all three victims days before each vanished. Lambert changed his name to Whitcomb and enrolled in college at Duke University. He earned his undergraduate degree in physics and also his master's and PhD. Now he runs a small computer engineering firm that specializes in systems design."

"A guy like that would know how to hack a computer," Novak said.

"My thoughts exactly," Andrews said.

"Let's have his address," Novak said as he checked his watch.

Andrews rattled it off.

"Thank you," Julia said.

"Keep me posted," Andrews said, just before he hung up.

CHAPTER FIFTEEN

Thursday, November 2, 11:30 a.m.

Novak and Julia arrived at the small office building on Grove Avenue. Julia was silent, tense. Few cases carried more emotional weight for her than the Hangman. She was glad Novak was helping her with the burden.

The office was nestled in a tree-lined section where older brick homes had been converted to offices. There was no sign out front indicating it housed an engineering firm.

"Stuart Lambert Whitcomb is supposed to be a genius," Julia said. "He went to Harvard on full scholarship at the age of sixteen and was top of his class until he had a nervous breakdown at nineteen. His parents brought him home, and after a hospital stay and a few prescriptions, they thought it would be good for him to work in a low-level job until he was a little older and could return to school. Got a job working the counter in a porn shop in the Bottom near where the bodies were found."

"Porn's not exactly a stable occupation," he said.

"No argument here. Andrews sent me a more detailed brief on the guy. Honestly, a little troubling how much Andrews can find out about a person online." She checked her file and pulled out a picture taken of Whitcomb in 1992. His hair was dark and thick and his face lean. What made anyone look twice were the eyes. Gray and penetrating, they had a haunting, unsettling quality. "He was twenty-one when this picture was taken."

Novak studied the image. "What kind of profile did the detectives get on Whitcomb?"

"Quiet. Withdrawn. Didn't speak much. His parents hired an attorney immediately and shut down the questioning. According to Andrews, he changed his last name to Whitcomb in 1992. Guess he needed a new beginning."

"What happened at Harvard? A breakdown can be defined many ways."

"There was an incident with a female student. She said he yelled at her in a chemistry class. The teacher called campus security, and by the time they arrived, Stuart had broken a beaker and had the woman cornered."

"Did they have a prior relationship?"

"Not according to Jim's notes."

In front of the building a huge oak was quickly shedding its brightly colored orange and yellow leaves. Below it was a wrought-iron bench and an urn full of bright-yellow mums.

"Nice view," she said. "Just like the view out my office window. Oh wait, I have no window."

"If you wanted a corner office and a view, you're in the wrong line of work."

"True." Her shoulders back, she climbed out, and together they walked toward the front entrance.

Inside, a young woman with blond hair and a pleasant round face smiled up at them as they approached. The decor was conservative with Oriental rugs, oil-painting landscapes on the wall, and mahogany furniture. It was a far cry from Stuart Lambert and the days of running a porn video shop.

"Welcome to SLW Engineering," the blonde said. "How may I help you?"

Both pulled out their badges.

Novak spoke first. "We'd like to speak to Stuart Whitcomb."

She studied their badges. "Mr. Whitcomb is in a meeting right now."

"Do us a favor and let him know we're here," Novak said.

"Can I tell him what it's in reference to?"

"The Hangman," Julia said.

"I don't understand," the receptionist said.

"He will," Julia said.

The woman vanished around the corner, leaving Julia and Novak to wait.

Less than a minute later, a slim man appeared. He was dressed in an expensive suit, tailored white shirt, and a red tie. His hair had grayed at the temples and his face had grown thinner over the years. But the eyes remained as sharp and haunting as in the '92 photo.

"I'm Stuart Whitcomb."

"Detective Tobias Novak and Agent Julia Vargas."

Mention of Julia's last name immediately drew his attention to her, but he made no comment as he waited for the receptionist to take her seat. Though she didn't look up, the blonde was clearly paying attention. "Come into my office, and we can have a conversation."

Novak motioned for Julia to walk in front of him, and together they followed Whitcomb down a long carpeted hallway filled with professional awards to his plush office. As she suspected, there was a large window that overlooked a pond. The geese were toddling past among amber leaves scattered on the neatly trimmed lawn. Peaceful, just as she'd thought. Also a bit boring.

They took their seats in front of a large ornately carved desk, which he sat behind. Carefully he threaded his fingers and leaned toward them a fraction. "What is this about?"

"We're reopening the Hangman case." Novak let the words sit there, seemingly content with however long it took for Whitcomb to respond. Nearly a full minute went by with the three of them staring at each other.

Finally Novak asked, "Jim Vargas interviewed you on numerous occasions, is that correct?"

Whitcomb's gaze held Julia's a beat longer before shifting back to Novak. "That is correct. Vargas and his partner, Ken Thompson, leaned on me pretty heavily. I always thought I'd have been railroaded into prison if not for my attorney. Once those detectives had me in their sights, they developed tunnel vision."

"Perhaps they had good reason to question you," Novak said. "You worked in a porn shop two blocks from where the three bodies were found."

"And," Julia added, "surveillance tape from a bar across the street from your shop recorded you making contact with all three victims."

"A lot of people came into that establishment," he said. "Consumers weren't streaming product then, so they had to procure it in person."

"How did an upscale kid like you end up in a job like that?" Novak asked.

"You've both read the files, I'm sure. After leaving Harvard, I needed some downtime to collect myself. I picked that store because I originally thought the chances of me running into friends or people I knew were slim. As it turned out, a few frequented the store. It was mutually advantageous for all of us to be discreet. No one was going to say, 'I saw Stuart Lambert working in a porn store while I was renting a BDSM video.' They left me alone, and I kept their secrets."

"You worked in the store a while."

"Two years. Well, twenty-three months and seven days," he corrected.

"That's one heck of a memory," Novak said, smiling as he shook his head. "I can barely remember what I had for breakfast."

"I have a good memory," Whitcomb said. "Not photographic, but it's exceptional."

"What kind of computer work do you do here?" he asked.

"Basically, we set up systems."

"Does that mean installing the wires and monitors?"

"That's a simplistic way of putting it, but yes, that's correct."

"What about web design?" Novak asked.

"Occasionally some of our clients need a site, and we handle it for them."

"And security? Can you, I don't know, test their systems and hack into it?" Novak asked.

"It's one of our services."

Novak grinned. "I don't know how you do it. I still struggle with my TV remote."

Julia thought she should be taking notes on Novak's rope-a-dope interview techniques. It wouldn't be long before he snared his prey. While Novak could distance himself from the brutal facts of the case, she found it much harder with this investigation. Her anger was just under the surface, and it was a struggle to keep her voice and facial expressions in check. Though she'd never admit it, she was glad to have Novak taking point this time.

Novak got to the heart of their visit. "Rene Tanner, the first Hangman victim, was caught on the security tape in your store."

"She was," Whitcomb said. "In fact, I remember Detective Vargas showing me a receipt from my store. It had been found in Rene Tanner's pocket. We all lived and worked in Shockoe Bottom. In many respects, we were in the business of sin." He picked up his glasses from his desk and with a tissue carefully cleaned the lenses. "As I also told the police in 1992, I do not remember any of the women specifically. I was polite enough but didn't care to get to know or bond with anyone. I was working in that place until I could get back into school."

"What was the area like then after the first murder?" Novak asked.

"No one panicked at first. Sure, people were talking about the killing. But it didn't have much of an impact on our business or the others'. In fact, business picked up a little. Folks were curious."

"And after the second killing?" Novak asked.

Whitcomb shrugged. "Most of my clients were men. And though we occasionally had slow nights, it didn't last long. For some of my customers, it would have been a turn-on."

Some men found pleasure in hurting women, a lesson Julia had learned. "The cops' first visit to your shop was routine. They were talking to all the businesses, correct?"

"That's correct. They asked for our surveillance videos, and the store owner promptly turned them over with the promise from the cops to not divulge he was releasing the tape with all his clients on it."

"Why do you think you were a suspect?"

Whitcomb kept his expression blank. "Agent Vargas, it sounds like you've read the files, so I bet you already know the answer, don't you?"

"I'm looking for your take on the story," she said.

He sat back. "The media got wind of the story, and because it was such a horrific crime scene, the police knew they had to get in front of it. After the second kill, reporters wrote about the two murders daily. I assume the pressure was building. The murder rates in the city were climbing then, and Richmond was getting tagged in the national media. Gene Tanner was cleared, so they needed another suspect."

"Media pressure is one thing," Novak said. "But the cops set their sights on a particular person. They must have had a reason for looking at you."

He shrugged. "I fit the profile. I'd had mental health challenges and worked in an establishment that featured BDSM videos. I was easy and convenient to blame."

"Didn't they also find your sweater at one of the crime scenes?" Julia asked.

Whitcomb cleaned the lenses of his glasses again. "I used to wear the sweater to work. One day, it went missing from the back room. Irritating, but hardly a reason to call the cops."

"When the third victim was murdered, you had an alibi?" Novak asked.

"I was with my parents. We were visiting my doctor. Why are you digging into this old case now? It's been twenty-five years."

"Mr. Whitcomb, can you tell me where you were last night?" Novak asked.

"Last night?" That question prompted a curious grin. "I was at home. But I thought we were talking about twenty-five years ago."

"Were you at home with anyone?" Novak asked.

"Susan Ramsey." He removed his cell from his pocket and rattled off the number. "Does that help?"

Novak scribbled down the number. "It does. Thank you."

"But why the questions about last night?" Whitcomb pressed.

"There was a murder last night," Novak said.

A gray brow arched. "Like that of the Hangman?"

"There were similarities," Novak said.

Whitcomb shook his head. "And so now you're coming back to the guy the cops tried to nail twenty-five years ago."

"We're just asking questions," Novak said.

"Cops don't just ask questions," he said. "They always have an agenda." He rose. "This interview is over. I'll need you to leave my office."

Neither Julia nor Novak budged. "All friendly questions here," Novak said.

Whitcomb shook his head. "It's not friendly. You're trying to entrap me."

"I'll be contacting Ms. Ramsey," Novak said. "When did she leave?"

"About eleven p.m." Whitcomb's lips flattened into a grim line. "I'm finished talking. You can address all your questions to my attorney. Now please leave or I make calls to your bosses."

Novak slowly closed his notebook, and in no particular rush, tucked it in his breast pocket. "I was hoping to keep this friendly."

"We aren't friends," Whitcomb said.

"We'll talk again," Novak said.

They left the office. Outside, Novak pulled sunglasses from his pocket and slid them on.

"What do you think?" she asked.

"I don't know. He's wary of police, but if he got a bad deal the last time, he's in for some more trouble really soon."

"He shut up as soon as you mentioned last night's murder. In the original cases, he spoke to the cops for hours before his parents hired an attorney."

"He's smarter now." Novak remained where he stood.

"Interesting guy," she said.

Novak stared at the building, his jaw tensing. "What do you think, Julia?"

"He's a nut in my book."

"He did something twenty-five years ago. He might not have killed those girls, but he was no angel. Can you get your buddy at Shield to dig a little deeper on that one?"

"Sure, I'll ask right now."

She texted Andrews the request, and he responded immediately. "He's on it," she said.

Novak listened to his messages. "My partner has found the hotel where Lana Ortega was staying. I'm going to check it out. Care to tag along?"

"Damn, Novak, that's the nicest thing anyone has said to me today."

"Julia, if that's the nicest, then you need better friends."

"So I keep telling myself." The stiffness released in her back as they moved toward the car. Inside, she settled into the seat. "You really think it's the same killer?"

"If it's not, then it's someone who knew a lot of details about the original killings."

"If it's the same guy, it puts my father in the clear."

"That's important to you."

"It is. I always said it didn't matter, but it does." She and her mother had lived their lives on the outside because of her father.

"We'll figure this out, Julia."

She tipped her chin up. "We certainly will."

CHAPTER SIXTEEN

Thursday, November 2, 2:45 p.m.

Novak parked a block away from the familiar upscale historic hotel located in the city center. When Bella had been younger, this was her place to visit at Christmas. He and his dad had made the trek with her each year. Neither Novak nor his father had liked the place—too fussy—but it was worth the trip to see Bella's excitement. Now that his dad was gone, he continued the tradition.

He and Julia walked past a flowing fountain decorated with a dolphin centered among arching streams of water. The hotel was well over a hundred years old and was considered the place to have tea or dinner. She didn't look in awe or that impressed. Instead, she studied the entrance in a tactical sort of way. The image of her balancing a teacup with a plate of biscuits made him smile.

"Why the smirk, Novak?" she asked.

"Imagining you here at high tea."

"Seriously?"

"It's not pretty."

She shrugged. "For your information, I had tea here at Christmas with my mother and aunt when I was ten. I liked the cookies, but the tea wasn't sweet enough, and my new shoes pinched. The entire experience wasn't a good fit. But I pretended to like it because my mom loved it."

"How do you and Cindy celebrate Christmas?"

"When I'm not on the job, I'm working a little behind the bar at Billy's. The holiday season is a big time for her."

"Where are you most at home?"

Slowly she shook her head. "Still working on that one."

"You don't have a clue?"

"Not really. Do you?"

"Thought I did. Now, I'm starting fresh."

Novak introduced himself at the front desk and showed his badge, and the clerk quickly hurried into a back room in search of the hotel manager.

Julia turned from the front desk to study the gleaming marble and lush carpets and furnishings.

A man behind them cleared his voice. They turned to see a man wearing crisp suit.

"I'm Mr. Young," the man said.

Novak made the introductions. "We'd like to see Lana Ortega's room. My partner should be here any minute with a search warrant."

"Yes, I've spoken to Detective Riggs. Let me go ahead and escort you upstairs. As he requested, we have not cleaned the room."

"Good."

They rode the elevator to the fifth floor, and Mr. Young hurried to room 521. He unlocked the door. "Would you like me to stay?"

"It's not necessary."

"I'll wait in the lobby for your partner."

"Thank you."

Novak and Julia watched him glance back at them before he stepped on the elevator.

"The manager was anxious to get us out of the lobby," Julia said. "Cops aren't good for business, I suppose."

"I look like a cop," he said as he pulled on gloves. "You do not."

She pulled latex gloves from her leather coat pocket. "I'll take that as a compliment."

He studied the rumpled bed. Lace underwear and a silk slip were tossed carelessly on the floor next to a pair of sparkling Louboutin high heels. A half-dozen dresses hung in the closet. "She liked the nice things," he said, studying a red dress that still had a $2,000 price tag.

"She was always dressed well. Benny expected her to look her best. One time she wore a sweatshirt and jeans, and Benny hit her. *Never again,* he told her."

"How long was Lana with Benny?"

"At least three years. She was eighteen when she met him. Came from a poor family. She was the oldest of six. Her catching Benny's attention was a coup for her family. The drug dealer and the girl from the projects, a gangster Cinderella story."

He crouched by the closet and studied the neat line of shoes. "You spend a lot of time with Lana?"

"Some. When she was upset she would sit at the bar and drink her pink cosmos. She wasn't smart enough to know she shouldn't have been talking to me or anyone about Benny. I mostly listened."

"What can you tell me about Lana?"

"She loved Benny, though I wouldn't describe it as a healthy relationship. He basically bought her from her family and considered her chattel. When a business deal or life wasn't going well, he liked to hit her. Even Lana didn't deserve that."

"What was your relationship with her like?"

"She liked me, believe it or not. She said I was a good listener and understood her problems."

"Ever consider Benny sent her to test you?"

"I did. I assumed every moment of that assignment was a test. I was so careful. I parsed every word I spoke." She picked up a silver watch on the nightstand and inspected it before replacing it. "I listened to her when she talked about her hopes and dreams. She always talked about going to school. She wanted respect, and there were moments when I thought if I found the magic words, she'd leave him and go back home to her family. But, of course, that wouldn't have helped my investigation much, would it? So the loving and beating continued on."

"Was she involved in his business?"

"No, but she wanted to be. She thought Benny would value her more if she could help him with his business. She was always bugging him about doing more." She frowned. "She would have done anything for Benny. Loyal to the end."

"Do you think he blames her for all his troubles?"

"Of course. Benny is a coward and a bully. He doesn't have the guts to put any of his troubles on himself."

"And he'd kill her?"

"Benny would boil his own mother in oil if he thought it would benefit him. It would be like Benny to have someone string her up to send a message to me."

Novak moved into the bathroom, staring at the counter littered with all kinds of beauty products. Bella always had her share of girl crap, but he'd taken it in stride. He'd counted the days until her bathroom wasn't an ongoing mess. Now that it was sparkling clean, he found the uncluttered counters, polished mirrors, and folded towels lonely and sad. Hard to believe one kid could eat up so much of his life.

"Look what I have here," Julia said from the other room.

He found her standing by an expensive suitcase, holding up a kilo bag filled with white powder. "Cocaine."

"Think she was distributing drugs for Benny while he's away?" Novak asked.

"She wanted to be a part of his business. This was her opportunity to prove herself to him. Show she loved him unconditionally."

"How would he react to that?"

She set the bag back in the suitcase. "If she didn't have his permission, not well. With his paranoia, he would see it as betrayal."

The hotel room door opened, and they found Riggs, dressed in a navy-blue suit, polished black shoes, and a dark silk tie. Riggs smiled as he extended his hand to Julia. "Julia, good to see you again. Any luck on the Hangman case?"

"Just getting into the case when Lana was murdered," she said. The ease in her tone evaporated as she spoke to his partner. She wasn't rude, but there was a layer of ice there that he'd heard when she spoke to everyone but her aunt and sometimes him.

"I saw the crime-scene photos," Riggs said. "Looks like the same guy, but makes no sense why he'd go dark for twenty-five years. Novak, I did get information on Alexi Popov. The old file hit my desk an hour ago," Riggs said.

"And?" Novak asked.

"Popov really was a nasty son of a bitch. He was convicted of drug trafficking, and thanks to Jim Vargas, the guy was sentenced to life in prison. He would have been looking at a death sentence, but the key witness refused to testify."

Julia straightened. "Who was it?"

"Rene Tanner," Riggs said.

Novak felt a rush as the pieces of a case fell into place. "Were the names Vicky Wayne, Tamara Brown, or Rita Gallagher mentioned in the files at all?"

"I haven't had time to read the entire file, but I don't remember any other Hangman victims on Popov's witness list," Riggs said.

"We have reason to believe Rene and Tamara were confidential informants for Jim Vargas," Novak said. "Rita worked at Billy's and was

Rene's friend. The only one without a direct connection to Jim Vargas is Vicky Wayne."

"Popov was in jail at the time of the Hangman murders," Julia said. "He died in his sleep ten years later in his prison cell."

"Guy like that had a long reach," Riggs said. "So after Rene decides not to testify, Popov decides to have her killed?"

"If he wanted to make a public statement, it was the way to do it. Anyone thinking about testifying would think twice," Novak said.

"The Hangman murders also were an opportunity to pull in Jim, who'd transferred to homicide. They all occurred in his jurisdiction," Julia said.

"Logical," Novak said. "But why Lana?"

"I don't know. Maybe Benny took a page from Popov's playbook and is killing two birds with one stone," Julia said.

"When you were undercover, did you ever find a connection between Benny and Popov's family operation?" Novak asked.

"No, but I know the Popov family still controls a large part of the drug trade. Benny wasn't the big fish. I was just using him to get up the food chain."

Riggs nodded. "Benny kills a potential witness and also sends a message to Agent Vargas that he's not forgotten her."

"It's time I paid Benny a visit," Novak said.

***

Novak kept a tight hold on his emotions as he and Julia showed their badges to the guard at the front desk of the Richmond Correctional Facility. They crossed from the carpeted reception area through the double doors that led onto tile floor, a clear signal they were now on the incarceration side. Standing in front of a set of small lockers, Novak opened one of the doors and stowed his gun inside. Julia did the same.

"I'm talking to Benny alone," Novak said.

Julia hesitated. "I'm not afraid to face him. And I can keep my temper in check."

"I didn't say you were afraid or unable to control yourself. But you'll be a distraction. Better I'm alone. He doesn't know me, and that might throw him off."

Her jaw tensed. "I'll wait."

He moved down the hallway and into a small visiting room furnished with one table and two simple chairs. He selected the seat away from the door and sat with his back to the wall.

He leaned back and unbuttoned his coat as he watched the door and waited for Benny Santiago to enter. He was struggling with his temper. This guy had hurt Julia. She'd dodged Novak's rape question when he'd asked her straight up, but he'd seen the tension rippling through her body. He knew exactly what had happened to her. And it now was his personal mission to make sure this animal never walked the streets again.

Outside the room, he heard the rattle of cuffs mingle with footsteps before a deputy opened the door. Benny was dressed in a loose-fitting jumpsuit that hung on his lean frame. His dark hair was slicked back, and a stubbled beard covered his face.

As another deputy stood behind him, Benny raised his gaze, his eyes narrowing as he looked at Novak. He waited while the deputy sat him in the chair across from Novak and cuffed his hands to the table. The deputy motioned for his partner to shut the door while he took several steps back.

"Who are you?" Benny asked.

"Detective Novak," he said.

Benny looked bored. "I don't know you. What do you want with me?"

Ignoring the statement, Novak addressed Benny's question. "Wanted to see what you look like." He let the answer soak in while he stared with no expression.

A nervous smirk lifted the corner of Benny's mouth. "Why the fuck would you care what I look like?"

"Like to know who I'm going to be coming after." His voice was calm, no hint of anger.

Benny slouched back in his seat. "You're really scaring me, Detective. Really. Why do I suddenly deserve your attention, Detective Novak? If you haven't heard, I'm headed to prison for a long time."

"When's the last time you saw your girlfriend?"

Benny grinned. "Which one? I got about five or six of 'em right now."

"Lana Ortega."

"Who?"

"When's the last time you saw Lana?"

Hearing Lana's name didn't seem to register with him. "I don't know."

"In the courthouse on Monday?"

"I couldn't say. There was a lot going on that day."

"Lana is a real pain in your ass, isn't she? She made a big scene that day. An important guy like you doesn't like big scenes. You like to fly below the radar. Thank God she's loyal to you, which is good considering how much she knows about your operation."

"Is she talking?"

Did he not know that Lana was dead, or was he playing some kind of game? Novak could play along for now. "She's friends now with the commonwealth's attorney and getting some nice gifts and favors."

Benny sniffed and glanced at his nails. "You going to tell me if there's a point to all this?"

"Why would a big shot like you need a woman like that as a punching bag?" he asked.

Benny leaned in. "I don't know what you're talking about."

Novak grinned. "You lost your shit thinking Lana betrayed you when it actually was the cop." He baited the hook. "And the funniest part is you could have taken off and not been caught with all that coke in the trunk of your car."

Benny's eyes narrowed as he looked at Novak. "You've been talking to Lana?"

"Lana says I'm a good listener." The lie tumbled over his tongue like the gospel truth. Lying to a guy like Benny was all part of the job. "And as it turns out, she can be pretty chatty when you treat her right. She's a good-looking woman."

Benny's lips pursed, and he mumbled an oath under his breath. "She wouldn't be stupid enough to talk to a cop."

Novak tapped his index finger on the table. "She did it before."

He tensed. "Lana has shit for brains, but she's loyal. She loves me. She wouldn't betray me."

"You beat her up pretty bad. Think that wins you long-term loyalty?"

His brown eyes narrowed. "What are you saying?"

"Maybe Lana is a lot smarter than she lets on."

"It was that cop that was spying on me."

"Correct, Benny. Lana had your back until you beat her up that night. After that, she cut a deal with the cops. I think Lana's show of loyalty to you at the courthouse deserves an Oscar."

"Fuck you."

"No, pal, but *that's* exactly what Lana is doing to you now."

Benny sat back, the chains of his handcuffs rattling. "You think I didn't know about Lana?"

"You didn't have a clue," Novak said.

"I've known all along she'd turn on me."

Novak leaned forward, his fists resting on the edge of the table. "Is that why you had her killed, Benny?"

Benny stared at him. "What the fuck are you talking about?"

Novak hesitated, letting him squirm in the silence. "I thought you would have heard. Lana is dead."

Benny shook his head. "The hell she is. I just saw her in court. You're jerking my chain. What the hell kind of game is this?"

Novak reached in his breast pocket and pulled out several pictures taken at the crime scene of her face. He laid them faceup, one at a time, like playing cards. At first Benny didn't look, but as the prisoner seemed to sense the detective's unwavering confidence, he looked down.

Benny simply stared. He swallowed. Finally, he reached for a picture. His cuffs prevented him from touching it.

Novak gently pushed the picture within Benny's reach.

Benny's gaze scanned the photo, but he didn't touch the image at first. Then he picked up the picture that featured Lana's pale drawn face, blue lips, and partly open eyes. He shoved the image away. "This is some kind of trick."

"No trick. I came here today to find out what you really thought about Lana and if you hated her enough to kill her."

He dropped the picture and leaned back. "I didn't kill her."

Novak gathered the pictures and slowly and carefully stacked them into a neat pile. He tucked them back into his breast pocket. "Now, because of Lana's murder, I'm wondering if your boss is coming after you next. I'm not sure you have the connections in prison to stay safe."

Benny drew in a breath, all traces of arrogance gone from his eyes.

"Now, if you say you didn't hang Lana, maybe Popov's crew was in on it?"

"Popov? Fuck." He sat up straight. "I don't associate with that crazy Russian family. Ever."

"So you know the family?"

"Who doesn't?"

"It might take me time, but I'll prove that you had her killed or knew she was going to be killed. And then your slick attorney won't be scrambling to get an appeal to keep you out of prison. She'll be fighting to keep you off death row."

"This is bullshit," Benny hissed. "I didn't kill her."

Novak rose, wondering now if Benny's righteous anger was real or another act. The dealer was smart. "Next time I see you it'll be in court, and the commonwealth's attorney will be filing first-degree murder charges." He leaned forward, knowing Benny was a cockroach whose number-one goal was survival. "What do you think Popov's family will do when they hear you've been copycatting a play from their game book?"

"I don't know what the hell you're talking about." Benny tried to stand, but the cuffs kept him in place. "You can't go spreading shit that I'm challenging Popov. This is bullshit."

"I can do whatever I want."

Benny's frustrated curses followed Novak out into the hallway. Novak smiled.

The door closed, and Novak turned to the deputy in the hallway. "He's going to want to call his attorney. Can you keep him in isolation?"

"Sure, how long do you want him to stew?"

"Let him stew for a day. And when he does meet with her, let me know, would you?"

"Will do."

Novak thanked the deputy and walked the hallway to the guard station. Both he and Julia collected their guns and headed straight to his car without saying a word. In his car, he started the engine as she stared out at large white clouds.

"How did it go?" she asked.

"I showed him a picture of Lana's face right after she was cut down. I certainly rattled his cage."

She tipped her face toward the sun. "Did he look surprised?"

"His face drained instantly. Not even a great actor could pull that off."

"Novak, he can fake it well enough when he wants to. Benny can also be charming when it suits. Above all, he's cunning. Though I'll say he's not very creative. And I don't remember him having an obsession with ropes." She rubbed her thumb against a silver ring on her index finger.

"He wasn't faking."

"Are the guards going to let him simmer for a while before he gets a phone call to his lawyer?"

"They said they'd keep him in isolation until tomorrow."

"Perfect. He hates being by himself. His paranoia and doubts will work on him."

Novak sat back, enjoying sitting alone with her. When she was around, he felt more alive.

"If not Benny, then who? Killing Lana wasn't random."

"No, it wasn't. We need to dig deeper into your father's case. Solve that one and we might get a double out of it."

"Even better."

His phone rang and displayed his partner's number. "Riggs."

"I found Rita Gallagher's brother, Brad. He works in Southside at a construction site." He gave the address. Novak thanked Riggs and pulled out, turning south to head across the river. "Brad Gallagher's been found."

"This should be interesting."

The drive took less than a half hour, and it was four thirty when they pulled into the gravel parking lot. By the looks of things, the construction company was renovating an older building, giving it a face-lift to fit the style of the new owner.

Out of the car, the two crossed the lot to the construction trailer, where they found two men. The one behind the desk was midthirties and wore a white shirt and dark pants that hung loose on his thin frame. The other was burly, midfifties, and sporting a gray crew cut and a dozen tattoos.

The men looked at the cops, and both stopped talking.

Novak pulled out his badge and introduced Julia and himself. "Looking for Brad Gallagher."

The older man stiffened. "That's me. What's the problem?"

"I'd like to ask you a few questions about your sister, Rita."

"Rita? She took off a long time ago."

"We found her body earlier this week," Novak said.

The second man looked at Gallagher. "I'll give you three privacy."

"Thanks, boss." When the trailer door closed behind him, Gallagher frowned. "What do you mean, *earlier this week*? Where was she?"

"Entombed in a basement. Appears she was murdered twenty-five years ago. When's the last time you saw her?" Julia asked.

"Early '92."

"We're trying to figure out who she might have been associated with," Novak said.

"Rita wanted to be rich, loved, and famous. And she'd do anything for any man who promised her any of those."

"Do you know who she was seeing?"

"She was running with a dangerous group. Russians. I told her to stay clear, but she just laughed."

"Popov?" Novak asked.

"Maybe. I stayed as far away from those people as I could." He rubbed his hand over his head. "One of the last times I saw her, she was excited. She'd been given an important job, she said."

"What kind of job?" Novak asked.

"I don't know. She wouldn't tell me. But said she'd be set after it was done." He shook his head. "I can't believe she's been dead all this time."

"We also hear there was a guy named Jack."

"I don't remember him." He drew in a breath, his frown deepening. "How did she die?"

"I can't say right now," Novak said. "Anybody you know who would want to hurt her?"

Gallagher shook his head. "It was a matter of time with Rita."

"What do you mean?" Julia asked.

"She was hot-looking and fun. She wasn't smart, but she was ambitious. Not a great combination. My guess is she finally crossed the wrong guy."

***

The Hangman stood on the street corner watching Billy's bar. The half-moon hung in the sky, and the stars were bright and sharp. The air had turned colder, and according to the weatherman it was supposed to drop into the low twenties in the next few days. He liked the cold, the promised stillness of the coming winter.

The first and second floors above Billy's were dark, but a single light shone on the third floor. He knew that was Julia's room. She was up late, working on her investigation. Tenacious. Dangerous. So much to admire. Even respect. But if he didn't act soon, she'd ferret him out of the shadows and destroy him.

Something inside of him itched to go to her and drag her from her room. He'd dreamed for months of wrapping his ropes around her soft skin and tightening the knots until she thrashed in pain and despair.

The sooner he placed her on exhibit, the sooner he'd know his secrets were safe. But now was not the right time for her to die.

"Can't rush this one," he whispered.

CHAPTER SEVENTEEN

Friday, November 3, 8:00 a.m.

Julia's alarm ripped her from the grip of a nightmare. When she startled awake, her heart was racing and her hands trembled as she searched for the blood she expected to see dripping from her fingertips. When she found none, her mind cleared, and flexing her fingers, she took a deep breath to steady herself.

She grabbed her phone and shut off the alarm. She checked the time. Lana Ortega's autopsy was scheduled for nine thirty. *Good.* She hadn't overslept.

Julia looked to the other side of her bed. She was sorry Novak wasn't there and also relieved he'd not witnessed the nightmare. It was one thing for him to suspect she might have issues; another to see it up close and personal.

Out of bed, she hurried into the bathroom and turned on the shower. When she stepped under the hot spray, she allowed the water to wash away the night sweats and the dream's lingering hold. She'd had this dream too many times, but it still took its toll. She prayed that solving the Hangman case would end it. If not, she wasn't sure what she'd do next.

Out of the shower, she dressed, fluffing her wet hair with her hands as she glanced in the mirror. Reflected back was a pale face with dark circles under her eyes. Extra concealer and blush covered both reasonably well, creating a refreshed look even if she didn't feel it.

While bread and cheese toasted in the oven, she clipped on her badge and weapon. When the oven dinged, she dropped the toast onto a paper towel, grabbed her purse, and headed out the back door. She paused at the top of the staircase and stared out over the alley, searching for any trouble. The morning was quiet and cold. Only then did she climb down the stairs and into her SUV.

She'd worked too late again last night. When she'd finally turned off her light at 1:00 a.m., her mind refused to settle. Ripe ground for the dream.

As she hurried toward her day, thoughts of Lana and their first meeting chased her. Julia had been working her first shift as a bartender at Benny's bar.

Lana was wearing tight silk pants, a black tank top, and high-heeled boots. Bangles jangling on her wrists and her perfume strong and spicy, she strutted into the bar. A few of the men tossed a look at her round backside, but no one did more than nod. She was Benny's, and no man was fool enough to poach.

"You're new here," Lana said.

Julia wore extra eye makeup, a fitted muscle T-shirt, and snug jeans. "The name is Jules, and I fill in when they need me."

Lana's hard gaze traveled quickly as she assessed Julia. "How old are you, Jules?"

"Thirty-two."

That softened her frown. "You're old."

Julia laughed. "One foot in the grave." This close, she could see beyond the makeup to the face of a young woman who would get chewed up and spit out by this life like so many before her. "I keep my walker behind the bar."

Lana laughed. "You're funny."

"It pays to have a sense of humor when you're old."

"Can you make a pink cosmo? The last bartender couldn't."

"I can." Julia squeezed lime into a silver shaker along with cranberry juice, Cointreau, and vodka. She shook it up and poured it into a martini glass. She placed a napkin on the bar and set the glass on top of it.

Lana's long fingers and red nails wrapped around the glass's stem, and she slowly raised the drink to her lips. "Very good."

"With age comes experience."

"I have plenty of experience, and I'm young."

"I can see you know what you're doing."

"By the time I'm your age, I'll be rich and living on a beach."

"A solid plan. How're you going to do it?"

"Benny is going to see how smart I am, and he's going to put me to work."

"Sounds like he's lucky to have you."

"He is."

Benny's office door opened, and he searched the bar until he saw Lana. He snapped his fingers, and she immediately set down the drink. Her smile widened, and she hurried toward him, wrapping her arms around his neck. He squeezed her bottom as he closed the door. There were other men also in his office. Julia wondered if the kid would see twenty-one, let alone thirty-two.

Julia ate as she walked from her vehicle the couple of blocks to the medical examiner's office. By the time she arrived, Novak was already gowned up and Dr. Kincaid and Tessa were standing at the head of the gurney in front of the sheet-clad body.

The trio looked over at her. "Agent Vargas," Dr. Kincaid said. "Welcome."

"Am I late?" she asked, glancing at the clock.

"No. We're a little early."

"Good."

Dr. Kincaid smiled and made some small talk, but Novak remained silent. He studied Julia, making no attempt to hide his concern. He was picking up somehow that it had been a rough night for her.

She'd be lying if she said she wasn't aware of him.

The sex between them had been surprisingly great. She didn't flinch, push him, or scream in fear, all the reasons she'd avoided intimacy since what had happened in Virginia Beach. He could make her feel like her old self. And when he was in her bed, she always slept soundly with no nightmares, at least so far.

But a few great turns in the sack didn't mean they were close. The detective thought she was a badass, and she wanted to keep it that way. Allowing him to see her vulnerable was unacceptable.

She shrugged off her jacket and suited up. By the time she reached Novak's side of the table, Tessa was making the Y incision.

Novak's gaze might have been focused on the autopsy table, but she knew he was thinking of her. Call it a cop's instincts, but she knew when people were paying too close attention.

The technician pulled away the sheet, revealing Lana's naked body. Julia flinched and steeled herself against the image.

Lana's head rested in a white plastic headrest that tipped her chin up and exposed her neck. Bleached blond hair flowed over the back of the table. Scrubbed clean of makeup, Lana looked older. The last year had aged her a decade. The ropes had been removed, but their ugly imprints on her chest, arms, legs, and of course neck remained.

Dr. Kincaid pulled the microphone closer to her lips and began. "Lana Ortega is an eighteen-year-old Hispanic female."

Eighteen. So the kid had lied about her age. That would have put her at sixteen when they met. *Damn it.*

Dr. Kincaid began her exterior exam. "The technician photographed the victim's bindings, and they have been sent to the state forensic lab." The doctor cleared her throat. "The subject has four tattoos: a heart on her right ankle, MR encircled by a heart on her right arm, a key on the inside of her left wrist, and a star on the back of her neck at her hairline. No needle marks on her arms or between her fingers or toes. She does have several scars. Several old ones on the underside of her left wrist."

"She told me she tried to kill herself when she was fourteen," Julia said. "She never said why, only that she took a straight razor to her wrist."

"You knew this woman?" Tessa asked.

"I met her when I worked undercover. Lana's boyfriend and his boss were my targets, and in an effort to learn more about them, I befriended her."

The doctor nodded. "There's a scar on the victim's cheek that was expertly closed with stitches. And there are small circular burn scars on her arms."

"Cigarette burns?" Novak asked.

"Most likely," Dr. Kincaid said. "Her teeth have veneers."

"She told me Benny gave her the new teeth as well as breast implants."

Dr. Kincaid frowned. "I'd say she's at least fifteen pounds underweight, and her dry skin suggests she was vitamin-deficient."

"She lived on cosmos and luncheon meat," Julia said.

"How long did you work undercover?" Tessa asked.

Aware of Novak's sharp gaze, she kept her focus on the doctor. "About three years. I had built a pretty good network in the underground beach community. When a task force was looking for someone to work in Benny's bar, I was a natural choice."

"I can't imagine what that must have been like," Dr. Kincaid said.

"It taught me to always think twice before I spoke," she said, forcing a smile. "Until a couple of weeks ago, I was still circling the block until I made the final trek home."

"Circling the block?" Dr. Kincaid asked.

"Hard to maintain a tail on someone if they take three or four right turns. Following anyone that closely will get you spotted."

"Good to know," Dr. Kincaid said.

"There are visible signs of bruising all over her body that match the ropes that bound her," Dr. Kincaid said. "The bruising around her neck is particularly pronounced, and that is due to the ropes that were bound there. There's also bruising on her wrists and ankles. Again, from ropes. And there's a deep slice to her left Achilles tendon. A cut like that would have incapacitated her immediately."

"In the original cases, the victims didn't suffer any cuts," Julia said.

"Maybe twenty-five years has slowed him down," Novak said.

"Unless I see something during the autopsy or in the tox screens, my first guess is that she suffocated," Dr. Kincaid said. "With her neck wrapped so tightly and her hands suspended, breathing would have become increasingly difficult."

"How long did it take?" Novak asked.

"Hard to say exactly, but at least a couple of hours."

Julia tried not to imagine the young woman's last hours.

Dr. Kincaid rolled the victim to her side. "Note her back is clear of any signs of bruising or lividity. However, her hands and feet are a dark purple, suggesting she was hanging when her heart stopped beating." Using the sharp tip of a scalpel blade, she flayed the lifeless flesh. From the underside of the right breast, Dr. Kincaid removed and inspected the large breast implant before laying it in a silver basin.

Using bolt cutters, Dr. Kincaid clipped the rib-cage bones, lifted the heart away from the body, and set it on a small table by the body. She inspected the organ. Slightly enlarged. Next, the lungs showed signs of stress. Asthma. Dr. Kincaid noted in the microphone that Lana's gut was inflamed. All the major organs were removed and weighed, and then tissue samples taken from each before they were repacked in the body.

"I've sent blood samples off for testing," Dr. Kincaid said. "We'll know in a few days what kind of cocktail of drugs she had in her system."

"A year and a half ago, her drugs of choice were vodka and triple sec. Benny didn't like her using the coke."

Dr. Kincaid inspected the lungs. "It looks like she recently discovered meth, but the tox screen will confirm it. Not enough at this stage to affect her teeth, but that would have been a matter of time."

The remainder of the autopsy was routine. The doctor confirmed Lana was not pregnant.

When Dr. Kincaid stepped back from the table so Tessa could close, Julia thanked everyone as she turned away, anxious to leave the room. Lana deserved a lot better.

Through the doors, she heard the doctor say to Novak, "All right. I'll get back to you with a report in a day or two."

"Thank you, Doctor," Novak replied.

As Novak pushed through the swinging doors, Julia stripped off her gown and reached for her jacket. Novak came up behind her and lifted the jacket's edge so she could slide in her left arm.

"I want to walk the Ortega crime scene again," he said.

She flipped up her collar and reached for her purse. "I'll come."

"Good. Mind if I grab a bite to eat on the way? I know a place near the scene." He grinned. "I haven't mastered the art of eating alone since Bella left for college."

"I ate but I'll get coffee."

"It's a date."

He made it sound easy. A coffee. But he was clever and used his calm voice and relaxed manner to draw in suspects and extract information, as he'd drawn her into his life.

He dumped the gown in the bin and slid on his coat, tugging the front sides until the jacket fell into a crisp line. He held the door for her, waiting for her to pass.

She arched a brow. "Novak, you're treating me like a lady."

"Last I checked, you are a lady."

"I'm a cop."

"And a good one." He grinned as he nodded toward the elevator. The doors closed, and they were alone. His size, the faint scent of his aftershave, the way he rubbed his thumb and index finger together made her aware of him.

She drew in a breath, trying to ignore him and a tightening wave of desire. She had lowered her guard with him, and she'd gotten away with it. To sleep with him again risked exposing all her shortcomings and fears.

Outside, she slid into the front seat, and seconds later he was behind the wheel. He drove across the river into the Manchester district and parked in front of a small street vendor.

"Sure you aren't hungry?" he asked.

"No. Go ahead."

They got out of the car, and he purchased a couple of bagels and two coffees. He handed her a cup and kept the bagels with extra cream cheese. Tossing his tie over his shoulder, he bit into the first bagel. As she stood in the parking lot, she stared out over the James River at the cityscape on the other side. A small boat floated lazily on the water.

"It's one of my favorite views of the city," he said, wiping his mouth with a paper napkin.

"I've been through this area enough but never stopped."

"I worked patrol in this district. Got to know the area well. Nice to see the new restaurants and new business." He finished the first bagel and offered her the second. When she shook her head, he bit into it. She sipped her coffee and was pleasantly surprised to discover it tasted good.

He smiled at her reaction. "Do you think I'd bring you anywhere that made bad coffee?"

She raised the cup to him. "Is it always this good?"

"Always. And the hot dogs at lunch are the best."

"Good to know." She sipped and stared more at the city. "So what's your next step in the Ortega murder?"

"We walk the crime scene. And then you know how it goes. Review credit card receipts, cell phone data, surveillance cameras. Any trail will help reconstruct her last weeks."

"She didn't have family in the area, but said she was from San Diego. Her whole world had become Benny."

"Friends?"

"You mean other than me?"

He wiped his mouth, crumpled the napkin, and tossed it on the plate. "She considered you a friend?"

"She did. I was paid to listen to her and pull information, so that's what I did. She was like a lot of kids. She wanted to make something of her life. There was a point at which I tried to help her."

"How?"

"Benny had smacked her hard and left a bruise on her face. I found her in the back office, trying to cover it up with paint and powder. I said she deserved better."

"Did she believe that?"

"She thought he was better. She thought bruises were the cost of doing business. Anybody else, and I might have hauled them to a shelter, but I couldn't do that for her without giving it all away."

"You were doing your job."

"Yes, I was. But it still sucked to see the pain on her face." She dug her finger into the side of the cup, not liking the fact the conversation was trained on her. "So tell me about you, Novak. I get tired of hearing about myself."

"My life has been work and my kid."

"No special lady in your life?"

His gaze sharpened. "No."

"Why not? You're decent looking."

"Decent?"

"You have a quality," she said, smiling.

"Thanks. I think." A smile tugged. "No special lady. What about you? Anyone in particular?"

Her smile faded when she realized he was watching and waiting for an answer. "No one in my life. I'm not easy to be around, if you haven't noticed."

He tossed his trash in a street bin. "Didn't notice."

She threw away her cup. "I thought you were a better liar than that."

He winked. "Let's have a look at that warehouse."

The site was three blocks away, and they opted to walk. Forensic and DNA testing could often seal the deal on a conviction, but knocking on doors and talking to people caught most suspects.

The area around the warehouse was quiet. Though there'd been some economic development in the Manchester district, this pocket was mostly untouched.

"If I were looking for a place where no one would bother me," she said, "it would be here. This is a good hundred yards from the next business."

Novak scanned the buildings as they passed. "There's a security camera on the grocery store and the gas station. Riggs is reviewing both."

"What about the architectural salvage yard? I know they have cameras."

"Four, as it turns out. They sent over tapes yesterday, and Riggs is going through them. Their system holds three days of video."

"Those would cover the murder window."

They approached the yellow crime-scene tape that blocked off the front entrance to the warehouse. Across the street a marked city car was parked, and the officer inside nodded to Novak.

He pushed open the door and flipped on the lights to the right, which slowly began to warm up, reluctantly spitting out more light. Their footsteps echoed in the large room as they walked toward the spot directly under where the victim had been hanging.

Julia stared up at the ceiling and suddenly found it difficult to breathe. She stepped back a few feet and collected herself.

Novak looked up at the beams with their new hooks. "It took work and planning to get those up there. He was here before the killing."

Julia nodded. "Scoped it out."

"Why Ortega?"

"She was killed because she knew me." She sensed Novak's full and undivided attention. "Did you notice the knots around her chest? The cops never released the knot configurations. The ones binding Lana were tied exactly like the first three cases. Only the Hangman would know that."

"Or someone who had access to the files."

She shook her head as she looked around the room. "It all feels so convenient."

"What are you saying?"

"I don't know." She mentally checked off all the obvious facts. "It feels off." She'd had the same feeling when she'd gone to Benny's bar that last day. She had no reason to believe any of it would go sideways, but it did.

"What do you suggest?"

"We talk to Benny's lawyer, Elizabeth Monroe. She's smart, slick, and will break any rule to get what she wants."

"You think she killed Lana?"

She shrugged. "She knows more than she's saying."

He was silent, and then, "Okay. I'll look into her."

She studied him. "Just like that?"

"You have good instincts, so yeah, just like that." He stepped toward her, his hands in his pockets. "Let's have a look upstairs."

"Sure."

They climbed a set of stairs that took them to a second floor packed with hundreds of boxes. "A redevelopment company bought the building two years ago, but the company went bankrupt. This place has sat unused for two years. The former owner must have been using the space as storage," Novak said.

"Why walk away from inventory?"

"Might have been more expensive to move. Nowhere else to store it."

She walked to a window that overlooked the James River. Outside, the waters slowly swept by.

As she turned, Novak squatted and pointed a light on the dusty wood floor. If anyone had been up here in the last couple of months, they'd have left impressions in the dust.

The floor by the boxes on the south wall looked well traveled. They both approached, and Novak put the light on the boards and then the boxes. The box on top wasn't as dusty, a sign it might have been opened recently.

"Have a look at this," Novak said. He handed his flashlight to Julia for a look.

She opened the top flap with the tip of the flashlight. The box was empty except for a couple of extra hooks that matched the ones in the downstairs ceiling. "Looks like our guy used this as his hiding place. Getting a little too lazy to cart his craft off-site."

"I'll call forensics and have them dust the box and the brackets for prints."

She stepped back, asking herself how much planning this killing had taken. "Yeah."

"How many more days do you have left to work the Hangman case?" Novak asked.

"It's back to the job on Monday, and after that, whenever I can find time. I still have this weekend to catch up with the third victim's family."

"Vicky Wayne."

"Yes. And I owe a visit to Shield to see if Andrews has been able to find anything else."

"Keep your head on a swivel."

"If I'm anything, Novak, it's careful."

"Define *careful*."

She shrugged.

They stood staring at each other. It was awkward. As if one should say more, but neither could find the words.

CHAPTER EIGHTEEN

Friday, November 3, 1:00 p.m.

Images of the crime scene plagued Novak long after he dropped Julia off. When he made his way into the squad room, he spotted Riggs pouring a fresh cup of coffee.

"I checked out that Hangman website," Riggs said. "Since this case aired on the news, the hits have rocketed up." He shook his head. "It's all a fucking game to people. No one stops to think about the women who were strung up."

"Any luck on the surveillance video from the Ortega crime scene?"

"I've been through them all. Saw drunks stagger past and a gang of kids, but no one hauling an unconscious woman."

"He had to get her in there somehow."

"He must have known about the cameras and found a way around them." Riggs flipped through a small notebook. "I did get the name of a guy who used to work undercover with Jim Vargas. His name is Nate Unger, and he might be able to shed some light on Detective Vargas."

"Nice work."

Riggs dumped a couple of tablespoons of sugar in the cup. "He lives about forty miles west. Off the grid or some shit like that."

"I'd like to talk to him," Novak said. "Julia also wants me to focus on Santiago's attorney, Elizabeth Monroe."

"Think the lawyer is cunning enough to off Lana and make it look like an old serial killer?"

"Hell if I know," Novak said. "But it's worth a shot."

"Did Vargas leave a suicide note?" Riggs asked.

"What brought that up?"

"Don't know. Just curious."

"He did not leave a note." He filled a cup for himself. "I've requested the files from the investigation of his death. I want to see for myself. Records should be on my desk sometime later this afternoon."

"Good."

"So what do you think about Julia Vargas?" Riggs asked. "She seems cool."

"Plays her cards close. But don't let that facade fool you; there's a lot brewing there. Reminds me of a coiled spring."

"A nice package, though."

Novak scowled.

Riggs laughed. "She's growing on you."

"I didn't say that."

"Didn't have to. You never call her Vargas. Always call her Julia. Nice touch, Tobias."

"You're full of shit."

Riggs chuckled. "Hey man, I'm happy for you." When Novak didn't answer, Riggs said, "It's okay if you do like her. About time, don't you think?"

Novak rubbed the back of his neck. "If Julia heard this conversation, we'd both end up with a couple of slugs buried in our chests."

"She'd probably like that."

"She's independent."

"Still trying to figure out if you two kids have a love connection?"

"It's not love."

"Whatever this is, as long as it makes you happy, I'm good with it."

Novak nodded to his partner, and the two headed to Novak's vehicle. While Novak drove them to Nate Unger's house, Riggs gave him the rundown on Unger's history.

"Some describe Unger and Vargas as the real-life Starsky and Hutch," Riggs said. "They were Wild West cowboys. Took chances that most cops would never consider."

"Why did Vargas switch to homicide?"

"Family. Wife and a kid are hard to weave into that kind of work. The time came for him to choose between the work and the family, and he did."

"And Unger?"

"He kept working the streets and continued to rack up arrests until his body gave out. Finally he took a desk job, which he barely choked on before retiring a couple of years after Vargas's death. Now he builds furniture and lives with the squirrels."

Unger's home was west of the city on rolling farmland in Louisa County. Locating Unger's place was a challenge, and it took a couple of U-turns to find it hidden off a rural gravel road. Novak drove cautiously on the dirt driveway. Dust kicked up and rocks popped under his tires as he made his way deeper into the woods. After rounding a small bend, he saw the log cabin.

Without cell phone connection and with no invitation, both understood the danger of rolling up on a former cop unannounced. They stayed in the car so neither would get shot. Shortly thereafter a slim man with long white hair appeared with a Remington twelve-gauge shotgun. Both Novak and Riggs slowly held their badges outside the SUV windows. "Detectives Riggs and Novak from Richmond homicide. Have a few questions about Jim Vargas."

Unger's eyes narrowed, but he slowly lowered the shotgun. "Jim Vargas? He's been dead twenty-five years."

"Yes, sir," Novak said. "Can we talk?"

"Sure. Come on over," Unger said.

"We've questions about one of his old homicide cases," Novak said.

Climbing out of the car and walking up to Unger, Novak said, "You worked with Vargas in narcotics, but we think you knew some of the homicide victims."

No hint of welcome in his gaze, Unger studied them an extra beat. "Never know who's going to come around here. Can't be too careful."

"You been out here a while?" Novak asked.

"Since my retirement in 1994. I've had more than a few reporters and cops ask me about Jim. These folks would always come out of the woodwork around the anniversary of his death for the first few years."

"I'm looking into the Hangman case," Novak said. "Vargas's daughter, Julia, reopened it. She wants to solve the case."

Mention of Julia's name softened his expression. "Last I saw Julia, she was about six. I hear she's making a name for herself as a cop."

"You keep up?"

"Sure. Her dad was my partner, so she was like family to me for a while. Some of the old-timers come out to see me every so often, we shoot the shit, and I catch up. Her operation in Virginia Beach went bad, I heard."

"No one's really talking about it," Novak said.

"If she's like her old man, she's tough, and she'll find a way to deal with it alone."

Novak didn't want her dealing with it alone.

"I understand why Julia might nose around in the case, but why you?" Unger asked. "Don't you have enough current cases to close?"

"I have two cases. Both appear linked to the Hangman."

"Hell of a coincidence," Unger said.

Novak left the comment alone. The old man was a pro and feeling him out. "Tell me about Jim Vargas."

Unger leaned his shotgun against the woodpile and picked up his ax. "Never saw a guy who was so good at slipping into the skin of another person. Even when we weren't on, he was. When he slipped into a character, he sometimes had a hard time getting out of it, if you know what I mean."

"What was his character?"

"A hard-nosed drug dealer. He could be the kind of guy who snapped bones if you didn't pay or broke rank. And don't ask me about specifics. I'm not trashing the guy or second-guessing what he did. He busted his balls to break up a drug ring, and sometimes he got his hands dirty."

"How long was he under?" Novak asked.

"A couple of years."

"He didn't get home much?" Riggs asked.

"No. The work was hard on his wife and kid. He knew the work was also changing him, making him harder, and that was costing his family. That's why he gave it up finally. It's why I never had a family."

"Can you tell me about the last cases you worked?"

"One was a cocaine operation. We'd heard there was a new dealer in the Washington, DC, area, and he was sending drugs down I-95. Jim worked the truck stops, selling to street criminals. He became a top-tier dealer, even getting undercover cops to buy from him. Word traveled around he was good. Deals and money started rolling in. Finally, a bigger fish approached him and wanted him to sell more. Jim agreed. Took us about fourteen months in that world to gather enough evidence to make arrests."

"Any details about those arrests stick out?" Novak asked.

"When the bust happened, the cops cuffed us also and hauled us away with the bad guys. We never broke cover on that case." He drove the ax into a log and split it. "There were times when we both wanted out, but we agreed to see the big case to the end."

"The big case?"

"Jim parlayed one of his drug arrests into a drug-running job for a Russian New York outfit looking to establish connections in Richmond."

"Is that the Popov case?" Novak asked.

"Yeah. I'll never forget him. Ruthless Russian son of a bitch."

"The case is a legend," Novak said. "Big bust. Too bad the bastard died in prison about ten years ago."

"I was hoping he'd rot for decades." Unger shook his head. "It's been nearly three decades since the case, and I still have nightmares about Popov and the men he killed. He never executed anyone quick or easy. Fingers, toes, dick cut off. Death for him was always about sending a message. He didn't think twice about going after the families of the people who challenged him. His tactics damn near worked until he figured out we were on to him."

"How?" Novak asked.

"The last men Popov killed were badly mutilated. He strung them up for all his crew to see. Their wives and kids were shot dead. Jim and I knew we were in deep shit. We'd had interactions with the dead guys. Popov knew there was a mole, and he didn't care how many innocents he offed as long as he found the mole. It was the first time I saw Jim really scared. So was I. But I didn't have a wife and kid. He did. He knew Popov would have killed them both in a heartbeat."

"Did Vargas lose his nerve?" Riggs asked.

"No one could have blamed the guy if he did. To be slowly chopped up into pieces. That kind of shit wakes you up in the middle of the night and has you looking over your shoulder. It changes you."

All three were silent for a moment before Unger added, "There was one guy Popov killed that really hit a nerve with Jim. The guy's name was Donnie Cameron. Donnie was a fuckup, but it was hard not to like the guy. He wasn't mean, only looking to make an easy living. Jim

213

and I knew another arrest for Donnie meant fifteen to twenty-five of hard time. It was a matter of time before Jim saw to it that Donnie was arrested." Unger shook his head. "Guy pissed his pants he was so afraid of going to jail."

"And Vargas offered him a deal?" Riggs asked.

"Jim was good at flipping people and getting them to talk." Unger steadied another log on the chopping block. "After he flipped Donnie, the information flowed. It was good for a while. We were making headway. And then Jim sensed something was off. He was sure he'd been followed. Kept saying it was a gut feeling. He didn't go home to see his wife and kid for long stretches. And when he did, he drove fifty miles out of his way before he circled back toward his home."

"And?"

"Nothing for weeks. Calm before the storm. After a couple of weeks, I thought Jim was overreacting, and then Donnie was found murdered. Hands and feet cut off. Balls shoved down his throat. All the information shut down. Jim thought he'd been made. The waiting was excruciating. He said he was packing it in. Had enough, done enough with undercover. Said he wanted more time with his family. We took what he had to the commonwealth attorney's office, and they moved forward with a prosecution of Popov. They had enough evidence to put him away for a long time. Popov was convicted, and Vargas transferred to homicide."

"You ever work with him again?"

"He came to see me while he was working that Hangman case. Asked me if my cover had ever been compromised in the Popov case. I didn't believe so. Jim was still worried Donnie had talked. Popov was the kind of guy who liked to serve his revenge ice cold. The Hangman killings would have been Popov's style. By then I'd quit the fieldwork, cut my hair, and was riding a desk, which is where I stayed until I got my pension."

"Do you remember which victims he asked you about?" Novak reached into his breast pocket for his phone as Unger watched him closely. He found the picture of Rene Tanner and handed the phone to Unger.

The old man squinted, then pulled glasses from his back pocket. "Yeah, I remember her. Rene Tanner. She worked as a bartender in the Bottom. Jim mentioned her and Tamara Brown during that last visit."

"They informed for Vargas?"

Unger handed back the phone. "He busted Rene on a cocaine possession charge. It was a large enough bust to ensure she spent ten to fifteen years in jail. Classic case of not wanting to go to jail and cutting a deal to get out of serving. Same with Brown. Busted and flipped."

"Rumor has Vargas and Rene sleeping together."

Unger let out a sigh. "Look, the work we did wasn't black-and-white, and living a lie all the time tossed a lot of gray in our lives."

"That a yes or no?"

"It's a yes. But it was an on-and-off relationship with them. It meant nothing to Jim, but Rene feared her husband would find out. The guy left bruises on her for a lot less."

"When Jim told you Rene and Tamara had been murdered, did you think it was odd they'd been targeted by a serial killer?"

"Sure. I worried about it. So did Jim. Who wouldn't as long as Popov was alive? But both women had been hookers, and they hung out in a rough section of town. Perfect hunting ground for a serial killer."

"How about Vicky Wayne? What did you think when she was found strung up?"

"Honestly, relieved. I didn't recognize her name, and I figured if she was connected to our old work, Jim would have told me."

Novak scrolled to her face and handed the phone to Unger.

Unger shook his head. "I don't remember her."

Novak located Rita Gallagher's photo. "How about this one?"

Unger studied the picture a little longer. "Yeah, I do remember her."

"Really, from where?"

He rubbed the back of his neck with a bent, lined hand. "There were so many women back in the day, but she was hard to forget. Built like a brick house. She could have any man."

"She worked in Amy Vargas's bar as a waitress. That's an odd coincidence," Riggs said.

"Jim set the job up. He told me she came to him. She wanted to go straight. She was tired of the life."

"He do that often?" Novak asked.

"Believe it or not, Jim cared about people. Said many were lost souls and he'd give a hand up when he could. If they didn't take it, so be it."

Novak closed his phone. "So she comes to him and tells him she wants to go straight, and he buys it?"

Unger shook his head. "I told him to steer clear of that one."

"Why?"

"Because Popov fucked her."

"Rita slept with Popov?" Novak asked.

"Yeah. Not for long, but yeah. He grew tired of his women easily." He split another log. "Why are you asking about Rita?"

"Rita's brother remembered her saying she had a big job that would make her serious money," Novak said. "Know anything about that?"

"I don't," Unger said. "Where's she now?"

"We found her body a couple of days ago. Looks like she was murdered about twenty-five years ago."

"When the Hangman was active?"

"We think she died within a day or two of Jim. We were able to connect her to Jim when we found a picture in her purse of Jim and his daughter, Julia. It was taken shortly before he died."

"She had a picture of Jim and his kid?" Unger asked.

"Know why?"

Absently he traced circles on the top of the wooden ax handle. "Last I saw Jim was October of '92. He admitted he and his wife had split over his affair with Rita, but were now trying to reconcile. He was torn up with guilt and shame." He curled his hands around the handle. "I told him she was trouble and to cut her loose. But he didn't. Couldn't. Said there were other factors."

"What other factors?"

"Didn't say."

"There's evidence to suggest that Rita was four or five months pregnant," Novak said.

"Shit, I had no idea about that."

"You think Popov knew Jim was sleeping with Rita?"

Unger set up another log on the block and sliced it in half with one chop. "Popov knew."

"How can you be so sure?" Riggs asked.

"After the arrest, Popov made a point to find out who had ratted him out. I always thought he never found out it was Jim and me." Unger drew in a breath. "But as I get older, I've gotten a little paranoid. I stay out here away from people because I still worry that Popov might have known more than I realized. The old man might be dead, but there are those willing to carry out one of his old vendettas to win the favor of the remaining family."

"What's that mean?" Novak asked.

"Keep a close eye on Julia Vargas. She is Jim's daughter, which makes her a target for the Popov family."

CHAPTER NINETEEN

Friday, November 3, 3:30 p.m.

Using information from Andrews, Julia found Vicky Wayne's mother, who lived in the south side of Richmond just over the James River. Parking in front of a brick rancher, she tugged off her sunglasses and walked across the small yard carpeted in weeks' worth of leaves. There was an old green van in the driveway and several kids' toys.

She walked up the concrete steps and knocked. Inside the house, she heard the hum of a kid's TV show and then the steady thump of footsteps moving toward the door. Seconds later, the door opened to an older woman with gray hair tucked back in a ponytail, tired blue eyes, and a drawn face. She wore jeans and a sweatshirt.

"Can I help you?"

"Are you Frannie Wayne?"

"Yes."

Julia introduced herself and showed her badge. "I'm reopening your daughter's murder case. I was hoping you had time to talk."

The old woman's face wrinkled into a frown. "My Vicky has been gone twenty-five years. Why would anyone care about that now?"

"I care," Julia said.

"Why? You were barely a child when it happened."

"My father worked the original case. I know it troubled him that the case was never solved."

"Might have been if he'd not killed himself."

"I understand."

The woman stared at Julia a long moment, as if sensing they both had a lot of hurt vested in this case.

"Could I come inside so we can talk?" Julia prompted.

"Let me see your badge again."

Julia held it up, allowing the woman to study it closely.

She sighed. "Okay, sure. I'm not certain I'll be of any help, but come on inside."

Julia entered the dimly lit house. The thermostat was turned up, and the air smelled stale. On one wall hung a collection of crucifixes. Some were simply made of wood, while a few were inlaid with silver or engraved with chapters and verses that Julia suddenly felt guilty not knowing.

She followed the woman past two glass cabinets filled with angel and small dove figurines.

"This is a lovely collection," Julia said, pausing to study the cases.

"After Vicky died, I was interviewed by some reporter. I said that Vicky liked angels and doves. People started sending them to me. At first I set them anywhere, but after a while so many came I bought those cabinets secondhand."

"How many do you have?"

"Hundreds, I reckon." She sat in the center of a worn sofa covered in a faded floral print.

Julia sat in a wingback chair covered in a plaid.

"I keep thinking, I'm going to reupholster these chairs," she said. "I used to do a lot of crafty things until my arthritis flared up. But lately, it doesn't make much sense. The furniture is comfortable, and I don't have the energy I used to."

Julia leaned forward with hands clasped together. "What can you tell me about Vicky?"

A faint smile tipped the edges of the woman's lips. "She was a firecracker. Wanted to set the world on fire. This house, my world, was never big enough for her. She used to love to dance. I paid for dance lessons when I could afford it, and she was good. Always practicing her steps. She wanted to be onstage."

"She danced in a club in Shockoe Bottom."

"She thought it was her chance to make it big. Vicky was so excited when she was hired. I wanted to come and see her dance, but she always made excuses. Time wasn't right. Or if we made a date for me to come see her, she'd cancel at the last minute because she was schmoozing fancy clients. Said it was all part of the business." Mrs. Wayne pulled a loose thread on her sweatshirt, twisted, and snapped it free. "I didn't know until a reporter called and said she was a stripper. I should have known better."

"Did Vicky ever say if anyone in the club was bothering her?"

"If there was someone, she didn't say. Always fine when I asked."

"Was she dating anyone?"

"She said there was a man paying attention to her. Said he was nice. Treated her well. I asked to meet him a couple of times, but again she always found an excuse."

"Do you remember a name?"

The old woman shook her head. "She never gave his name."

"What was he like?"

"She said he was tall, good-looking. Never said what he did for a living. I do remember he wanted her to quit the club and find another job. She said leaving the job was not an option. She owed her boss money, and dancing was helping her pay off her debts."

"What did she owe him for?"

"Costumes, room and board, things like that, she said."

"Do you remember the name of her boss?"

"No. But her club was on the street where those other girls were killed. The police asked me a lot about Gene Tanner. Wanted to know if he knew Vicky."

"Did he?"

"I don't know, but the cops said he had an alibi," she said. "The police said he was in . . ." She paused, then seemed to remember. "In Atlantic City when that other girl died. They said there was no way he could have killed her." She sat back, her gaze tired and dull. "Why are you talking to me about this after all this time?"

"I'm talking to everyone associated with the case. Sometimes a new perspective helps. Folks are more likely to talk after time passes. What scared them at the time of the murder no longer intimidates them."

The woman frowned.

"Did Vicky keep any kind of diary? Write any letters? Was there anything that the cops might have overlooked?"

"I still have the letters that her married boyfriend wrote her. I was ashamed when I found out she was taking her clothes off for strangers, but then to know she was chasing after a man who belonged to another woman, well, I was mortified. I should have destroyed them, but I couldn't bear to lose any more of Vicky."

"You didn't tell the police about the letters?"

"No, I didn't," Frannie said. "And I wouldn't be telling you this now if my mama were still alive." She pushed herself up. "It would have broken her heart to see how her granddaughter turned out."

"Can I see them?"

For a long moment she didn't speak. "You're right about time. It has a way of breaking some of the chains. I might as well give the letters to you."

Julia rose, electrified by the idea of new evidence. The letters might be of no significance, but they might also be very important.

Mrs. Wayne opened a drawer at the bottom of one of her display cases and pulled out a small box wrapped in a faded red ribbon. She rubbed her hand over the top, releasing dust and whatever spell it had on her daughter's secrets. "If this helps you catch the man who killed her, then share it with anyone who wants to read 'em. It would be nice going to my Maker knowing my Vicky can finally rest in peace. There are also pictures in there. I never knew who anyone was, but like the letters, couldn't throw them out."

"I'll guard this carefully. I'll get these back to you."

"No, keep 'em. I've been hanging on to Vicky's belongings for a long time, and now it makes no sense to keep any of it."

"Thank you, Mrs. Wayne."

"I should thank you, dear."

"I'll call you if we have a break in the case."

"Please do. That would be nice."

Julia left Mrs. Wayne's house with the letters and drove back to her aunt's bar. The afternoon crowd had filtered in, and there was a low buzz of conversation. She found Aunt Cindy slicing lemons and limes for the drinks that night.

Julia visited with her briefly, then headed upstairs to her apartment. She set her purse down long enough to tug off her boots and shrug off her jacket. She always kept basic forensic supplies on hand to restock her pockets before heading to a crime scene. She spread out a thin sheet of plastic on her kitchen table and tugged on latex gloves before setting the box in front of her. Carefully she untied the ribbon and laid it aside in a neat line on the plastic. She removed the top.

Inside the box were four envelopes. The first three held letters. Each was written on white stationery from a local hotel. None of the letters were postmarked, but each was dated in blue ink. The first was January 18. The second was August 2, and the last October 15. In the last envelope were five faded snapshots. Each of the photos featured Vicky. Bright eyes, wide smile, and hair that curled away from the edges of her face. She was at a party filled with people.

The letters were addressed to Vicky Wayne in a thick handwriting that reminded her of her own style. There was no return address on the front or back.

She removed a letter and opened it. It read:

Dear V. Always thinking of you, babe. Always. J.

She sat back and stared at the boldly scripted letter *J.* "Please tell me this isn't Jim Vargas." She read the next letter.

V. You're in my heart. We will be together forever. I will take care of you. J.

And the third letter.

V. Can't stop thinking of you. You're the only woman I trust. Meet me at our place. J.

Our place. Julia remembered the medical examiner's autopsy notes. Vicky Wayne's body had been found in the Shockoe Bottom warehouse on October 25, 1992, and the pathologist had estimated at autopsy that she'd died near October 21, 1992. Had J lured Vicky to her death?

She sat back, staring at the letters. The author of the letters could have expressed sincere loving feelings, but he could also have been feeding the insecure young woman exactly what she needed to hear. Vicky was loved. J would care for her. Trust. Julia paused. She'd done the same with Lana. She'd told the woman what she needed to hear to win her trust. It's what an undercover officer did.

What troubled her were the dates on the letters. Her father had joined homicide in the summer of 1990, so if J was Jim Vargas, could he still have been using her as a confidential informant? Or was *J* for *Jack*? Or maybe even the Hangman, who was trapping another victim?

She sat back, staring at the bold script that could have been written by her father. It would take an expert to tell for sure. Her gaze shifted to the photographs, and she searched for any sign of her father's face. Several men and women had their faces turned from the camera. In the background, there was a large window with a view of the city skyline. That view would have been taken from the Manchester district on the other side of the James River, looking toward Shockoe Bottom. Lots of puzzle pieces, but no clear picture.

She dug her cell from her pocket and dialed Andrews.

He picked up on the second ring. "Vargas."

"I've come across letters that belonged to the third Hangman victim. Her mother never showed them to the cops. The content of the letters is not revealing, but I'd like them dusted for fingerprints and tested for DNA, and a handwriting analysis."

"I can do all that. Why the handwriting analysis?"

She could well be throwing her father's memory under the bus. "The letters are signed by *J*, but I can't be sure my father wrote them."

"Why would your father be writing letters to her?"

"They read like love letters."

"Can you bring them to me today? I also have items I'd like to discuss with you in person."

She checked her watch. "I'll leave now and be there as soon as I can."

"I'll wait for you."

She repacked the letters and pictures in the box, secured the lid, and tied the ribbon.

Northbound traffic ended up being lighter than she'd expected, and he was waiting for her in the lobby when she arrived. They shook hands and rode the elevator to the fifth floor. Dozens of computer monitors in his office displayed everything from stock reports to current local and international news.

He moved to a light table and handed her latex gloves before he tugged on his own set. Gloved up, she set the letters and photos on the table.

Nerves tightened her gut. "Do you have samples of my father's handwriting?"

"Yes. Your father's police files will supply ample samples. Any idea why he was writing this woman?"

"I don't know for sure if it was Jim. The letters suggest an affair or maybe manipulation, but beyond that I don't have a theory," she said. "He's not in any of the photos."

"There's no mention in your father's notes about him knowing Vicky Wayne before her death," Andrews said.

"That doesn't mean much. I'm learning he kept a lot of information off the books because he worried about information leaks." She didn't like the path the facts were creating, but she would keep her word and play them all out until the end. "Tamara Brown's sister recognized Jim's name. She said Tamara was working with him. Rene Tanner was one of his informants. And now maybe Vicky had a connection."

"I did find out that the department authorized several payments for Rene Tanner, a CI who was assisting him on the Popov drug case."

"The Popov case was a huge bust for my father and the department. He put Popov away along with some of his lieutenants."

"I read about it."

"So a serial killer targets Vicky, Rene, and Tamara after Jim left undercover and moved to homicide?" Julia asked.

"The odds are against such a coincidence."

She handed him the photos. "Vicky's mom gave me these as well. I don't recognize anyone in the pictures but Vicky."

Andrews studied an image. "I have facial-recognition software. The view out the window is interesting. My guess is that it was taken from the south side of the river."

"I would agree," she said.

"Let me examine the letters and pictures. When I have an update, I'll let you know." He moved to a desk cluttered with digital devices, including a printer. He removed a sheet of paper from the tray. "And Mr. Vic Carson has returned to Richmond. He's at his memorabilia store now."

"The Hangman website creator."

"I've researched him more since we last spoke. About ten years ago, he started blogging about famous murder cases and the methods of murder they employ. He went into detail about hangings, including knots. He never named the Hangman in the entry but heavily alluded to the case. He went into detail about the position of the bodies and the victims. Some of what he discussed came from not only public records but also police files. Someone on the inside fed him information either out of carelessness, stupidity, or greed."

"How old is he?"

"He's forty-nine now. Twenty-four at the time of the murders."

"What about DNA? Have you examined the clothing found at the original crime scenes?"

"I have. And I pulled several hair fibers from two of the victims' clothes. Being tested as we speak. A day or two longer and I'll likely have results. Call me."

"And you'll let me know about the letters?"

"I will."

"Thanks, Andrews. I do appreciate your work on this case."

"Shield Security takes its commitments very seriously."

Andrews escorted her out of the building, and as she headed out of the lot, she felt no closer to catching the Hangman. The case was a tangled mess. Before she second-guessed her decision, she called Novak.

He picked up on the first ring. "Julia."

The deep timbre of his voice had a soothing quality. "I'm leaving Shield now. Vic Carson is back in town. Thought I'd pay him a visit. Care to join me?"

"I would like that very much. Meet me at my office."

***

Unmindful of the hour, Andrews called Dr. Kincaid at the medical examiner's office. When he found out she'd left for the day, he dialed her private cell. When she answered, she was shouting and sounded rushed. In the background he heard the sounds of a rock concert.

"This is Dr. Kincaid," she said.

"Garrett Andrews with Shield Security."

"Wait a moment, let me get to a quieter spot." Muffled sounds followed before he heard a door close. "Sorry about that; I'm at a club. How did you get this number?"

"It's what I do."

"Right. What can I do for you?"

He'd never met Dr. Kincaid in person but had seen pictures of her in the media and online. He tried to imagine the highly professional woman in a club with rock music pulsing around her. Was her hair down? Was she wearing glasses? The image he conjured was appealing.

"I'm working with Agent Vargas on the Hangman case," Andrews said.

"Yes, I heard."

"I would like to review the autopsy report for her father, Jim Vargas."

"He was a suicide. Why would his death be relevant?" Her voice had lost the breathless quality and was back in control.

"It may not have any bearing on the case. But he was the lead investigator, and he was mentioned as a possible killer. I have reexamined all avenues of this case, but not his death. Can you secure the records?"

"It might take a day or two to retrieve them from archives. I can't release them to you. But you can come by my office and look at them."

"As soon as you have them, call me. I'll drive down immediately and review them."

"Anything else I can do for you, Mr. Andrews?"

The downbeat of the background music pulsed. "No, that will be it, Dr. Kincaid. I look forward to your call. Thank you."

He hung up and turned toward the pictures Julia had retrieved from the Wayne home. He'd scanned them, and they were each now displayed on three large computer monitors.

Vicky stood in the foreground of all the photos. In all she was smiling and staring at the camera. She wore a halter top and hip-hugger jeans that showcased large breasts and a narrow waist. A belly button ring winked from her navel. Her gaze was aimed directly at the camera in two images, but in the other two she looked to her left as if someone had caught her attention.

However, his interest shifted from the young girl who had less than one month to live to the background—the Richmond city skyline. As Julia Vargas had theorized, it had been taken from across the river toward the old tobacco warehouse district. A construction site beside a partly built skyscraper gave him the timeline he needed. It had been taken approximately October of 1992. A newspaper and police report search revealed that there'd been three private parties in the Manchester district in that month. The events had been newsworthy because they'd attracted several hundred people. The cops had raided one of the parties and made dozens of drug arrests. No one had been able to pinpoint who had set up the party.

He enlarged the faces in the background and noted there were six men and sixteen women who'd been captured by the picture frame. Some faces were too blurred or turned in such a way that facial recognition would not be possible. But there were at least four men and nine women among the set of pictures that he had enough facial points to analyze. He isolated each face and fed them into the program.

He rose from the workstation and moved to the break room to pour a fresh cup of coffee. He already knew it would be a long night. But he didn't care. Chasing killers who thought they'd gotten away with murder filled him with purpose, and for a few hours the ghosts he'd left behind in Iraq didn't taunt him.

***

The Hangman dug a ring of keys from his pocket and opened the basement door to his work space. He pushed open the door, clicked on a light, and then immediately closed the door behind him. The room was as he'd left it. Workbench filled with a collection of power tools, hooks, and strands of a half-dozen strips of rope.

He adjusted a light at his workstation and sat on a stool. Reading glasses on, he clicked on his computer and searched for mention of the Hangman in the news. There'd been brief accounts of an unidentified female found dead in a city warehouse. The article ended with: *Police still investigating possible motives.*

He sat back and pulled off his glasses. The media had mostly ignored the first murder two and a half decades ago. A lone woman of questionable virtue had died in the city. And no one cared. By the second death there was some interest, and by the third he'd had everyone's attention.

General apathy this go-around confirmed to him that people really didn't change that much. They didn't see danger or crisis until it was in their face. Too late.

Maybe if Julia hadn't rattled cages with her undercover investigation, or if she'd left the Hangman alone, it would be different. But she'd done both, and he could no longer ignore her. To prove to everyone, especially Julia Vargas, that the Hangman had never gone away and the Popovs never forgot, he would have to kill again.

"This one might be the charm," he muttered with a smile.

He glanced up at a bulletin board in front of his workbench filled with dozens of faces of women who could die tomorrow and no one would notice. There were so many lost souls ripe for the picking.

But the images faded from focus as he zeroed in on the center image. This was an older picture, taken over twenty-five years ago. He pulled the thumbtack out and studied the face of the young girl and her father. Jim Vargas and his daughter, Julia.

He remembered that bright fall day. He had followed Jim and his daughter to the soccer park, curious about the man who had been so sure and cocky when the media had interviewed him on the newly dubbed Hangman case, which brought the total to three deaths.

"We're still sifting through evidence," Vargas had said. *"We have several solid leads and expect an arrest soon."*

He took the statement as a direct challenge, and that had prompted him to track Vargas and his kid. He'd watched Jim taking pictures of his girl. The kid was cute. Kept tugging on her soccer uniform.

"Want a picture of the two of you?" he had asked, smiling, watching for a reaction.

Jim had grinned, surprised and happy to see him. *"What brings you out here?"*

"Fresh air."

And so he'd snapped three pictures of Jim, the great cop who thought he couldn't be stopped, and his little pride and joy. The

Hangman had left the park that day convinced Jim didn't know shit about the Hangman's identity. He was in the clear. He now had the advantage.

He'd never expected to slip into the Hangman's skin again to kill. But if the last twenty-five years had taught him anything, it was that life had a way of circling back around and flexibility was key to survival.

To re-create his past pattern, two more women would have to die. The knots and displays would have to be more graphic and more intricate. He wasn't sure if he'd re-create the original displays, but the endgame was a given: Julia Vargas would die just like her father.

CHAPTER TWENTY

Friday, November 3, 6:30 p.m.

Novak found Julia waiting for him in the lobby of police headquarters. She was leaning against a wall, eyes closed, her arms folded over her chest. Her hair looked a little messy, as if she'd run her fingers through it too many times, and she held a fresh large coffee in her hand. She also looked tired. He guessed she'd not eaten, something she'd pretended to do earlier but had avoided. Hadn't she said caffeine and nicotine were her two major food groups?

He moved toward her, and when she didn't open her eyes, he touched her gently on the arm. Her lids snapped open. For a flash, she stared at him, her eyes vacant and afraid. And then, just as quickly, the look was gone and she was in control.

"You okay?" he asked.

A slight shrug and a half smile followed. "Never better."

"Ready to talk to Vic Carson?"

"Let's go."

When they arrived at Carson's shop, the parking lot was at least half-full. Inside, there were a dozen people milling around either playing vintage games or rifling through bins to find games to buy.

Novak showed his badge to the kid behind the register. "Looking for Vic Carson."

"He's in the back, fixing a game. Want me to call him up?"

"We'll go back there."

"Yeah, sure."

As the pair moved toward the back, Novak commented, "None of these customers were alive in the nineties."

"Ancient history comes alive," she joked.

"If the nineties are ancient, what does that make me?"

"Novak, you're timeless. An old soul."

He winced. "That hurt, Julia."

She shrugged. "I bet you read the classics, smoke a pipe, and yell at the kids to get off your front lawn."

He laughed. "Only two of the three."

"Which one did I get wrong?"

Shrugging, he pushed through the swinging door. "Hang around and find out." He paused. "What do you do on your off-hours?"

"Work at animal rescue shelters, bake cookies, and channel thoughts about world peace."

"Seriously." He wanted to know more about her.

"Run, weapon train, help Cindy at the bar. Nothing really noteworthy."

"You might want to expand your interests."

She paused, studying him closely. "Like what?"

He wanted to give whatever it was between them more time and nurturing. "How about we try a date?"

A brow arched as if she were waiting for a punch line. "Are you serious?"

He didn't hesitate. "I am."

She relaxed into a smile. "Maybe."

As they moved along the hallway, he noticed she ran her finger along her belt until her right hand bumped her service weapon. Novak did the same. As routine as this visit felt, both understood routine could turn deadly on a dime.

At the end of the hallway, he found an open door and a workshop filled with dozens of old gaming systems. Many were dismantled and picked clean for parts.

In the center of it all was a large man with shoulder-length graying hair cinched back in a ponytail. He wore a black Pac-Man T-shirt and faded jeans.

"Mr. Vic Carson?" Novak asked.

The man looked up. Thick, dark-rimmed glasses made his gray eyes look large. "What is it?"

Novak introduced himself, holding off on Julia's introduction. He didn't want the Vargas name to be a distraction. "I hear you're the creator of the Hangman website."

Carson set down a small screwdriver and pulled off his glasses. "Why would you say that?"

"I have it on good authority you created it," Novak said.

Carson sniffed. "There a law against setting up a website now?"

"No law against it. But it draws attention when anyone shows an immense interest in serial murders."

"The twenty-fifth anniversary is this year. And as you can see from the crowds outside, there's a yearning for the nineties and their murder and mayhem."

"Your website is detailed."

"Again, no law against it." Carson looked at Julia. "Detective Novak, are you going to introduce me to Agent Vargas?"

"You know me?" Julia asked.

"Sure. How could I not?" He moved around the counter, and after wiping his hand on a rag, extended it to her.

She didn't accept it. "How long have you been stalking me?"

"*Stalking* is a harsh word," he said.

"Then what is it?" she asked.

"I'm simply a curious admirer. Your father was the lead investigator. I researched him extensively."

"Did you know the original victims? You lived in the city at the time."

"No, I did not. But I frequented Shockoe Bottom a lot and spent time in the bars near the crime scenes. I read all the newspaper accounts."

"You have an alibi for the nights they died?" Julia asked.

Carson smiled. "As a matter of fact, I do. I was working in Roanoke that fall doing temporary work."

"That's three hours west of here," Novak said. "Easy to drive down and back in a day."

"But none of the victims died quickly," Carson said. "And all the shrinks I talked to about the Hangman said he liked to watch his victims die. Doesn't make sense to string up a victim and then leave before the main event."

"The main event," Julia said.

"Do you know a woman named Lana Ortega?" Novak asked.

"No, should I?" Carson asked.

"Where were you on Tuesday night?"

"I was in California at a convention. I travel to promote the site, which brings in new customers both here and especially online. Keeping both my passions afloat takes work. Again, why are you here?"

"I think your site might have inspired someone to resurrect the Hangman," Julia remarked.

Carson held up his hands. "I don't like the direction this is headed."

"What direction is that, Vic?" Novak asked.

His eyes narrowed. "I read the news and listen to the scanners. A woman was found in the warehouse district. Was she strung up?" His eyes glistened with interest.

"Does the idea of that excite you?" Novak asked.

"It's strictly business for me, Detective," Carson said. "If a new Hangman case emerges, it will be a boon to my business. And before you ask, none of my subscribers mentioned the killing to me. Besides, the bulk of my patrons simply have a fascination with death. They're harmless."

"Do you have a list of these followers?" Julia asked.

"You have a warrant?" Carson replied.

"You sell rope out front?" Julia fired back.

"Sure. It's a novelty item. All of it can be bought in any hardware store." He studied Julia. "I've watched news footage of your old man. Intense like you. Reminded me of a wound spring. I guess not a huge surprise when he shot himself. Is this discussion now your effort to clear his name? There are still plenty of people who thought he was the Hangman."

"You have theories about the Hangman that you wrote about on your blog?" Novak asked.

"Sure. Who doesn't?"

"Enlighten me," Novak said.

Carson shrugged. "Any profiler will tell you the Hangman killings were more than murder. The killings were a statement, a form of art. He likes to be noticed. My guess is if this body you found is displayed like the others, he's feeling irrelevant. Forgotten."

"Irrelevant?" Julia asked.

"For whatever reason, he stopped killing, but with the silver anniversary approaching and people like me ginning up interest, he discovers he wants to be noticed again. Tuesday night would have been Halloween, and Jim Vargas died on November 1."

"You sound like you know him pretty well," Julia said.

"Hard not to seeing as I've crawled in his head enough times."

Julia's expression didn't change. "How did you get hold of the video footage shot at the original crime scenes?"

Novak watched Carson closely, and the subtle tightening of the man's left hand and the micro shift in his gaze told Novak that Julia had struck gold.

Carson smiled. "Footage was sent to me. Like manna from heaven. I couldn't pass on it. Which one of you pulled it off my site?"

"Who sent it to you?" Novak asked.

"A fan. I received a CD in the mail. Old-school, but effective. And I can put it back up."

"So you still have the CD?" Novak asked. "I'd like to see it."

"Again, I need you to get a warrant."

"I'll get one," Novak said.

"Until you do, you both need to leave. I have work to do."

"I'm asking you to not upload the video again," Novak said.

"Freedom of speech," Carson said.

"When I came in here," Julia said carefully, "it was strictly a fact-finding mission. But it's growing more personal for you by the second. If I find out you're hiding the identity of the killer, I'll charge you as an accessory to murder."

"Is that a threat?" Carson asked.

"Nope," she said, smiling. "It's a statement of fact."

He folded his arms. "And you two can count on one thing."

"What's that?" Julia asked.

"He's going to kill again."

"Why do you say that?" Novak asked.

"One death of a woman nobody cared about falls out of the news quickly. Two deaths, a little harder to ignore, and three—well, that's a pattern no one can overlook."

***

Julia was quiet during the drive back to her place. Seeing Carson's callous infatuation with death shouldn't have troubled her so deeply, but it did. Lately she was all raw nerves. When Novak suggested he drive her home and she retrieve her car from the station in the morning, she'd agreed.

When Novak parked, she reached for the door handle. "Keep me updated."

He turned toward her but made no move to stop her. "I'm an open book."

A smile formed on her lips. "Written in what ancient language?"

White teeth flashed in the dark. "Pot calling the kettle black, Julia."

"No arguments here. Maybe keeping our personal secrets is best."

"Why do you say that?" His tone turned low, deep, serious.

"The truth has a way of spoiling things, so I tend to avoid it."

"There's no hope without truth. It's ugly, but it's better to know."

She shook her head as she shifted her gaze to a point in the distance. A part of her wanted to talk to him. Confess her fears. Bare her scars. But that part was overruled by too many well-seasoned barriers. "Be careful what you ask for."

This time he laid a hand on her shoulder. "What truth are you hiding, Julia?"

For a second, she was quiet as she absorbed the heat of his touch. Here, alone with him, she thought maybe she could be more herself. Not be so on guard. But as she lowered the veil, she caught herself. "Nothing too interesting."

He was taking her in. "You're interesting to me."

She arched a brow. "That's because you want to get laid again."

He didn't break contact. "Guilty as charged."

She liked his touch. It was steady. Nonthreatening. Gentle. "If you promise not to talk about feelings, you can come up."

He leaned forward and kissed her on the lips. When she leaned into the kiss, his hand went to her waist. "Let's go upstairs."

He'd made no promises about the long term. Neither had she. But that was good. Better that way. "Right."

He shut off the ignition and followed her up the back staircase to her apartment. Desire tingled in her as she tossed her keys aside and turned to face him. He didn't rush toward her, though she sensed a simmering heat that hinted at how much he wanted her.

She dropped her purse to the floor and shrugged off her jacket. "I'm not made of china, Novak."

He closed the distance between them and cupped her face in his hands as he kissed her again. There was nothing angry or punishing about his touch. He wanted her to want this. She threaded her fingers through his hair and pressed her breasts to his chest.

"This is all I've been able to think about since the last time," he said.

"One-track mind."

He traced his hand along her neck, then outlined her collarbone. Each time he touched her, he was gentle, his desire securely in check. That restraint made her want him more.

She unknotted his tie, pulled it free of his collar, and tossed it on the floor. She unbuttoned his shirt, smiling when she saw the white undershirt. "My, my, Mr. Clean."

He pulled his shirt and undershirt from his waistband but let her shrug the shirt from his shoulders. He traced a finger down her chest to the V of her sweater. He cupped her breast, and her mouth went dry.

"Where can I put my weapon?" Novak asked.

"No pun intended." She nodded toward a dresser by the door. "I put mine in the top drawer." She unclipped her weapon and opened the drawer.

He laid his beside hers along with his badge, phone, and cuffs. She closed the drawer and locked it. Quickly he pulled her into his arms, and she stiffened. Not a flinch, but a tensing.

He kissed her, his hands on her hips. Again, she sensed he controlled his desire. She tugged off his undershirt, smiling as she thought that Mr. Clean had a hot body.

He grabbed her hand and led her toward her bedroom. "Not so fast this time."

She followed, wanting to feel the desire and get lost in an orgasm. She was in a rush. He wasn't. "I thought you liked it that way."

"I like it this way, too." In her room he kissed her before reaching for the hem of her sweater and pulling it over her head. Gently, he traced the edge of her bra and then unfastened the snap between her breasts. He slid off the bra and lightly kissed her breasts. She pulled in a breath as she reached for the buckle of his pants and undid it. The zipper slid down, and she pushed her hand into his pants and cupped his hard erection.

He groaned as he pulled her hand away. "Taking our time, remember?"

"We can do that later."

He shook his head. "I want to enjoy you." He unfastened her belt, and the buckle slipped free of its sheath. The sharp tip glinted. "Surprise, surprise."

"Never a dull moment."

He tossed the buckle aside and slid the denim down over her slender hips. She stepped out of the pants and pushed them aside. She stood naked before him, exposed, a state that did slightly unsettle her. The last few times it had been dark, hurried, and with enough desire to crowd out fear.

Now, he wanted to go slow? Fine. He'd suffer.

She wrapped her arms around him, savoring the way the hairs on his chest teased her nipples. She shoved off his pants and heard them fall to the floor. He stepped out of them as she pulled him toward the rumpled sheets of her bed. He sat, and she crouched in front of him and slowly ran her hand along the inside of his naked thighs. She tugged off one sock, then leaned forward and kissed the inside of his leg before kissing the tip of his erection. He sucked in a breath, burying his hands in her long hair and gripping it in a tight fist. She pulled back and removed the second sock.

"You said slow," she said.

"Taking off socks will never be the same."

She licked the inside of the other leg and ran her tongue hungrily along his erection. When he groaned, she did it again before she pushed him back on the bed, straddling him. She brushed against his erection but only enough to tease. They were going slow after all, as he wanted.

She licked his nipple and then kissed him on the lips, skimming her hand over his flat belly.

He placed his hands on her bare hips. "You're going to make me regret slow."

"Your choice, not mine."

With a grumble, he rolled her on her back. "Next time, we will go slower. Right now, I can't get enough of you."

For an instant, she lost the sense of control and tensed. Cold fear threatened to extinguish the fire. He hesitated. Strong fingers caressed her clitoris in small circles as he kissed her on the lips. Round and round he went, coaxing the sparks into a flame. She relaxed back into the pillows and groaned.

He nudged his knee between her legs. "Open for me."

She didn't hesitate and spread her legs. He pressed his erection just inside her. She was wet and tight, but having him close still tugged at bad memories. Closing her eyes, she ran her hands over his back, grabbing his buttocks and trying to hang on to her desire. Her throat tightened with tension as the beauty of this moment slipped away.

He thrust fully inside her now, kissing her on the lips. "Don't go anywhere. Stay with me. Open your eyes."

She gripped his shoulders and opened her eyes. She met his gaze, dark with longing but with no traces of anger.

"It's you and me," he said. "No past. Only right now."

She nodded, hating the tears that welled in her eyes and spilled over the side of her cheeks.

"I can stop," he whispered.

"No. Don't."

He moved inside of her and began to rub her center. Slowly, desire flashed and urgency returned. She tipped her hips toward him and ground into his palm as he slid in and out at a steady rhythm. Heat flared. Her body built toward the sweet release she realized she now needed from him. And then in a blink, an explosion washed over her, and she gripped his back. He shoved deeper into her, and they both came.

When he collapsed against her, his heart thumped quick and hard, matching her own beat for beat. Absently, she traced her hand over his back, now slick with sweat.

"Not bad, old soul."

He grinned against the hollow of her neck. "Like to think I have moves."

"You do."

He rose up on his elbows and pushed back her hair from her face. "You okay?"

"More than okay."

"You tensed again."

She'd shared her body, but feelings were a whole different matter.

"You can talk to me."

She tried to wriggle free and thought he might hold her too close, but he rolled on his side and let her put distance between them. She didn't go as far this time, choosing to stay on her back, inches from him.

He traced circles around the delicate lines of a scroll tattoo inked above her hip bone. "When did you get this?"

She smiled. "Spring break. Junior year of college. Made sense at the time."

"Sexy." His fingers moved over her flat belly to a scar by her left breast. "What happened?"

"Part of my adventures in Virginia Beach with Benny."

"You can talk to me about it."

Instead of answering, she rolled to her side and swung her legs over the edge of the bed. She searched the floor for her shirt. Now that the desire had burned itself out, her skin cooled and she was feeling too exposed. When she moved to stand, he grabbed her wrist. Not an unbreakable hold, but firm enough to let her know he wanted her to stay. Because she had a choice, she stayed.

"You're always running," he said. "I can feel your heart racing."

A sigh leaked over her lips. "Cindy says I've been on the move since I was a small kid."

"Where are you running to now?"

"To get my shirt. I'm cold."

"Not away from the question?"

"That, too."

He released his grip, shifted his weight under the covers, and held up the blanket for her.

Novak didn't push, but waited. Always steady, coaxing.

She dropped the shirt and slid under the covers beside him. He touched his body close to her, banding his arm around her waist. His erection hardened and pressed against her buttocks.

She chuckled. "So soon?"

"The tattoo did it for me."

He pushed against her ass, and his hand slid, trying to coax her forward a fraction so he could enter. She moved for him, opening easily and surrendering to the pleasure. After a while, they collapsed against each other, and she nestled close to him. For the first time in a long time, she drifted off peacefully to sleep.

***

When her cell phone rang, Julia jolted awake. She was aware of two things. The sun had not risen, and she wasn't alone in her bed. She glanced over at Novak, who lay on his back, his hands draped over his eyes.

"Not my ringtone," he said.

Novak. In her bed. *Shit.* She scrambled out of bed and found her cell in the pocket of her pants. She fished it out. Dakota Sharp. *Great.*

She cleared her throat. "Vargas."

"Vacation ends as of Monday," he said.

She searched the room for her digital clock and read the display. 6:01. "This could have waited until later, but Sharp works all the time."

"Didn't want you filling up your dance card for Monday."

"Sure. Fine."

"Any word on the Hangman murders?"

"Not yet. But there are a couple of new leads."

"Any connections to the Ortega case?" Sharp asked.

"Several. Hopefully I'll have plenty to share by Monday."

"Right."

Novak rose up out of bed and moved toward her. He wrapped his arms around her and squeezed her ass.

She inhaled and tried to wiggle away, but he held her tight.

"If you don't have hard leads on the Hangman case by Monday, turn the case over to Novak. He's a solid detective."

She cleared her throat. "Solid, understood."

When she hung up, Novak took the phone from her hand and tossed it on the pile of clothes on the floor. "Duty calls?"

She tipped her head back so her hair fell away from her face. "Sharp reminding me I'm back on the job as of Monday. Time is running out for me and this case."

Novak kissed the hollow of her neck before his lips moved to the exposed side of her left breast. "You have some time to spare, don't you?"

She relaxed into his touch, knowing none of this was smart. Hard to climb out if she fell in too deep. "Maybe a little."

"Good. Now we can try even slower."

CHAPTER
TWENTY-ONE

Saturday, November 4, 8:30 a.m.

Andrews received an early-morning call from Dr. Kincaid. She had Jim Vargas's autopsy files in her office, was working today, and would be on hand to answer questions. He told her he'd see her in two hours. He pushed away from his computer screen, showered, and dressed and was on the road in fifteen minutes.

He'd not formally met Dr. Addison Kincaid but was aware of research she was privately doing on a cold case that was of great interest to him. Her work was the reason he'd pitched the idea of a cold case team to Shield Security's founder, Joshua Shield, who had been more than willing to chase killers who'd gotten away with murder. He hoped Dr. Kincaid would come to value the work he was doing now and trust him with her case before he had to force the issue soon.

When he arrived at her office, he found her sitting at her desk, her head bowed over graphic images of a body midautopsy. He cleared his throat, and she looked up, dark-rimmed glasses accentuating green eyes.

"Garrett Andrews," he said.

She rose and came around her desk. "I didn't hear you. I get lost in thought."

And he moved quietly. He shook her hand, knowing the scars on his palm grated her smooth skin. "Thank you for getting the files so quickly, Dr. Kincaid."

"Certainly." She adjusted glasses that framed her face nicely. "I had a chance to look at the autopsy report."

"Any conclusions?"

She turned toward the desk, pulled a file from a neat stack at the corner, and crossed to a small conference table. Extending her hand, she invited him to sit. As she moved past him, a subtle perfume drifted around him.

She opened her file to an explicit picture of Detective Jim Vargas lying on the autopsy table. His face was intact, his eyes closed, his mouth agape. However, in the center of his chest was a bullet wound.

"When we see close-range shots to the head or in the mouth, it's often an indication of suicide, not homicide," she said.

"You've seen gunshots to the chest in a suicide?"

"Not as often, but yes."

"Were there scratches or bruising to suggest any kind of struggle?"

"No. I looked at all the pictures and read the medical examiner's notes. No other signs of fresh injuries, though X-rays detected several broken bones that had healed and an old cut that had been sewn up. Crime-scene photos suggest he was sitting in a chair that was at his kitchen table."

"Gunpowder residue on his hands?"

"Yes. There was gunpowder residue on his hands and chest, which is consistent with him holding the gun close to his chest. The investigators theorized that he placed the gun's muzzle to his chest using both hands and fired. He was wearing a T-shirt at the time of the shooting."

"Really?"

She flipped a page to another picture that showed a close-up of the wound. "Although he was wearing a T-shirt, there is still gunpowder stippling in the entrance wound as well as on the garment."

"Again, consistent with suicide?" Andrews asked.

"It proves that the gun barrel was less than a quarter inch from his body."

"Not pressed against his skin?"

"That's correct. Again, consistent in a suicide."

"Angle of the shot?"

"Slightly downward. The bullet traveled through the chest, including the heart, exiting the body. Death was immediate."

"Suicides are slightly upward, so the bullet misses the rib cage, hits the heart and possibly the aorta, correct?"

"Yes, typically." She showed him another image featuring Vargas's body turned on his side so that the medical examiner could document the exit wound. "The bullet was a nine-millimeter jacketed hollow point, a nasty one. It's meant to expand upon impact to decrease penetration and disrupt more tissue. The medical examiner noted the forensic team dug the slug out of the kitchen wall."

"No signs of a struggle."

"None was found by the patrol officers," she said.

"Were they first on the scene?"

"Detective Vargas's wife found the body and immediately called Ken Thompson, who came straight to the house. He reported that he called the paramedics immediately."

"Was there an estimated time of death?"

"Liver temperature put death around five p.m."

"And when did paramedics arrive?"

"About seven."

Two hours between the time the shot was fired and paramedics arrived. Plenty of time to collect a note or clean up evidence that might have been incriminating. It was natural to protect a partner, especially one who could no longer defend himself.

"If you had to make the call on his death certificate, would you have called it a suicide?" Andrews asked.

She flipped through more pages. "The medical examiner spoke to Amy Vargas and asked if there had been any mental health issues or talk of suicide. She'd said no. Though the couple was separated, she said they'd been talking about reconciling. She said he knew she was coming by the house with their daughter the day he died. No one reported him making farewell declarations, nor did his everyday routine or spending habits change." She shook her head. "The gun was found one foot from the body, which investigators believe was the result of the weapon recoiling after the bullet discharged. There was some sign of alcohol in his system, but not enough to impair. Jim Vargas's death has the hallmarks of suicide, and I can certainly understand why the determination was made."

"But what's your opinion?"

Absently she tapped the file with her finger. "My next comment needs to be treated with the utmost discretion."

"Understood."

"I would have given Vargas the benefit of the doubt. I would have marked it as undetermined."

"Why?"

"Given what I've learned about this man, who was one tough cop, I don't see him racking a hollow point into his weapon and pulling the trigger knowing his wife and kid are coming by the house and will find him. He would have known the bullet would blow out his back and project blood everywhere." She pressed her index finger to her abdomen. "The trajectory of the bullet bothers me. Why fire down toward the heart? Most suicides fire up into the heart to avoid bone."

"There was gunpowder residue on his hands?"

"Yes. But it was noted that Detective Vargas had gone to the shooting range that morning. The residue on his hands could have also come from that. But as you may know, residue degrades quickly after an hour and is all but gone after six hours."

"Thank you, Dr. Kincaid. You've been helpful."

"Mr. Andrews, it's just an opinion. Take it for what it's worth."

"Understood. I value your opinion."

"Why are you questioning this autopsy's findings?"

"I've read Jim Vargas's case notes and watched several of his crime-scene videos. He was chasing a serial killer. It makes no sense why a man like that would leave the game via suicide. He put himself through hell to make the Popov arrest. And then he kills himself and gives Popov the only thing the mobster wanted more than freedom? I don't buy it."

"Popov was incarcerated at the time of Jim Vargas's death," she said. "And you have no proof Popov knew Jim had been the mole."

"A man like that gets to where he is by knowing whom he can trust. And he would have had a reach that extended far beyond prison walls."

Absently she touched the ring encircled by a chain around her neck. "Have you discussed this with Julia?"

"No. And I won't until I have all the DNA retesting results from the Hangman case. That will be tomorrow. And I could be off base. Jim Vargas was a chameleon, and if anyone could have hidden a darker, homicidal side, it would have been him."

"Jekyll and Hyde."

"Maybe."

"Call me if I can help any further."

"Thanks." He rose, shook her hand, and left.

In his SUV, Andrews checked his phone and searched for Ken Thompson's address. The man was suffering from the early onset of Alzheimer's, but it was possible he might shake loose a memory or two. He drove the twenty-five minutes crosstown and parked in front of the neat rancher house. It was almost noon, so not too early to make an unannounced call.

He approached the front door and rang the bell. Seconds later he heard the movement of footsteps. The door snapped open to a slender woman in her midfifties. Silver hair was tied back in a neat ponytail. A light flannel shirt and jeans hung loosely on her body.

"I'm Garrett Andrews," he said. "I'm working with Julia Vargas on the Hangman case."

The woman's gray-green eyes narrowed. "She didn't mention your name."

"I'm assuming you're Wendy Thompson."

Again, prudent hesitation consistent with someone who'd worked for the police. "That's correct."

"I'd like to speak to your husband, if I may."

"About what?"

"His partner, Jim Vargas."

Her grip tightened on the door. "I don't see how this will help with the Hangman case."

"It may not," he conceded. "But the death of Jim Vargas has always been shrouded in question, and your husband was the first man on the scene." ·

"You understand he's not well."

"And I promise to be careful with him, Mrs. Thompson. My intent is not to upset him."

"I'm not comfortable with this, Mr. Andrews."

Footsteps sounded behind Wendy, and her husband appeared.

"Mr. Thompson," Andrews said. "Garrett Andrews. We met the other day."

Thompson stared at him a long moment before he said, "Mr. Andrews. At Shield."

"That's right."

Wendy glanced up at her husband. "Ken, he wants to talk to you about Jim."

Thompson patted his wife on the arm. "Sure, I'll help Mr. Andrews in any way I can."

Wendy laid her hand over his. "Are you sure it's wise?"

Ken squeezed her hand. "I forget details, but I'm not an invalid yet. Let me help this young man while I still can."

Her jaw tightened, but she yielded, pushing open the screened door. "Come in, Mr. Andrews."

The house was a modest one-story. The walls were an antique white and covered with dozens of pictures that chronicled both their lives and careers. They'd traveled extensively, but did not have children. He thought about the blank walls of his own home. It wasn't that he didn't have memories; he simply did not want to remember.

He followed Wendy to a sunporch that overlooked a modest backyard. Ken indicated to Andrews to take a seat on a floral sofa while he moved toward a recliner. "Wendy, would you excuse us?"

"Ken, I really think I should stay."

"It will be fine, honey. Mr. Andrews is here to help Julia, and I told her I'd do whatever she needed."

Her gaze flickered to Andrews in a silent warning before she left.

Ken sat. "Excuse my wife. She's worried about me. The diagnosis has really upset her."

Andrews sat. "Understandable."

"I have to remind her daily I'm still here for the most part and am not crippled."

"Good to hear. I'm counting on your memory."

"What do you want to know?" Ken asked.

"Tell me about the day Jim Vargas shot himself."

Ken took in a deep breath and sat back. "How does this relate to the Hangman? Jim wasn't the Hangman."

Spoken like a loyal partner. "Understood. But I think his death is linked. Tell me about the day."

Ken's hands formed a steeple, and for a moment he didn't speak. "It was a Saturday," he said. "Rainy. Dreary. It had been warm the few days before, but the weather had shifted suddenly and turned cold. I had gone for an afternoon run and was stepping out of the shower when my phone rang. It was Amy, and she was hysterical. I could hear Julia crying in the background. She said Jim was dead. I thought she'd made a mistake. I'd seen him that morning at the shooting range. We'd closed a homicide in the early hours of the morning and went by the range to blow off steam." He closed his eyes. "Amy screamed to come. I lived minutes away and it took no time to get there. I found her in the living room, holding Julia close. Amy was trying not to cry, but Jesus, who wouldn't be a wreck. I went into the kitchen, and Jim was slumped over the kitchen table. He had an exit wound the size of my fist in his back. Blood was everywhere."

"How long had he been dead?"

"He was still warm. I'd say less than an hour."

"And the weapon?"

"Nine millimeter. One foot from his body on the floor."

"Did he leave a note?"

Ken dropped his gaze and didn't speak.

"It's been twenty-five years," Andrews said. "There's no one left to protect."

"There's Julia. I always swore I'd protect her."

"She deserves to know the truth, and from what I've seen, she can handle anything."

"She was a kid," he choked out.

Andrews waited. "What did you do?"

Thompson didn't speak as he raised his gaze.

The hair on the back of Andrews's neck rose as it did when something wasn't right. Thompson had information. A secret he'd carried inside him for over two decades. Maybe if not for his illness, he'd have taken that secret to his grave, but Andrews could see the weight of it on his shoulders now.

"Tell me," Andrews coaxed softly. He wasn't a patient man but understood the value of pausing. He would press eventually, if necessary.

Thompson leaned forward and clasped his hands. "He did leave a note."

"You took it?"

"I did. It was bad enough that Jim had killed himself, but he didn't need the world knowing all the grim details. The press and brass would have swarmed all over it, and it would have ruined his legacy and humiliated his family."

"What did it say?"

"He confessed to being the Hangman."

Andrews sat still; his breathing slowed. He didn't blink. "He said that in the note?"

"Yes. But the note made no sense to me. The handwriting was shaky."

"Did you save it?"

"No. I shoved it in my pocket as the paramedics arrived. As soon as I got home, I burned it. I know that was a mistake. I should have saved it. But I couldn't let the world think that my partner killed all those women."

Andrews subdued frustration. "Do you recall exactly what it said?"

"I do. It said: *I'm the Hangman.*"

"That's precise. Are you sure that's what it said?"

"It's burned in my memory. And not a day goes by that I wish I could forget it. Of all the memories that are slipping away, that one has its hooks in me."

"You never told Julia."

He rubbed the back of his neck. "Shit. I never told anyone until this moment."

"Why now?"

"I can't tell Julia. I can't put this burden on her."

"I'm going to have to tell her," Andrews said.

"She won't believe you. She'll need hard forensic data to ever be convinced that Jim was the Hangman."

Andrews mentally shifted. "What did the note look like?"

"What do you mean?"

"Tell me about the note. You said *shaky handwriting*. What type of paper did he use? What was the color of the ink that he used? Were there stains on the page?"

"It was written on the back of a Chinese take-out menu. Dark ink. Uneven handwriting scribbled across the menu. There was a dark stain in the upper-right corner. Looked like food or coffee."

"Had he ordered Chinese that day?"

"I saw later in the refrigerator that there was beef and mixed vegetables in there."

"Where was the note?"

"On the kitchen table, stuck in the bowl of apples."

"Was there a back door to the kitchen?"

"Yes. And it was open when I arrived. I asked Amy about it, but she said she freaked out and might have opened it when she ran outside."

"Did you look out the back door?"

"Sure."

Andrews sensed someone behind him and turned to see Wendy standing in the door. She was staring at her husband as if seeing him for the first time.

"Ken," she said. "Is this true?"

He nodded. "It's all true."

"Jim left a note?"

"Yes."

"What about the back door?" Andrews pressed. Staying focused on the facts was more important than Wendy's reaction.

"I shoved the note in my pocket. Their backyard was bordered by woods, and I briefly searched, hoping to see someone, something, or anything to help explain what had happened. I didn't want to leave the girls alone too long. When the paramedics arrived, it all rolled on from there."

Wendy went to Ken, knelt by his chair, and wrapped her arm around him. "Honey, why didn't you say something?"

"I wanted to protect Jim and Julia," he said. "I couldn't believe he'd killed those women."

"When you were partnered with Jim, did you ever wonder if he was connected to the Hangman murders?" Andrews asked.

"Jim knew all the women from his undercover work, and he knew the murders weren't random. But he never once made me think he'd killed them."

"He never made a note of his relationship with them in his files."

"Like I told Julia, he hated writing down his thoughts. He didn't trust that the information wouldn't be compromised." Ken clenched his fists as his gaze sharpened. "But I never once had any gut feeling about him wanting to hurt those women. They had helped him, trusted him, and he wanted to repay that trust by helping them straighten out their lives."

"Stay here," Andrews said. He moved into the living room and dialed Tobias Novak's number. Though Julia was his contact on the case, this suicide fell within the jurisdiction of the city police, and that meant Novak.

On the second ring, he heard a crisp "Detective Novak."

"Garrett Andrews with Shield Security."

A pause. "What can I do for you?"

He recapped what he'd learned.

More silence. "Are you certain he's not confused?"

"He appears lucid. Actually, he appears quite in control."

"Does he know about the Ortega murder?" Novak asked.

"It didn't come up. And Ortega's death doesn't mean Jim didn't commit the original three."

"I'll get Julia, and we'll be right over. Can you stand firm?"

Julia. Not Agent Vargas. Interesting. "Of course."

***

"I don't want to believe Jim was the Hangman," Julia said.

Novak studied her solemn expression. "We haven't ruled out a copycat."

She shrugged her shoulders, chasing away the tension that'd been building since he'd told her about his conversation with Andrews. "I don't buy it. Ken is confused."

"Let's take it one step at a time."

"I said I'd follow the case until the end, and I meant it."

Julia and Novak arrived at the Thompson house twenty minutes after Andrews called. Inside, they found Ken, Wendy, and Andrews. Wendy sat next to Ken on the arm of his easy chair. Andrews stood a few steps back, making some notes on a small pad.

When Julia entered the room, Ken looked up at her, his eyes filled with a mixture of pain and fear. "Honey, I'm so sorry," he said.

She knelt beside him and took his hand in hers. She had only one shot at this and couldn't badger him into recanting his story. "Ken, don't worry. Don't get upset. Tell me what you told Andrews."

"Your father left a note." He dropped his voice to a whisper. "He confessed to killing those women."

"Why did he kill them?"

"I don't know. The guy worked side by side with me every day trying to solve the case. None of it made sense."

"So you think my father really wrote that note and then killed himself?"

"The scene looked like a classic suicide. There was no sign of struggle or that anyone else had been there."

"Maybe it was someone he knew," she said. "Maybe it was someone who could get close to him. My mother and he had been separated for a couple of months. Maybe there was someone else."

"He never told me about seeing anyone."

"You destroyed the note," she confirmed.

"I didn't want anyone finding it. I was afraid for you and your mother. She'd have lost her widow's benefits if it could be proved he was the Hangman." His wrinkled brow knotted into a frown. "I wanted to protect him, you, and your mother. I wanted to do right by everyone."

"Why let me go to Shield if you found the note?" Julia asked.

"Because I need the truth before I die." He slowly shook his head. "The suicide never made sense to me."

"Was he depressed or sad in the days leading up?" Novak asked.

"No. Not at all. That's why I hid the note."

"You didn't think to send it in for analysis?" Novak followed up.

"The media and the brass were still hungry for a close." He met Julia's gaze. "It would have made it all so easy to pin it on him. And you and your mother's life would have been devastated. You have to believe me. I did what I thought was best for you."

"What if he was murdered?" Julia asked. "What if that note had been a clue to the killer?"

Ken shook his head, his watery gaze lost. "I thought about that later. I wished I'd saved the note. But I didn't."

Wendy stepped forward, her arms crossed over her chest. "This is enough for today. It's time for his medicines, and he's tired. It gets worse when he's tired."

Julia rose, keeping her frustrations in check. "I want to talk to you again, Ken."

"Sure, honey. Sure," he said.

She kissed him on the cheek and stepped outside. The morning sun warmed her face, but she didn't feel it. She was numb.

Novak came up behind her. She resisted the urge to lean into him, ask him to wrap his arms around her, and hold her tight. Andrews walked up.

"What brought you here, Andrews?" she asked.

"I went to see Dr. Kincaid. She allowed me to see your father's autopsy file."

Her gut tightened. "And?"

"The findings were conclusive enough," he said.

"What's that mean?" she asked.

"Most of the indicators suggest suicide." He also relayed Dr. Kincaid's personal opinion and doubts.

"And now we have a note that no one saw and our only eyewitness is a guy suffering from Alzheimer's. So basically, we have a few maybes, but no solid facts," she said.

Andrews appeared unfazed. "I consider it progress." His phone chirped, and he checked the message. He raised a brow as he read. "I'm running those pictures you gave me of Vicky Wayne through a facial recognition scanner."

"And?"

Novak was listening.

"I have two faces that the program identified," Andrews said. "Vicky Wayne and Rita Gallagher. So we know Rita knew Vicky or was at least at a party with her shortly before they were both killed in the fall of 1992."

"Have you completed your handwriting analysis of the letters Julia gave you?" Novak asked.

"I did. I do not believe they were written by Jim Vargas."

"So Vicky's boyfriend wasn't my father?" Julia asked.

"He didn't write the notes," Andrews said.

Wendy pushed through the front door.

"How's Ken?" Julia asked.

"He's upset and withdrawn into himself. He does that now when he's stressed."

"Do you have a minute to answer questions?" Julia asked.

"I'm not sure what I can add."

"What was your opinion of Jim Vargas?" Novak asked.

"No matter what anyone said or what Ken thinks he remembers, Jim was one hell of a cop. A good man. He hated being away from you and your mother. But he said someone had to be willing to sacrifice and do the hard work."

"Some men like Jim get addicted to the rush of the job," Andrews said. "Sometimes a more normal life is too mundane without the constant adrenaline rush of undercover work."

Julia watched Wendy closely. A tension seemed to ripple through Wendy's body that made Julia think she was on guard. "Do you think Jim could have been the Hangman?"

"No." A nervous laugh rumbled in her chest. "That is absurd. I don't care what Ken thinks he remembers. Why would Jim kill those women?"

"He knew them all," Julia said.

"He was your father, Julia. How can you say this?"

"I didn't see him growing up. I never really knew the man."

"I'm sorry for you, because he was a great man. People don't realize what kind of sacrifices men like Jim make. He gave up so much. And I can't stand to hear him run down," Wendy said.

"You're loyal to Jim," Novak said.

She glared at him with watery eyes. "He was my husband's partner."

"You married Ken right after Jim died, right?" Julia asked.

"So? Ken and I were engaged when he and Jim worked together."

"But when you talk about Jim Vargas, it's as if it were yesterday," Novak said. "You sound like his champion."

Wendy raised her chin. "I cared about him."

"Did you and Jim Vargas have an affair?" Novak asked softly.

Julia wasn't surprised by the question and stood waiting for the answer.

Wendy flinched. "Why would you ask that?"

"I'm not passing judgment, Wendy," Novak said, softly. "I'm trying to solve a case."

Julia was silent.

Wendy shook her head as she looked at Julia. "You're all off base on all of this."

She'd not denied an affair. And in Julia's experience, when someone was innocent, they made it immediately clear. "Wendy, is it true? Were you and Jim having an affair?"

"Amy was my friend."

Julia leaned in, stripping the emotion from her voice as she struggled to maintain some emotional distance. She said, "It's okay. It's in the past."

Wendy looked at her, and for a second she looked ready to speak before she shook her head. "All you need to know is that Ken is wrong," she said. "Jim didn't leave any note. And he didn't kill himself."

Still no denial. Whatever superhero fantasies she'd had for her father grew more and more tarnished. No one spoke as they waited for Wendy to continue.

"Jim created the image of the ladies' man," she said. "The image suited his undercover work. He wasn't the man people thought he was."

"He was having affairs," Novak said.

"He was lost and lonely after Amy left," Wendy countered.

"Rita's the reason Amy left," Novak said.

"You didn't know him. He wasn't perfect, but he cared so much about his family and his work."

Her mother had endured so much to hold her marriage together. She could see now why Cindy hadn't liked the man. "Who was Jim Vargas?" Julia asked.

A tear slid down the side of Wendy's cheek. "A good, dedicated man. And that's all I'm going to say. Now you all will have to excuse me."

When she vanished into the house, Andrews stared after her for a long moment. "She's expressing signs of guilt."

"Agreed," Novak said.

"For the affair?" Julia asked.

"Or something much worse," Novak said.

CHAPTER
TWENTY-TWO

Saturday, November 4, 2:00 p.m.

Novak didn't like leaving Julia at the Thompson house, but she'd insisted she wanted to stay longer. She'd find her own way back.

Too restless to go home, he went by the office and found a note from Riggs. He'd located Charlotte Gibson, Rita Gallagher's former roommate. The woman now used the last name Cramer and lived south of the city. She was married and the mother of two. Novak snatched up the note and drove across town.

Thirty minutes later, he parked in front of a two-story colonial house. The yard was cut and edged; the leaves were raked in a large pile at the curb.

He rang the bell, then stepped back and off to the side. He'd picked up the habit as a uniformed officer, learning early in his career that routine could turn deadly in a blink. He'd witnessed an officer being shot through a door while serving a warrant.

The door opened to a short, heavyset woman. She wore jeans and a gray sweatshirt and had pulled her hair into a ponytail. Impatience in her gaze suggested he'd caught her on her way out.

"Mrs. Cramer?"

"That's right."

He held up his badge. "Detective Novak with the Richmond Police."

Her brows rose with worry. "Is everything okay? My husband? The kids?"

"They're fine, ma'am, and I'm sorry if I alarmed you. I'm investigating a murder case."

"Murder."

"Rita Gallagher?"

"Rita." She shook her head slowly. "I haven't heard her name in years."

"Do you mind if I ask you about her?"

She checked her watch. "I need to join my husband at my son's soccer practice in twenty-five minutes, but I have a little time."

She pushed the door open, allowing him into a meticulously clean and organized living room decorated in a colonial style. The walls were filled with pictures of kids ranging in age from infancy up to high school. She extended her hand to a wingback chair, and she settled on the edge of a couch.

"You and Rita were roommates?" he asked.

"Yes, how did you know?" She shook her head. "I was still single then and hadn't met my husband yet."

He sat and removed his notebook from his breast pocket. "We located Rita through the address on her driver's license. That led to the apartment complex, and they gave us your name."

"Maple Tree Apartments. That takes me back. I had a lot less responsibility in those days. Can't remember what it's like to kick back by a pool and drink wine on a Saturday. Why're you asking about Rita?"

"Her remains were found Sunday night, but judging by the receipts we found on her, we think she's been dead since November of '92."

"She's dead?" Charlotte shook her head. "When she first vanished, I was so mad at her. She stiffed me on the rent for several months. I ate peanut butter sandwiches so I could make good on the entire rent. I kept expecting to hear from her. I knew she could be a free spirit, but she always turned up eventually."

"Did you file a missing persons report?"

"No. I thought she and her boyfriend, Jack, took off for good. She always talked about living at the beach with him. Rita fully expected him to marry her."

"But," he said, sensing her hesitation.

"He was married, I think. I met him once or twice. Charming and attractive, but a little aloof. I assumed he was hiding a wife and kids."

"When was the last time you saw Jack?"

"Well, I had a big party to celebrate a new job, and he came by. She had begged him to come and was thrilled when he walked in."

"Do you have his last name?"

"No. That's what always bothered me. He was just Jack."

"Do you have any pictures of him?"

"I might from that party. I'm a scrapbooker, and I know I have stuff from then."

"May I see it?"

She glanced at her watch. "Sure. Be right back." She vanished through a set of double doors and was gone less than a couple of minutes when she returned with a bright-red leather-bound book. She laid it on the table and opened it, flipping through detailed pages until she reached the page decorated with balloons and marked "First Real Job." She tapped on two images. "That's Rita, and in the other picture is Rita with Jack."

Novak studied the face of the woman who looked like the one in the driver's license he'd found with her body. His attention shifted to the boyfriend. He was tall with thick blond hair that brushed his shoulders, but his face was turned partly away, ensuring the camera didn't catch his face. "Mind if I snap a picture with my phone?"

"Go ahead. And I have the negatives." After he took a picture she flipped to the back and tugged out a packet of negatives. She found the corresponding strip and handed it to him. "Keep it."

"Thank you." He thought about Andrews's facial recognition scanner. If Jack was in the system, Andrews was the man to find him.

"How did she die?"

"She was struck in the head with a blunt object and perhaps suffocated."

Unconsciously her fingers rose to her mouth. "That's terrible."

"When was the last time you saw her?"

"It was only a few days after my party. October 30. Funny I should remember that. The rent was due the next day, on Halloween, and she asked if I could cover her portion until the middle of the following week when she was paid. It took every penny I had to do it, but she swore she'd get me the money. She was a waitress in a bar then, and I knew she made good tips and was good for the money."

"Did she need financial help often?"

"It was always close with her when it came to the rent, but she managed to make it."

"What was Rita like?"

"Fun girl. When she was around, it was always a party. The guys loved her."

"Anything else about her boyfriend, Jack?"

"He was nice enough. She catered to him. Did whatever he said. Do you think he killed her?"

"I don't know. I'm chasing all the leads I can now."

She frowned. "I did find drugs in the toilet tank after that party. It was the middle of the night. And the toilet wouldn't stop running. I lifted the lid and found a white bag. I'd never seen the drugs before, but it didn't take a chemistry degree to figure it out. I asked her about it, but she swore she didn't know anything. Someone at my party must have stashed it there. When I told her I was calling the cops, she begged me not to. She said she had been arrested before and didn't know how the cops would take this discovery or who would come after them."

"What did you do with the drugs?"

"I flushed them down the toilet. I was terrified of having that in my apartment."

"Did you know about her arrest record?"

"No. I didn't. In fact, I was really upset about it. I don't think I'd have roomed with her if I'd known."

He found the picture of Jim Vargas with a young Julia on his phone and showed it to her. "Did you ever see this guy before?"

"No, but I've seen this picture. I remember finding it in her nightstand. It was a few days before she disappeared. It was on her nightstand."

"Did she ever say who the picture was of?"

"Said it was another guy she was dating and his kid."

"She was seeing someone else other than Jack?"

"Like I said, the guys liked her."

"Can you think of anyone else who I can talk to about Rita?"

"She worked at a restaurant called Billy's. I think it's still in business."

"I've spoken with the owner. Any other friends?"

"There was one woman named Rene. They went out a lot. But I never got a last name."

She was the second person to confirm that Rene Tanner and Rita had been friends. He thanked Charlotte for her help, left his card, and slid behind the wheel of his SUV. As he turned the ignition, his phone rang. "Novak."

"Natasha Warner. I have some forensic results for you."

"I'll be right over."

***

Novak swung by Natasha's office. He found her hunched over a shirt laid out on a light table.

"You got something?"

Natasha pushed away from the table. "Found DNA at the Lana Ortega crime scene."

"And?"

"The DNA we found on the ropes binding Lana Ortega matches DNA on a similar set of ropes you and Julia Vargas brought in. I believe they were found near her residence."

"Correct, it was a noose left as a calling card for Julia by the back door of Billy's. Are you sure about the DNA match?"

"I was as surprised as anyone when the system came up with a hit, so I retested. After analyzing your sample and the ones from the Ortega crime scene, I'd say with 90 percent certainty they share the same touch DNA."

"Does the DNA sample match any already in the CODIS?" CODIS was the FBI criminal justice DNA database.

"No. But I'm confident that the same person handled both sets of rope."

"Do me a favor. Get these results to a fellow named Garrett Andrews. He works with Shield Security. He's retesting the ropes from the Hangman cases."

"That was twenty-five years ago, Novak. Good luck with that."

"I know. It's a long shot." Novak pulled out his phone and texted Andrews's contact information to Natasha. "Andrews found some hair samples on the clothes of two victims and is retesting."

"Okay."

"Have you gotten any hits on the Rita Gallagher crime scene?" Novak asked.

"I pulled several hair fibers from her clothing that don't belong to her. I found a surprising match."

"Who?"

"Jim Vargas."

CHAPTER
TWENTY-THREE

Saturday, November 4, 4:00 p.m.

Julia had made her way back to her place, but was headed out the door again to revisit Ken after his nap when she saw Novak push through the front door of the bar. Oddly, she was glad to see him even though his jaw was clenched. Something was chewing on him.

"Out with it," she said. "Or you're going to grind all your teeth out of your head."

A wry smile tugged at his lips. "Am I that obvious?"

"You are. What happened?"

"The DNA on the rope that you found in the back alley behind Billy's matches DNA found on the ropes binding Lana Ortega's body."

Any lightness was crushed under the weight of worry and anger. "I suppose that shouldn't be a surprise."

"I've asked Natasha Warner to get with Andrews and compare DNA notes. I want to know if the same killer is at work on both ends of the timeline. If so, your father is innocent. If not, a copycat can kill you just as easily as the original killer."

Acknowledging her fear would do her no good. "Of course."

He moved to within a foot of her. He wore a subtle aftershave that she'd come to associate with him. He knew he'd put a lot on her plate, and yet she sensed there was more.

"Hit me with both barrels," she said. "I know there's another shoe to drop."

"A thumbprint was pulled from the inside of Rita Gallagher's pendant. It belongs to your father."

She studied him without any hint of emotion. "And?"

"I also found Rita Gallagher's roommate, Charlotte. I showed her the picture we found in Rita's purse. The picture of you and your father."

"Okay."

"We'll get to the bottom of it."

She looked around the bar that had once felt so familiar and safe to her. Now she felt exposed, vulnerable. "I'm fighting blind, and I know time is running out before he kills again." She hated hearing her voice crack with emotion.

He nodded toward the door. "Get in my car."

"Why?"

"A time-out."

"A what?"

"A break."

"We can take a break upstairs," she said.

"Somewhere else," he said. "Neutral territory."

She didn't have the reserves to argue. "Sure."

In his car, she didn't pay much attention to where they were going. He didn't speak, and neither did she. They ended up in a suburban neighborhood populated by houses that weren't large but looked solid and well kept. Novak parked in front of a two-story white colonial. The yard was neatly trimmed and the leaves raked. Nothing fancy about the gardens, but the beds were edged and mulched.

"Where are we?" she asked.

"My house."

He was bringing her to his home, which for a guy like him meant a new level of commitment. There were so many logical reasons to say no.

Out of the car, Julia shook her head. "Never figured you for a yard guy."

He opened the front door and clicked on the lights. "I can thank my dad for the green thumb. I hated yard work as a kid, but now I find it peaceful."

"Hard to escape genetics."

"But not impossible."

Like the yard, the inside of the house was neat and organized. Everything in its place, unlike the clothes she'd tossed over the chair in the corner of her bedroom, the shoes scattered on the floor next to a pile of laundry looking for some care. The only item out of place was the framed citation he'd received at the awards banquet. It leaned against the wall.

"Why haven't you hung your award?"

"I'll get around to it."

"I never asked why they gave it to you."

"For doing my job."

She laughed. "Novak, spill."

"Last year there was a little girl who went missing for seventy-two hours. Evidence suggested it was a homicide, so I was called in."

She snapped her fingers as some of the events came to mind. "I was working undercover but heard rumblings about that. You found her in an odd place."

"Under the floor."

Now she remembered. The lead detective had narrowed down the address where the girl was found. He and several uniforms, with the suspect in tow, had gone to investigate. They couldn't find the child. The detective had asked for a few minutes of privacy with the suspect. No one argued or asked questions. Five minutes later the detective left the rattled suspect in the squad car and charged back into the house. He pried up the floors and found the little girl bound and gagged. That detective had been Novak.

Well, *damn*, Mr. Clean was a badass. "How'd you get the guy to talk? I heard there wasn't a mark on him."

"I can be convincing."

She followed him toward the kitchen. Bright and clean, of course, it looked out onto a backyard. On the stainless-steel refrigerator were pictures of a young girl. First grade, no teeth, middle school braces, and cap and gown.

"This must be Bella," she said.

"That's my girl." His tone was full of pride and love.

"She doesn't look like you."

"No." An edge sharpened the word. He leaned against the counter, arms folded as he regarded her. "No, she looks like her mother."

"How did her mother die?"

He pushed off the counter and turned to set up the coffee machine. "Suicide. She drove her car into a lake. Bella was strapped in her car seat. It's a miracle someone saw it happen and was able to save Bella."

The news surprised her, but the anger and fear lurking behind his words didn't. She understood the feelings so tightly linked to her own father's death. His frustration over her tendency to hide feelings, especially in light of what he knew about her father, made sense now. "Does Bella remember any of this?"

"I don't think she has direct memories. But she's not fond of water. It was such a chore to get her to take swimming lessons when she was a kid that I backed off."

"She ever learn?"

"She did. I taught her myself."

She let her purse slide off her shoulder onto the polished counter. "For me it's apples. I can't stand apples."

"Why apples?"

"It's the memory I associate with my father's death. Apparently I used to love them, and he'd filled a bowl with them because Mom and I were coming home. All I remember is his blood on the apples."

"Ken mentioned the note your father supposedly left was lying in the bowl of apples."

"He said it was in the bowl of apples?" She shook her head. "As many times as I've remembered that moment and those apples, I never remembered a note."

"A traumatic event like that can do things to a person's memory."

"I suppose." She leaned her hip against the counter. "And for the record, no matter how bad it's gotten for me, I've never considered Jim's option. Not for a second. What about Bella?"

"Never," he said.

"Good."

He filled a filter with coffee, then poured water into the back of the machine and hit "Brew." "So Jim's excited about your return home. Buys apples. Writes a note. And then shoots himself with a hollow point?"

She was silent.

"Doesn't make sense. A guy who loved his kid, but then sticks a suicide note in the gift he bought especially for her?"

She pressed her fingers against her eyes. "I don't want to think about it anymore today."

He poured her a cup of coffee. She reached out to accept it, and their fingers brushed. Tension and energy snapped like a live wire. Her gaze lifted, and his expression derailed her train of thought. Desire sparked.

She set the coffee cup on the counter. She was here now, standing close to a man who looked ready to devour her.

His body looked relaxed as he leaned against the counter. What gave him away besides his face was the white-knuckle grip he had on the counter.

"Looks like you could snap that countertop," she said.

He glanced at his fingers and slowly released his grip. "I'm not good at waiting, but I'm trying not to rush you."

"Again treating me with kid gloves. Look, something bad happened to me, but I'm not broken."

He brushed her hair from her face. "You're definitely not broken."

"Are you sure about that?"

He pushed off the counter and gently cupped her face. The calluses on his fingertips made her skin tingle. "Very."

She pressed her lips against his. Tension rippled through his body as he leaned into the kiss. Her desire growing, she pressed her breasts to his chest and wrapped her arms around his neck. His hands slid to her waist. His erection pressed against her. She knew it took all his discipline for him to hold back. And she loved him for it.

Julia deepened the kiss, her desire for him fanning the flames. "I'm not delicate, Novak."

"I'm very aware of that," he growled.

She kissed him again, and this time she felt his fingers fist around the folds of her shirt.

"Do you have a bedroom?" she asked breathlessly. "Or are you a kitchen-counter kind of guy?"

A chuckle rumbled in his chest. "I'm an anywhere-you-want-it guy."

"Bedroom, now."

He leaned in, his hands on her hips, and kissed her again. Then, taking her by the hand, he pulled her up the stairs to the master bedroom.

He didn't turn on the light, allowing the waning afternoon sunshine trickling in through the blinds to guide him. "You sure about this?"

"I am." She unhooked her weapon and badge from her belt and set them on the dresser. He did the same. She kicked off her shoes, unfastened her pants, and stepped out of them. He watched her undress down to her bra and underwear before he closed the distance and cupped her breast. He kissed the hollow of her neck.

"This feels so good," she said.

"I'm only getting started." He tugged his tie and then quickly pulled it free. Her long fingers unfastened his buttons, and he shrugged off his shirt. She ran her hands over his T-shirt. "Please tell me you don't iron your undershirts."

While kicking off his shoes, he pulled the T-shirt over his head, revealing the flat belly that she still couldn't resist touching. He slid the strap of her bra off her shoulder and kissed the top of her breast. With him, she never felt the anger and fury that Benny had unleashed when he'd touched her.

She slipped off her panties and stood naked before him.

He tugged her toward the bed, sitting on the edge. His erection pulsed against her, and the overwhelming desire she'd thought had died elbowed aside all her fears as she took control.

She knelt in front of him and ran her hand across his pants zipper. He reached to unfasten his belt buckle, but she brushed his hand aside. She was in charge. She unfastened the buckle and slid the zipper slowly down while looking into Novak's eyes. She pulled his pants down and freed his erection. Slowly, she sucked. He moaned with pleasure as she slid her mouth along the shaft. He ran his fingers through her hair. When he groaned as if he might release, she playfully pushed him back on the bed.

"In the nightstand," he said.

She opened the drawer and found the packet of condoms. She tore open the wrapper, and with trembling hands, slid it over him.

He lay back on the bed and moved to the center. She climbed on top of him and slowly lowered herself onto him. He hissed in a breath but didn't rush her as she adjusted to the sensations bombarding her body. This was good. This was so good.

His hands slid up her flat belly to her breasts and then her shoulders. He pulled her toward him and kissed her. One hand gripped her buttocks, and then he banded a hand around her waist and rolled her on her back.

She stilled, wondering if she could handle this. His erection pulsed against her clitoris.

Sensing her stillness, he raised his face and studied her closely. "You okay?"

"Let's take it slow this time."

He rose up on his elbow, then slowly pressed back inside her. The sensation was different but good. He pressed in to the hilt and held steady. His fingers brushed her center, and she hissed in a breath as a bolt of desire rushed her senses.

"You're pretty good at this, Novak." Her voice was so breathless she barely recognized it.

A smile curved the edge of his lips. "I like to think so." He drew circles and moved in and out of her. Involuntarily she arched into his touch and gripped his buttocks. She lost track of how long he touched and caressed her. He brought her to the brink several times, but each time backed off. By the time he pushed into her, she was throbbing with need. Cupping his face, she kissed him, tilting her hips up so she could take all of him.

When her release came, she arched and moaned, letting loose tension and fears that had been building for years.

"Good?" he whispered close to her ear.

"Better than good."

He moved inside of her, driving her back into the mattress. He came and collapsed against her. He lay on top of her, their hearts beating furiously.

He rolled on his back beside her. Neither spoke as they caught their breath.

"Thanks, Novak. I needed that." She laughed.

***

Ken arrived at the city jail after visiting hours. He'd not been here in over a year. Wendy would be pissed when she found out he'd taken the car out alone, but assuming he got back safely, he'd deal with her then.

He moved up to the front desk and grinned at the guard as he pulled out his badge that he'd broken out of the shadow box the department had given him when he retired. He didn't recognize the guy and hoped they'd never met. He didn't need a lot of time here, but he needed to get inside.

The deputy glanced at the badge. "What can I do for you, Detective?"

"I'd like to talk to one of your inmates. Won't take long. Just pulling together details."

"Sure. Who?"

"Benny Santiago."

"Sure. Might be a minute. Get checked in and I'll buzz you in at the door."

He did as told, and when the door buzzed, he moved through it, realizing how much he missed the job. Retirement hadn't been optional. It sucked. He settled in an interview room, asking the guard not to tape the session.

He sat in his chair and leaned back as if he had all the cards in a high-stakes game. He tugged at his cuffs and then the front of his jacket, which had gotten tight in the last year.

The door opened, and a shackled Benny Santiago was ushered into the room. The deputy locked the prisoner's handcuffed hands to a metal ring secured to the table.

The dealer showed no emotion. That was the way guys like Benny played it. Show nothing. But Ken knew the gears in the dealer's head were spinning as he tried to figure out what the hell was going on.

Benny slouched back in his chair. "What do you want?"

Ken waited until the guard left. "To see you. And to let you know that I'm the guy who's going to kill you."

That prompted a grin. "Really? How you gonna do that, old man?"

"Won't have to raise a finger," Ken said. "See, I was in the game a long time. Made a lot of connections, both friends and enemies."

"There a point to this?"

"I know the prison where they're sending you. I made calls and asked a few of my buddies who work there if they could spread the word about you."

The grin faded. "What have you done?"

He was old, his memory abandoning him more each day, but there was still enough left of him to hurt this bastard. "By the time you arrive, the right people will know you sold them out for a reduced sentence."

"I didn't tell no one shit."

"Benny, that's not what they're hearing. These very nasty guys think you snitched like a little bitch."

"Fuck you."

Ken didn't flinch. In this moment, he felt like his old self, and it felt fucking good. "No, pal, fuck you."

"Why you doing this?"

"You made a mistake when you hurt Julia Vargas."

"I didn't know she was a fucking cop."

"Doesn't matter. You did, and now you will pay." Chuckling, Ken stood and moved to the door.

Benny's chains rattled against the ring and he tried to jerk them free. "You can't do this!"

"It's done. You're a dead man."

"I'll tell. They'll come after you."

"Maybe the cops will. But I don't give a shit. I got nothing to lose, Benny."

***

Novak liked seeing Julia in one of his white shirts, which skimmed her long, tanned legs. He'd slipped on gym shorts. A frozen pizza cooked in the oven as she sipped coffee.

"So, what have you heard about what happened with me and Santiago?" she asked.

Novak sensed she was trying to figure out if she could trust him with more than her body. He pushed aside a surge of pure outrage over what he now suspected Santiago had done to her. "I heard it was rough."

"Yeah, it's common knowledge he beat the hell out of me. It took several weeks for the bruises and cracked ribs to heal."

He was silent as he waited for her to keep talking.

The word she'd yet to utter made her flinch. "A friend of mine is a forensic nurse at a local hospital. I saw her the next day. She did the full work-up, including evidence collection. Her unit will hold the evidence for two years in case I decide to use it. Other than a bad memory or two, he gave me no other nasty extras."

Without saying the word, she'd admitted to him what happened.

"Why didn't you press charges?"

"I couldn't handle my coworkers seeing me as a victim. The beating was bad enough. The other would have made it unbearable."

He closed the gap between them and wrapped his arms around her. She stiffened and pulled away. He let her go, dropping his arms.

She ran a trembling hand through her hair. "I'm not a victim, Novak."

"You're certainly not."

She hesitated. "I've never been good at intimacy. And what happened in Virginia Beach didn't help."

"You did a good job of it twenty-five minutes ago."

That startled a shaky laugh out of her. "Come on. You know that's different. Sex and intimacy aren't the same thing."

"What we shared, well, let's say it was charged with a lot of emotion."

"Maybe." She shrugged and threaded her fingers through her hair again. "Standing here like this, Jesus, talking . . . it feels far more intimate than I'm comfortable with."

"But you're doing it."

"I've created the impression of intimacy, but is it really there?"

"Who else have you spent time like this with lately?"

She didn't answer.

"Who?"

"No one."

He carefully took her face in his hands. "So this is different."

"Yes," she whispered. Suddenly her gaze glistened with tears. She tipped her head back. "I hate tears. Hate them."

"Why?"

"I saw my mother cry over my father enough times. Tears don't fix problems." And still they filled her eyes. She tipped her head back farther. "I'm getting all girlie on you. When emotions get sticky, it's usually the signal to leave."

"Whose signal?"

"My signal."

"Why leave? It's getting good."

When she tried to pull her head free, he tightened his hold on her face enough so she knew he wanted her to stay, and yet loose enough so if she really wanted to break free, she could.

She drew in a ragged breath. "I don't want to talk anymore. I can't."

Novak kissed her, showing instead of telling her that he wanted her again. "So we don't have to talk."

She wrapped her arms around him, her body pressing against his. "I might stay. If you can convince me it's worth my while."

He was rock hard as he smoothed his hand up under the shirt and cupped her breasts. He knew when he touched her, she wanted him.

He backed her up onto the counter as he pulled a condom from the pocket of his shorts. As he slid it on, she kissed him and opened for him. He pulled her to the edge, freed himself, and with one thrust pushed deep into her. She wrapped her arms around his neck and leaned back.

This time, not able to hold back or go slow, he was faster, more urgent. He needed her to know how much he wanted her. Her body tensed.

"Open your eyes," he said. "See me."

She hesitated, then looked at him.

"If you don't want this, say it." He continued to move inside her. "Tell me what you want."

She didn't speak at first but then whispered, "You."

"I won't hurt you. Ever."

She moistened her lips. And reached for her center as if she simply wanted to lose herself in the sex again.

He grabbed her hand, raised her fingers to his mouth, and kissed the tips. "Do you understand that I'll never hurt you?"

"Couples say that to each other. We're not a couple."

His hand slid under her hair to the back of her neck, and he tugged her closer. He nipped her bottom lip with his teeth. "Us a couple? The thought never crossed my mind."

She opened wider for all of him. "I mean it. Not a couple."

He pressed inside her. "I thought you didn't want to talk."

She didn't argue as her hand slid back to her core and she whispered, "Don't make promises you can't keep."

He captured her hand yet again and halted her race toward orgasm. "We're in this together."

She tried to tug her hand free.

"Tell me you understand," he said.

"Fine. I get it."

"You get what?"

"What I've known all along. You're a good guy. But that has never been the issue."

He released her hand and watched as she began to touch herself again. This time when they came, it was together.

***

Julia dreamed of the pop of gunfire. Bright-red blood splashed on her face and hands. She looked up and saw her father lying in his own blood. The air was sharp with the acrid scent of gunpowder. Behind him stood the monster that vanished when she screamed.

She sat up in bed, swallowing a scream as her heart pounded in her chest. "Shit," she muttered.

Julia pushed her hair out of her eyes, searching for her bedside clock. It wasn't there. She wasn't in her bed. *Where the hell . . .*

Novak clicked on a light. He was awake, alert. "What's wrong?"

She shook her head. "Sorry to wake you."

He smoothed his hand over her rigid spine. "You're shaking."

She pressed her fingertips to her temples, trying to soothe the pounding in her skull. "Just a dream. I can handle it."

He sat up and put his hand on her back. "Does it have to do with Santiago?"

His touch was gentle and strong. Calming. "No. Ironically, I never dream about him and what happened."

"Then what?"

"It's always the same. The day my father died."

"When did the dreams start?"

A silence settled around her, and she couldn't find her voice.

"After the rape?" he asked.

She winced. "Yes."

"What's in the dream?"

"I hear gunfire and smell the gunpowder. There's blood under my feet. And then I see the monster recede into the shadows."

"The monster?"

"No face. No name. Just a shadow. Moving away and vanishing."

"The police report states your mother found your father's body."

"That's what she told me at first. She kept telling me I didn't see anything. But the shrink the department chief made me see after Benny suggested I try hypnosis. It must have opened a door, because that night I had the dream."

"Did you talk to the doctor about the dream?"

"I did. It made no sense to me, but he said Jim's death was so traumatic that it was logical a new trauma would bring it back to the surface."

Absently he rubbed a calming hand against the small of her back. Christ, sex with Novak was becoming a habit, and she was telling him all her secrets. These complications were unwise on so many levels.

Her phone rang, giving her a reprieve. She cleared her throat, but didn't pull away. "Agent Vargas."

"This is Andrews."

She glanced at the clock on her phone. 5:02 a.m. "You're up early, or should I say late?"

"Is this a bad time?"

"Not at all."

"I've traced the sender of the e-mail that contained footage of the original Hangman case."

"Who?"

The mattress shifted as Novak sat up.

"Elizabeth Monroe."

"Santiago's attorney?" she asked, looking at Novak. "That doesn't sound like a mistake she'd make."

"It took some digging. She hid the source information behind some very sophisticated firewalls."

"So why send the video to Carson?" she asked as she tipped the phone so Novak could hear.

"I dug into her past as well as her career. She used to be an attorney at Ricker, Davis & Michaels. That firm defended Alexi Popov in his drug-trafficking trial."

"What does that have to do with the Hangman?"

"I'll let you figure that out." Papers shuffled. "I'll have DNA workups for you today. When can you be here?"

She rubbed the sleep from her eyes. "One p.m. I want to have a chat with Monroe first."

"Tell Novak to join you when you come here."

She glanced at Novak. "Why do you want Novak?"

"He's investigating the case of Rita Gallagher, correct?"

"Yes."

"I might have information for him."

"We'll be there in a few hours."

CHAPTER
TWENTY-FOUR

Sunday, November 5, 8:00 a.m.

Novak studied Julia's rigid features. Her face showed no signs of emotion when they arrived at Monroe's office. Any traces of the emotionally exposed woman he'd seen an hour ago were gone. It was critical to her that the world didn't see any of the vulnerability she'd shown Novak. But as long as she let him in, he could live with that.

Monroe's West End office was sleek and modern with neatly manicured landscaping. The guard at the front desk didn't seem impressed by the badges, and given Monroe's client list, Novak imagined they looked tame in comparison. After a ten-minute wait, another guard appeared and escorted them up to the top floor, where they were placed in a conference room.

An attractive woman dressed in a designer navy skirt and white blouse materialized at the door. "Ms. Monroe will see you now."

The pair followed the woman along a carpeted hallway decorated with original works of art that would have cost more than six months' worth of the entire police department's payroll. They found themselves in a spacious corner office with a large bank of smoked windows overlooking a lake. The furniture was tasteful, expensive, and antique. Sell that and he could put Bella through college and graduate school.

The woman behind the desk wore black, her blond hair combed back into a smooth ponytail. She looked midforties, but a bio suggested she was at least a decade older.

Elizabeth Monroe stood from behind her desk. "Agent Vargas, what a surprise on a Sunday morning."

"Ms. Monroe."

"I wasn't expecting to see you again until I filed Mr. Santiago's appeal."

"I thought so, too."

"And who's this?" Monroe asked, regarding Novak.

"Detective Novak, Richmond City Police," he said.

Her handshake was firm, but her skin cold to the touch. She moved to a stylish upholstered chair and crossed her long legs. "Please have a seat."

Julia glanced at Novak, and he knew she was ready to come out swinging. He moved toward the sofa and sat, hoping Julia would follow his lead. She did.

"What can I do for you two?" Ms. Monroe asked.

"Have you heard about a case called the Hangman?" Novak asked.

"Of course. As part of my preparation for Agent Vargas's testimony in the Benny Santiago trial, I did extensive research. Her father was the lead detective on the case. Some even argued he was the Hangman."

Julia was stoic, but tension radiated from all her muscles.

"You have a reputation for being thorough, Ms. Monroe," Novak said. "You must have viewed some of the original footage taken at the Hangman crime scenes."

She smiled and brushed imaginary dust from her skirt. "I wouldn't have had access to that."

He held her gaze. "You have a few connections in the department."

"All I can say is that I did my due diligence when it came to deposing Agent Vargas." She knitted her fingers together. "What is this about? Cut to the chase."

"Vic Carson, who operates the Hangman fan site, received original footage of the crime scene. He posted it, though it's since been removed."

A delicate brow arched. "How does that relate to me?"

"The e-mail sent to him with the video attachment came from your company's server."

She shook her head, smiling. "I find that very hard to believe."

"We traced it to your firm," Julia said.

Monroe swung her gaze toward Julia. "How, when it never came from this office?"

"A private company with sophisticated software offered to assist," she said.

The smile hardened. "I don't know what you're talking about."

"Of course you do," Julia said. "Why'd you send the video to Vic Carson? Why do you care about the Hangman case?"

Monroe remained silent.

Novak followed up. "Have you heard about Lana Ortega?"

Her focus remained locked on Julia. "I did hear about her death. That's unfortunate. Ms. Ortega was one of your informants, and my sources told me you took a very personal interest in her. You thought you could save her."

Julia's expression remained steady. "Some people can't be saved."

"I find it interesting that Lana's death mirrors the Hangman's work," Novak interjected.

The attorney looked genuinely surprised. "What would that have to do with me?"

"We can prove you sent the video to Carson." Julia held up her hand as Elizabeth began to rebut. "For the moment, let's not argue that."

"Your premise is flawed," Monroe said.

Julia continued. "I'm not worried now about how you gained access to the files, only that you did. You used my father's death during my cross-examination to discredit me. It didn't work. But never let a crime go to waste, right? You decided to use the Hangman to clean up a few loose ends. First you sent the video to Vic Carson to stir up interest in the old case. People might think the Hangman saw the video and it sparked his desire to kill again. And then you used the Hangman to deal with Lana Ortega."

"Why would I do something so foolish? My case will soon be on appeal. For now, the commonwealth won, and Mr. Santiago is going to prison until I win the appeal."

"Benny Santiago has a long memory," Julia said. "What better way to get back at the girlfriend who talked too much than to have his attorney kill her? What better way to rattle me than to kill her like the Hangman?"

Novak admired Julia's cool, direct tone. He knew this case was emotionally charged for her, but her theory was logical and on point.

Monroe was silent for a moment before responding. "These theories are interesting, but I don't have any more time to waste on conjecture." She rose. "Thank you for stopping by."

Novak remained seated, willing to run with Julia's theory. "Now that I know where to dig, there's going to be no stopping me. I'm going to prove you had Lana Ortega killed."

Monroe's gaze sharpened. "I did not have that woman killed."

"The evidence is telling a different story," Julia said.

Monroe pointed a manicured finger toward the door. "You need to leave now."

Novak relaxed back into his chair as if he had all the time in the world.

"Who left the rope outside my house? That you or the person you hired to be the Hangman?" Julia asked.

Monroe reached for her phone. "I'm calling security."

Julia rose slowly. "I'm coming back with a warrant."

Novak, taking his lead from Julia, stood. "Looking forward to seeing you again, Ms. Monroe."

They were escorted back to the main lobby and rode the elevator to the first floor. Outside, the air was crisp and the sky a vivid blue.

Julia exhaled as she reached for her cigarettes. "Do you believe her?"

"She's a hard one to believe," Novak said.

"I hope it isn't true. If she hired someone to copycat the Hangman, that means Jim could still be guilty."

"Or maybe she took a page from her former boss's playbook."

Julia studied him. "You think the Hangman was *hired* to kill those women?"

"Everyone who was murdered had talked to your father. A man like Popov would have assumed they'd snitched on him and shown no mercy."

"But it could still be Jim."

"If it had been Jim, Monroe is the type of shark who would have found a way to use that information for leverage against you by now."

Julia nodded. "I've watched her in court. She painted Benny as a choirboy and tried to make me look unstable. She suggested Jim killed himself because he failed to catch the Hangman."

"And that adds weight to your theory. Monroe reminds everyone that the Hangman escaped justice so that when she had Lana killed in the style of the Hangman, no one would question her or Santiago," Novak said.

They walked to the car, and when they closed the doors, Novak scanned his messages. One from Riggs reported more credit card information on Lana Ortega.

Novak summarized the contents to Julia. "Lana's credit card charges show she visited the same bar a dozen times during Benny's trial. The place is called the Edge and is located six blocks from her downtown hotel. I know it. Mostly folks on business travel with extra cash and a wandering eye."

"We're close. Let's have a look."

It was midmorning, and when they pulled up in front of the Edge, there were few cars parked in front of the brick building. Inside, the round tables and booths were empty. With the lights on, all the scars showed. It would take dim light and a lot of alcohol to create charm here.

He knocked on the bar. "Hello?"

"What can I do for you?" The gravelly voice came from a gray-haired man wearing jeans, a black shirt, and boots. He looked like he would have a Harley parked out back.

Novak held up his badge and introduced himself and Julia. "I'm working a case." He liked to avoid the word *homicide* at first. People had a way of shutting down when he did. "Have you seen this woman? Her credit card receipts said she recently spent a bit of time here."

He looked at the picture. "Sure. That's Lana. She's a fun girl. Always has the guys sitting around her laughing or lusting. She's good for business. I sell more booze the nights she's around."

"Did she spend any time with any one man?" Julia asked.

"She had a lot of men around her," he said. "Like I said, she's hot, and men like that look, especially if they're trashed."

"She was here a dozen times according to her credit card receipts. Any reason in particular?"

"Some of the regulars noticed her. She received lots of attention, and she liked it. Some tried to score, but she wasn't interested. Is this about the other cop?"

"What other cop?" Novak asked.

"He sat beside her on two different nights while I was bartending. The cop said he was working on a case and needed her help."

"What case?"

"I didn't catch what he said. But I did hear her call him Jim once or twice."

"Jim?" Julia asked. "Anything about Jim that you recall?"

He pulled in a breath. "What's going on here? Why do you cops care about Lana?"

"Lana was murdered the other night. I'm looking for her killer."

The bartender tensed. "And you think this cop did it?"

"I'm not sure he was a cop," Novak said.

"I saw his badge. And I've seen enough badges and cops to know when I see the real thing. He was a cop."

"And his name was Jim?" Julia repeated.

"Yes."

Novak opened his notes and scrolled through the pages. "Do you have surveillance footage from Monday night?"

"Yeah, sure."

He turned a page. "I have Lana's last credit card visit here on Monday night at ten p.m. Can I see it now?"

"Sure. Come on in the back."

Novak followed him into an office. He opened a cabinet where the surveillance equipment was stored. The bar owner punched a few buttons on the computer and selected the 10:00 p.m. time stamp. In the far left corner of the image sat Lana at the bar.

"Can you back it up?" Novak asked.

"I have a thirty-day storage backup, so I can make you a copy of all the nights she was here if that will help."

"That would be great."

"Give me a second."

Fifteen minutes later, Novak had digital footage covering seven separate nights.

"I found your guy," the bar manager said. He selected a Thursday night and hit "Forward" to the spot where Lana sat at the bar. She was laughing with another woman, a martini glass raised to her red lips. Blond hair was teased high and fell over her bare back in a cascade of curls. The woman beside Lana, a dark, smoky brunette, wore her hair loose around her shoulders. Her black dress plunged deep in the back.

"Do you know the woman Lana is talking to?" Novak asked.

Julia leaned in and studied the image, frowning but silent.

"I do remember her. Set of tits that every guy in the bar noticed. She called herself Bonnie. Those two acted like old friends and were pretty wasted."

Novak watched the video feed of a man approaching the bar and sitting to the right of Lana. His back was to the camera.

"That's your man," the bar manager said, tapping the screen.

Novak watched as the man ordered a mixed drink and within a few minutes was talking to Lana. She grinned at him. Bonnie was also engaged in the conversation. The man was careful to keep his face turned from the camera so that it never captured a good view.

"Have any idea what they were talking about?" Novak asked.

"No. I was slammed with customers, but I could see all three of them were having a good time. They ended up leaving together. I figured the ladies had set up some kind of date with him."

"Do you have credit card information on Bonnie?"

"Let me look." He punched into the computer. "Yeah. Bonnie Jenkins. Computer doesn't save the credit card number. I remember the guy put a fifty-dollar bill on the bar for his orders. Left a nice tip. Does that help?"

Novak recorded the name in his notebook. "It's a start."

Julia and Novak thanked the bar manager and after leaving their cards stepped outside. Julia drew in a breath. "Andrews can find Bonnie Jenkins quickly."

"Call him."

Julia dialed Andrews's number. When he picked up, she told him what she needed. He asked her to stand by. One minute later he had the address of a motel where Bonnie was staying.

"He's a handy guy to know," Novak said.

"So I'm discovering," she said.

Bonnie's hotel was located on Route 1 about fifteen miles north of the city. The area was known for its run-down motels, drugs, and prostitution. When Julia had been in uniform, she'd assisted local police a couple of times in the area.

Novak drove them to the motel, which was a two-story brick building located behind a gas station and a fast-food restaurant. It was one mile from the interstate, which meant plenty of traffic from truckers and the endless stream of drug dealers and human traffickers who traveled the I-95 corridor.

They made their way to the small office located closest to the parking lot entrance. Novak pushed the front door, allowing Julia to pass before him. The office smelled of stale cigarettes and booze. There was a condom machine to the right and a vinyl sofa patched in several spots with duct tape. Behind the counter stood a reed-thin man with reddish hair and a pockmarked face. They showed their badges to him, but he barely glanced at them.

"I'm looking for Bonnie Jenkins," Novak said. "Is she registered here?"

"Yeah, Bonnie's here." He sniffed, reaching for a cigarette and a lighter. Smoke swirled around his head.

"What room?"

"I can't be giving out customers' room numbers," the manager said.

"I can get a warrant," Novak said.

"And in the meantime, I can have a dozen state police cruisers parked in your lot, lights flashing. That will do a lot for business," Julia said.

"We have reason to think she might be in danger," Novak said. "At the very least, she's a material witness in an active murder investigation." When the manager hesitated, Novak added, "I might slow walk that warrant, so her state police buddies can hang around and meet the neighbors. And when it does arrive, I won't be in a happy mood because of the delay. I hate to think what I'll find in your office if I get the warrant to cover that."

Cigarette dangling from his lips, the manager rose. "No need to get shitty. I'll let you look inside the room." The manager coded a key card for the room and led the way to the elevators.

They walked up the stairs to the second floor, and the manager knocked hard on the paint-chipped door. "Ma'am, it's the management." When there was no answer, he swiped his key and switched on the light.

"Ma'am, it's the management," he said again.

Novak reached past him and pushed open the bathroom door. Makeup was arranged neatly on the counter along with a collection of hairbrushes as well as a straightener and curling iron.

"When is she supposed to check out?"

"Today," the manager said.

Novak edged open the closet and found a half-dozen dresses and several sets of heels. "Has housekeeping been in the room today?"

The manager raised a two-way radio to his mouth. "Housekeeping. Has room 206 been turned over?"

After a pause. "No. Waiting for front desk to confirm checkout."

"Which was fifteen minutes ago," Julia said. "Did she call for a late checkout?"

"No."

"So where is she?" Julia asked.

"You really are going to have to get a warrant before I let you go any further," the manager said. "I could lose my job over this."

Novak flexed his fingers. "I'll be back this afternoon with one." He handed the manager his card. "If she returns, call me. And don't let housekeeping in here."

"Sure," the manager said. "I can do that."

When they were in his SUV, Julia said, "She's met this guy who's likely calling himself Jim Vargas. She might be able to tell us who he is or at least what he looks like." She reached for her phone and called the local sheriff's office. She explained who she was looking for and asked for a deputy to watch the motel for the next couple of hours. "Great. Thanks. Call me if you see her."

Novak checked his watch. "We'll need to hustle to get to Shield by one."

The drive to the Shield office took just under two hours with the light Sunday-morning traffic. During the drive, Novak put out a BOLO—be on the lookout—for Bonnie Jenkins. When they arrived, Andrews met them in the lobby and escorted them upstairs.

"I have the DNA results from the original cases," he said.

"Great."

"Any luck on Bonnie Jenkins?" Andrews asked.

"As of a couple of minutes ago she has not returned to her motel room. She doesn't have a cell phone registered to her, so we aren't able to ping her location. But we have local cops watching out for her."

"I've kept a flag on her credit card. If she uses it or takes a cash advance, I'll be notified."

"Good."

Andrews pressed several buttons, and a large screen behind him illuminated. Pictured were the three Hangman victims of '92. "DNA was found on the clothes, which were left in piles at the crime scenes. We pulled hair fibers from two of the three victims. One was from Tanner's and one from Wayne's clothes. The original team did an excellent job, and it's unfortunate those samples were ruined. However, I could confirm that the hair fibers I found were from the same individual."

"That's not a big surprise," Novak said.

"Yes, we expected those results." Andrews clicked a button, and the images on the wall switched to Rita Gallagher's picture. "But what was a nice surprise was a match to the fibers found on Rita Gallagher's body."

"What about the DNA found on Lana Ortega's clothes?" Julia said.

Andrews's eyes sparked with what could be called excitement for him. "It matched what I found on the Tanner, Wayne, and Gallagher bodies."

"The same man killed all five women?" Julia asked. "Which means, Jim wasn't the Hangman?"

"Correct," Andrews said.

Julia stood very still, drawing in a breath and releasing it slowly. She tipped her head back, rubbing the side of her neck. "Shit."

Novak could see Julia wrestling with her emotions as she kept her head tipped back and balled her fingers into a fist. Julia's father had been vindicated.

If they'd been alone, he'd have pulled her into his arms and congratulated her on her good work. But they weren't alone, and he knew she needed to stay in control.

"So why the change in tactics for Rita Gallagher if it's the same murderer?" Novak asked, deliberately speaking to give Julia a moment to recover. "She was hit on the head and tucked away in a root cellar where no one could easily find her."

"I can't tell you that," Andrews said. "But this is a very meticulous killer. Each time he killed, he planned and executed like a professional."

"No plan with Rita," Novak said. "He wasn't planning on killing her. Something happened. She figured out who he was or discovered something she shouldn't have."

Julia cleared her throat as she stared at the picture of the redhead projected on the screen. "What are we missing here? Maybe she was working with the Hangman."

"Explain," Novak said.

"She'd dated Popov, and then she starts working in Billy's and gets access to people in Jim Vargas's life. He was the cop who brought down Popov. Rita told her brother she had a big job coming up. She seduces Jim. She steals a picture of Jim and me. We know she made friends with the victims. Maybe it was her job to lure those women to the Hangman."

"What better way to get rid of three women who consorted with an undercover cop," Novak said. "They become the target of a serial killer."

"The presence of sandwich particles at the original crime scene suggests the killer broke for a snack," she said. "He was on the job and took a lunch break."

"The Lana Ortega killing was as public as the first three," Novak said. "Monroe knows who the Hangman is. Somehow she found out about him from her days at Ricker, Davis & Michaels. She decided to use the Hangman to kill Lana. Then she found another use for the killer."

Julia finished his thought. "To come after me."

***

Elizabeth Monroe's Sunday was going to hell fast, and if she wasn't careful, she'd have a lot more bad days ahead of her. As she stood on the steps of this elegant house, she knew it was time for her to cut her ties with the past and forget she'd ever read about the Hangman in her late boss's files.

She glanced back at her SUV, wishing she had brought her driver. But no one could ever know what she was doing today. She slid her hand into her coat pocket and wrapped her fingers around the grip of the unregistered .38 snub-nose revolver pulled from a crime scene decades ago.

She knocked on the door. Footsteps sounded on the other side of the door, and she straightened, tightening her hand on the strap of her purse. The door opened to a towering man with white hair. He was handsome and well dressed with the build of a onetime collegiate athlete trying to fight time's effects on his joints. He'd asked her to meet him here.

"We need to talk," she said. "The cops are getting close."

"Getting close to you?"

"If they get me, they will get you."

"The cops don't scare me."

"What about the Popov family? I've had some interesting conversations with them lately."

His expression grew harder. "What did you say to them?"

She considered shooting him in the doorway but thought of security cameras or prying eyes from some distant neighbor walking his dog. If not for the files she had on him, she'd be afraid of what he'd do to her. But he knew if anything happened to her, the cops would find out about him. And once the Hangman secret was out, the Popov family would be forced to handle him like they did anyone who failed them.

Monroe stepped inside. He stood silent, staring at her. He could be vicious, but she'd made a career controlling men like him. His usefulness had passed, and she was anxious to get rid of him and close this chapter.

As her hand slid into her coat pocket, a smile flickered across his face. It was a stupid smile. Her fingers tightened around the gun's grip.

His smile vanished, and his eyes grew hard. She sensed the shift, and as she yanked the gun from her coat, he pulled a knife from his pocket. With the lightning reflexes of a snake, he jabbed the sharp tip through her side and into her lung. She stumbled back and steadied the gun. Pain rocketed up her side as she took aim. He moved easily out of her line of sight as she fired. He knocked the gun out of her hand, and she staggered to the side and against the wall. Breathing was nearly impossible now. She stared at the spot of blood moistening her silk blouse.

"Why?" she stammered.

"I knew from the beginning you were going to try something like this. Takes a snake to recognize a snake." He picked up the gun and tucked it in his waistband. "I haven't survived this long without over-thinking every scenario."

"If I don't make it back, you'll be exposed," she said as she pressed a trembling, blood-soaked hand to her midsection.

"I don't give a shit about that anymore." He hauled her forward. Her knees buckled, but he held her steady. "I have one more job to do, and then I'm free of all my debts." He grinned. "Even if you hadn't tried to kill me today, I'd have killed you anyway."

"You'll go to prison."

He pressed the barrel of the gun to her temple. "I won't."

Her gaze met his. Pain and fear stripped her confidence, leaving only desperation. "I have money."

"I've been paid enough already. I only need you."

She could feel her life draining away. "Why?"

"You're an important piece of the puzzle now. Not only will my debts be paid, but anyone who knew me as the Hangman will be dead."

"What does that mean?" she asked.

"I need bait for the trap, and you're it." Blood dripped on the floor and on her leopard-print shoes.

***

Novak's gaze settled on Julia. As she reached for the car door handle, he grabbed her hand and gently pulled her toward him. "We'll figure this out."

She studied him close.

"I need to talk to Ken," Julia said. "He's the last real link to my father and the case."

"And you've called his house twice and left two messages. We'll catch up with him within the next few hours and get to the bottom of the note." He kissed her. "I'll call you soon."

Novak watched her climb the back staircase and vanish into her apartment before he pulled out of the alley. En route to his office he received a call from Riggs.

"We found Bonnie Jenkins," he said.

"Where?"

"In a bar on Southside. She's at the station now. We're giving her coffee and food to sober her up."

"Great. Don't let her leave until I get there."

Blue lights flashing all the way, he made it to police headquarters in fifteen minutes. He found Riggs standing outside an interview room, his hands in his pockets.

"How's she doing?" Novak asked.

"She's still drunk but making more sense."

"Have you asked her about Lana?"

"Nope. Thought I'd save that conversation for you."

"Let's do it." Inside the small interview room, he found Bonnie Jenkins in a chair hunched over a metal table. Her hands cradled a cup of coffee, and beside her was a partly eaten doughnut. When he closed the door, she looked up.

Her skin was pale, her eyes heavily made up. Her tousled hair was brown, and one false eyelash was coming loose. She wore a red dress with spaghetti straps and a tight bodice.

"Bonnie," Novak said.

"Why am I here? I've been drunk in public before, and I've never been brought to a room like this."

He pulled up a chair beside her. He didn't want the table separating them or her thinking he was the enemy. "I'm hoping you can help me."

She sniffed and straightened. "With what?"

"You know Lana Ortega?"

"Sure, Lana. We partied together a few times. Where is that bitch, anyway?"

"She's dead," Novak said, matter-of-fact.

Bonnie blinked and sat back in her chair. "What?"

"She was murdered a few nights ago. You may be in danger, so we want your help."

"Shit. How?"

"Hanged, suffocated, and carved on. Very gruesome and not done quickly."

"That's messed up. Was it a john?"

"We don't know yet, but I don't want him finding you."

"I haven't seen her since Monday."

"You and Lana met another cop in the Edge bar. Do you remember him?"

"Yeah. Jim. He bought us a few rounds of drinks."

"What did Jim look like?"

"Like a cop. Okay-looking. Suit. Typical cop."

"If I had a sketch artist sit down with you, could you describe Jim?"

"Did a cop kill Lana?"

"We don't think he was a cop, but I have to be sure. Will you work with me?"

"Yeah, sure."

"What did Jim talk to you and Lana about?"

"He was more into her than me. Said she was his type. She loved the attention to flirt, but it never got serious with anyone."

"Did he talk to you?"

"A little. But he was always more interested in Lana." Her brow wrinkled with a frown. "When Lana left the bar that night, he left with her."

"They say where they were going?"

"Another bar."

"Was it Billy's?"

"Maybe. I'm not sure."

"Did either one of them return to the bar?"

"I don't know. I hung around a little longer and then found someone else to party with."

"Okay. Drink up that coffee, and I'll get the artist."

"Could I get a chocolate doughnut? Not crazy about the sprinkles."

"Sure. Anything you want."

***

"I don't like the name *Hangman*," he said as he coiled the rope around Ms. Monroe's neck and secured it tight. "No imagination. I put time and effort into the knots, and no one appreciates the effort."

Monroe stared at him, her eyes wide and full of fear, her voice silenced by the rag in her mouth secured with a strip of duct tape. She struggled to breathe with only one good lung now.

He ran the strand of rope around her wrist and secured it to a pole that crossed over her shoulder blades. Both her arms were now stretched out into a T. The pole was suspended by another rope that stretched up and over a rafter in the ceiling of the garage behind the main house.

"I like this setting. Perfect place for our party." He removed the duct tape and pulled the rag from her mouth.

"Please," she said.

"It takes planning to make these scenes work. It's not just tying knots. And honestly, it was never about the money."

She looked at him, her brown eyes bright with tears. A moan rumbled in her throat.

He moved back to his bag and pulled out another length of rope. Winding each end around his fists, he tugged. He knew it was strong, but also knew she was watching. Little things like this could ratchet up the terror. "You understand this is not personal," he said as he approached her. "It's that you fit the criteria, which is important to the endgame. Without the right trail of bread crumbs, I won't catch the right bird."

"What are you talking about?" she whispered.

"Julia Vargas. She's the prize."

"Killing a cop . . . you're overplaying your hand."

A grin tipped the edge of his lips as he looked at the ropes in his hands. "I'm not always logical, if you haven't noticed."

"Why her?"

"Partly because it's a job. Partly because she thought she could catch me, like her old man. She needs to know she can't. Like you need to know you can't control me."

He wrapped the rope around her neck, and she closed her eyes. Tendons tightened and bulged. He secured the rope at the base of her neck, then began to wind it around and around until it formed a high collar that brushed the underside of her chin.

"It might not feel tight now, but once I suspend you, your good lung won't be able to take in air as well. The angle combined with the rope is going to take its toll. You would suffocate in a matter of hours. The best you can do is relax into your bindings and allow death to release you. Struggling brings only more pain and worry."

He moved to the rope looped around a large hook and began to pull. She rose up on tiptoes, and her little pink-painted toes fluttered above the ground. A sound gurgled in her throat. He watched as her feet kicked. When her eyes rolled back in her head, he slackened the rope and allowed her body to crumple to the floor.

"Don't. Please," she gasped. "I can pay."

He crouched beside her, watching the color return to her pale face. "I have no doubt you could pay me more. But you must know that this stopped being about money a long time ago." He stared up at the rafters. "I'm running out of places to display my work, so I guess this is going to have to be a private collection."

She moistened her lips; her gaze steadied on him. "I'll get you whatever you want."

He pulled the rope taut, forcing her to rise up on her knees, her feet, and then her tiptoes. "Nothing you have that I want—well, except for your life."

"Please," she rasped.

He jerked hard on the rope. It tightened around her neck, cutting into the flawless white flesh, and she gagged as her feet rose up off the ground again. She was now suspended several feet above the ground. He tied off the rope and stepped back, savoring the twitching and jerking of her muscles as they begged for oxygen.

Such a rush!

CHAPTER
TWENTY-FIVE

Sunday, November 5, 7:00 p.m.

"Found a few videotapes that might be of interest," Cindy said to Julia as she came down the back stairs to the bar.

"What tapes?"

"Found them in storage at my house. They were taken of your parents and you. Looks like your birthday party."

Julia eyed the three dusty tapes sitting on the edge of the bar. "I haven't seen these before, have I?"

"I don't think you have. When your mom showed up with you after your father died, she had lots of boxes that I shoved anywhere I could find. I found these tapes in the back top closet under a stack of blankets. Like I said, I have stuff squirreled all around there."

Julia set her purse beside the tapes and carefully picked one up. One was marked "Julia's 7th Birthday." The others were not labeled. "Do you have a player?"

"I do. It's in the back in the cabinet next to the pool table."

"Great. I'll grab it and move it upstairs."

"Don't know what you're going to find. I hope they're still intact."

Julia heard the hesitancy in her aunt's voice. "It's okay. And thank you for these."

"I can sit with you while you watch."

"No, I'm fine."

Cindy rested her hands on her hips. "I've been worried about you since you started all this."

"Why? I've investigated cases before."

"Not involving your father. I know it's been hard to hear people talk about him."

"Actually, it's been therapeutic. Even if some of it wasn't what I wanted to hear. For so long it was like he didn't exist. Now he seems more real."

Cindy's expression turned wistful. "I never realized you wanted to talk about him. You never asked."

"Whenever I brought up his name, it always led to someone being sad or hurt. So I stopped."

Cindy reached out and took Julia's hand. "You can ask me anything you want about your father."

Julia patted her hand. "I've discovered he was one hell of a cop, but a complicated man. I can understand now why you might not have liked him."

"It was hard not to like Jim. He was a charmer with a devil's smile. And your mother loved him with all her heart. And every time he told her he was sorry, I think he really meant it. He couldn't stay put anywhere for long."

"What was it like when he was working undercover?"

"Lonely for your mom. You were so young then. He'd be gone for weeks at a time. I think part of the reason he gave that life up was you. He hated seeing you cry when he left. He gave up undercover to work homicide, and they were happy for a time, but then he started staying out late. He said it was the Hangman case, but Amy had her suspicions."

"Cases like that can eat up a lot of a cop's life. He could have been telling the truth."

"I think it was true at first. He was working long hours with his partner. I gave him the benefit of the doubt. And I know he missed his old job. Once his ex-partner came by the bar, and they must have talked a couple of hours. I thought he was coping with the new life, but one night your mom brought you by the bar and asked if I'd watch you for a few hours. Said she was going for a drive. When she came back, she was crying. She'd been following your father."

"She saw him with another woman?"

"She never would say. Only that you two would be staying above the bar and that she wasn't going back. Jim came by the next day. He was upset. I'd never seen him this upset, but this time he looked broken. Your mother told him she wanted a divorce."

"When was this?"

"Several months before he died."

"What made her decide to go back?"

"Jim Vargas had the devil's charm. He could make anyone like him. And he set his sights on winning your mother back. She said the marriage was over. He said it would never happen again. He told me the same thing, and as much as I knew about the guy, I even believed him. Like I said, the devil's charm."

"And you never found out who he was seeing?"

"No. Didn't matter. If not this girlfriend, it would have been another later. As much as I wanted my sister to be happy, your father was doomed to make her miserable."

"Was it Rita?"

"Could have been. Those two got on well together." She nodded toward the three tapes. "Have a look at those, and if you have more questions, you know where to find me."

"Thanks."

Julia changed into sweats and a T-shirt and then went to the pool-room, where she dug through a cabinet until she found a dusty VCR. In her room she plugged it into the outlet, and after a few minutes of trial and error, had it connected to a small television.

She didn't have a remote, forcing her to pull up a chair close to the television so that she could hit "Play." She chose the video that read "Julia's 7th Birthday," hoping to start with something upbeat. She pushed the video into the machine, and her fingers hovered over the "Play" button before she pressed it. Julia sat back, folding her arms over her chest as the static crackled. Then the image of a backyard popped onto the screen. She knew from pictures that it had been her parents' home. She recognized a tall oak and the gray privacy fence. Her parents had bought the house when her father transferred to homicide. Balloons tied to the back fence wafted gently in the breeze, and in the background a neighbor's dog barked.

In the next frame, a little version of herself ran out into the yard. She was wearing shorts and a blue-and-white-striped T-shirt, and her hair was short and curly. She was laughing, running toward the balloons. The camera panned to the right, and her mother's voice said, *"Today is Julia's big day. She's seven years old."*

Julia hit "Pause" and replayed the section, this time closing her eyes as she listened again to her mother's voice. It had been so long, and she'd forgotten what her mother sounded like. When she looked at the screen again, her mom was panning the camera toward a group near a smoking barbecue grill. There were more children running around, their laughter bubbling up as they played with Julia.

The adults gathered on the small back porch were cops. Some were in uniform as if they'd swung by after or before a shift, and others were in plain clothes. One man had long hair and a thick beard and looked like he belonged on the streets rather than at a kid's birthday bash. Novak had visited her father's former partner and told her of the meeting. She'd bet money that was Nate Unger.

Her father stood at the grill. He held a spatula in one hand and a bottled beer in the other. Beside him were Ken and Wendy. As Julia studied Ken and Wendy, she was struck by the change in appearance of both over the years. Wendy could only be described as hot. She wore her clothes tight and her thick blond hair loose around her shoulders.

Ken looked into the camera. *"Are we going to get the cake?"*

Her mother's laugh drifted from behind the camera. *"Very soon."*

"How about now?" Ken asked. *"Starving."*

"Sure. I think the kids are more than ready."

Julia wished her mother had turned the camera around so she could see her face. Instead, her mother set it down and followed Ken. The footage continued to roll.

Jim Vargas continued to grill and sip his beer while Wendy moved closer to talk to him. As she spoke, too quiet for the camera's microphone, Jim's body tensed. He looked toward her. She tried to touch his hand, but he pulled away. The movements were so small, anyone at the party could have missed their interaction.

She hit "Rewind" and replayed the footage. Wendy reached for Jim. He tensed and pulled away, quickly glancing toward the door.

Ken's voice boomed from behind the camera. *"Birthday girl! We have cake!"*

A gaggle of squealing children ran from offscreen. Wendy put several steps of distance between her and Jim and smiled brightly. The camera rocked and the picture jumped as her mom settled the camera back up on her shoulder. The kids came running toward the cake, and seven-year-old Julia dashed to the head of the table. Jim lit the candles, and everyone sang "Happy Birthday." Wendy snuggled close to Ken, and he kissed her on the cheek. Life went on; the moment was gone. The tape stopped.

***

Julia arrived at the Thompson house after eight. Ken often went to bed early because his meds made him sleepy. Julia was counting on this when she rang the bell. She wanted privacy when she spoke to Wendy.

Wendy came to the door. Her smile was hesitant. "Julia? You all right?"

"Is Ken awake?"

Wendy glanced quickly behind her as if there were a problem. "No, he's asleep for the night."

"Good, I want to talk to you about my father."

"Look, whatever Ken told you about a note is also news to me. I can't help you with that."

"It's not about the note." When she dealt with suspects or witnesses in her professional life, she'd never had trouble asking the hard questions, but she did now. She liked Wendy. Remembered all the times she'd seen her while growing up and how nice the woman had been to her.

"Can we go to the front porch in case Ken wakes?" Julia said.

Wendy stepped out onto the porch. "Now you're making me nervous."

"Sorry. That's not my intent. I found this old video," she said, pulling her phone from her pocket. "It's my seventh birthday. You and Ken were there."

"I remember that party. Such a fun afternoon. It was a lifetime ago."

Julia had taped the video on her phone. She played it for Wendy. "Have a look."

The now-gray-haired woman with a sick husband was transported back to a more joyful time. Julia closely watched Wendy's expression grow strained as the tape played.

"Wendy," Julia said, accepting her phone back. "I couldn't help but notice how close you were to Jim."

"He was Ken's partner. Makes sense we'd be close."

"Being a cop has developed an innate radar in me. I can tell when there's more to the story."

"What do you mean?"

"It's the way you touched his arm and his reaction. You two shared a secret."

Wendy pushed back her bangs with the back of her hand. "You're reading too much into an old video."

"I don't think so." She glanced at the screen and hit "Play." Again the scene of Wendy touching Jim's arm, him flinching and glancing around, played. "He's afraid you two will be seen together by his coworkers, his wife, his daughter. He's worried they'll see something."

"I've been married to a homicide cop for twenty-five years. I know a fishing expedition when I see one."

"I watched that tape a dozen times since my aunt gave it to me an hour ago, and as much as I wanted to find another explanation, I can't."

Wendy rubbed her forearm. "You're being ridiculous."

"Did Ken know? Would his reaction to this video be the same as mine?"

Her lips thinned into a grim line. "Do not bring Ken into this. It wouldn't be fair given his state."

"My aunt suspected Jim was sleeping around again and that's why Mom left him. Some think he was sleeping with Rita Gallagher or Rene Tanner. You never denied you were having an affair with him."

Her brows knotted. "You misunderstand."

"How do I have it wrong?"

"Jim loved your mother, and he adored you. He never would have hurt you."

"I don't think his intention was to hurt my mother or me. He'd been on his own so much while he was doing his undercover work, and he got lonely. Mom accepted what happened between them while they were apart, but when he joined homicide she had dreams of a conventional marriage. But old habits for Jim must have died hard. And he still worked long hours, often side by side with you."

Her face paled. "You have it all wrong."

"It must have been painful for you when he died. I can see that you cared for him."

Tears glistened in Wendy's eyes. "Julia, you need to let the past stay buried. There's no good that will come from it."

"My intent is not to hurt anyone. You worked in close quarters with my father. What happened then?"

She tipped her chin up. "I was good at what I did."

Julia pressed. "You worked side by side with him for months. Long hours. You fell in love and slept with him."

She jabbed a finger at Julia. "I didn't sleep with him."

"But you did love him," she said softly.

"Yes. I loved him. But not how you think. We didn't sleep together."

"Did you love Jim enough to destroy forensic evidence linking him to the murders? You worked in the lab then."

"What?"

"There were whispers for years that Jim was the Hangman. It was the reason he supposedly shot and killed himself. But no one could prove it because the DNA samples from the three murder scenes had been compromised due to improper storage."

Wendy drew in a breath. "What are you saying?"

"Did you destroy evidence to protect Jim?"

"Jim wasn't the Hangman," she said. "Anyone who knew him knew that."

"You didn't answer my question."

"Because I'm not answering that question."

"What were you trying to tell Jim that day? Did you tell him what you found at one of the crime scenes? Did you tell him that you loved him?"

"No!"

"It wasn't idle chatter, Wendy. What was it?"

She clenched her fingers. "I told him Rita was trouble. I was at Billy's to see Amy when I caught Rita coming out of your aunt's office at the bar. I confronted her. She said she was using the phone, but she was lying. I told her to stay away from Jim."

"What did she do?"

"She laughed in my face. Said she could make Jim do whatever she wanted."

"If Rita had a hold on Jim, what did she expect from him?"

"I don't know. But whatever it was, it wasn't good. Men didn't see her as the manipulator she could be. What you saw in that tape was me telling Jim to watch his back with her."

"Her autopsy revealed she was pregnant. Maybe this was all about the baby."

Wendy frowned. "I didn't know about the baby."

Rita had been nearly twenty weeks along and had hidden her pregnancy. Julia didn't speak, sensing Wendy had more to tell.

Wendy rubbed her hand over the back of her neck. "Rita knew Jim and Amy were struggling. They'd never really had a traditional marriage, and they were discovering it was harder than they thought to live a normal life. Rita wanted Jim to herself. She was fun and so exciting. And she was good at twisting him around her finger. He was such a fool. There were times I thought she took the job at Billy's just to be close to Jim."

"Did he remember her from his undercover days?"

"With a body like that, do you think any man would have forgotten her?"

So Rita had intentionally come back into Jim's life? "Rita told all her friends she had a boyfriend named Jack. Is that true?" Julia asked.

"If Jack was actually real, I never saw him." She touched her fingers to her temple. "When Ken told me Jim was dead, Rita was the first person I thought of."

"Why?"

"She didn't like hearing no. I could picture her losing her temper. Ken went to look for her, but she had vanished."

"So who killed her?"

***

Julia stood on the street in front of the house where Rita Gallagher's body had been found a week ago. Yellow crime-scene tape was strung across a rotting wooden front door. The floor-to-ceiling windows by the door had been broken by the fire department and were now boarded up with plywood. Several signs planted across the front lawn warned that this house was an active crime scene and not to be entered.

"What was your angle, Rita?" Rita, like Jim, had known the Hangman victims. Had she taken the job at Billy's to meet Jim and perhaps be close to the other victims? "Was it your job to lead those women to the Hangman? Did Jim figure out what you were doing? Did you kill him?"

Across the street, a door creaked open and then shut. Julia turned to see an old woman easing herself into a chair on her front porch. The woman waved her over.

Glancing both ways, she crossed the street and stopped at the base of the concrete steps. Rows of potted plants were crammed on the front porch around the woman's chair. Once painted a fresh white, the porch had grayed and chipped, and the Astroturf that covered the cement front steps curled up at the edges. A security door covered the historic wooden door. Bars protected the first-floor windows.

"Yes, ma'am."

"You're police."

"Yes, ma'am. Agent Julia Vargas with Virginia State Police."

"Etta Greene." She adjusted her glasses and squinted. "You're here about that body the police found the other day?"

"I am."

"Thought so. You have that look."

Julia smiled. "I'll take that as a compliment."

"You have an air about you. Like you're in charge."

Julia nodded. "What can I do for you?"

"The cops came by the other day and were knocking on doors and asking questions. I wasn't here, but I still have the card from Detective Novak."

"He and I are working the case and need all the help we can get. How long have you been in this house, Mrs. Greene?"

"Seventy years. My folks moved here when I was a child."

"That's saying a lot. I bet you've seen some changes in this area."

She picked at the folds of a white crocheted shawl. "It was a nice place when we moved in. A real community. And then the area went downhill bad and stayed down for the longest time."

"I never policed this area when I was in uniform, but I heard stories. Happy to see the new development coming back."

"And young families. We're getting more and more young families." She adjusted the folds of a thick purple housecoat. "It's good to hear the laughter of children again."

Julia glanced at the house across the street. "You heard about what we found in that house the other day?"

"I arrived home from my grandson's this afternoon, but I heard."

"We think the woman found in that house died about twenty-five years ago."

"The early nineties," she said, more to herself. "I remember that time. My mother was real sick, so I had to quit my job for a time and was home a good bit."

Julia rested her hand on her hip. "You remember what was going on with that house at the time?"

"Like a lot of houses on this block, it was home to druggies and homeless people. Some of those houses closer to the river were getting fixed up, but not this street. It was rough. I didn't dare go out at night. Mr. William Delany owned that house in the early nineties, and after he died he left it to his son. I saw the son, Marcus, a lot. Came and went around the clock. He'd show up at odd hours. Carrying boxes. Had a redheaded girl with him all the time. Often, there was another man with him, but I didn't catch his name or his face."

"That's a good memory. You remember the woman?"

"Pretty. Big laugh. Big chest." She sniffed. "I never spoke to the woman, but I didn't like Delany. He was rude and left his trash in the yard. Made me so mad I would go over and pick it up."

"You happen to catch the name of the girl he was with?"

"No."

"You remember what she looked like?"

"It was usually dark and hard to see, but the one I remember wasn't a big woman. A white girl."

Julia pulled her phone and found Rita's picture. "How about this woman?"

Mrs. Greene took the phone, squinting. "Make the picture bigger."

Julia swiped the image with her fingers and enlarged Rita's face.

"Got great-grandkids who have phones like that. They're always looking at it rather than playing outside. They type messages, snap pictures, and play games. Don't think anyone talks on 'em. My phone is attached to the wall, where it should be." She studied the image while adjusting her glasses. "Can't say for sure if it was her. But this one reminds me of that woman."

"I'm still amazed you remember back so far. Twenty-five years is a long time." She wasn't questioning her honesty, but the story of the body had been in the paper, and memories, though helpful, weren't always reliable.

"I remember them real well because the last time I saw them together was the night my mama died. The ambulance came, and I was so upset. And then I heard that woman cackle as she and Mr. Delany staggered into the house. They saw the damn ambulance taking my mama away, but they didn't stop to give their respects. Some moments stick hard in your memory."

"You're sure it was Marcus Delany? I understand he had a guy living in the house." She flipped through her notes. "The guy's name was Scott Turner."

"No one else lived in that house but the younger Mr. Delany. The others came and went."

"You sure? This Turner fellow could have come and gone at odd hours."

"I know my street, young woman. Especially in those days with me being home so much. It's like now. I don't work no more, but I know my street."

She showed her a picture of Jim Vargas. "Did you ever see this man?"

Mrs. Greene leaned in and studied the image. "No."

Julia cleared her throat, surprised by the emotion that cut through her body. "What day did your mother die?"

"November 2, 1992."

November 2. One day after Jim Vargas had died. There'd have been no way Jim Vargas could have killed Rita if Etta Greene had seen Rita here on November 2 with Delany.

"Did Delany come back to the house?"

"That next week was mighty busy making the funeral arrangements for Mama. Fact, I don't think I ever saw Mr. Delany again until the week before last."

"He was here over a week ago?"

"The Thursday or Friday before last, I think it was. He looks a lot like he did back in the day. Fit. Hair is grayer, but he looks about the same."

"What was he doing here?"

"I don't know. He went inside the house and was in there for about a half hour, and then he came out and left."

"You're sure about the day?"

"I went to see my grandson that next Saturday afternoon."

The fire started the following Sunday night around seven. Natasha had said there might have been a delay device that had set the fire. But why set the fire for forty-eight hours later? Why bring everyone here? Did he know Rita's body would be found? Or did he want her body found?

"Thank you, Mrs. Greene. I appreciate your time."

"Think it helped?"

"It was a big help."

"You going to tell Mr. Novak? I was gonna put a call in to him, and then I saw you. Now I reckon he won't have to call me."

"I'll tell him." She handed Mrs. Greene her card. "And if you think of any new information and can't get Novak, you can call me."

"Sure will."

Julia crossed the street to her car and slid behind the wheel. She dialed Novak. He answered immediately. "Julia."

"I paid a visit to Etta Greene. She lives across the street from Delany's Church Hill house."

"What were you doing there?"

"It all circles back to Rita. So I wanted to see the house again were she was found. Mrs. Greene saw a woman that looked like Rita with Delany the night Rita disappeared. It was the night Mrs. Greene's mother died, so she remembers it clearly. It was November 2."

"Assuming it was Rita, why would Delany kill her?"

"I think Rita's job was to set Jim up. And maybe after he was dead, she was of no more use."

"Where are you now?"

"Headed to Delany's residence. I need to talk to him."

"I'm on my way. Don't engage unless I'm there." His voice was tense with worry.

"I think Rita might have shot Jim."

Novak repeated his demand. "Don't engage until I arrive."

"Understood."

CHAPTER
TWENTY-SIX

Sunday, November 5, 10:00 p.m.

Julia arrived at the entrance to Delany's driveway a half hour later. She cut her lights and drove slowly down the drive. The house was dark, silent. She parked and cut her engine. Without the heater running, the fall air quickly chilled her.

She dialed Andrews's number. He answered immediately. She didn't bother with pleasantries, sensing they annoyed him anyway. "What can you tell me about Delany? Where was he during the Hangman murders?"

"Stand by." Keys tapped in the background. "He was the primary investor in a real estate development in the West End. Came close to filing bankruptcy when it took longer than he'd anticipated to fill up the units."

Moonlight bathed the two-story brick home and its well-manicured lawn. "What saved him?"

Keys tapped. "He was able to attract a new investor. The influx of cash bought him enough time. He ended up turning a significant profit on the development and moved on to his next project. Why do you care?"

"He was seen at his Church Hill home with Rita Gallagher the night after Jim died. Rita was linked to all three Hangman victims along with Jim. I'm at his place right now."

"Who's your backup?" Andrews asked.

"Novak is en route."

"I assume you'll wait until he's on scene."

"You sound like Novak."

"He's a reasonable man," Andrews said.

"I'll be fine." She studied the dark house. "It doesn't look like Delany is home. Can you ping his phone to confirm his location?"

"Stand by." More keys clicked in the background. "His phone is pinging from his home address."

"I can't imagine he's in bed this early."

"This guy might be smart enough to leave his phone at home so he won't leave an electronic trail."

"What about his vehicles?"

Keys clicked. "All have antitheft packages. He has three registered in his name, and his company has six trucks. Delany's cars are in his driveway. And five of the six trucks are at the corporate offices."

"Where's the sixth?"

He hesitated. "In the Manchester district near the warehouses on the river."

"Warehouses. He's killing someone now," she said.

After a heavy silence, "Update me immediately when you and Novak have made contact."

"Will do."

She checked the time on her phone and dialed Novak.

"Where are you?" Novak demanded. Frustration sharpened each of his words.

"At Delany's." She recapped the information Andrews had shared. "I'm headed to the Manchester district now."

"I'm rerouting."

"I'll call you right back."

"Don't hang up."

"I have to go." She ended the call, but as she reached for the ignition key, she spotted the flicker of movement in the garage. A light clicked on, and she watched a man pass in front of the garage window. Behind him she could swear she saw a dangling body.

"What the hell?" Hand on her weapon, she got out of the SUV. She moved closer, not fully believing what she'd just seen.

Julia pulled out her phone and dialed Novak. He didn't answer. The woman's body had twitched. She was dying. "Pick up." On the fourth ring she shoved the phone in her back pocket and drew her weapon. She pushed open the garage door and stood back, surveying the area, knowing this could be a trap.

A woman was suspended from a beam in the center of the large garage. Blood soaked the woman's chest and dripped down her body to the concrete floor. Julia scanned the room, taking in a workbench with neatly arranged tools, lawn equipment tucked in a corner, and a collection of six racing bicycles in the other. A door that appeared to lead into the house was closed. There was no sign of anyone else.

Heart racing, Julia dashed toward the end of the rope, which was tied off around a support beam. She shoved her gun in her holster, and rising on tiptoes, reached for the knot. The body faced away from her, making it impossible to see the victim's face.

She dug her nails into the rope and tried to wedge her thumb under the outside loop. After the outer knot, there were two more knots to undo before the rope would give. More digging and pulling and the second knot came loose. The woman's body was limp now.

A squeak of hinges and movement in her peripheral vision had her backing away from the rope and drawing her weapon. She steadied the gun in front of her with both hands as a man with long white hair and a slim build came in the side door. Even as very faint memories tugged at her, she couldn't place him. Where and when had she seen him before?

She leveled her gun. "Put your hands where I can see them." The last knot held firm as the woman's body now dangled gently. "Untie her! Get her down!"

He looked amused as he glanced toward the lifeless body. "Which is it? You want me to get my hands up or cut her down?"

Julia's fingers tightened on her grip of the gun. He had an air about him that screamed *cop*. "Release the rope!"

He glanced up at the woman, then looked at Julia with a smile before moving toward the last rope.

Her phone rang, her heart hammering as she watched him. She started to reach for her phone. "Who the hell are you?" she demanded.

Laughing, the man tugged at the rope, and the last knot came free. The woman slammed to the concrete floor in a heap. The impact of the body distracted Julia for a split second. It was enough time for him to unwind a second rope she'd not noticed when she'd entered.

Overhead, three-inch-diameter metal pipes rattled and then fell about her, driving her reflexively to a crouching position while covering her head. Two struck her shoulder and back. She staggered to rise just as the man landed a punch squarely to her stomach. Pain rocketed through her body.

"You working with Delany?" she wheezed.

He gently lifted her chin upward and pointed her focus to Marcus Delany's lifeless body, which lay crumpled in a darkened corner. There was a bullet wound in the chest.

"Not anymore."

"Why?"

"He owed Popov a debt. He thought no one cared after the old Russian died. But the family never forgot, and I collected the last installment," he said.

She stared into his eyes, and old memories reached out from the past. The hair was whiter and the lines around his face deeper, but she knew him.

The moment's hesitation cost her. He was old, but his reflexes were lightning quick. She never saw his left punch rise up and connect with her jaw. Pain shot through her head. She staggered, then dropped to the floor. And blacked out.

***

Novak stared at the phone display, wondering why Julia had called him and was now not picking up. He dialed her number a third time, and when he still got no answer, he called Andrews, who picked up on the first ring. "Andrews, this is Novak. Where's Julia?"

"Five minutes ago, she was on her way to the Manchester district."

"Ping her phone."

"Stand by." The seconds ticked by at a painfully slow pace. "She's still at Delany's. Why hasn't she left?"

"This isn't good. She just called me and now is not picking up. I'm headed to Delany's now."

"I'm on standby."

"Understood." He ended the call and shoved his foot against the gas pedal. He'd barely traveled a mile when his phone dinged with a text. Riggs had sent him a snapshot of the police artist's rendering done with Bonnie Jenkins.

He gripped the phone as he stared at the very familiar eyes. Bonnie Jenkins had described Nate Unger.

***

323

When Julia's eyes opened, a thick fog enveloped her brain. Her body was racked with pain. She lay very still and slowly unhooked her belt. She tugged the buckle free and gripped the sharp edge in her fist.

She blinked until her vision cleared enough for her to realize she was lying on a cold concrete floor. The room was dimly lit now, and rope coiled around her wrists, binding them in front of her body. She fought, twisting her hands as she rolled on her back. Beside her lay the lifeless bodies of Elizabeth Monroe and Marcus Delany. Julia swallowed her panic. She pushed herself up, shoving back a wave of nausea.

Julia's skin tore and burned as she struggled to pull her hands free of the ropes. The ropes didn't budge. Her weapon, badge, and shoes were gone.

She pushed up into a sitting position and forward onto her knees. Pulling in several slow, deep breaths, she concentrated on her breathing until it settled. Gritting her teeth, she lumbered into a standing position like a boxer taking an eight count after a knockdown. She staggered, then righted herself. How long had she been out? Was Novak headed toward her or toward the warehouse in the city?

The same man came around the corner, his arms loaded with rope. "You're awake. I thought you'd be out longer. I'll give you credit. You figured this out faster than I anticipated. I thought we'd have more time to play. Me leaving you little clues like attorney Monroe here. But no matter. I'll get you both loaded up, and we'll head to the staging area."

The distant memory crystallized. "You knew my father."

"It's been a while since we saw each other face-to-face. I think you might have been ten or eleven."

Her head spun, and she drew in air to settle her tight stomach. "Unger. Jim's undercover partner."

He grinned. "That's right. We worked undercover for three years together. He was a great cop. A bit too honest for his own good, but I still liked him."

"You came to my birthday party."

"That's right."

"What do you mean Jim was *too honest*?"

He grabbed Monroe's body and dragged it toward an SUV. Hefting the dead weight, he loaded her in the back and covered her with a tarp. "He never took a bribe. Not once. Dedicated son of a bitch. Nothing would stop him from putting Popov behind bars. I used to tell him that he needed to bend and learn to look the other way. But he wouldn't listen."

"That arrest made both your careers."

"And would have ended my life if I hadn't learned to bend."

She twisted her hands, trying to free them from the ropes. "What did you do?"

"I saved Popov's ass. If not for me, I think the old bastard would have gotten the death penalty."

All the victims had worked with Jim as confidential informants. Rene gave up information that led to Popov's arrest, but before his trial she refused to testify. "Did you see to it Rene didn't testify?"

"I had a chat with her. She was smart and knew when to back off. Popov got life in prison, but that wasn't enough for Jim. He was working on Rene, trying to get her to testify in another case against Popov."

"But she was murdered by a serial killer."

"What are the chances of that?"

The chances were almost zero. "You are the Hangman."

He touched the tip of his nose and grinned. "Good guess."

"And you killed the others to cover up her murder?"

"I did." He studied her, genuine curiosity glistening in his dark eyes. "How did you figure out to come here and look for Delany? I was careful."

"Rita Gallagher." Her throat was dry, and her jaw ached. She wouldn't be surprised if he'd broken it.

He looked sincerely interested. "What did little Rita tell you?"

"Delany's Church Hill neighbor saw him with a redhead the night her mother died. It was November 2."

"That was twenty-five years ago. How could anyone remember that?"

A wave of pain rocketed through her jaw. She blinked, clearing her vision. "Delany and Rita showed up at the house just as the ambulance arrived for her mother. Her mother died that night, and she never forgot. So Jim couldn't have killed her."

He shook his head. "And to think I went out of my way to make sure she was found."

"You set the fire?"

"I did." He seemed to enjoy discussing secrets that he'd carried for over twenty years.

"Delany brought her to you. You were waiting at the Church Hill house." Etta remembered seeing Delany, but on the night her mother died, she'd missed seeing Unger slip inside.

Unger moved over to Delany's body and kicked it. "He owed Popov a big favor. The old guy bailed Delany's ass out after he lost his shirt in the real estate market. His payback was the house in Church Hill. What a pile of junk, but real estate is all about location. We ran a lot of drugs there with no interference, and of course made it Rita's final resting place. Delany was told never to sell it, but I guess he thought enough time had passed and he could do what he wanted. He was wrong."

She shook her head, wincing with pain and trying to stay conscious. Her mouth was dry, her throat raw. The cold metal of the buckle dug into her palm. "Rita was having an affair with Jim."

"She was Popov's little handmaiden. Her job was to lure those women to the warehouse and seduce Jim. She said, by the way, that he was an easy lay. He was bored and restless. Domestic life didn't suit him so well."

"Did she kill Jim?"

He nodded. "She was supposed to bring him to the last warehouse, but he wouldn't go. He was waiting on you and your mother." He pouted. "Poor Jim wanted to be good, but it just wasn't in him."

"How could she shoot him with his own gun? Jim wasn't a fool."

"She said since he'd gotten back from the firing range, he had cleaned the gun and reloaded it. He'd stepped away, and when he came back into the kitchen she'd come through the back door. She was holding the gun and pointing it at her temple. He lunged to stop her and she turned the gun on him. He staggered, and she lowered him to the chair and staged it to look like a suicide. You should have seen her. She was so proud of herself. She had no idea she had messed up my plans."

Jim had not shot himself. The news was too much to absorb right now. "His partner said there was a note."

"Rita wrote it. She was good at copying handwriting. But good old Ken came to the rescue and took it. Loyalty between partners is very touching."

"The letters to Vicky?" she asked, more to herself. "Rita wrote them to trick Vicky."

"Yes."

Her jaw throbbed. "So Rita came to you?"

"Like a good little girl hoping for a reward."

"Why did you kill her?"

"Because she was there to tape each of the Hangman murders for Popov to see. But most importantly because she shot Jim. That was my job. Popov had been clear about what my job was. And I thought he'd skin me alive. I lost my temper and hit her hard with the butt of my gun. She dropped to her knees. She was barely breathing, but I hit her again, and when she fell I pressed my hand over her nose and mouth."

"And you left her in that room?"

"I wasn't sure what to do at first. Then I thought I'd leave her. I knew one day I would have to double back for you. If you'd not reopened the case, her body would have."

The download of information was almost too much to process, but she kept talking. Andrews would figure out where she was. She had to believe that this time help would arrive before it was too late. "You were hired to kill those women, but why come after me?"

He stepped forward, the overhead light accentuating the hard angles of his face framed by white hair. "It was part of the deal with Popov. But the old man was dead and the family didn't seem to care, so I was almost tempted to let this part of the deal slide, until Elizabeth Monroe came to me."

"She knew all the details of the original deal. She told you to murder Lana," Julia said.

He wagged his finger at the woman's dead body. "She wanted to resurrect the Hangman. She needed a loose end snipped. She said she'd pay me if I said yes and tell the Popovs I was going to the cops if I said no."

She moistened her dried lips as she pushed through the pain throbbing in her ears.

He picked up a water bottle, twisted the top off, and moved toward her. He held the bottle up to her mouth. She staggered back a step. She needed to buy time. Feed his ego. Listen to him talk. Anything.

"Why the public displays?" Warm blood oozed under the ropes as she twisted.

"Hide in plain sight. If I murdered Rene and the others with no style, it would have looked like Popov ordered the hit. Women murdered in a fetish style would create sensation and divert attention. Sad for poor Rene, but no one cared she was dead."

He was right. The media coverage had been sparse after Rene's body was found. He stood a few steps from Julia. His gaze sparked with delight. "I waited a couple of weeks before I strung up Tamara. Frankly, I was a bit annoyed no one had paid attention to Rene. I worked hard on my display of her body. I took even more time with Tamara. I wanted people to pay attention, and I needed Jim to wonder if Rene's death was attached to him."

"Rita led them to where you wanted to murder them."

"She was an eager little helper. She was devoted to me and to the idea that she was helping Popov. And you know, I got used to having her around, and I missed her after she was gone. She was fun."

She tried to turn the buckle blade upward so she could saw it against the ropes. "Was this all about the money?"

His gaze sharpened. "You sound like your father."

"Did he know you worked for Popov?"

"He was smart as hell. It was a matter of time before he put the pieces together. You remind me so much of Jim. Smart and determined."

"Did you kill those women for the money?"

"Popov's people came to me. Threatened to skin my mother and siblings alive if I didn't take the money and do the job. I knew he meant it, so it was an easy choice."

"You could have gone to your superiors. You didn't have to kill for him."

He shook his head. "You don't say no to a family who will cut your family to pieces and mail them back to you bit by bit."

"But now?" She was feeling steadier on her feet. She purposefully let her shoulders slump and rocked back and forth as if unsteady.

"As I said, Monroe opened it all back up. And I couldn't trust that she hadn't spoken to the Popov family. Killing you will mean something to them and maybe earn me a little goodwill in the face of whatever Monroe might have said to them."

"Kill Jim's only child. It's something Popov would have ordered if he were alive."

"Something like that." He shrugged. "Frankly, I enjoy all this far more than I should." He put down the water bottle and tested the length of rope with a tug. "I always thought it interesting that you became a cop and did undercover work like your old man and me. The apple doesn't fall far from the tree."

"So what happens next? Do you string me up and watch me suffocate?"

"Basically, yes." He turned to get busy.

She pushed the knife against her ropes. "You think you'll get away with this?"

"The Hangman will retire. Or perhaps find a new place to play. You even said it yourself that the Church Hill neighbor saw Marcus Delany with Rita. He will vanish after tonight, and the cops can spend their time chasing him."

She pulled hard against the ropes. Frayed threads broke, and her hand, scraped and bloodied, slipped free. She pulled the other free and waited as he moved toward her. If he wanted to string her up, he'd have to get close. Heart hammering in her chest, she watched as he readied to close the distance between them.

She lunged toward him.

***

"Where is she, Andrews?" Novak demanded.

"Still on the property, as is her vehicle."

Novak gunned the engine, arriving at Delany's seconds later. He parked behind Julia's car, killed the lights, and shut off his vehicle. Out of the SUV he stripped off his jacket and spied the darkened house. He called Andrews. "Her vehicle is here. Can you pinpoint her location?"

"Only within a hundred feet of the property. Not a specific building. How long before backup arrives?"

"Less than a minute or two, but I'm not waiting. I'm moving in toward the main house now."

"Understood."

As he approached the main house, he could see there were no lights on. To the right and behind it was a large garage. Lights glowed from the window. Adrenaline pumped, narrowing his focus. Weapon in hand, he approached the garage, praying Julia was still alive. When he found her, he'd give her hell for being such a cowboy. "Jesus, Julia, you have got to be okay."

He was less than a few feet away when he heard a scream.

***

Julia slashed her buckle knife across his eye and face, cutting into soft flesh. Blood gushed from the wound.

"Bitch!" he screamed as he cupped his hand to his eye.

She lowered her head and drove her body into Unger's chest. The unexpected blow caught him off guard, and he hit the concrete floor hard. But he immediately rolled to his side and righted himself. His gaze burned with fury as he growled.

"I'm going to string you up and make sure it takes hours for you to die."

She pushed past the pain in her body and gripped the knife at her side. "You're not stringing me up like your other victims."

When the gunshot echoed in the garage, she froze, fearing Unger had fired at her. She stared at her attacker. His cool detachment had been replaced by anger. Seconds slowed. Time almost stopped.

As the rush of adrenaline ebbed, she realized she'd not been hit. It was Unger who'd been shot. He staggered back, a bloom of blood growing quickly on his chest. He drew in a ragged breath and raised his hand to his chest. He stared at his bloodstained fingertips and looked as if he couldn't believe what he was seeing.

He raised his gaze and looked past her. His face twisted into a snarl, and he lunged forward. Another shot followed from behind her, hitting him again. He fell back to the ground.

She couldn't pull her attention from Unger's body, which lay sprawled on the floor. Her heartbeat drummed in her ears, and her vision narrowed.

"Julia!" The sound of Novak's voice snapped her back to the present. "Are you okay?"

"No." Julia sucked in a breath as her vision cleared. Her hands were trembling as adrenaline surged in her body again. Sweat dampened her shirt.

Novak pushed past her, gun still drawn, and rushed up to Unger, his weapon pointed at the man. He checked for a pulse.

"Is he dead?" she asked.

"No pulse." Novak rolled Unger onto his belly and handcuffed him. He turned to her. "Julia, are you hurt?"

Her mouth was dry, her head pounding. "Nothing I won't survive. Is he dead?"

"Yes."

Her adrenaline crashed, and tears clogged her throat. "Good."

Gently he touched her cheek. "You are not okay."

She managed a shaky nod. Novak had been her partner on this case, her team, and he'd saved her. Swells of gratitude and relief collided. "Scrapes and bruises."

He wrapped his arm around her, pulling her close. "You did it, Julia. Your father would be proud."

She leaned into him, burying her face in his chest, inhaling his scent. All the years of wondering about her father and living under his shadow and the Hangman's were over. She'd seen it through. "I got him."

EPILOGUE

Thursday, December 21, 8:00 p.m.

The holiday rush at the bar commenced in early December. People busy with family and festivities came to Billy's for drinks and a little conversation before heading back into the holiday storm, as Julia called it. She always requested the holiday shift. It was tradition. It was home.

Her bruises had faded, as had the rope burns on her wrists. She'd tried to argue she was fit for duty, but her boss had ordered her to take time to decompress. "I don't want to see you until after January 1," he'd said.

The downtime had proved to be irritating. She'd visited with Ken a couple of times. Wendy had been guarded at first, but Julia assured her she wouldn't press for an investigation into Wendy's handling of the evidence. Wendy and Ken needed each other now, so she was willing to leave everything associated with the Hangman in the past.

Julia had tried to take it easy, but finally the vacation was too much and she'd grabbed an apron and moved behind Cindy's bar. Her aunt had not been happy, but Julia convinced her she'd go mad if she binge-watched another television series.

Julia and Novak had been seeing each other regularly over the last six weeks. He'd encouraged her to leave a toothbrush and several of her things at his house, and when they weren't together, they spoke daily. It was peaceful. The two of them were in their own little world.

A week ago, he'd delivered unexpected news. Benny Santiago had been knifed to death two days after arriving in prison. She'd have been lying if she said she'd not felt relief. He was one less demon to worry about.

When Bella came home for Thanksgiving, Julia had made herself scarce, letting the two enjoy their holiday. And now as Christmas loomed and Novak's daughter had returned, she'd retreated again. Again, she told Novak to enjoy his kid and to not worry about her. They'd find each other again in January after the New Year. Julia had plenty to do with helping Cindy behind the bar.

"Why are you here?" Cindy asked as she straightened the red Santa hat perched on her head.

Julia grabbed a couple of empty tumblers from the shelf and filled each with two fingers of bourbon. "I'm helping you, remember? The holidays get crazy, and your regular help always flakes."

"Thought you'd be with your man."

"He's not my man, Cindy. And his daughter is home from college. It's their family time."

"And they can't include you? I gave 'em a pass at Thanksgiving, but not now."

"I didn't give him the chance to ask. Told him I was busy and working here."

"I can judge men pretty well. Novak is a good man, and you're important to him. You should be with him."

"I'm the chick he dates. And that's okay."

Cindy shook her head. "Why do you still keep your distance?"

"I'm not keeping my distance."

"You're just hedging your bets because you think he'll leave like Jim."

"I'm not."

"Then why aren't you together now?"

Julia couldn't give her a good answer. "Cindy, the guy wants to spend time with Bella. I can't begrudge that. I'd have loved it if Jim had wanted to spend a holiday with me."

Julia served up the two drinks, wiped down the bar, and refilled the peanut bowls. She liked the familiarity of the bar. It was easy to lose herself in the mundane work and take her time processing what had happened only six weeks earlier.

Nate Unger had created the Hangman when Alexi Popov had told him to destroy Detective Jim Vargas. Popov didn't want Jim to simply die; he wanted Jim's family and life stripped from him, his reputation ruined. Rita had also been enlisted. Her job was to seduce Jim and turn his personal life upside down. When the cops searched Unger's country house, they'd found a collection of videos that had been made during the hangings. In several instances, Unger panned the camera around the warehouse and captured Rita standing in the back, smiling. Waving.

Andrews dug into Unger's bank accounts and discovered he'd been paid over $1 million for his Hangman work. Most of the money had been wired into numerous small accounts. Judging by the account balances, he'd not spent much money over the years. He never really cared about it. It was the one truth he told Julia.

Unger had slipped into the Hangman persona as easily as he had his undercover identities. He lost himself in the role, became the person, and this time discovered he liked the monster.

When Julia had reopened the Hangman case, she'd never realized she was racing an unseen clock or that the Hangman was coming after her. Lana and Elizabeth had been chosen because both were loose ends. Unger saw Julia's death as insurance—a show of loyalty—to guard against anything Elizabeth might have said to the Popov family about him.

The front door opened, and Cindy glanced up, her frown fading. "So look who just walked into my bar."

Julia turned to see Novak and a young girl with curly red hair and a petite frame enter the bar. She recognized Bella from her pictures, and her nerves jumped. She could chase a bad guy down a blind alley at night, but meeting Novak's kid made her stomach knot.

She smiled at them, and though tempted to use the bar as a buffer, came around it to greet them.

She wiped her hand on her apron and extended it to Bella. "You must be Bella."

"Julia," the girl said, grinning. She shook Julia's hand. "Great to meet you! Dad's told me a lot about you."

"What brings you two here?" she asked, looking to Novak, who stood behind his daughter with his hands on her shoulders.

Bella laughed. "Dad's been champing at the bit to come see you."

She glanced at Novak, who didn't look the least bit put off by his daughter's openness. "I thought you guys had a special tradition at Christmas. Did you make it to tea?"

"Yeah, and it was fun, sort of," Bella said. "At least for me. Dad always looks like someone is shoving bamboo shoots under his fingernails."

"We were hoping you'd join us for a late dinner," Novak said. "Part of the tradition is that we get a real meal after our plate of girl sandwiches."

"I don't want to intrude," Julia said. "Better you two have your special time."

Novak moved around Bella and kissed Julia lightly on the lips. "Come with us. I know you haven't eaten."

"I had nuts and crackers."

"Oh, please," he said.

"We can get pizza," Bella said. "There's a great Italian place near the university."

"She's determined to feed me, just like you," Julia said, smiling.

"She's never been good at taking no for an answer," he said.

"Maybe you can tell me what it's like to be a cop," Bella said.

Julia shook her head, holding up her hands. "I think your father might have a nervous breakdown if I do. He has visions of you in a plush, safe office. He mentioned something about encasing you in Bubble Wrap."

"Not happening," Bella said. "I'm going to be a cop."

Novak let out a long, not-too-pained breath. "Maybe you can scare her away from the job."

"I love what I do," Julia said.

"Then, that's a yes?" Bella asked.

Julia glanced back at Cindy. "Mind if I take off?"

Cindy nodded toward the door. "Get out of here."

Being part of a couple, a family, felt awkward. But she wanted it to work. She wanted to spend more time with Novak, and she liked Bella already.

"Let me get my coat." She moved to the back office and grabbed her belongings. She glanced up at the picture of Jim and Amy. "Wish me luck."

As she turned, she found Novak leaning on the doorjamb. Crossing the small room, he reached for her coat and helped her put it on, a gesture she allowed only when other cops weren't looking. He kissed her cheek. "I love you."

She heard Cindy and Bella in the hallway, but she didn't pull away. His words wrapped around her heart and warmed her in a way she'd never felt before.

"I love you, too," she whispered.

He turned her to face him and kissed her on the lips. This time his touch wasn't quick but lingered an extra beat. "Did I hear you correctly?"

She moistened her lips and grinned. "Maybe." Julia walked out into the bar and found everyone staring at her.

Novak came up behind her, unmindful that they were the center of attention. He squeezed her shoulders. "You said you loved me."

Julia faced him. "Don't let it go to your head."

"Say it again, out here for everyone to hear."

Her gut clenched. "Novak, we're in public. And your daughter is watching."

Novak's gaze didn't waver. "And your point?"

She flexed her fingers against his forearms. She moistened her lips, wondering why this had to be so hard for her.

He traced circles on her shoulders with his thumbs. He would stand here all night until she said the words.

"I love you," she said, loud enough for Cindy and Bella to hear. Several of the regulars in the room started to holler encouragement. "And I'm not saying it any louder."

Novak laughed and kissed her on the lips, tugging the folds of her jacket closed. "Baby steps, right?"

Julia nudged him close. "Exactly."

ABOUT THE AUTHOR

Photo © 2015 Studio FBJ

New York Times and *USA Today* bestselling novelist Mary Burton is the popular author of twenty-nine published romance and suspense novels, as well as five novellas. She currently lives in Virginia with her husband and three miniature dachshunds.